SAVING
A ROB MADDEN NOVEL
VENGEANCE

I0680828

SAVING
A ROB MADDEN NOVEL
VENGEANCE

LT. COL. JOHN WITZEL
(USAF, RET.)

WILDCATTER PUBLISHING   Omaha, NE

© 2018 John Witzel. All rights reserved. No part of this book may be used or reproduced by any means, graphic, electronic or mechanical, including photocopying, recording, taping or by any information storage retrieval system without the written permission of the publisher except in the case of brief quotations embodied in critical articles and reviews.

Wildcatter Publishing books may be ordered from your favorite bookseller.
www.wildcatterpublishing.com

Wildcatter Publishing
c/o CMI
4822 South 133rd Street
Omaha, NE 68137
wildcatter@conciergemarketing.com

Paperback ISBN: 978-0-9911029-3-8
Mobi ISBN: 978-0-9911029-4-5
EPUB ISBN: 978-0-9911029-5-2

Library of Congress Cataloging Number: 2018901882
Cataloging in Publication data on file with publisher.

Printed in the United States of America

10 9 8 7 6 5 4 3 2

This suspense story is set in dangerous and unstable Yemen in January through December of 2009, well before the Yemeni revolution and Arab Spring. Although this latest adventure of Rob Madden is fiction, I have attempted to portray the locale, circumstances, and characters as authentically as possible.

Critical to this story are true, real life terrorist groups that at this period occupied Yemen including: Al-Qaeda of the Arabian Peninsula, Shi'a Houthis, and the Islamic State (ISIL). All of the terrorists' personal names mentioned in this novel are strictly fictional, but their actions and affiliations are very real. Of note, many of the 176 terrorists released by the Yemeni government were at one time prisoners at Guantanamo Bay, Cuba, and their terroristic acts continue today.

Although many actions and situations described are fictional, our military members, plus our allied partners, face grave dangers everyday attempting to restore peace in the deadly chaos of Yemen.

"The angels have chosen
to fight their battles below"

ALAN JAY LERNER, "CAMELOT"

For those engaged in the fight
against terrorism

CHAPTER

1

"Thank you, Mr. President, for allowing our brothers back in jihad fighting the Great Satan and the infidels," an emotional Abu-Amr yelled to his fellow al-Qaeda cell members. "Soon all of our brothers will be freed from Guantanamo and return to spill the blood of the infidels and Crusaders. *Allaahu A'lam,* God knows best!"

Hunkered down in the basement of the Al Wadi refugee center in downtown Minneapolis, the four Brothers of the American Jihad were intensely focused on a recent TV cable news story about a terrorist bombing at a uranium mine in a place called Tres Rios, New Mexico. The men rubbed their long beards contemplating what Tres Rios meant and where it was.

The members spread maps across the filthy living area and began internet searches trying to find Tres Rios and determine which organization's sleeper cell would take responsibility for the explosion and destruction of such a critical American nuclear facility. It was a common trait among terrorist groups to have deadly competition among themselves. Who, in American terms, could produce the "biggest splash" for name recognition and donated dollars for their cause?

"Allahu Akbar!" All in the basement were chanting, "Allahu Akbar!" and hailing the actions of their fellow al-Qaeda brothers as a new stage began in their fight against America and the Great Satan.

"It is a blessing from Allah that our brothers became martyrs to destroy and stop America's ability to create nuclear bombs to use against the Islamic states and Arab nations. Allahu Akbar," screamed Wadi el-Hage.

"Someday," he yelled, "we will also have nuclear weapons to even the score with the infidel murderers of our people." He hoped it would be his organization obtaining the first of such weapons.

"Our al-Qaeda brothers' sacrifice has made it possible for our own nuclear bombs," Karmin Curien shrieked as he jumped up from his desk, which was cluttered with Arab newspapers and magazines.

As the excitement intensified at the Al Wadi refugee center, all eyes were on the National News Network and the Arab Al Jazeera cable news.

All the major networks were reporting on the uranium mine explosion and the many terrorist organizations emerging and taking responsibility for the act—from Hezbollah and Hamas to the Muslim Brotherhood and al-Qaeda. All terrorist groups were taking credit for one of the most brazen acts of terror since 9/11—the destruction of an American nuclear mining facility. The implications for both American allies and known terrorist organizations were obvious to all listening—a major threat to world peace and something once unthinkable—the Western world held hostage to a terrorist group with nuclear weapons.

"Our brothers have earned a great victory for Allah and Islam and will be rewarded as faithful martyrs," the leader announced to the other cell members, who continued to chant "Allahu Akbar!" The uncontrolled frenzy of excitement carried on while information was streaming on the National News Network with live reports from the site of the explosion. Al Jazeera was reporting events in New Mexico with their Islamic affiliate station in Albuquerque, New Mexico.

"Silence, all!" ordered Abdullah Saleh as all turned from their rituals and focused on the large HDTV. The screen showed the barren desert terrain typical of the New Mexico high plains. The camera zoomed to a massive, disfigured rock formation on the side of a hill and gigantic boulders and rocks scattered at the foot of the mesa. The impact of the explosion and its sign of growing terrorist activity in the United States was obvious.

"This is Jose Hernandez with the National News Network reporting from Tres Rios, New Mexico, where four known al-Qaeda terrorists infiltrated a major uranium mine complex and blew part of it up." Hernandez motioned the camera to focus on the explosion site on the side of the cliff.

"Reports are unconfirmed that under all the rubble and rock is the mine's security officer and his staff. Eyewitnesses to the explosion say there was gunfire between mine security personnel and the terrorists just prior to this massive explosion."

Touching his earpiece, Hernandez acknowledged a message from his producer. "Just a moment, ladies and gentlemen. We have a witness to the explosion and the firefight."

He turned to his right, where a man was walking toward him. "Sir, what is your name and what can you tell us about this horrific incident?" Hernandez poked his mic toward a broad-shouldered, bearded man wearing dust-covered overalls. The man neared Hernandez and spit a chew of tobacco onto his shoes. Hernandez winced.

"Well, yes, sir, my name is J.C. Skinner. I was just getting off my shift at the main processing center over yonder." As Skinner pointed, the camera followed, zooming in to the mine entrance. Skinner spit another wad of tobacco.

"That over there was the mine's security office," he said, pointing to the explosion site. "Mister, let me tell you there was plenty of action going on there last night, with tons of gunfire and tracer bullets flying all over the place and lighting up the whole area. It was just like a firefight I had in Iraq." He spat out more tobacco juice, which landed near the cameraman's boots.

"Mr. Skinner, thank you for your service to our country, but can you tell us anything else you saw besides the gunfire and tracer bullets?" Hernandez asked.

"Funny, just about the time when all the shooting began over yonder, I saw a pickup truck hauling ass out of there," Skinner said as he rubbed his gray, dirty beard.

"Please, Mr. Skinner, tell our viewers more about the truck and what happened to it."

"Well ya see, sir, this truck was racing out of there from that security compound, and folks was firing at the truck like it was a moving target at a county fair," Skinner continued. "Just over yonder, about a couple hundred yards where it sits."

Hernandez motioned for the cameraman to get a good shot of what appeared to be a burned-out pickup truck near the explosion site.

"Man, when those terrorists' tracer bullets hit that truck right in the fuel tank, the whole area lit up like a NASCAR racetrack on Saturday night," a grinning Skinner explained, shaking his head. "Don't see how no one coulda survived riding in that truck. They told me the truck belonged to one of those crazy wild guys working at the security facility," Skinner added.

Hernandez could not believe what he heard and anxiously asked Skinner to explain what he meant by "crazy wild guys."

"Well, ya see, it appeared to most of us miners that these fellas on mine security were different and really didn't look like no security experts, but more like the motorcycle outlaw types."

Hernandez pondered that statement for a moment and wondered about its significance. Something here was bizarre, and he, Jose Hernandez, was going to make exclusive news of these events as described by Mr. J.C. Skinner.

Known al-Qaeda terrorists travel to New Mexico to blow up a uranium mine and get into a firefight with mine security members who are viewed as crazy wild guys belonging to motorcycle gangs, Hernandez thought to himself with a puzzled but excited look on his face.

The cameraman could read Hernandez's intentions and began preparing for a taped interview with Skinner that could be edited and viewed later.

Hernandez wrapped the report with this: "We'll interrupt our regular programming as we learn more on the uranium mine explosion here in Tres Rios, New Mexico. This is Jose Hernandez with the National News Network."

Hernandez and the cameraman asked Skinner to join them at a wooden picnic table on the edge of the gravel mine parking lot. For the next half hour, Skinner described to Hernandez his impressions and what he had heard about the "crazy wild guys" in security—especially about the chief of security, Billy Hemrod, the son of the mine's chief executive officer. Hernandez sensed there was something more to this story than a band of marauding terrorists out to destroy a security facility at a uranium mine guarded by what appeared to be drug-dealing thugs.

"Mr. Skinner, we certainly appreciate your time and information," Hernandez added, "and yes, you will be on Albuquerque's channel 10 tonight at 6:00 and 10:00 p.m."

As Skinner walked away, he turned and said, "One other thing, Mr. Hernandez. Not sure if it means anything, but many of us swear we saw Rob Madden leaving the security complex earlier in the evening."

Hernandez stopped making notes in his folder and gave Skinner a curious look. "Who is Rob Madden?"

Hundreds of miles away from the Al Wadi refugee center in Minneapolis, in a small, cluttered apartment just off the University of Michigan–Dearborn campus near Detroit, another al-Qaeda sleeper cell was beginning its morning routine of monitoring message traffic on the internet and watching Al Jazeera programs.

Sahim Abdul, the cell leader, reviewed the current overseas directives from al-Qaeda leaders in Yemen and almost fell off his chair when he read about the uranium mine explosion in New Mexico.

"Kareem, turn on the news now!" Sahim shouted to the newest member of the cell.

The loud barking of orders by Sahim immediately drew the attention of other members, who were brewing tea and preparing for their prayers. All gathered around a bulky old TV.

"Silence!" screamed Sahim as the screen showed the barren, dusty landscape of northern New Mexico as a TV broadcaster reported from Tres Rios.

"We break into our normal programming to provide you with an update to the attack on a uranium mine at Tres Rios, New Mexico. Jose Hernandez is on the scene with the latest on this terrorist attack on America."

Members of the cell sat in silence trying to determine the magnitude of what they were hearing. Was this possibly the work of Humza Aldawasari, their brother who was recently released from Guantanamo prison in Cuba and who vowed to kill his brother's assassin, Rob Madden, in Tres Rios?

"Quiet, everyone!" Sahim ordered.

As the news updates were becoming more detailed and accurate, it was obvious to all in the al-Qaeda sleeper cell that the terrorists were indeed Humza Aldawasari and the three other cell members who accompanied him to Tres Rios to settle the score with Rob Madden.

Sahim's mind raced back to the tense, divisive discussions the cell had with Humza regarding this decision with no authorization from al-Qaeda leadership abroad—especially with the ambitious plan to obtain a nuclear bomb. He realized that this personal, irrational trip by Humza could jeopardize years of planning by several al-Qaeda cells to obtain a nuclear bomb from Pakistan and deliver it, through Mexico, to the United States.

"Brothers, we have no time to lose. It is critical that we destroy all the documents in this room, to include computer hard drives and files—now. Do it!" ordered the cell leader.

Regaining his sense of the consequences now facing his little cell of "terrorists in training," Sahim forcibly pushed the quick destruction and burning of any incriminating documents that could trace Aldawasari to their location. He also knew the al-Qaeda cell protocol if the apartment were raided by law enforcement, and he hid the appropriate booby-trapped explosives within the rooms.

CHAPTER
2

BOOM, BOOM, BOOM. Explosions from stun grenades rocked the neighborhood as three teams of FBI SWAT units converged on the al-Qaeda cell's Detroit apartment. More grenades were forced into the apartment's broken window to stun the occupants, who became disoriented after the grenades exploded.

SWAT team members stood ready on the side of the apartment complex—locked and loaded on high alert with full body protection, gas masks and MP5 submachine guns.

Screams could be heard from occupants of adjoining apartments as two team members rushed the apartment entrance with a special operations battering ram that quickly dislodged the door, allowing a SWAT team to rush the apartment yelling, "FBI, STAND WHERE YOU ARE."

KABOOM. An explosion in one of the back bedrooms rocked the building and blew two SWAT members out of the apartment onto the littered street. Several other SWAT members lay injured on the debris-strewn floor. The assault team members still able to act readied their MP5s to take out any surviving cell members.

Moving forward, cutting through the debris and smoke with his powerful flashlight, team chief Joe Dejka noticed a slight movement to his right, inside of what once was the small kitchen. He recognized Sahim Abdul, the cell leader

"Stay back!" he said to the remainder of his team inside the smoke-filled apartment.

Dejka then saw the disfigured body of Sahim attempting to enable a switch with his only functional hand on what appeared to be an explosive vest. The team chief fired his weapon repeatedly into Sahim's head and arm, hoping to keep Sahim from activating the vest. Either Dejka and his team were going to survive, or they all were going to be blown to bits, along with most of the adjoining apartments. The now headless, armless Sahim was no longer a threat.

The chief noticed a large canvas bag next to the terrorist. He took a moment to inspect what appeared to be documents the deceased cell member was hoping to take with him to paradise.

After confirming the deaths of all cell members, Dejka ordered his team to leave and allow the FBI bomb ordnance specialists to enter what was left of the apartment. The forensic identification team would follow to identify the dead cell members and recover computers and any additional documents.

Dejka contacted the FBI's deputy director of operations and provided him with a quick update on the recent raid and the status of wounded team members. He also mentioned finding the canvas bag filled with documents, files and computer disks.

Hearing of Dejka's discovery, the deputy director could not believe their luck and ordered Dejka to remain exactly where he was. Dejka was told his new priority was to safeguard the bag until an armed FBI escort arrived to ensure its safe delivery to FBI headquarters.

"This is urgent," the deputy director said to the FBI director's executive officer. "I need a confidential meeting with the director immediately."

While newly appointed FBI Director Al Schmid was being briefed on the recent raid on the al-Qaeda cell's apartment, chief Dejka's bag of al-Qaeda documents had arrived at the FBI headquarters and was being sorted, analyzed and interpreted by terrorism specialists from the FBI, CIA, and military intelligence agencies.

After two days of extensively researching the documents in the bag, an FBI message traffic decoding specialist reviewed several times what he considered a priority and top-secret document. Realizing the sensitivity of this particular document, he asked to speak with his supervisor in a secure, confidential location—his supervisor would understand once he reviewed it.

After the document was reviewed by higher-ups, the decoding specialist was warned not to mention anything to anyone about what he had discovered.

The supervisor, breaking all rules of protocol and FBI procedures, urgently requested a meeting with the bureau's deputy director. After much reluctance by many middle management department heads, the supervisor was granted a short meeting that immediately resulted in an interview with FBI Director Schmid in the top secret briefing room adjacent to his office.

Top-level directors were ordered to attend the hastily scheduled briefing.

"So what you are telling me in brief," Schmid clarified, "is that somehow al-Qaeda has been able to transport a small tactical nuclear weapon from Pakistan, via Mexico, to somewhere here in the United States." He peered over his glasses at the assembled directors and demanded, "Do we happen to have any idea how this happened or where it is now?"

"Director Schmid," CIA Director Adams replied, "for weeks we have been monitoring sensitive, top secret message traffic in Pakistan between various military units and intelligence agencies concerning the location of a certain tactical nuclear bomb. It seems no one can account for it."

Schmid scoffed.

"Much of the disappearance is centered on their nuclear arsenal at the Tarbala Nuclear Underground Depot at Khyber Pakhtunkhwa, Pakistan," Adams added. "This is a hotbed for global jihadism, and it's reasonable that a terrorist group penetrated the depot as employees and worked a successful plan to heist it from the facility—must have taken years of planning."

"Al, from the documents you uncovered, do we know who may be responsible for leading and financing this possible terrorist action?" the CIA director asked.

"From what we are able to glean from the documents so far, it appears the top al-Qaeda leader in Yemen is calling shots on this threat—Khalid Azzam. The information you are receiving today is strictly need-to-know," Schmid advised, "so be very discreet in sharing what you heard today to any members of your staff. We don't need to alarm the public—yet. We have got to get to Azzam immediately, regardless of what it takes."

Schmid turned to the CIA director and asked, "How soon can you get an operation going in Yemen?"

CHAPTER

3

Terrorist Threat Integration Center, FBI Headquarters, Washington, D.C.

"Humza Aldawasari and his fellow terrorist assassins looking to kill Madden are now international heroes in most Arab countries," a stunned FBI Senior Special Agent Tom Krupski told fellow agents. The threat team was meeting in a top-secret security facility with several high-level agency directors and their staffs reviewing intelligence from the CIA and FBI.

"And Billy Hemrod, the drug kingpin and his thugs using the mine as a drug lab, are now considered heroes for fighting terrorists and attempting to defend the uranium mine from being taken over by terrorists—how in the fuck did we miss this?"

All those in the center were shaking their heads in amazement and embarrassment wondering whose head would be on the chopping block for this screw-up.

"Shit!" David Black shouted loud enough for all to hear. "We have literally stirred up a hornet's nest with every fucking terrorist group taking responsibility for the raid."

The center's executive officer opened the door and peeked around it, looking directly at Black and Krupski.

"Sirs, you're wanted by the deputy director," the executive officer said. Black and Krupski knew they were to be sacrificial lambs for this unforeseen catastrophic event.

"No good deed will go unpunished," Krupski mumbled to Black as they headed for the director's office for what was sure to be a monumental ass-chewing and possible reassignment or forced retirement.

Two hours later, both men emerged looking down and frustrated, knowing full well the consequences of their actions. Their new task was to produce a plan of action and gain more intelligence on terrorist groups claiming they were actively targeting nuclear facilities.

Black and Krupski had been briefed that documents uncovered at a recent raid on an al-Qaeda cell produced evidence that a Pakistani nuclear bomb could be somewhere in the United States. From the center's analysis of recent al-Qaeda message traffic, it was evident that the leader in Yemen was going to use the current excitement of destroying a uranium mine and obtaining a nuclear bomb as a rallying cry for recruitment, financing and holding the United States hostage.

To senior al-Qaeda leader Khalid Azzam, this dream come true fell right into his lap—thanks to the federal law enforcement agencies and lax security at a Pakistani nuclear storage depot.

Senior officers and agents from the alphabet agencies, CIA, FBI, DIA and DEA, met that afternoon and concluded the only way to gain human intelligence on Azzam's possession of and ambitions for nuclear weapons was to send a clandestine team to Yemen. Special Operations teams were attracting too much attention in country, and their operations were in many cases compromised by the local tribal network.

Also, the collateral damage and ill will they were causing with the local populace were creating even bigger problems for the military. The use of the very dependable and reliable drones was discussed in neutralizing Azzam; however, he had his leadership and recruit training facilities adjacent to a bona fide school, mosque and makeshift village. Any strikes would surely bring many civilian and student casualties.

The officials concluded the meeting with a recommendation that a small indigenous team of contractors could track Azzam to his base and possibly call in a drone strike when he was sighted leaving the school. Another option was for a two-man team to infiltrate the school area and personally kill Azzam and grab any documents or computers in his possession to possibly find where the stolen nuclear bomb was being stored. Planning for the team went into the night and included representatives from all military intelligence and federal law enforcement agencies.

After much planning and discussion, the agency heads met in the morning and finalized their plan, with the DEA and CIA directors recommending Robert Madden as the team chief for Operational Plan "Paradise Bound"—the close, personal interrogation and execution of al-Qaeda leader Khalid Azzam.

"Why Madden?" Schmid asked the meeting of agency directors.

"Sir, allow me to answer that question," DEA director Mike McGinnis offered.

"Rob Madden is a retired Air Force Combat Controller who served a tour of duty in the badlands of Yemen calling in drone strikes on al-Qaeda leaders, including the successful assault on Anwar Aldawasari and a friend of his—a royal prince from the United Arab Republic."

"Yes, I do recall reading about that incident a few years ago," Schmid said. "Weren't Madden's wife and daughters murdered due to some involvement Madden had with the drone strike on Aldawasari?"

"That is correct," McGinnis said, "and besides being fluent in Arabic, experienced in drone operations in Yemen, the single most important reason Madden is perfect to lead this mission is very simple."

The rest of the agency directors stopped taking notes and looked up at McGinnis, anxious to hear the most important reason for selecting Madden.

"It is confirmed via various al-Qaeda communication chatter that Azzam ordered the brutal murder of Madden's wife and daughters," said McGinnis. "I believe Mr. Madden will be more than willing to return to Yemen and settle the score."

Gathered around a large conference table, all the directors nodded their heads in agreement, knowing inside they would make the same decision—to settle the score.

"Anyway, after news of this disaster at the uranium mine and Madden supposedly just walking away just prior to the explosion, I am sure some al-Qaeda sleeper cell will be out again gunning for Madden," McGinnis said. "He just might be safer in Yemen than in the States."

"Where is Madden now?" asked Schmid.

"From my undercover agent, Bonnie McCord, I understand Mr. Madden is packing it up at Tres Rios and heading west to Stanford University to begin a doctoral program in education," McGinnis said.

"Shit, what was a guy like that doing in Tres Rios, and how did he get involved with one of your DEA agents?" the CIA director asked.

"Trust me, gentlemen, it is a long and interesting story to say the least, and I wish we had the time to share the details with you," McGinnis replied.

"The urgency now is to brief Madden on the mission and get him to safety out of Tres Rios, so he can begin preparing for this mission," Schmid said.

"I'll have Special Agent McCord have a talk with Madden and make the deal. She can, uh, be awfully convincing," McGinnis laughed, knowing there were rumors of a budding romance between the two.

The FBI's Krupski asked, "What about Madden? Does he just walk away from Tres Rios and move on to Stanford University? Every terrorist group and their brother are going to be gunning for Madden now. Just getting him out of New Mexico alive will be challenging enough."

"After he has a short talk with Bonnie," McGinnis said quietly. "He just might change his mind."

"Regardless, if Madden can't pull this off, which I hope he does," said CIA Director Adams, "our last option will be to execute a massive air attack on Azzam's position—and screw the collateral damage."

All members nodded their heads in agreement.

CHAPTER

4

"Do you hear me, Rob? We know who killed your wife and daughters. We also know where the murderers are."

Madden, still holding the cell phone in his shaking hands, was trying to grasp what DEA Special Agent Bonnie McCord had just told him. Sitting back in the squeaky kitchen chair he mostly used for grading his students' assignments, Madden was motionless as McCord emphatically yelled, "Rob, do you hear me? Are you okay?"

A moment passed. Madden didn't know how to react to the sudden news he had been waiting to hear for more than three years. Three years ago, his loving wife and two young daughters were targeted and murdered by terrorists as payback to Madden for his Special Ops work in Yemen.

A variety of law enforcement vehicles were idling, with their lights flashing in preparation for escorting Madden to the highway and the Calico County line.

"Come on, Rob, let's get you going and out of town on your way to Stanford, Dr. Madden," yelled Sheriff Russell Wells outside Madden's trailer. Law officers from all over the county wanted to participate in a star-spangled goodbye to the tough school teacher who was shanghaied to teach school but in turn changed all their lives for the better.

"Hey, Wells, what's the problem here?" shouted Deputy Sheriff Kelly. "We got places to go besides sitting out here waiting for Madden. Could you get him moving?"

"Okay, let me see what the holdup is. You stay put until I find out what the hell is going on here," Wells told Kelly and the rest of the officers.

Exiting his patrol vehicle and heading up the broken wooden steps leading to the trailer entrance, Wells knocked on the door and took a quick look inside through the screen door. Shedding his aviator-style sunglasses, Wells could make out Madden sitting on his kitchen chair with a cell phone clutched in his hand. Sensing something had changed, Wells calmly asked, "Hey, Rob. It's me, Russ Wells. Is everything okay?"

After no response and hearing a loud voice coming from the cell phone in Madden's hand, Wells waited a minute while surveying the inside of the trailer.

"Hey, Russ, would you please get Madden packed in his car so we can get this over with?" was among the pleas coming from the agitated parade of officers.

Turning away from the door of the trailer, Wells looked at the assemblage, put his finger to his lips and waved his hands downward, motioning the others to keep quiet until he could figure out what was happening with Madden. The other officers took notice of Wells's instructions and turned off their patrol cars and flashing lights, waiting for further word.

Over the past year, Sheriff Wells had had an adversarial relationship with Madden. Granted, Wells knew he was mainly responsible for Madden's detour from earning his degree from Stanford University to teaching school at the impoverished Tres Rios Rural School—Madden had no choice.

But now, Wells desperately wanted to get Madden on his way to Stanford—no more detours. If Wells had to drive him there himself, he would. He figured he owed Madden the right to finish his mission and pursue his dream. *What a crazy school teacher,* he thought.

"Rob, may I come in?" Wells asked through the trailer's screen door.

The last thing Wells wanted was to be on the receiving end of Madden's temper. Too many times, he had witnessed the results of Madden's vengeance, or as he put it, "corrective action." For obvious reasons, Wells would be cautious with his approach.

"Rob, it's Sheriff Wells, may I come in?"

Looking up at Wells with red, quivering wet eyes, Madden nodded his head and returned to staring at the cell phone in his hand—not making any effort to speak with the person on the other end. Wells heard a woman's voice asking, "Do you hear me, Rob? What's the matter? Do you hear me?"

Madden made no move to reply to the caller—just a blank stare at the phone. This continued for several minutes, until gradually Madden regained some composure and lifted the phone to his ear and quietly, slowly told Bonnie McCord he would get back to her.

With that, Madden turned off the phone and put it on the kitchen table. Wells sat motionless, trying to determine what could have happened on the phone call to cause such a sudden change in Madden's behavior. This was to be a happy and rewarding day for him, but what tragedy had befallen Madden?

After a few minutes of silence with a deadly stare, Madden turned, red-faced, to Wells and said in a whisper, "Russ, there may be some significant changes for me starting today—that's all I know."

"Okay, Rob, is there anything we can do to help you?" Wells asked uncharacteristically.

"Yes, I appreciate the gesture of the local law enforcement officers' escort out of Tres Rios, but things might have changed. Please ask them to leave—maybe another day."

"Sure, Rob." Wells grabbed his radio mic from his shoulder strap. "Return to normal duty. No escort today. Thank you."

All officers acknowledged and were now more confused than ever why no escort was needed. As much as they all respected Madden, they were more than anxious to get Madden on his way. He knew too much about Billy Hemrod, the uranium mine, and their past activities, especially with Hemrod, the drug kingpin.

"Russ, would it be all right with you if we delay my departure for a few days? There are a lot of issues that came up that I need to get sorted out."

"Not a problem, Rob, you take all the time you need here and let me know if I can be of any assistance," Wells said, with about as much sincerity as was possible from him.

Silence followed for a few more minutes as Madden stared out the trailer window at the inspiring New Mexican high plains with their clear, majestic colors.

"Rob, would you like some coffee, maybe a Coke?" offered Wells.

"Thanks, Russ, coffee would be fine."

Being very familiar with the kitchen—he and his deputies had supplied all the necessities Madden needed in the past year—Wells found the coffeemaker and started the brew. Finding a couple of clean mugs in the dishwasher, Wells filled them and took one to Madden while he placed a small amount of cream in his. From his many associations with Madden, he knew he liked it black.

"Thank you," Madden said, sipping his coffee while still staring out the window. "How many times have I had coffee with you and your law enforcement brethren here in this trailer?" Madden surprisingly asked Wells.

"Many times, both under good and bad circumstances, but the coffee was always good, wasn't it?"

"Yes, as long as you paid for it, Russ," Madden said, calmer now, and slowly moving to face Wells.

Both nodded.

Wells knew he had added much stress and agony to Madden's short stay in Tres Rios since he arrived almost exactly a year earlier. Wells recalled Madden's routine rest stop on the interstate highway on his way to California and how he, by bad luck, encountered the out-of-control local drug kingpin, Billy Hemrod, beating his wife at the nearby casino restaurant.

Training kicked in, and Madden instinctively stopped the attack and broke Hemrod's arm. Little did he know that the kingpin owned the town, the police, the sheriff and the schools. Due to lack of teachers in Tres Rios, Madden was given a choice—teach at a rural school for a year or go to state prison for assault. He fulfilled his year of teaching and was rumored to be responsible for the deaths of the kingpin and a group of terrorists at the uranium mine.

This day was to be a new beginning for Madden, Wells, the Tres Rios Rural School, and the local law enforcement/security officers of Calico County. Something was amiss, and Wells was trying to read the situation—with intentions to help.

"Rob, I don't know what happened this morning, but I get the impression it was tragic—is there anything I can do to help?"

"No, Russ, just allowing me a few extra days here would be extremely helpful."

"Fine. Is there anything you can tell me? What has changed to delay your departure?" Wells asked, more curious than caring.

"In due time, you will know, in due time," mumbled Madden.

Getting up from his broken kitchen chair, Wells picked up Madden's mug, refilled it with coffee and put his own mug on the counter.

"I'll be going now, Rob, so contact me if you need anything."

"Thanks, Russ. You'll never know when I may need a favor from you."

Sheriff Wells had a sixth sense that favor would be needed sooner rather than later.

"See ya, Sarge, and please keep me updated." Wells affectionately said his goodbye, walked down the steps to his patrol car and headed out of the parking lot for the gravel road to Tres Rios, leaving a cloud of dust in his wake.

Approaching the main highway back to town, Wells noticed a car going the opposite direction heading toward Madden's trailer. Slowing almost to a stop, Wells was curious who was driving the Ford SUV with New Mexico plates. Upon passing the vehicle, he noticed that the driver looked like one of the escort girls from the Flying Buffalo Casino Truck Stop—lots of makeup and lipstick. She waved at Wells as she passed and blew him a kiss.

Oh well. We've given Madden everything he needed since he's been here, might as well have some company now—what the hell. Enjoy! Wells thought to himself.

The Ford SUV slowly traveled to the trailer's parking lot and came to an abrupt stop in front of the trailer.

CHAPTER

5

"Yes, I just arrived at Rob's trailer," announced Special Agent Bonnie McCord over a cell phone to her superior at the DEA operations headquarters.

"Okay, Bonnie, you know what you have to do—get it done and keep me advised immediately to his reaction." Pausing for a minute and reflecting, he added "You and I both know this has to be done—there is no way out for us or Madden."

"Yes, I understand," replied McCord, hanging up and mentally preparing herself for her meeting with Madden.

From their off and on professional association through the past three years, McCord had a special liking and attraction for her old mentor, Madden. He saved her life in the jungles of Colombia fighting the FARC, and she in turn saved his from the local drug lord fixed on revenge. Sometimes she would smile and fantasize about going off with Madden to Stanford University and starting a new life with him in Florida—he with his doctorate in education and her setting up a law practice somewhere.

Still smiling about her dream, she put on her professional game face. McCord looked at herself in the rearview mirror to ensure she still looked presentable in her present uniform. Now laughing at herself in the very black and alluring, maybe sleazy, attire of a blackjack dealer from the Flying Buffalo Casino, she still could not get used to all the makeup she was required to wear.

"Okay, Rob, let's get down to business," she said to herself as she slid out of the SUV in her short black leather skirt and stiletto heels.

She saw Madden through the screen door, just sitting and staring out the window—occasionally taking a sip of coffee.

"Knock, knock, knock." McCord hit the side of the door at the same time announcing her arrival.

"Rob, it's me, Bonnie. May I come in?"

Slowly turning his head toward the trailer door, Madden could not make out or understand what he was seeing. Recognizing what appeared to be an attractive and scantily dressed woman at the door, he was not sure but could have sworn it was Bonnie McCord.

"McCord, get in here," Madden said, still eyeing her and confused what the hell she was doing looking like a cheap cocktail waitress from the casino. Answers would come later, he suspected.

As McCord entered, Madden instinctively rose to greet her. McCord could not hold herself back. She immediately ran to Madden and held him tightly in her arms, with her head on his shoulder. Surprised at this reception and rather enjoying it, he also held McCord while both enjoyed this short, romantic interlude. Nothing was said for a few minutes as uncontrollable tears ran down both faces.

"Yes, Bonnie, it's good to see you, but we need to talk," Madden whispered to McCord as she let go of Madden, fixed her attire and grabbed a small tissue from her purse to wipe a few tears from her eyes and the heavy mascara that was surely running down her face.

"Let me guess, Bonnie, your people, the Feds, sent you to tell me who they believe killed my family. Is this correct?"

"Rob, please, why don't we sit down at the table here and have a nice talk, and I'll explain what I know," McCord suggested.

"Would you like some coffee?" Madden asked. "The sheriff was just here, and he made a pot."

"Yes, Rob, that would be good," she replied as she moved a pile of books from a kitchen chair.

Getting his anger and emotions calmed down and checked, he was now going back to his old Air Force sergeant role—*let's keep it cool and react with reason, stay cool.* Of course he wanted to explode and yell, "Enough, who killed my family? Tell me now!"

McCord found herself a clean mug and poured herself some coffee, returned to her seat at the table and opened a professional portfolio binder she had brought.

"Bonnie, would you please do me a favor before we begin?" Madden tried not to stare at McCord's cleavage or be distracted by her sensual attire, which included black fishnet stockings.

"Sure, Rob, what do you want?" she asked, looking at Madden flirtatiously over her reading glasses.

"Would you please go into the bathroom and change your clothes? I have a clean sweat suit in the bathroom you can wear. Would you mind?"

"Sure, Rob, give me a minute," she mused as she almost forgot the effect her appearance could have on men, and she did enjoy the attention from her year of working at the casino.

"What are you doing still wearing that casino outfit? I thought you were through with your undercover work since the explosion," he asked McCord as she was changing in the bathroom.

"Rob, this is my last day. I thought you might get a kick out of what a working girl looks like." The smell of her perfume lingered in the trailer's kitchen as Madden waited for McCord's return from the bathroom. Madden wanted to sneak a peek inside her portfolio; however, she knew Madden and had taken it with her in the bathroom.

"Okay, Rob, is this better?" McCord modeled the slouchy sweats as if in a fashion show.

"Thank you, much better," he said, with an approving nod.

After both sat down at the kitchen table, McCord opened her portfolio and adjusted her reading glasses. Madden was anxious to get started, and bad memories were starting to return. He was ready for answers.

"Now, Bonnie, why don't we get right to the point? You called me this morning, out of nowhere, and explained that you know who killed my family—who are they and where are they?" He stared at the portfolio in her hands as he seemed to become more agitated.

"Yes, Rob, we do have information on the killers of your wife and two daughters and feel very confident we know where they are," McCord said sternly. "However, when I attempted to contact you this morning with the information, I received no response, no reply—nothing."

She paused. "I completely understand your needing time to digest and prepare yourself for receiving such critical information, but I would have appreciated some sort of callback from you.

"I was worried about you and your reaction to the news— that's why I'm here now," she said softly, momentarily touching his arm.

Madden's sudden urge to vent in anger was subdued by McCord's gentle touch. "Enough, Bonnie, let's get down to what I need to know—who and where are the killers?" Madden almost demanded now.

"All right," she said, opening a report from her portfolio. She began briefing Madden on the conditions he would be required to agree to before receiving such classified and sensitive information.

"Conditions, what conditions?" Madden angrily asked. "I busted my ass and nearly got killed to hand over Hemrod and his drug operation to you and your DEA friends, to include some damn terrorists, and now you want conditions before you'll hand over the names of the killers to me? I can't believe this," he shouted, pointing at McCord.

She was expecting such a turn in the conversation and attempted to defuse it.

"Rob, you and all of us know if we had not tracked and stopped Humza Aldawasari and his terrorist cell, you certainly would be dead now—no doubt!"

He jumped on that: "What bullshit. Your guys were tracking him since his little sleeper cell in Detroit. You could have taken him out before he left Michigan. But no. You have to bring him all the way down to Tres Rios, New Mexico, with me as the bait. Am I wrong in any of this?" Madden's voice was gradually rising.

"Yes, Rob, you certainly were used as bait, as you call it, to bring Aldawasari out of Detroit," she acknowledged. "That was not our call, at least from the DEA's perspective. We just wanted Billy Hemrod and his drug and distribution operations out of business, completely."

She explained, "The Aldawasari project was dreamed up by the higher ups at the FBI and CIA. We just assisted as ordered, Rob. And there's one other item you need to know," she said, lowering her voice and staring at Madden.

"Not sure if you knew, but my undercover assignment as a blackjack dealer at the casino saved your life," she said. "I figure you owe me, Rob."

Breathing less heavily and with his composure coming back to normal, Madden thought hard about what McCord had just told him, trying to put all the pieces together, including the mysteries that shrouded his year at Tres Rios.

"Rob, Hemrod's bust was planned for years—even prior to you ending up here, you damn do-gooder."

He stared at her.

"Did you ever figure out who stole Hemrod's truck and distracted his doped-up gang just prior to them almost breaking your arm?" McCord asked, not expecting an answer.

"Yes, Bonnie, I do remember that—very close call." Madden was now almost grinning.

"There are also a few other incidents where I interceded on your behalf and you had no way of knowing, but it sure was exciting," McCord reminisced. "One other thing you need to know. We had wiretaps on Hemrod and his crew since we started operations here, from the very beginning, and paid informants in the area."

"Yes, I'm listening, please go on," Madden said, now interested in her review of events.

"It is obvious, with all of the voice recordings we obtained in the past year from Hemrod and crew, they disliked you immensely, and if not running their little drug operation, they were planning to take you out before you had a chance to leave Tres Rios."

"Bonnie, before you continue, would you like some more coffee?" Madden offered as a gesture of conciliation.

"Sure, many thanks," she replied, handing Madden her cup as he found his way to the coffeemaker.

With refills of coffee, Madden took his seat across from McCord and opened a box of Girl Scout cookies he received as a going-away gift from one of his students.

"Thank you," she said, taking a sip. "Let me be quite clear about one thing, Rob. If we had not been here working the sting on Hemrod, you would be dead."

"Were the police or law enforcement around here involved in this plot to do me in?" Madden asked.

"No, in fact, Sheriff Wells and his people had warned Hemrod on numerous occasions to leave you alone—nothing was to happen to you."

"Do you know why the sheriff and the other officers wanted to give you this wonderful, going-away escort out of the county?" McCord asked sarcastically.

Madden shook his head no.

"Because they had heard of plots to kill you from various sources and through some sense of honor, if you can imagine any of these jokers having honor, liked you and wanted to get you out of town without incident," she said and grabbed a Thin Mint out of the cookie box.

"So don't be telling me that the Feds, the DEA or I had anything to do with your challenges here at Tres Rios. You should bless your lucky stars and your very good friend Bonnie McCord that you are alive and departing Tres Rios," she said with a smirk.

Taking another sip of his coffee and also grabbing a cookie from the box, Madden sat back, stared outside for a moment, then looked back at McCord.

After a stressful year at Tres Rios and plenty of intense, stress-relieving workouts, he remained a lean, muscular man of just under six feet. The New Mexico sun turned his light complexion somewhat darker and had lightened his short brown hair. Many said he resembled the actor Robert Redford with his easy swagger and charismatic personality and smile. It was difficult to believe a guy with his almost boyish good looks served in Special Forces and survived.

McCord was enjoying Madden's company. She also was staring at him—the kitchen was quiet. While training with Madden in Colombia, McCord had pulled her long brown hair back in a ponytail, and the tom boy appearance in her military uniforms gave her an all-American, girl-next-door appeal—a stark contrast to the sexy bombshell sitting across his kitchen table in a loose-fitting warm-up suit.

Perhaps it was her piercing green eyes that quickened his heartbeat. Or the slashing scar, now fading, across her left cheek from a bullet that grazed her while fighting revolutionaries with him in Columbia.

Madden thought the scar added to McCord's mystique. Even at a sturdy five-foot-five, she was one woman you did not want to tangle with. She had been married once while serving as a lawyer in the Air Force, but eventually the marriage dissolved, and McCord went off to join the DEA for a little adventure. She had many male suitors, but her DEA was now a priority—ambition and power had taken over Bonnie McCord.

"All right, where do we stand?" Madden broke the tranquility as the cool, dry desert breeze whispered through the trailer's screen door. "This morning, I was just about to leave Tres Rios, my loving second home as you well know, to Stanford to complete my doctorate in education, and surprisingly I receive a phone call from you saying you know who killed my family, and you know where they are. Am I correct?" Madden worked to be as calm as possible, but still was confused about where McCord was going with her "conditions."

"Yes, that is correct," McCord confirmed.

"Now, please bear with me, but let me assume the reason you're not telling me who the killers are is that you suspect I'll simply want to go after them and make them and their families suffer. Is this correct, Bonnie?"

"That's part of it, but we both know you have options," she noted.

"One option, I suspect, would be to take that portfolio away from you, pull the information I need and take care of business my way—without involving the Feds or taxpayer dollars." He looked at her. "Just a public service to my country, very clean and easy."

"Trust me, Rob, I'll give you this portfolio today with no problems, but it only contains a summary of the conditions. There is not a shred of information here regarding what you are looking for," she assured Madden.

"I suspected as such, but wanted to see your reaction," Madden bluffed.

Birds outside Madden's trailer were starting to make their normal, noisy visit to the large cottonwood tree adjacent to the parking lot, near the old wooden picnic table. Madden had enjoyed hearing their chirping in the early morning and evening. It was always calming to hear the birds' chatter.

"Let's see, option two. Right now I could get in my packed Honda Element and head to Stanford University, finish my degree, and worry about settling the score at another time," Madden suggested. "I have good people counting on me to earn the degree and get back to work in Florida."

"So what's stopping you, Rob? I know you well enough to know this would never work for you. Remember the old Sgt. Madden?"

"Ah yes, the old Sgt. Madden—what would he do in this situation?"

Madden was almost laughing at himself regarding where this conversation was going with Special Agent Bonnie McCord. She was now more relaxed, drinking her coffee and playing with her hair—knowing all the answers.

"You know, Bonnie, this little get-together of ours reminds me of the meeting I had with Sheriff Wells and County Attorney Raymond Garcia when I first arrived here—do you know about the deal they offered me?"

"Yes, we know all about it. Let's see, you were given a choice between state prison for breaking the arm of one of Tres Rios's favorite sons—Billy Hemrod, the drug kingpin, or teaching school at Tres Rios, right?" The beaming grin on McCord's face said it all.

She continued, "For your information, Rob, we had been monitoring Wells's office for a long time and knew of his involvement with Hemrod's group for some time. You should have taken the state prison choice. We could have gotten you out in an afternoon," McCord kidded, enjoying the dialogue with her old instructor and mentor.

"Well, it seems like I'm in a game that has already been called—so why don't you tell me my options," Madden said, resigned to the fact he was going nowhere without the help from the Feds, or the Feds were going nowhere without his assistance.

"Okay, let's talk!" McCord shifted her personality to the professional DEA Special Agent she was and grabbed her pen and portfolio, sat up straight and adjusted her glasses.

"Okay, Special Agent, what's the deal this time?"

Without using notes or documents, McCord slowly updated Madden.

"As you well know, in the world of the al-Qaeda organization, Anwar and Humza Aldawasari were considered top leaders. You were a marked man after being named responsible for the death of Anwar with that drone strike you authorized in Yemen." McCord looked Madden in the eyes.

"However, no one in their right mind thought that al-Qaeda would actually pursue or mount a vengeance strike against one of our military or Special Forces teams here in the United States—it just is inconceivable." She tapped her pen on the table.

Listening while drinking more coffee was nothing new to Madden.

"We know where you are going, we know they found a way to murder my wife and daughters." Madden's annoyance began to show as he was more than familiar with McCord's briefing.

She said, "We had initially thought al-Qaeda was satisfied with the deaths of your family, but his brother Humza Aldawasari was not."

"Ah yes, he is the character that you and your friends allowed to travel all the way from Detroit to good ol' Tres Rios, to seek me out and kill me for the death of his brother Anwar," Madden added. "Many thanks for letting me know this prior to his showing up. What were your people thinking?" Madden asked.

McCord realized the update brought up past wounds. She listened.

"Now I suspect the government will let it be known that I am responsible for the deaths of two of al-Qaeda's top leaders," shouted Madden as he jumped up from the table and looked outside the trailer, rubbing his head.

Calmly, McCord responded, "Rob, they already suspect you were involved in the disappearance of Humza. The FBI had been monitoring his little sleeper cell in Detroit, and there is no doubt they believe you alone were probably responsible for his demise—that and his traveling companions."

"Well this is just great," a frustrated Madden angrily said. "Let me guess, getting down to brass tacks, I suspect you're here to warn me of the dangers facing me from another al-Qaeda vengeance team."

McCord, almost in tears, stood up and put her arm around Madden's shoulder and firmly held him while she guided him back to the kitchen table. "Please, Rob, please sit down."

"Damn it, Bonnie, who is responsible?"

"The same people who are right now planning your assassination on the road between here and Stanford

University," she said. "And according to our informants and phone monitoring, the momentum and enthusiasm for your death is building every day with the disappearance of Humza."

Surprised by the quick response from McCord, Madden sat back for a minute. He grabbed a small notebook from the kitchen counter and began looking at its calendar. The ever-present pictures of his late wife and children were proudly displayed on the kitchen wall. Looking up from his notebook, he stared at the pictures for a few more moments. McCord sat motionless, glancing back and forth between her portfolio and Madden's face.

"I am expected to begin my studies at Stanford in two weeks. I'm going to Stanford."

The only sounds came from the chirping and gaggling birds outside in the trees and the steady tick-tock metronome sounds of the kitchen clock.

"Unfortunately, no, Rob," McCord answered with a few tears and trembling lips.

Just sitting in his chair nodding his head, resigned to the fact he was not leaving for California, Madden asked, "What is next, Special Agent?"

She got up from her chair and knelt next to Madden, stroking his hair and resting her head on his arm.

Surprised by the sudden show of affection, he reached down to embrace her shoulders. They held each other tight while Madden gradually placed his hands on her wet face.

"It's okay," he assured her in almost a whisper. He broke the embrace and asked, "Bonnie, if I am not going to Stanford, where am I going?"

Backing away now and grabbing a Kleenex from a nearby box on the kitchen counter and wiping away tears, Bonnie said, "Rob, this afternoon you are to drive to the Northern New Mexico Printing Company in Albuquerque and wait for further instructions."

"Hold on. Wait just a second. Hear me out," Madden vented, realizing the magnitude of direction given him now was weighing on the many other complicated issues facing his future—

especially his commitment to Dr. Tessa McDonald and the Crestview Public School System in Florida that was sponsoring his doctorate degree.

"How am I going to explain all of this to Dr. McDonald and her school board?" Madden asked as he got up from the table and went to his briefcase.

"Rob, may I ask what you are looking for?" she asked.

He continued searching for a document he wanted to show McCord.

"Rob, please, just tell me about the document. You don't need to show me."

"Dr. McDonald and Stanford University were kind enough to permit me a one-year delay to begin classes. One year, Bonnie— you know all of this."

"Rob, we have already taken care of explaining to Dr. McDonald and the officials at Stanford the many reasons why we need to extend your delay in beginning your studies," McCord explained. "It very much hinges on national security and your quest to see your family's killers held accountable."

He looked up.

"What's it gonna be, Rob?"

Turning away from his briefcase and looking at McCord, resigned to the fact there were no other options, Madden said, "All right, give me some time to gather my thoughts and make a few phone calls, and I'll be on my way to Albuquerque."

"Thanks, Rob, let's see what adventure awaits us." She looked at her phone and noted the time. "I suspect I better get back to the casino and put my papers in to quit—no use hanging around with Billy Hemrod and his gang no longer around." She put her coffee cup in the sink.

"Oh, Rob, one other thing I forget to tell you," she said.

"No more surprises," Madden said, "I have just participated in the killing of a drug lord and his gang to include an international terrorist and his loyal followers, and I have just been recruited by the Feds to participate in an operation that includes dealing with the terrorists who killed my family."

McCord just stood listening, entertained by this drama.

"And please don't forget, we now have terrorists coming after me to avenge the killing of the Aldawasari brothers—al-Qaeda's finest. Could it get any better?" Madden said, now trying to make light of all that had happened. "Oh yes, it does. The fine people who sponsored my degree will now be waiting two years for me just to start the program—if they remember who I am after two years."

"Rob, while you're reminiscing about your good times in Tres Rios, I'm going back to your bathroom and get back into my casino uniform. Is that fine with you?"

"Sure, make yourself at home," Madden said.

Madden heard the water running in the bathroom as McCord was changing. He also heard her singing away as she had in the primitive quarters at their forward operating base in Colombia while stationed together. He turned on the radio to the local country western station—he was tired of listening to the all-Spanish stations with their accordion and mariachi music—always about wanting or waiting for love.

Madden reflected on the sudden change of his plans. *And it could have happened,* thought Madden, *so close to happening.*

He was almost in a trance, dreaming, when he heard the door of the bathroom open to see Bonnie McCord with a large bath towel wrapped around herself.

"Rob, I need to talk to you," she softly said.

Madden, as if drawn to the Siren's song, joined her in the hallway. Without a word, he gently embraced her face with his hands and leaned down for a passionate kiss that had been years in the making.

As she wrapped her arms around his neck, leaning into the kiss she had been hoping would finally happen, Madden loosened the towel with his right hand, scooped up her still-wet body with his left and moved her into the small bedroom.

Only the chattering birds outside heard the passionate cries and lovers' talk.

McCord got out of bed, leaving Madden gently snoring. She showered again and donned her tight-fitting, sleazy black casino uniform.

She returned to the bedroom to sneak in a farewell kiss and found him propped on his right side, smiling. She sat down next to him, and his free hand traced the outline of her thigh.

"That was nice." Madden didn't know what else to say.

The typical McCord went immediately back to business— her mission.

"Now Rob, there is one other piece of information you need to know before you head for Albuquerque this afternoon."

"Bonnie, what now?"

"When you cross the Calico County line, you will be arrested by the Feds and taken into custody in Albuquerque. A wrecker truck will be there to carry your Honda to the federal impound. Any questions, Rob?" McCord had withheld this information for last, not knowing how he would react.

"This dream of going to California sure is taking a beating, and this takes the cake," he said.

Thinking for a while and resigned that there was no use arguing or questioning, he simply nodded.

"Thank you for the heads up. Anything else?"

"Rob, you know this is all for show," she said, "because there are still elements out there that we believe are credible in wanting to see you gone. So we are just being very careful. And remember Hemrod had many state and county officials on his payroll. We're not sure how much they knew about you or acts of vengeance they might take to keep incidents quiet here at Tres Rios—you might know too much in their eyes."

Madden never considered this, but McCord, with her vast knowledge of the conversations going on between Hemrod's organization and the outside, must have suspected something was amiss and that there was a possible threat.

"Yes, you do have a point," he said, resigned to the fact McCord was correct. "I may know a little too much about Billy Hemrod that others in the state may not appreciate."

McCord stood up from the bed.

"Okay, Mr. Madden, thank you so very much for your time this morning. I hope I was not an inconvenience to you," she said in her professional tone. And then, "One more hug?"

Madden found his boxers on the floor and put them on. He stood. Bonnie embraced him and whispered in his ear, "Tell me you care for me."

"I do," he said softly, "I do."

"Now look at me!" McCord ordered as she moved Madden's face directly in front of hers. "Wait for me, Rob, wait for me."

"I have nothing else to do," he jokingly replied.

"Smart ass," she said, giving him a quick pat on his butt.

"One minute she's a professional deadly agent seeking my services to track down terrorists and killers, the next, she's a romantic siren seeking affection—oh, how exciting," Madden said with a smile.

McCord grabbed her portfolio and opened the screen door to leave, giving Madden an unexpected kiss on the cheek while rushing to her SUV in the parking lot. Madden stepped outside and waved goodbye, not knowing when he might see her again.

"I didn't think it would be this tough being a public-school teacher," Madden called after her.

CHAPTER

6

As Bonnie McCord was just about halfway down the dirt road in the quarry heading for her last day at the Flying Buffalo Casino, she noticed a rather strange, loud car coming from the other direction, also with a large dust cloud following its progress. As the car neared McCord's SUV, she recognized a familiar face—Hank, Madden's school fix-it man. With McCord knowing who all the players were in Madden's world at Tres Rios, she suspected Hank just knew her as a painted-up blackjack dealer at the casino.

They eyed each other, passing with mutual friendly waves. McCord continued her drive to the casino, and Hank drove to the trailer's parking lot, parked the car and looked around. Madden's Honda was still in the parking lot, and the screen door of the trailer was open.

Hank rapped on the screen door and said, "Mr. Madden, you should have been long gone by now,"

"Hey amigo, over here!" Madden shouted at Hank while sitting in his favorite makeshift wooden chair under the cottonwood tree.

"Shit!" a very startled and surprised Hank yelled as if he had seen the second coming of Jesus.

Regaining his composure, Hank smiled and waved at Madden, who was visibly amused at Hank's reaction.

"Hank, do us both a favor. Get us some coffee out of the trailer and come on back here and talk with me," Madden said.

"Sure, boss, good idea," replied Hank as he opened the screen door of the trailer to the kitchen and made more coffee. It appeared to Hank that someone had already been drinking coffee that morning with Madden. Also, he smelled the fragrance of a woman's perfume lingering in the air. A peek down the hall at the jumbled bedsheets confirmed his suspicions.

I'll be darned, boss must have gotten a going-away present from the casino, Hank assumed and smiled.

"Here you go, boss, just brewed," Hank said as he handed the coffee to Madden.

"Thanks. Surprised to still see me?"

"Yeah, I thought you would be long gone by now, with the sheriff's escort and all of that—what happened if I may ask?"

"First, it is good to see you, and what are you doing here?" Madden inquired, still smiling.

"Well, I was asked by your old friend and school superintendent, Dr. Kramer, to come out here after you left and clean the place up for the next teacher showing up," Hank said, "and here you are—please say you decided to stay."

Madden bellowed out a laugh at that comment and slapped Hank on the back—both grinning and laughing knowing that would never be the case.

"Nice of you to say, but I think I have been destined for something else," Madden said.

"I thought you would have been at the New Mexico border by now heading to California, surfing or seeing all the movie stars." Hank laughed. "But no, here you are, what gives?"

"Hank, do you remember the movie *The Godfather* several years ago, where the Godfather was known for giving offers somebody could not refuse?"

"Sure, I do remember," Hank said. "That was a great movie. Did you get an offer you can't refuse?"

"Unfortunately, yes, I have." Of course, Madden really did not know where he was going, except to the Northern New Mexico Publishing Company in Albuquerque, a DEA front.

"Hank, please listen to me good," Madden began, "if anyone should ask if I left for California, please let them know I just departed today. However, I was detained for a few days by the Feds wanting more information from me on the mine explosion. Apparently, they think I know something about that," Madden added.

Both men were now taking long sips of their coffee.

"Okay, continuing on to California sounds good to me," Hank said, trying to make light of the situation. "Sunny beaches, warm weather and pretty girls."

"Right, I got it made," Madden confirmed, knowing full well he was probably going from the frying pan into the fire by avenging the killers of his family.

"Hank, I hope the next teacher enjoys this place as much as I have," Madden said, almost getting sentimental as the New Mexico wind started to kick up. "I'm going to take a leak, and then I'm heading out."

"It has been an interesting year for both of us, wouldn't you say?" Hank observed.

"Yes, but I don't want to do it again, that's for sure."

"Buena suerte, Hank, and will keep in touch." Madden shook his old friend's hand.

Hank went to his car to get his tools, and Madden walked into the trailer for the last time. While washing his hands and grabbing for a towel, Madden saw a pair of woman's black panties hanging from the overhead light. It did not take a village idiot to determine that they were most likely left by Bonnie McCord while she was changing in the bathroom. Granted, he was sure she had left them to get a rise out of Madden, and her desired effect was just that.

"Oh, Bonnie, why are you doing this to me?" Madden muttered to himself. He grabbed the panties and stuck them in his back pocket.

Getting in the Honda, he rolled down the window and yelled out to Hank the old military saying, "Hank, it's been real, it's been fun, but it hasn't been real fun."

He headed down the gravel road one last time, leaving the typical swirl of dust behind him.

CHAPTER
7

"Thanks, Tres Rios, for the memories," shouted Madden out the open window of his Honda as he turned onto State Highway 605 heading toward Interstate 40 like he did almost exactly a year before.

He drove by the Tres Rios Rural Elementary School and noticed the new construction and additions to the once lone school building.

"What a change," he thought, wiping a tear from his cheek, or maybe it was road dust.

He slowed to look at the uranium mine, where forensic work continued. The security complex headed by Hemrod and his team was no more, with what appeared to be the whole side of a cliff burying the facilities and the old mine shaft—used by Hemrod as a large drug lab and regional distribution center.

Investigators were still milling around the explosion site, going through the mountain of rubble probing the cause of the explosion that killed Hemrod's crew.

Wonder if they will ever know that Humza Aldawasari and his terrorist cell are also buried in that mass of rock and debris? Madden smiled to himself.

He smirked and thought, *I taught Bonnie McCord all she needed to know about using explosives.*

Cranking up George Strait on CD and his favorite song, "Amarillo by Morning," Madden drove off to what was supposed to be Stanford University, but he knew differently—there were paybacks and a deal with the Feds to be dealt with.

"I get them before they get me," said a now serious Madden talking to himself.

Madden topped a hill on Highway 605 and noticed a small cluster of large, nondescript SUVs with blacked-out windows. Along with the SUVs was a rather large wrecker truck capable of carrying a large vehicle on its platform bed.

Bonnie had told him to expect this reception, so Madden slowed as a man stepped out from one of the SUVs and waved his hand to get Madden's attention to slow down and stop. He was wearing cowboy boots, a slim pair of cowboy fit jeans, a white starched Western shirt and a Stratton cowboy hat—a typical outfit for law enforcement officers in the Southwest. Madden also noticed a .45 automatic pistol wrapped in a holster around his belt and a law enforcement badge identifying him as a U.S. Marshal.

Madden stopped the car and lowered the window. The officer slowly walked over to the driver's side of the Honda. Wearing the typical aviator sunglasses worn by Southern law enforcement officers, the marshal smiled at Madden, and Madden smiled in kind at his reflection in the marshal's glasses.

"Well, good afternoon, Mr. Madden, how ya doin' this great day?" the officer asked. "Could I trouble you for your driver's license and registration?"

"Any trouble, officer?" Madden almost laughed at the smiling officer as he handed over the documents.

"Oh, Mr. Madden, we have nothing but problems. How would you like to take a little trip with me down to the Calico County sheriff's office for a little talk?" The marshal let Madden know that he knew his history and reputation.

A year earlier, the sheriff's office was Madden's first stop after being arrested by the Tres Rios law enforcement officers for fighting and beating up Billy Hemrod. The officers interrogated Madden with fists and nightsticks until it was determined he was attempting to defend Hemrod's wife and family from being assaulted. The police tried to correct their mistake, but it was too late. Hemrod wanted Madden in jail.

"No thank you, been there! Done that! Anything else?" replied Madden, enjoying the exchange with the marshal.

"Well, if that is the case, how about we load your vehicle here on that wrecker and you can ride with me to…let's see, Stanford University sound good to you?" the marshal jokingly asked.

"Stanford would be fine," Madden said, nodding his head in agreement and walking with the marshal to one of the SUVs while the crew from the wrecker loaded Madden's Honda.

As Madden slid into the backseat, he recognized a familiar person sitting in the backseat with him.

"Rob Madden, great seeing you. Would you like a Coke or a sandwich? We have plenty," the stranger offered.

"Yes, I remember you," Madden recalled, "aren't you Steve Webb, a DEA Special Agent?"

"Excuse me, Rob." He learned forward and directed the driver, "Nancy, would you go ahead and take us the drop-off site?" Nancy, also a U.S. Marshal, was wearing Southwestern cowgirl attire.

"Yes, sir, we are on our way," she announced as she and the small caravan headed east on Interstate 40.

Both men shook hands and recalled their past associations with each other in Tres Rios while helping themselves to the chicken sandwiches, potato salad, and soft drinks.

"Steve, I should be traveling west this morning toward California, but here I sit going the opposite direction with my friends from the DEA," Madden said, politely getting to the point.

"Don't forget the U.S. Marshals," Webb added.

Nancy turned around for a second and smiled at Rob while monitoring the radio frequency with the other vehicles.

Madden laughed. "Sorry, and the U.S. Marshals."

"Okay, Webb, what's the deal? Where are we going?" Madden asked.

"And what does all this cloak-and-dagger stuff have to do with me finding out who killed my family?" Madden's emotions were beginning to rise.

"Rob, everything will be brought to you in good time," Webb continued. "We are just as intensely interested in finding the killers as you are, trust me. We also lost some agents to the same group that murdered your family."

Webb looked intently at Madden. "That's all I will say right now about their identities, but believe me, we know who did it, and we have some excellent intel regarding where they are."

"Then just tell me," demanded Madden with an intense stare back. "I'll take care of them."

"You're going to have your chance, that's for sure," said Webb, finishing off the last of the potato salad and grabbing another Coke out of the cooler.

"You want another?" Webb offered.

"Yeah, why not? I'm not going anywhere but with you anyway," replied Madden.

Handing Madden a Coke and a napkin, Webb stared out the window at the beautiful high plains, mountains and plateaus of northern New Mexico, wishing he were somewhere else.

"What the hell you lookin' at?" Madden asked.

"Sorry, just daydreaming. It's been a long and stressful year here," Webb answered.

"Listen, asshole, you think you've had a long and stressful year? You're preaching to the choir, pal," Madden said. "You haven't been through shit compared to what I've had to deal with in Tres Rios."

Webb smiled and replied, "I guess I deserved that, Rob."

Breaking the silence except for the occasional chatter on the caravan's law enforcement frequencies, Madden asked, "Webb, where are we going? And, uh, more importantly, where am I going?"

Webb picked up his briefcase, put on his reading glasses and began reviewing a document.

"Rob, we are taking you and your car to the Northern New Mexico Publishing Company in Albuquerque. It's one of our covers here in the state, and we use it for a host of different operations," explained Webb.

"That's nice. Curious minds would like to know what I'm going to be doing at this company."

"First off, we have a small apartment unit within the facility you will be using tonight. It is fully equipped with a small kitchen, bathroom, washer and dryer—everything you need," Webb said.

"Your Honda will stay within the building and will be waiting for you when you complete your mission and are on your way back to Stanford, school teacher," said Webb, trying his best to ease Madden's concerns.

"Great, just great," Madden said. "How long am I going to be your guest at this publishing company?"

"Tomorrow afternoon, you will depart Albuquerque from the Albuquerque International Sunport airport with a destination of Washington, D.C.—to be exact, to the Pentagon."

"Now we're getting somewhere," Madden responded.

"Rob, when we get to the building, I'll brief you further on some additional information about your mission. All right with you?"

"Why not? I have nothing else planned," joked Madden.

The caravan of vehicles made its way to a typical looking industrial warehouse near one of the many exits to the airport. At the vehicle entrance, a rather fat and aging security guard checked the identification of the drivers and proceeded to open doors to allow the vehicles to enter. He immediately closed them once all were in and parked.

The passengers exited the vehicles as the towing crew began unloading Madden's Honda. The marshals drove their SUVs and the wrecker out of the building at a side exit, leaving Madden, Webb, two other DEA agents and the Honda Element.

"Rob, mind if we hitch a ride with you to the publishing company?" Webb asked.

"Oh sure, why not?" Madden said, "any more James Bond secret agent stops you want to make on the way?"

Madden was directed to the Northern New Mexico Publishing Company headquarters located next to the state fairgrounds, not far from the University of New Mexico. Webb instructed him to drive down the ramp to the underground parking, and Madden was guided where to park. The agents got out and helped Madden carry some of his personal belongings to a small, makeshift apartment in the basement of the building.

After putting the boxes and suitcases in the apartment's living room, the two DEA agents bade Madden goodbye and good luck. Webb stayed behind and made himself at home at the pinewood kitchen table, where he again began pulling more files out of his briefcase.

Madden was busy arranging and sorting through his clothes—seeing what needed to be cleaned.

"Why don't you take care of the cleaning later?" Webb suggested.

"Sure, later," Madden said.

Before taking his seat at the table, Madden grabbed a small notebook and pen. The way things were going, he figured he might need it.

"Again, thanks for your patience today. I realize you must have a thousand and one questions regarding this whole operation—especially your conversation with Bonnie McCord this morning," Webb began.

"Not a problem, Steve. I always like it when the Feds send seductive female agents knocking on my door enticing me to join them," replied Madden, remembering he still had McCord's panties in his back pocket. He reached into the pocket and was relieved to find they were secure.

"This is very important for you to know, especially for your own safety and that of others associated with you," warned a stern-faced Webb.

"We'll get into a few details of your assignment later, but for now I need to explain to you the groundwork that has been or is being laid as we speak. We have built a pretty elaborate façade, with the assistance of Stanford and Crestview Public Schools regarding your enrollment at Stanford. Working with university officials, they will be showing that you enrolled and began your studies as scheduled. But that could not be further from the truth."

"Why?" asked Madden, dumbfounded.

"We'll get to that in a minute," Webb said.

"If anyone happens to be looking or searching for you at the university, they will see you are registered and attending classes, but will never find Madden the ghost. The hope and goal are that those searching will continue to do so, with frustrating and confusing results until you return to the campus to begin your studies," briefed Webb.

"What about Crestview Public Schools? I am sure Dr. Tessa McDonald, my boss, will suspect something is amiss," Madden said.

"Rob, in a few days, Dr. McDonald will be briefed by the FBI, CIA and DEA regarding this arrangement."

"So let me get this straight, you want the world to think that I left Tres Rios as scheduled and am on my way to Stanford where I enrolled and am attending class?" a curious Madden asked.

"Yes, and Dr. McDonald will assist us by confirming, to all who ask, that you are indeed in California, and she speaks with you by phone on a regular basis," acknowledged Webb.

"We are going to provide you with a special cell number that cannot be traced by any of the phone companies. You are to make a regular schedule of calling Dr. McDonald. Make normal conversation with her as though you were a Stanford student."

Webb continued, "Again, in your conversations with her, she will know all that you are saying is bullshit, and she in turn will give it right back to you, knowing the situation."

"Well, the $6 million question is why the phony attendance—why the façade?" Madden was anxious to learn the answer.

"When you get to the Pentagon, your questions will be answered."

"All right," a frustrated Madden replied and added, "Webb, I am sure you are well aware of the deal I made with the Feds regarding my 'volunteering' to help—I want first crack at my family's killers, you got that?"

Webb didn't reply.

CHAPTER
8

"Dr. McDonald, you have a call on line 3," said Brenda Willis, administrative assistant to the Crestview Public School superintendent, cracking open the office door to deliver the message.

Dr. Tessa McDonald was discussing the recent district test results with her staff and principals and was annoyed by the interruption. "Brenda, would you please take a message, and I'll get back to them immediately," McDonald replied, returning to dissecting the test scores of the district's students and wondering what would prompt Willis to disturb her in a meeting when she knew better.

"Yes, ma'am," replied Willis as she closed the door.

The test score meeting ended an hour later, with all staff and principals returning to their normal office duties. Dr. McDonald filed a few documents and wrote a few notes to herself before stepping out of her office to talk with Willis about interrupting the meeting.

"Brenda, what is so important that you needed my attention in that meeting?" she asked.

"Dr. McDonald, I thought you might like to see this message immediately," Willis replied, handing McDonald the standard message slip.

Like the hundreds of messages sent to her every day, Dr. McDonald nonchalantly took the slip from Willis and headed into her office. Sitting back in her chair, with piles of folders everywhere—including on the small conference table that adjoined her desk— the superintendent glanced at the slip and immediately sat straight in her chair to read the words again under the reading light on her desk:

"Dr. McDonald, FBI Special Agent Nic Goettemoeller called and would like to speak with you at your earliest convenience." A phone number was written on the form along with the date and time of the message.

"Brenda, would you please step into my office?" McDonald called out.

Willis appeared in the doorway within seconds.

"Thank you, Brenda, please come in and shut the door," said McDonald, holding the message in her hand.

"Yes, you did the correct action in interrupting me in the meeting, and I have to pat you on the back for not announcing to the members the nature of this call," an apologetic McDonald said.

Willis had been McDonald's admin for more than ten years and knew and respected her boss. She realized this was no ordinary matter. In past years, McDonald had been contacted by various law-enforcement agencies regarding students, parents and even school teachers, but the FBI was a little different and usually a lot more serious.

"Brenda, you have been through this before. No mention of this message to anyone," McDonald said. Willis nodded her head and left the office, closing the door behind her to ensure McDonald would not be interrupted that morning.

"Now what?" a frustrated McDonald gasped as she dialed. Preparing herself for the call to the FBI, the superintendent's mind was racing with the different scenarios that she might be presented with: from teachers with child pornography problems to gang activity within the school. The more she thought about possible reasons for the call, the more she worried about the outcome. She reasoned that she and her staff had enough problems working minor miracles to give an exceptional education to their students.

"Good morning, Federal Bureau of Investigation, Mobile Field Office, how may I direct your call?" the operator answered.

"Good morning, I am Dr. Tessa McDonald with the Crestview Public Schools in Walton County, Florida, and I have a message from a Special Agent Nic Goettemoeller."

"Thank you, ma'am, I will connect you, and have a nice day," the operator said.

"Right, have a nice day," McDonald repeated to herself as she waited on the line for Goettemoeller.

"Good morning, Dr. McDonald, and thank you for returning my phone call from this morning," Goettemoeller said. "I hope I am not interrupting you. I trust you are extremely busy."

McDonald was amused at the niceties.

"Special Agent Goettemoeller—" McDonald started to say.

"Oh, please call me Nic," replied Goettemoeller.

"How can I help you?" McDonald said, her brain running at full speed attempting to be ready for anything the FBI needed to know.

"Thank you for your assistance. Are you familiar with a student of yours named Marvin Banister?"

"Yes, Nic. I am thoroughly familiar with Marvin Banister and his family," a stunned and surprised McDonald replied. She could write a book on Banister's family history—several delinquency problems, fighting in the classrooms and drug problems. And that's not including the many law enforcement problems with the parents. In the past, McDonald was interviewed by local police, state police, the DEA and several other agencies regarding the Banister family.

But never the FBI.

"What have the Banisters done now?" she thought.

"We would like to talk with you about the Banisters here in our offices in Mobile. Is that possible? Maybe this Saturday afternoon at two o'clock?" Goettemoeller politely asked.

"I am to be at our school's high school track meet this Saturday," explained McDonald, "because we are in competition for state championships in a couple of events. Is it possible we could discuss any issues you have in my office?" she asked, wondering why the FBI wanted her to travel to Mobile just to talk about the Banisters.

"Dr. McDonald, I can tell you this: yes, it is imperative we speak with you as soon as possible, in person, at the Mobile office," Goettemoeller stressed, adding, "if you need transportation, I can arrange for an agent to transport you to and from where you live."

"All right, Nic. I'll be at your office at two o'clock Saturday, just email me the details," she said, resigned to the fact the FBI wanted her in Mobile.

"I will. You're only about an hour away," he said. "Also, please don't go to any trouble researching or refreshing yourself with your Banister case files or records—we have everything we need here. We just want to get your take on a certain situation, okay?"

"Fine, I'll be there," she said, thinking of all the events and commitments she had scheduled for the weekend, and now the FBI wanted to speak with her in Mobile.

"One other thing," Goettemoeller assured McDonald, "your visit is critical in helping you and your school. See you Saturday."

"What?" she said into a dial tone.

She opened the office door. "Brenda, please clear and reschedule my appointments for this Saturday. It appears I am going to Mobile."

CHAPTER
9

"Robert, I just got off Interstate 10 heading up North Water Street," Tessa McDonald relayed on her cell phone to her husband. "I'll give you a call when I leave Mobile. Bye, love."

Tessa found herself at the FBI field office in the federal building. She checked her watch after parking in front of the building and discovered she was 15 minutes early.

"Oh well, let's get this over with," she told herself as she grabbed her briefcase and cell phone, slid out of her Buick and headed for the building's main entrance. She noticed the parking lot was almost empty. Momentarily stopping just outside the entrance, she remembered all the activity on the Mobile Ship Channel many years before when she studied in Mobile. She smiled and headed for the entrance.

She noticed the standard security checkpoint and what looked like retired police officers manning it, somewhat more relaxed on a Saturday afternoon and, like her, wishing they were somewhere else. After being cleared through security, she made her way to the reception area where a young black man received her in a most cordial manner.

"Good afternoon, I am Dr. Tessa McDonald. I have an appointment with a Special Agent Nic Goettemoeller."

"Yes, welcome to the Mobile FBI Field Office. Agent Goettemoeller is expecting you," the young man said. "May I see a photo ID, please?"

He handed her ID back and said, "Make yourself comfortable in the visitor's lounge," and pointed down the hall.

She was beginning to enjoy the lounge with its coffee machine and tray of pastries, two TVs tuned to cable news, and a host of magazines and newspapers.

McDonald had many tasks she could have been working on with her laptop while waiting but decided to enjoy all the creature comforts the FBI offered.

The rumble of an elevator could be heard with the distinct ding of its arrival at the first floor.

McDonald turned to see a pleasant-looking man in his mid-40s, athletic build with some graying hair, smiling and coming her way. In her mind, she thought this is what FBI agents should look like.

Gathering her purse and laptop and finishing off the Danish pastry, she got up and swiped away any crumbs on her lips.

"Dr. McDonald, good morning, ma'am. I'm Nic Goettemoeller and I want to thank you for meeting us here in Mobile," he said. "How was your trip in? Any problems?"

"No, Nic. No problems." They shook hands.

"I would like to escort you up to our briefing room, where there will be a few more agents interested in speaking with you," he said, leading McDonald to the elevator.

Goettemoeller made small talk with McDonald about the weather, her school duties and her family. McDonald joined in the conversation but was conscious of what she should say—she would indeed be careful in the FBI field headquarters.

Arriving at the third floor, Goettemoeller guided her to a secured conference room with two serious-looking security guards at the entrance. Goettemoeller signed McDonald into the sensitive compartmented information facility, or SCIF. She was asked to leave her laptop at the security desk.

As McDonald walked into the SCIF, she noticed a few other men and women drinking coffee and having side discussions.

"Good afternoon, everyone," Goettemoeller said. "Could we get everyone to take their seats, please."

He turned to Tessa and said, "Dr. McDonald, if you would be so kind as to sit here," and escorted her to a seat that had a professional nameplate with "Dr. Tessa McDonald," written name on it.

She looked around and saw others in the room also had nameplates and designations where they worked.

My gosh, all of this attention for that worthless Banister family, McDonald thought to herself.

"I would like to make a few introductions," Goettemoeller began.

"Dr. McDonald, this is Senior Special Agent Curtis Lee with the FBI headquarters in Washington." Lee rose from his chair and shook McDonald's hand.

Goettemoeller gestured. "Also, Senior Special Agent Paul Kenny with the DEA in Virginia and Special Agent Ryan Meyers with the CIA, also in Virginia." Goettemoeller concluded with introductions of the various other staff personnel in chairs surrounding the conference room. Each got up from their seats and introduced themselves to McDonald.

"Nic, why don't you get us started with an intro and preliminaries," Lee directed. McDonald, now nervous and dumbfounded at all the high-ranking federal law enforcement people in this one room, found herself at the head of the table.

The Banisters must have really done it now, McDonald thought to herself.

The conference room grew quiet as the lights dimmed and a huge lighted screen dropped down from the ceiling bearing a large FBI symbol. Goettemoeller went to a lighted podium at the front of the room.

"Dr. McDonald, again welcome, and we are glad you are here. We definitely need your help," he said. "Please keep in mind anything said in this room is to stay only in this room—this is critical. The information you are about to hear is highly classified and cannot be permitted to leave this room. Do you understand?"

"Yes," she confirmed in as loud a voice as her nervousness allowed.

"Dr. McDonald, I will be upfront and say you were not asked to come here to discuss Marvin Banister or his family—it was a deception to give others, yourself included, a bona fide reason for your visit here today. We did our research and found the Banisters were problems with your school district in the past, and it made sense the Feds would be interested. There are other important matters we need to discuss with you that are highly sensitive and could be potentially dangerous."

"What?" she stammered. "May I ask what the hell is going on here, if you have no interest in the Banisters?"

The faces around the room showed tight smiles, as if understanding her concerns.

"Dr. McDonald, we understand a Mr. Robert Madden is employed with the Crestview Public School System," Goettemoeller began.

"Where is this going, Nic?" she asked calmly. "Yes, he is one of our stellar elementary school teachers who was selected to receive a full scholarship for a doctoral degree in education from Stanford University last year."

She began to relax. "Last year on his way to California, he got into a conflict with a drug lord in New Mexico who was beating up his wife. Rob stopped the fight, but unbeknownst to him, the drug lord owned the police and the town, also..."

"Thank you, Dr. McDonald, we are all very aware of what transpired with Rob Madden after he left Florida for Stanford."

"Well, last time I heard from Rob a few days ago, he was packed up, completed his teaching commitment and was on his way to Stanford," she said. "I had heard there was a terrible mine explosion near where Rob lived that accidentally killed the drug lord and his gang. That's all I know."

Silence filled the room as most of the attendees were now looking at Goettemoeller with expressionless faces—only Lee, Kenny, and Meyers knew Madden's exact status.

"Tell me, Rob is on his way to Stanford, is he not?" a worried and concerned McDonald said to everyone in the room, as if

Madden were one of her sons. "Damn it, would someone please assure me that Rob is on the road to Stanford as we speak?"

"Dr. McDonald, since the mine explosion in New Mexico and Madden's last day at school in Tres Rios, unfortunately many things have changed for Madden and us," Lee explained.

"Let me make a few points to you if I may," McDonald said, unwilling to wait for the official line. "First, Mr. Madden works for me and is obligated to my school district and the state to earn his doctorate and return to his duties at the Crestview Public Schools as soon as he completes his degree."

She looked at each of the attendees. "Second, the administration at Stanford has been very generous in postponing the start of Madden's academic studies until now, a year later than planned.

"Third, and let me remind you again, Madden does not work for the federal government. He works for me, and I am the one accountable for his actions. Right now, he is to get his ass to Stanford University."

She paused. "For me to be here, with you people, high-level officials with the Feds, I am beginning to think something happened, something changed. Am I correct?"

"Yes," Meyers said, "there have been some changes since Madden's last day at Tres Rios that have turned all of our worlds upside down. Our operations against active terrorists, your concern for Madden's status with Stanford, and his safety, and Madden's decision to assist and join with us in an upcoming project all happened, coincidentally, at the same time."

Turning to Meyers at the other end of the table, McDonald yelled, "What are you talking about, Agent Meyers? Would you please be a little more clear? Where is Rob Madden and is he on his way to Stanford?" she demanded, pointing her finger at Meyers.

Lee looked at Goettemoeller and then nodded to Meyers.

"Again, everything you hear discussed in this room is top secret," Meyers said. "Do you understand, Dr. McDonald?"

"Yes, yes, I understand. Get to the point."

"A few days prior to Madden's scheduled departure from Tres Rios, federal agents raided the house of a terrorist sleeper cell in Michigan and were fortunate enough to recover many highly sensitive documents including computer hard drives and external drives filled with information.

"The result of the raid identified the terrorists who were responsible for the deaths of Rob Madden's wife and two young daughters," Meyers said calmly.

The conference room grew even quieter, with most members now staring back and forth between Meyers and Dr. McDonald.

"How sure are you, Agent Meyers?" asked a now startled and surprised McDonald.

"There is no doubt. From what we learned from the information obtained in the cell's safe house, we know who the killers are," Meyers said. "We also recently had one of the cell leaders confess to the killings, with the confession including detailed information about how they were planned, executed, and those responsible."

A morbid silence again filled the room as Dr. McDonald was trying to determine why she was being briefed on such sensitive and terrifying information. Why did she need to know?

"Also, the same operation that provided us with the terrorist organization that was responsible for the Madden family murders resulted in additional information we were not expecting. They were not satisfied with the revenge killing of Madden's family and are now targeting him." Meyers stopped there.

"So, let me get his straight. The people who killed Madden's family are now targeting Madden himself?" McDonald grabbed for her purse for a tissue to clear the tears from her eyes.

"Oh my God," she said, her lips trembling. "Why, why would this terrorist group suddenly want to extend their revenge to Madden?" she asked. "I had the impression they were satisfied with killing his family, with the satisfaction of seeing him suffer for the rest of his life."

Goettemoeller took his seat, and Agent Lee went to the podium carrying a large folder.

"Ma'am, I realize you are receiving a lot more than you ever expected at this meeting; however, there is still more you need to know about, and the reasons will become obvious to you in a few minutes." He put on his reading glasses and opened the folder.

"I am not sure if Rob Madden had mentioned anything to you about a certain Special Forces operation he was part of in Yemen. In short, then Senior Master Sgt. Robert Madden was responsible for targeting known terrorist Anwar Aldawasari in a CIA drone strike," Lee said.

"Everyone has heard of Anwar Aldawasari—he was one of the most wanted terrorists in the world," McDonald said. "I do remember that was in the paper many years ago. You're telling me my Rob Madden had something to do with that?"

"Yes, Madden literally pulled the trigger on Aldawasari, and he is responsible for the killing of a United Arab Republic royal prince at the same time."

"So you are telling me, my star school teacher is responsible for killing Aldawasari and a royal prince," McDonald commented, now totally intrigued by what she was being told.

"The royal prince just happened to be joining Aldawasari at a deserted airfield in Yemen for a traditional Arab hawk hunt," Lee recalled. "Madden did not have permission from his superiors to execute the strike, but fuel was low on the drone and a decision had to be made then and there—either cancel the mission or strike. Madden took it upon himself to strike, taking full responsibility later for his actions. No one was to face disciplinary action except him," Lee said, looking up at McDonald from the podium.

"Hence, payback for the deaths of Aldawasari and the UAR royal prince came in the way of a sleeper cell being ordered in Miami to take vengeance on Madden's family while he was serving with the Air Force in Colombia," Lee continued.

"We had intelligence from other sources that the sleeper cell was satisfied with the elimination of Madden's family, and they considered the score even," Lee said. "Do you have any questions?"

"Why are they suddenly after him more than three years later? I thought you said they were resigned to the fact the score was settled?" asked McDonald.

McDonald could feel an uneasiness among the members in the room, but she wanted answers.

"This is sensitive information, but the mine explosion in New Mexico also killed Anwar Aldawasari's brother, Humza."

"How in the world did Aldawasari's brother end up in New Mexico in exactly the same place Madden was living?" McDonald quickly asked. Then she figured out the reason.

"Oh my God, he was heading for Madden—wasn't he?"

"Yes," Lee confirmed, "after recently being released from the prison in Guantanamo, he was traveling with a group of known cell members from Detroit. From what we can gather, he was acting alone without permission from his superiors in the organization. In fact, he was instructed not to proceed with his vengeance toward Madden. It was considered too risky and served no purpose, but he went anyway," Lee answered.

"Agent Lee, could we take a short break? I would like to use the bathroom," McDonald said.

"Certainly, we'll take five minutes and continue where we left off," Lee answered. He then left the podium to take some messages outside in the lobby. The other agents and staff also rushed to the lobby to pick up messages and use the bathrooms.

Returning, Dr. McDonald was stopped by a few agents asking her advice regarding school issues. Surprised at the questions, it dawned on her that these federal agents were not the cold-blooded mercenaries the media would portray, but genuine family members concerned with the well-being of their children in school.

Gradually, a larger circle of people surrounded McDonald and listened intently to her wisdom on school issues such as violence, drugs, testing, and teacher accountability. Most of her audience were taking notes and swapping business cards with her. McDonald was more than happy to help and surprised at the enthusiasm in their questions.

"Okay, could we have everyone return to the conference room?" Goettemoeller said. The members gradually found their seats. The federal officers knew what was coming next, but McDonald had no clue.

"Please secure the door and the alarms—security, are all present and accounted for?" Goettemoeller asked the security guard monitoring the door and the systems.

"Yes, sir, all secure," replied the guard.

Goettemoeller took his place at the podium while the lights were being dimmed and all eyes turned to the overhead screen.

"Before we continue with the remainder of the briefing, Dr. McDonald, do you have any questions regarding what you have learned so far?" Goettemoeller asked.

"Yes, one question. Was either Anwar or Humza Aldawasari responsible in any way for killing Madden's family?" McDonald asked, now totally immersed in this unbelievable mystery affecting her teacher and friend.

"No, ma'am," Goettemoeller explained, "as we now are sure, Anwar was killed by the drone Madden was working with several years before the incident to his family. And Humza, our sources and monitoring indicate, knew of the operation against Madden's family but took no part in it. Humza was more intent on tracking down Madden to revenge the killing of his brother. We're not sure if he even cared about Madden's family."

"If I may speak directly to the point," Agent Lee spoke from his seat at the conference table. "Currently, we have two of the top terrorists in the world now dead—both, in some way or form, connected to Madden," Lee momentary stopped to review some files.

"My gosh," McDonald commented without thinking about her audience, "Rob seemed like such a nice, clean-cut school teacher, and in his prior life he was chasing and killing terrorists."

"Let's just say he was part of a large team whose mission was to track and eliminate known terrorists—and that included bad guys in Colombia," Lee said, looking up from his file to respond to McDonald.

"Dr. McDonald, I am sure you are asking yourself why federal law enforcement officers would ask you to attend a meeting where we review Robert Madden's past," Lee began.

"That is all well and good," she said, "and I am of course intrigued by all of you and the information you provided me on this wonderful Saturday afternoon. But why don't we get to the point?"

She stared Lee down and asked, "Where is Rob Madden?"

Quiet filled the room, all eyes on the McDonald and Lee ping pong match.

"Robert Madden is not on his way to Stanford University. He's—"

McDonald stood and was now literally yelling at Lee. "Then why don't you just go after these murderers and take care of them—isn't that what we pay you to do?"

More silence from the peanut gallery.

"You assholes told Rob Madden who killed his family, didn't you, didn't you?"

The security guards started to approach McDonald. Lee waved them away.

"Please, Dr. McDonald, there is much more you need to know, so you'll understand," he said. "Please, sit."

McDonald plopped into her seat with a blank stare.

Shaking her head with disgust, she said, "Let's get this over with. I'm getting sick just being in the same room as you people. You knew full well Rob would go to the ends of the earth to find the killers and there you go, handing him the names—what are you thinking?" she cried. "He just wants to move on with his life, teach school, earn his doctorate, and try to forget the past. What are you thinking?"

"For your information, yes, we could have kept this information from Madden and we would have done our best to take down those responsible for the murders ourselves, again without Madden's involvement. And that is what we initially wanted to do," Lee confessed.

"However, we have very good intelligence that the same people we are after are also on Madden's trail," he said. "In other words, Rob Madden could have left Tres Rios, fat, dumb and happy, dreaming of completing his degree, but in reality, his life would be in grave danger if he continued on to the university."

"What are you talking about, Agent Lee?"

"The terrorist group that initially killed Madden's family has now turned their attention to Madden because of the Aldawasari brothers—Madden now has gained some notoriety in the terrorist world as an infidel who needs to be taken care of immediately," Lee said.

"Dr. McDonald, we don't want you hearing on the national news that a car, loaded with explosives, was somehow detonated next to Madden's car, and maybe killed others around him. Like the detonation that killed his family."

She nodded, "Where do we go from here?"

"Ma'am, again, I am Paul Kenny with the DEA." McDonald just acknowledged him and nodded. Kenny stood, running a hand through his black hair on the longish side for a federal agent.

"I was the agent in charge of our operation in New Mexico that brought down the drug lord Billy Hemrod and his team of drug distributors. Believe me, it was by sheer accident, fate, whatever, that found Rob Madden in our sting operation in Tres Rios."

He continued. "We know for a fact that if we had not been on the scene there, Rob Madden would be no more—Hemrod and his associates would have taken Madden out prior to him even reaching the county line.

"Madden knows this, but we all were surprised to see Humza Aldawasari enter the picture looking for Madden. Nobody was more surprised when we had the opportunity to take down Hemrod's operation and Aldawasari all in one night with the assistance of Madden."

McDonald got up and helped herself to a cup of coffee.

"To the point, Dr. McDonald, for your benefit, we saved him from Hemrod and Aldawasari in New Mexico, and we are protecting him from a terrible fate if he continued his journey to California," Kenny said. "So please, stop thinking we, the Feds, are somehow interfering with Madden's life."

McDonald sipped the coffee and considered the facts.

"We would just as soon have been very pleased if Madden would have walked out of that casino, where he got into a fight with the local drug boss, but you can see where we and Madden are," Kenny explained.

Resigned to the fact that all that was briefed to her made perfectly good sense and she was somehow embarrassed now for creating such a scene not knowing all the facts, she contemplated what she now knew about Madden's past—and his questionable future.

"Thank you for the thorough briefing and, may I say, I apologize for my outburst to you—I just did not know," a somber McDonald replied. "Why do I need to know all this information?"

Lee looked and nodded to Goettemoeller, prompting the junior agent to answer McDonald's question.

"Dr. McDonald, you may be relieved to hear that Rob Madden is not on his way to Stanford University, but is now traveling to a secret DEA facility in Albuquerque, New Mexico."

Goettemoeller continued. "Upon leaving Tres Rios, DEA agents detained Robert Madden and escorted him to the facility where he is currently being housed—plus his car and personal belongings."

"Is the threat against Rob that bad where you have to detain him in New Mexico? Why not just let him go back to Florida?" an inquisitive McDonald murmured.

"Yes, the threat is that bad and very real." Agent Ryan Meyers of the CIA broke into the conversation with his assessment.

"We have solid intelligence that a sleeper cell in California was planning actions against Madden, and we certainly do not want to send him back to Florida—especially to a school," Meyers explained.

"Please get to the point. What do you want me to do for you?" asked a frustrated and tired McDonald. As senior CIA officer in the room, the middle-aged Meyers had waited patiently. A veteran of the war on terror, he wore his worry in his creased face and graying hair.

"With what information we have and to protect and at the same time use the services of Madden in apprehending these terrorists," Meyers noted. "We would like for you to create a façade that your stellar school teacher is physically at Stanford working on his degree."

Others in the room were now just as intrigued as McDonald with this request as lower-level agents turned to colleagues with questioning looks and whispers.

McDonald sat quietly. Thinking.

"Stanford University officials have already been briefed on this situation and have agreed to have a Mr. Robert Madden registered as a doctoral student for this year—of course this will result in an administrative error at the end of this year, if anyone is ever asking," Meyers explained.

"If I may ask you, Agent Meyers, you're telling me that Stanford has agreed to carry Madden as a student, for the records, even though he is physically not there?" McDonald asked.

"The bad guys looking for Madden will research the social media sites or even have a mole at Stanford to confirm he is indeed enrolled but will never find him because he is flat not there," Meyers responded.

"I see where you're going with this. I'm already carrying Madden on my books—how long can I expect to carry this ghost of Madden?" asked McDonald.

"We expect no more than three months," replied Lee. "If the situation is not resolved within three months, either the terrorists we are looking for will be no more or—Madden.

"Also, expect periodic phone calls from Madden providing you with all the niceties and updates on his studies," Lee advised. "For God's sake, do not let on that anything is amiss or different— just your normal conversation with Madden as if all was good, do you understand?"

McDonald nodded.

"Also, Agent Goettemoeller will provide you with a telephone number and mailing address at Stanford for Madden. All are valid contact information, but Madden never answers the phone or returns mail. Again, all bogus."

"My God, you think of everything," McDonald replied.

"We have to. Madden's life could depend on it, and we have a bunch of terrorists we cannot wait to break up and apprehend. We cannot leave anything to chance," answered Lee.

"I understand," she said.

"Expect no contact from us when you leave this building, but in the event you feel something is amiss or someone may be asking too many questions about Madden, I recommend you use a commercial pay phone and call Agent Goettemoeller. He's your point of contact," Lee strongly emphasized.

"Are you permitted to say who you believe killed Madden's family?" McDonald asked, knowing the question would not be answered.

Silence fell upon the conference room.

"I'm sorry, ma'am, for your safety and the safety of Madden, we cannot provide you any information," Lee said.

"Thank you, I understand," McDonald responded.

Goettemoeller rose to the podium and thanked all of the members for their attendance, especially on a Saturday afternoon. He also reminded the group of the classification of the briefings, knowing all were professionals who knew the drill. All organized their briefing books, stretched and began heading for the elevator.

McDonald was following the crowd when Goettemoeller caught up with her and asked her to return to the conference room for a moment. Looking at her watch and feeling a bit tired, McDonald shrugged and followed Goettemoeller back into the conference room where Lee, Kenny, and Meyers were waiting. Upon McDonald's arrival, the security guard shut the door behind them.

"Thank you for your time and assistance in this matter," Lee said. "You can see how important your involvement is."

"Yes, of course," McDonald replied. "I was totally surprised regarding the briefing. I had no idea."

"There is no way you could have known," Kenny said.

"This may be a small request, but we must emphasize again your reason for being here was to discuss Marvin Banister and his family's involvement and his problems with your school. It's important that message is relayed to others at your school if asked about today," Kenny stressed. "A pleasure meeting you."

McDonald shook hands with all three men and confirmed again what was expected of her—she bid farewell and was about to leave.

"Nic, would you please escort Dr. McDonald to her vehicle?" Lee requested.

"Be happy to, Curtis. If you'll follow me, we'll get you down to your car and back to Florida."

Once in the elevator, Nic said, "Dr. McDonald, I apologize for all of the questions, especially what we put you through today."

"No problem, but there is one other thing you can do for me," said McDonald.

"Sure, what?" Goettemoeller asked.

"Give my star teacher back to me with a degree, safe and sound," McDonald sarcastically said.

Goettemoeller nodded and smiled. "We'll see what we can do."

Late afternoon in Mobile and the lights of the barge traffic on the Mobile Channel were twinkling on this warm, humid Southern evening. As McDonald walked across the parking lot of the federal building, she had a sixth sense someone was watching her. Or maybe it was nothing. After all, she suspected she was just tired after the secret briefings and maybe she had been immersed in too much "cloak and dagger." Maybe her imagination was getting the best of her.

Laughing at herself for being suspicious, especially in the parking lot of the FBI, McDonald headed for Interstate 10 and home. As she pondered how she'd deal with Madden's ghost, she didn't see a large, black Chevrolet SUV pull out of an adjacent lot near the ship channel.

CHAPTER

10

"I quit!" screamed Bonnie McCord as she tossed her dealer's apron and name tag on the casino human resource director's messy desk.

The stunned director just stared at McCord, who had abruptly turned and walked toward the parking lot while the other employees and dealers stared in amazement—or was it amusement?

"Hey, do you want your back wages?" the director called after McCord.

"Shove it up your ass," McCord answered back. "I've had enough of this damn casino, and people are getting killed all over the place here."

Shaking his head, the director said to no one in particular, "She was such a good and dependable employee—wonder what got into her?"

Special Agent Bonnie McCord headed for Interstate 40 that would take her to the Albuquerque airport for her final destination: DEA headquarters in Arlington, Virginia.

"One more assignment, and I take a break," she told herself.

After a week of debriefing her actions and reports during the Tres Rios operation, McCord was assigned to DEA graduate courses in overseas undercover operations. McCord's superiors were impressed with her performance reports but somewhat concerned that she might require more field work prior to her next undercover assignment in South America. The assignment was considered dangerous. Two undercover agents were already compromised and barely made it back to the United States.

McCord, feeling somewhat smug and confident after her past few assignments, including the stint as a dealer in a casino, had enthusiastically volunteered for the next assignment. She knew she was a rising star at the Agency and was prepared to do whatever necessary to rise to the top in the DEA hierarchy—she would show them!

McCord registered at the Advanced Special Tactics School (Undercover) at the DEA Training Academy at Quantico, Virginia, for the Advanced Agent Training Course followed by an extended stay with the Practical Applications Unit where she would hone her already successful undercover skills.

Rob Madden was never far from her thoughts.

CHAPTER
11

"Shit, man, how old are you?" Madden teasingly commented to the fresh-faced DEA agent driving him to the DFW airport.

The driver just smiled, shook his head and said "Thanks for asking, pops."

Madden sat back and grinned at the reply.

"You know what, driver, they could have easily had me travel from Kirkland Air Force Base, right next to Albuquerque, to Andrews in D.C. in a government airplane," Madden suggested. "But, no. I get to travel commercial with this ugly ass corporate getup on. Let's see, what does the shirt say? Buckey's Gas and Pizza."

"Mr. Madden, due to the nature of your current task, I understand it is safer for your current identity to travel undercover versus your presence at Andrews Air Force Base—too many bad people taking pictures there of VIPs coming and going," noted the young agent.

"Here I am, traveling to some of the worst and most dangerous places in the world and I'm wearing a Buckey's Gas and Pizza shirt to get briefed on my assignment," Madden said.

"Sir," the agent replied as he maneuvered the government SUV through the high plains of West Texas, "you are assigned a first-class seat to Reagan National."

Madden thought maybe things wouldn't be so bad after all.

The drive from Albuquerque to Dallas was a pleasant diversion for Madden as he stared out the window. As a boy growing up,

Madden always remembered the desolate country and the many fond memories that were associated with the Southwest.

As the quiet DEA agent driving the government SUV listened to a country-western station, Madden relaxed and mentally prepared for the new challenges ahead. He wanted nothing more than to seek a merciless vengeance on those responsible for killing his family—even deviating from the CIA's rules of engagement he had agreed upon with Bonnie McCord.

"Sir," the DEA driver calmly spoke to a napping Madden. "Mr. Madden, we're here."

Madden awoke puzzled and awkwardly looked around at his surroundings while stretching from the long drive from New Mexico.

"Sir, we're at the airport. Do you need assistance with your luggage?"

"Agent, my name is Jack Erickson," Madden politely reminded the driver.

"Yes, sir, my fault," the rather embarrassed agent nodded as he parked the car in front of the outbound flight terminal.

Buck Buchanan, the "buck" in the Buckey's Gas and Pizza Corp., had been helpful to the CIA, FBI, and DEA in the past few years in providing employment to agents traveling across the world needing a valid, legitimate cover. Buchanan got a kick out of assisting the Feds as though he was actually working some James Bond 007 adventure. Thus the logo on Madden's shirt, and any residual sales of gas or pizza at Buckey's convenience stores was always a bonus.

Agents were schooled to say, "Yes, ma'am, best homemade pizza in the Southwest," the standard reply to strangers asking about the gas and pizza logo. Madden truly enjoyed the charade and often laughed at himself after all he had been through. Now he was a leader in thick-crust pizza.

Madden picked up his luggage and headed for the check-in desk.

"Mr. Erickson, good morning. Could I see your identification, please?" asked the perky, cute ticket agent. Of course Madden thought, after being in Tres Rios for a year, any woman would probably look good to him. Smiling, he showed the airline agent Jack Erickson's driver's license.

"Very good, Mr. Erickson, I see you have a first-class ticket—can I check your baggage for you?"

"Greatly appreciate it," a smiling Madden replied.

"It is pretty obvious Buckey's people travel in style," noted the agent.

"Ma'am, when you're selling the best thick crust pizza in the world, we have to go above and beyond," Madden replied with a tip of his head.

"Mr. Erickson, please proceed through security and make your way to gate B12," she smiled and pointed the way. "Here is your boarding pass and your luggage claim tag. Have a good flight."

Madden knew his lifestyle would soon be changing to the very deadly and serious, but for now, he was truly enjoying being part of the Buckey's Gas and Pizza team.

He held the Dallas Morning News in front of his face, but his mind was far away from the local news scene. Here he was, a retired Air Force senior master sergeant from the Air Force, a Combat Controller no less, with an Air Force Cross. A certified public school teacher who was on his way to Stanford University to earn a doctorate in education when he was detoured while making a stop in New Mexico to a town called Tres Rios.

He was partly responsible for the killing of a drug gang operating a drug lab and distribution center, and as a bonus he assisted in killing four terrorists bent on killing him for his work with drone killings overseas.

The nightmare is always there—the murder of his wife and two children at his home base in Florida by a terrorist sleeper cell. He was confident he would settle the score soon—there was no doubt. If he needed to deviate from the agreements he made with McCord and the Feds, so be it—the parties responsible would be brought to justice on Madden's terms.

I hope the Feds are correct, Madden thought to himself, *because whoever they have on their priority strike list will be no more.*

"Hey, mister, is that a gas pump and pizza on your shirt?" a bewildered girl about 10 wearing a Mickey Mouse shirt and a long pony tail asked with a large smile and the biggest blue eyes.

Startled by the sudden presence of a girl who closely resembled one of his own deceased daughters, Madden came close to tears and gave a big grin. "Sweetheart, you bet it's a pizza—do you like pizza?" Madden asked the girl.

She nodded.

The girl was immediately found by her mother, who profusely apologized for her daughter disturbing Madden.

"Ma'am, not a problem, you are blessed to have such an active and healthy child," Madden said while tears ran down his face. Nobody in the waiting area understood why.

CHAPTER
12

"Ladies and gentlemen, we will be arriving at the Washington Reagan Airport in a few minutes. Please ensure your seats are in the upright position," the young, tired flight attendant announced to the anxious passengers in the cabin.

Madden was just waking up from a fitful nap and reviewed the underground Metro's map to the Pentagon stop. It had been a while since he had been to the Pentagon and like the true military professional he was, he always tried to avoid the place. Too many politics, too many ass kissers and way too many "yes" people.

Shaking his head and laughing, he picked up his Buckey's corporate carrying case and took his turn heading off to the exit. People stared at the noticeable and obnoxious gas pump and pizza on the corporate shirt of an unusual first-class passenger.

Arriving at the Pentagon's main entrance and visitor check-in—as just another food service company rep wanting to service military installations—Madden made his way to a reception area where visitors met their escorts for entry into the building for their scheduled appointments.

"Are you Mr. Erickson with Buckey's Gas and Pizza?" asked a young Marine second lieutenant.

"I am Jack Erickson with Buckey's, and it is a pleasure to meet you, lieutenant," Madden added laughing, "I didn't know they still made second lieutenants."

As a rite of passage for all veterans, second lieutenants are a source of bad jokes and the butt of all humor in all branches of the service. They carry all the privileges of an officer, but due to their lowest rank in the officer corps, they are treated more like apprentices until they obtain more rank and experience.

The young officer was already annoyed that he had to serve as escort for this lowly food vendor, and now this remark about second lieutenants added to his disgust.

"Yes, sir, I am a Marine-commissioned second lieutenant," the now irritated Marine replied, looking forward to dropping this vendor off at his scheduled appointment.

"What's the matter, lieutenant—couldn't you get in the Air Force?" Madden asked, having fun provoking the Marine.

"Please follow me, Mr. Erickson," the Marine said, trying to avoid punching this visitor in the mouth.

After walking the many hallways and through several security checkpoints, the lieutenant escorted Madden into the Department of Defense (DoD) Services Administration department on the second floor of the Pentagon.

"Mr. Erickson, this is your area for your appointment. Have a great visit," the lieutenant said sarcastically.

"Thank you, lieutenant, and good luck to you," Madden replied, almost sorry he gave the lieutenant such a bad time. But he reasoned the young officer was a second lieutenant, and it went with the rank.

"Mr. Erickson, I am Dwight Trumble," an officious civilian employee announced as Madden stood up and shook hands. Trumble stared at the shirt.

"So your company, Buckey's, wants to sell pizza and gasoline to our military bases," Trumble announced so all around the waiting area could hear.

"As our proposal stated, we are one of the nation's most established pizza bakers in the Southwest, and our gasoline distribution system is second to none, with competitive pricing to boot," Madden proudly announced—putting on a good show for all listening.

"Okay, then, Mr. Erickson, please follow me back to my office and we'll sit down and talk about your proposal with my contracting staff." Trumble showed Madden down the crowded corridor of office cubicles to an executive elevator next to Trumble's office.

Trumble entered a code on the keypad, the elevator doors opened and both men entered.

Trumble pressed what looked like a basement button. When the elevator door opened, Madden noticed an entire area of sophisticated entry checkpoints and elite security guards manning the area. From Madden's past, he was impressed by the professionalism and behavior of the guard. They were truly elite.

"Well, Mr. Madden, here is your destination. Brig. Gen. Dave Klug will escort you further." Trumble shook Madden's hand, turned and amusingly added, "Good luck with your pizza and gas sales—God-ugly shirt."

A clean-cut, older gentleman with short white hair and wearing a well-fitting, green Army formal uniform with plenty of ribbons, medals, and badges approached Madden.

"Good afternoon, Mr. Madden, good to see you again—I suspect you will feel right at home down here in the Sensitive Compartmented Information Facility, or SCIF as you know it," Klug said.

"Let me see, is it Brig. Gen. Klug or Mr. Klug? Sometimes I really get confused now that I am retired," mused Madden, remembering Klug from his days in the Air Force stationed in the Middle East. Madden remembered Klug as a pretty good officer who took as many chances as he did and paid the price.

"So, Brig. Gen. Klug," Madden asked, "whose ass did you kiss to get the star?"

"The same asses you kissed to win that Air Force Cross of yours," Klug replied.

Both men let out a roar of laughter, slapping each other on the back and causing the security guards to take notice of the commotion.

"Rob, I see you have your luggage with you." Madden looked at Klug and nodded. "I recommend you go on into this vacant conference room and change your clothes—don't think your present attire is appropriate for your briefing," Klug said as he stared at the logo on Madden's shirt.

Madden emerged wearing a nondescript coat and tie.

"Are you ready to go to work, school teacher?" Klug asked, always respecting Madden's decision and dedication to become a public school teacher after retirement.

"Yes, sir!" Madden replied. Nothing else needed to be said. All knew the reason Madden was there—he had made a deal.

CHAPTER
13

Briefings in the Pentagon's basement SCIF were considered ultrasensitive and top secret. Before entering the SCIF, Madden was searched for any recording devices or other electronics by a notably impersonal security manager who was known for treating all visitors to his sanctuary with the same service with no smile—from a lowly private to a four-star general.

"Mr. Madden, you are authorized to enter the SCIF," instructed the manager. "Please remember all notes and working papers must be filed and submitted to the administrative assistant prior to your departure."

"Yes, I understand all," Madden said professionally. He had been in the SCIF often during his military days.

Many military staff members were already seated with a few DoD civilians and contractors. Madden recognized a few from the past, but surprising to him were all the young faces.

"My gosh, am I getting that old where full-bird colonels look like kids?" Madden commented to his escort, Klug.

"It's a new generation's game now," Klug agreed. "We are getting old."

Klug introduced Madden to all of the members in attendance for the briefing.

"I have been eagerly waiting to meet you, Mr. Madden, it's an honor," Curtis Lee, the senior FBI agent-in-charge, introduced himself to Madden and added, "It appears you had some real excitement at Tres Rios. Glad you lived to tell about it."

"Were you the asshole who planned that little adventure in New Mexico?" Madden asked.

"Rob, I was one of them and I would like you to meet the other two assholes who made it possible," motioning to two seated civilians. "Ryan and Paul, come on over here and meet Senior Master Sgt. Rob Madden—our man in New Mexico," Lee instructed.

"Rob, good to meet you. I'm Ryan Meyers with the CIA and am so very relieved all worked out to our satisfaction," Meyers said. "You did a great job for everyone in that town…and school."

Paul Kenny gave Madden a strong embrace that startled him. "School teacher, nice to finally meet you. I'm Paul Kenny, senior special agent for the Drug Enforcement Agency and like Lee and Ryan, very glad to meet you."

Klug took his seat at the head of the conference table, and the SCIF was secured and locked.

"Sir, the room is secured," the SCIF manager announced to the general.

"Good afternoon, ladies and gentlemen, and thank you for your attendance at this afternoon's briefing. And a very special thanks to our visitors today from our partners from the FBI, DEA, and CIA," Klug said.

"Also, I would like to recognize a special visitor today: Mr. Rob Madden. Would you stand and be recognized by our members?"

Madden briefly rose and then sat down quickly.

"Col. Warren Weaver, please begin the briefing," directed Klug.

Suddenly the lights dimmed, and a large tactical map of Yemen was projected on a screen that had been electronically lowered from the ceiling.

Madden stared at the map and knew it well from his six months of temporary duty in Yemen working as an Air Force Combat Controller with a Special Operations CIA team tracking terrorists for the drones to target and kill. Madden was considered one of few operators who knew Yemen well and understood its culture and language.

Yemen, Yemen, whispered Madden to himself, *God's hell on earth, Yemen.*

Madden also knew the devil lived there, and he was going to kill it before it killed him.

"I would like to provide you with a brief summary of Mr. Madden's experiences in Yemen," announced Col. Weaver.

All eyes were now on Madden as the colonel read the intense and dramatic after-action reports of his Yemen operations. Madden was too aware of the summary as his mind raced back to those God-awful days.

"Please, for the benefit of the audience, I am very familiar with Yemen," Madden snapped and thought to himself, *How many times do we need to review this?*

Yemen was responsible for the deaths of my wife and two daughters at the hands of terrorists. Yemen was responsible for the exceeding of my orders and killing a notorious terrorist and a United Arab Republic royal prince by a U.S. drone attack. Yemen was responsible for my being denied a significant and prestigious promotion to chief master sergeant. Yemen was responsible for being a center of refugees for just-released al-Qaeda prisoners from Guantanamo, Cuba. Yemen was responsible for…

The list went on in Madden's mind. So many tragic events when he first set foot in Yemen eight years ago.

"Could we please move on?" Madden politely asked.

Feeling like jumping up and asking the colonel to stop, Madden sat motionless like the professional he was, just staring ahead in an imaginary land—attempting to daydream about Stanford and the promising years ahead—possibly with Bonnie McCord.

"Gen. Klug, that completes the briefing," Col. Weaver concluded.

"Thank you, colonel, please take a seat. Any comments or questions by anyone?"

There would be no questions, no comments—all were aware of Madden's performance in Yemen.

"Very good," said Klug as he rose and headed for the speaker's podium on the right side of the map of Yemen still being displayed on the screen.

"Everything we discuss today in this briefing room is of the highest level of Top Secret, No Dissemination." Klug warned. "There will be no note-taking or working papers of this briefing—does everyone understand?"

The SCIF was silent, with all eyes focused on Klug as he nodded his head to the colonel who operated the PowerPoint.

Suddenly displayed on the screen was a picture of a Middle Eastern man in his late forties, with long black hair and a rather grayish black beard and mustache. The man was wearing the traditional al-Qaeda dress, including tribal scarf and head gear. An AK-47 assault rifle was cradled in his arms. By his side was a long, dual-bladed knife traditionally carried by al-Qaeda terrorists.

The glow of the lights on the conference room table was now a small nuisance as all were stretching forward to capture every detail of this man—one of the world's most dangerous terrorists. There was not a person in the SCIF who did not know who the man was, but his portrait on the screen was bigger than life. Why now?

After the initial surprised reaction by the audience, members were attempting to reason the significance of showing the portrait at this meeting. A few of the attendees knew only too well the significance of beginning the briefing with the photo of this terrorist.

"Meet Khalid Azzam," Klug said. "He is now living, training, and conspiring with his al-Qaeda members in Yemen with his powerful tribe, the Awlakas, in a remote mountain valley in eastern Shabwah."

A detailed map suddenly appeared on another screen showing features of eastern Shabwah.

Madden sat staring off in the distance, knowing full well of the conditions at Shabwah, an area often described by the local tribes, military, and oil companies as the "triangle of evil." He continued his long, expressionless stare as Klug continued his briefing. Bad memories entered Madden's mind—bitter recounts of betrayal and the hardships endured while tracking terrorists at Shabwah. He knew too well where Klug was going.

"Khalid Azzam is technically an American citizen who is making his home in Yemen," briefed Klug as the audience was now commenting among themselves on what Klug had just said.

The targeting of a "signature type" terrorist such as Azzam was known to be rather routine, and he was recently placed on the CIA's authorized kill list. However, Azzam was still considered a U.S. citizen, and his death would be a political hot potato in the United States and around the world.

"Khalid Azzam was born in Arizona, where his father earned a doctorate in agricultural sciences at Arizona State University," Klug told the group. "Upon earning his degree and years of teaching at several prominent universities, he was asked to return to Yemen and serve as the Yemeni president's advisor on agriculture."

Klug consulted his notes. "Azzam returned to the United States and earned degrees in civil engineering from the University of Michigan and Indiana State University. He attended the universities on a student visa with scholarships from the Yemeni government," Klug continued.

"Interestingly enough, he spent his summer vacations during college training with the mujahideen in Afghanistan. What makes Azzam so very popular and dangerous is his fluency in English, his advocacy of jihad and mujahideen organizations and his knowledge of computers—especially the use of worldwide social media. Please hold any questions until we complete this briefing," Klug said, as many hands were raised at this point.

"Besides having links to the 9/11 attackers, I would like to read what one Yemeni official familiar with counter-terrorism operations stated: 'Azzam is the most dangerous man in Yemen. He's intelligent, sophisticated, internet-savvy, and very charismatic. He can sell anything to anyone, and right now he's selling jihad and death to America, death to America.'"

Klug looked up from his notes. "I know many of you have questions, but there is another reason why we have placed Azzam on the authorized kill list. Please listen up. I'm not sure if you are all familiar with the 2004 drone strike on al-Qaeda leader Anwar Aldawasari."

Madden's ears started to burn.

"Aldawasari was planning a hawk hunting trip with many of the United Arab Republic's royal family members near a small airport in southern Yemen. As opportunity would have it, we had a Special Forces CIA team tracking the whereabouts of Aldawasari in the vicinity. Apparently one of our high-priced informants got it right—didn't they, Mr. Madden?"

Klug looked directly at Madden while the rest of the members were now on the edge of their seats.

Madden just nodded his head, reliving every second of that day in his mind.

"Again, I repeat, many of the details you are about to hear are highly classified and would cause great embarrassment and threat to the United States if any of the following is leaked. You shall see and hear why," Klug warned his audience.

A hush filled the SCIF as everyone strained to hear more—this briefing was far beyond anything they knew of Azzam and Robert Madden.

"Senior Master Sgt. Madden's Combat Controller team was coordinating the drone attack on Aldawasari when suddenly, unannounced, a royal United Arab Republic aircraft circled the small airport and landed with a royal prince who immediately embraced Aldawasari." Madden's stare told the story as Klug continued the after-action report.

"The team was in contact with DoD and the Joint Operations Commander regarding the sudden appearance of a royal prince in the company of Aldawasari. Permission was requested by the team to take both of them out—the attacking drone was running very short on fuel and could not stay in the area much longer—a decision had to be made," Klug continued, "and Sgt. Madden made it—the strike goes."

All were now stretching to see Madden and his reaction to Klug's sensitive briefing.

"Madden paid the price for the team by authorizing the strike, for which he would pay dearly in many ways, again, many ways."

Madden didn't move a muscle.

"First, Madden was on the promotion list for chief master sergeant, the top rank for the enlisted force, which he lost due to a concession to the United Arab Republic royal family for Madden's participation in the death of a royal family member."

Klug continued. "Second, due to Madden being appointed the scapegoat for the operation, while taking the hit for his team, intelligence confirms that members of the Aldawasari clan who survived the drone attack are responsible for the deaths of Mr. Madden's wife and two daughters."

Madden desperately tried to control his rage and anger hearing again a recounting of the killing of his family, but showed no outward emotion as all eyes were on him.

"Azzam was with Aldawasari at the drone strike but somehow survived," briefed Klug, "and he swore revenge for those responsible."

"A wounded Azzam barely made it back to his camp in Yemen's rugged Shabwah region, which is known for attracting al-Qaeda militants seeking refuge among local tribes who are unhappy with the Yemeni government," Klug said.

"With clandestine financial support from the United Arab Republic, Azzam was able to sponsor an assassination team to take down Madden's family as a payback for the death of the royal prince and Aldawasari."

The audience was fixated on the photo of Azzam now displayed on the screen, with quiet whispers being heard among them.

Madden had heard this briefing many times, with updated intelligence each time he heard it.

The more intelligence the better, Madden whispered to himself as his mind was developing his plan for the demise of Azzam, *because his passing will be very painful.*

"Many of you are asking the same question at this juncture: why target Madden's family and not Madden? Madden was spared by Azzam at the insistence of the United Arab Republic—

it would have created an enormous amount of political tension with the United States, and it certainly would have placed the fingerprints of the killing on the UAR—an obvious connection."

Klug paused and looked at the group. No one moved. "The killing of the family could be reported as a mistaken terror act or just a random killing by local thugs that happens every day in our country. Regardless, an al-Qaeda sleeper cell in Miami was instructed to manage the operation with financial support from the numerous Muslim charities that had indirect ties with the UAR. However, targeting Madden is a different story—there would be a link to the UAR, and the UAR did not want to open old wounds with Madden's murder."

Lucky for me, Madden thought, *because now it's my turn.*

"Azzam was specifically instructed to take no acts of vengeance against Madden—killing his family was considered payback enough."

"Let's get on with the operation plan," Madden said, ready to move forward.

Klug nodded to Madden.

"Before we get into the details of our operations plan for confronting Mr. Azzam, one other interesting situation happened recently that confirms our suspicions and intelligence regarding Azzam's following his directives from the UAR," Klug said.

"Aldawasari's brother, Humza, was released from Guantanamo two years ago and made his way via Yemen, Germany, and Great Britain to an al-Qaeda sleeper cell in Detroit. Swearing revenge for his brother's death, Humza obtained the name of the one responsible as posted on numerous social media websites. By chance, the sleeper cell found the whereabouts of Madden, and Humza, with no permission or authority, and took off on his own to kill Madden. It was a foolhardy venture that was totally tracked by the Feds and ultimately he was killed, with the rest of his cell, at a uranium mine explosion not far from where Madden was living in New Mexico."

A low murmur took over the room. For the majority of the audience who did not know the circumstances behind the deaths of Madden's wife and children, shock and disbelief were evident on their faces.

"Robert Madden was scheduled to leave his teaching obligation in New Mexico and be on his way to Stanford University to complete his doctoral degree, but he has so graciously volunteered to delay his studies in education and help us find and target Azzam in Yemen."

Klug looked over at Madden who just nodded, a smirk on his face.

CHAPTER
14

"Mr. Ryan Meyers from the CIA will brief us on this joint task force effort to establish contact with priority target Azzam," Klug announced and took his seat.

Meyers was a former Army Ranger sergeant who had an extensive background working with the CIA in tracking known terrorists. With a medium-sized, stocky frame, close-cropped haircut, and weather-tanned face, he appeared to be someone Hollywood would call up from central casting for the role. Just put him in military battle dress uniforms instead of the smart gray suit he was wearing, and he'd look the part even more.

Upon his retirement after twenty-two years in the Army, Meyers was asked to join the CIA as an operations analyst—in layman's terms, a hired gun to track terrorists. Like Madden, he was also familiar with drone operations and setting up one of the first drone bases in Africa for strikes in Yemen. Again like Madden, he was called back in the Yemen/drone world to track and kill this "signature target" who was a proven deadly menace to the United States abroad.

"Good afternoon, I am Ryan Meyers, and I represent the CIA in this clandestine operation called Paradise Bound."

The operation's name received a short chuckle from the members present, yet all knew the significance.

"Let me begin by laying out a step-by-step concept briefing for Paradise Bound."

Immediately, the large screen showed a photo of a nondescript air strip.

"This is Camp Lemonnier in the eastern African country of Djibouti. It is one of our Third World bases originally established by the French Foreign Legion and was recently used as a staging area for U.S. forces a few years ago," Meyers said. "Over the past few years, DoD has secretly transformed it into one of the busiest drone bases in the world."

The audience was now turning in their chairs for a more close-up view of this new base and mission.

"The 500-acre base, with its complement of over 300 Special Ops members, is truly dedicated solely to counter-terrorism. Numerous drones fly out of Camp Lemonnier daily with the main flight plans to Yemen to intercept and target signature terrorist targets," explained Meyers.

"The Special Operations commander, Col. Robert Graham, in charge of the drone operations at Camp Lemonnier, is present today to provide an overview of the camp's responsibility in providing drone support to Mr. Madden and his team in Yemen. Col. Graham, we welcome your briefing."

And with that brief introduction, Meyers yielded the podium to a tall, thin, muscular man, whose dark tan signaled that he had recently spent considerable time in the desert. He approached the front from the visitor's section of the SCIF.

The colonel was wearing his formal Air Force blue uniform with an endless array of fruit salad—multi-colored ribbons decorated his blouse, giving him a look that the military calls "command presence."

Not one for formalities, Graham began, "This briefing is classified Top Secret with No Foreign Dissemination—our mission at Camp Lemonnier in Djibouti is very sensitive in nature and requires your attention in keeping my briefing in this room."

So this was the mysterious Col. Graham. All knew or suspected he was the DoD's point person for drones in Africa from the many classified reports coordinated through DoD. But Madden was one of the few in the room who had ever seen him in person.

Graham shuffled his notes, but momentarily stopped and stared at Madden, who in turn was staring at Graham—the exchange of cold, steely stares was not missed by anyone present.

Both men had crossed paths in the past when Madden was operating in Yemen and Iraq. Madden had remembered that Col. Graham, at the time a major, was assigned to be the official military investigating officer for the drone attack that killed Anwar Aldawasari and the royal prince from the United Air Republic in Yemen. In the official Air Force Inspector General's report, Graham was highly critical of Madden's performance and judgment during the operation that created a stir of embarrassment for the State Department and the United Arab Republic.

As Madden recalled, Graham was the only officer on the board of inquiry after the incident to recommend that Madden be court-martialed for dereliction of duty and disobeying orders from a superior officer. The bad blood between the two men had existed since of the release of the inquiry. Graham continued to believe Madden should have been held accountable for his actions.

Graham moved his gaze away from Madden and directed his attention to the large briefing screen with a satellite picture of the small, cramped airport.

"Camp Lemonnier is located in the eastern African country of Djibouti—an impoverished former French colony with fewer than a million people. It has no natural resources, and it's incredibly hot all year." The screen now showed a sunbaked Third World outpost with desert-camouflaged tents and buildings.

"Camp Lemonnier was originally established by the French Foreign Legion and for the past fourteen years has been a contingency staging area for U.S. Marines. Over the past four years, the United States has secretly changed the mission of the camp to one of the busiest predator drone bases in the Middle

East." Graham paused for the screen to change and show another satellite picture of the drone operations centers.

"Joint Special Operations Command has been tasked by the president to execute highly sensitive counter-terrorism missions," Graham proudly announced as though he was the single most important person on the mission.

Madden sat quietly listening to the briefing thinking to himself, *Still an ass kisser, huh, Graham.*

"I have over three hundred Special Operations members who plan raids and coordinate drone flights from inside this high-security compound at the camp, and as you can see, it is filled with various antennas and satellite dishes ringed by guards and concertina wire." He used a laser pointer.

"In addition to the primary counter-terrorism mission, I have about four thousand U.S. troops, civilians, and contractors who are assigned to the camp, where they train foreign militaries, gather intelligence and provide humanitarian aid across East Africa as part of the campaign to prevent extremists from taking a hold in Africa," Graham said.

"Col. Graham," Gen. Klug interrupted the briefing. "Would you please explain to the audience about the method you use to determine drone targets—I'm talking about the Disposition Matrix."

So now there was a matrix to determine terrorists to be hit, Madden thought. *Screw the matrix. Azzam is on top of my matrix list and anyone around him—just get me to Yemen.*

Graham hesitated for a moment at the briefing podium, obviously feeling uncomfortable briefing the highly classified and elaborate targeting database referred to as the matrix.

It was considered the playbook to define and explain in detail how decisions were made for targeted killings and considered a political hot potato, both in politics and the military.

"Col. Graham, please brief the matrix," Klug repeated, to the point of almost ordering the colonel.

"Yes, sir," Graham replied.

Madden was now on the edge of his seat thinking, *What the hell is so special about this damn matrix?*

"The Disposition Matrix is a database that records and files biographies, locations, friends, associates, family, and affiliations of suspects. It also creates action plans and strategic plans for finding, capturing and/or killing suspects including subjecting them to ways of surrendering information." All eyes were focused on Graham as he continued his grudgingly delivered briefing.

"The matrix directs our drone operations in Afghanistan, Pakistan, Somalia, and Yemen, and will extend our hunt to include Algeria, Egypt, Mali, Libya, Iran, and throughout East Africa."

"Col. Graham, please brief our audience on the different types of strikes authorized by the Disposition Matrix." It was an order, not a request or even a question from a noticeably frustrated Klug.

"Yes, sir," a red-faced Graham dutifully began. "There are three types of strikes available for engaging a particular target. The Personality Strike is a targeted attack on a particular individual who is confirmed to be a terrorist leader. The Signature Strike is against an individual who is believed to be a terrorist but whose identity may not be known. The Terror Attack Disruption Strike, like the Signature Strike, again refers to strikes against terrorists whose identity is unknown but is executed to thwart or stop what intelligence proves to be an imminent attack on a friendly government," Graham said.

"And for Mr. Azzam, what type of matrix strike is he classified as?" asked Klug.

"Sir, I am not at liberty or have the authorization to answer that question," Graham answered.

Klug stood staring at the colonel with disgust, not understanding his unwillingness to answer the question.

Madden interrupted the heated exchange. "Doesn't make any difference at all how he is classified in this Disposition Matrix, we're going take him and his associates out just as soon as possible. Just have a drone available to support us if you would please, Col. Graham."

"Mr. Madden, please don't forget, I'll be the final authority in any strike from a drone on target Azzam. Do I make myself clear on this point?" Graham directed his ire at Madden. "I don't want us to get in another embarrassing international incident where unauthorized personnel exceed their authority and disregard the orders of their superiors in the execution of drone strikes—do you understand, Mr. Madden?"

The audience in the SCIF was stunned at the unusual exchange among Klug, Madden, and Graham—it was obvious to all that there was some bad blood and history between these two, but who didn't like some heated dialogue?

"Col. Graham, thank you very much for your briefing and updates," Klug said, signaling very tactfully that he had had enough of Graham's outburst. He added, "Immediately following this briefing, I would like a word with you and also with you, Mr. Madden."

Col. Graham nodded his head and mumbled, "Yes, sir," as he sat down.

Regardless of his disdain and dislike for Col. Graham, Madden was truly in awe of what he had been hearing and the advancements in drone operations and bases—especially so close to Yemen as Camp Lemonnier in Djibouti was in East Africa. He was reflecting on the early days in using the drones, when only a few were operational, and it seemed to take forever for them to reach their targets with the long distances needed to travel, which frustrated Madden at the time with the minimum time on station.

He was jarred from his daydream as the CIA's Meyers continued with details.

"—also, the standard package of communications equipment, weapons, and regional clothing have already been packaged and crated for your final destination at the Midland Oil Company depot at Marib, Yemen. The crate is marked 'seismographic equipment' and is waiting for you at your secure storage area," explained Meyers.

"Mr. Madden, you have used the communications equipment in the past; however, you will be thoroughly briefed on any new updates and frequencies at a later specified date," he said.

"Mr. Meyers, for the benefit of our team, would you please explain what you meant by regional clothing?" Klug, knowing that many supporting agencies on this mission needed to know the clothing factor, asked for a brief rundown.

"With due respect, does this audience need to know the clothing disposition?" a very concerned Meyers asked.

"Brief the clothing and why—now!" a very annoyed Klug commanded. "Hear me out, ladies and gentlemen, when I ask for information regarding this mission, I don't want any hesitation in the answer," he warned. "We are all a team, and we certainly need to know what each other is doing to support Madden and Col. Graham, so be quick with your answers."

"I understand, Gen. Klug," Meyers said, picking up where he left off concerning the clothing disposition.

Madden was also perplexed about the clothing issue and wondered what was so sensitive about oil field work clothes that consisted mostly of blue denim work pants, cotton shirts, gloves, boots, hats—typical roughneck wear in the field. At least he wouldn't be wearing a shirt with a gas pump and pizza on it.

"The clothing disposition in the supply crate forwarded to Midland Oil Company in Marib—" Meyers stopped for a few seconds, knowing the sensitivity and the political ramifications for what he was about to brief.

"Mr. Madden will be supplied with various clothing items that reflect the populace of the region to include clothing typically worn by al-Qaeda of the Arabian Peninsula, Houthi rebels, security forces backing the current government, plus appropriate regional documents identifying Mr. Madden as a member for each of the organizations."

Meyers paused and looked to the general to continue. "One extremely important note about the regional clothing items, they all have embedded electronic beacons hidden within their lining. Where and when the clothing is utilized for the mission, our operations team, whether drones or satellites, will be able to track and identify those clothing articles Madden is wearing," he concluded, securely holding his top secret briefing folder and preparing to head to his seat.

Madden sat back with his eyes closed, attempting to make sense of what he just heard—especially about the regional clothing. All of the conference members were now staring at Madden.

"Hope they got my size right," Madden said, shaking his head in amazement.

"Mr. Meyers, will you please brief the main purpose and use of the regional clothing?" a very impatient Klug demanded.

"Yes, sir. Depending on the circumstances Mr. Madden faces in targeting Khalid Azzam for the drone attack while in oil field attire, he may need to blend in with the local populace in the Nisab district of Yemen's Shabwah province," he said.

"Granted, Mr. Madden currently has a very good knowledge of the Arabic language and is familiar with the terrain and culture of Yemen, having spent a few months there tracking assets," Meyers said. "From oil field worker to a devoted believer in jihad, Mr. Madden will blend in well. The Nisab district is a rugged area that has long been outside the control of Yemen's central government, or for that matter, any other challenging force."

"Let me get this straight." Graham said, immediately rising from his seat. "You're telling me that Madden is expected to change his disguise from a foreign oil field worker to one of an al-Qaeda jihadist? That's impossible. How does he do it?"

As much as Madden despised Graham, Madden was thinking along the same lines to himself, *And how am I supposed to carry my com gear plus weapons in one of the most dangerous and chaotic cesspools in the world?*

"Mr. Meyers, let me get this straight." Madden was now standing, facing Meyers and attempting to stay as calm as possible. "You want me to change from oil field worker to an al-Qaeda jihadist, put on some sort of al-Qaeda garb that you issued and just hike over near Azzam's camp and call in a drone strike."

The conference room turned silent except for the muffled sound of cool air flowing through the ventilation ducts and the occasional whispered comment from one conference member to another. Madden remained standing, expecting an answer.

"Mr. Madden," Meyers said, "your name and purpose for being there will allow you easy access to Azzam."

"Name and purpose will get me through some of the worst cutthroats in history? How does that work?" Madden demanded.

"You will be given a new identity and documents to support your background," the CIA guy replied, "a new identity of Johnny Snow from Minneapolis, Minnesota."

"Who in the hell is Johnny Snow and how is his name going to help me evade capture by these jihadist thugs?" Madden shook his finger at Meyers, thinking he was in some fantasy world or on drugs.

"Last year, Mr. Madden, one of our roving CIA intelligence teams in Yemen captured a middle-aged man named Johnny Snow, a United States citizen, who had found himself in Yemen and enlisted in al-Qaeda," Meyers said.

"Mr. Snow was recruited for the jihad through the various al-Qaeda social media sites in the United States and made his way to Yemen, where he received rudimentary military training including how to use the Kalashnikov rifle, the AK-47."

Meyers continued. "In your mission portfolio, we included the information we received from Mr. Snow's debriefing with the CIA that will assist you with your cover—if you decide to use it."

"Do the al-Qaeda leaders have any clue that he might have been captured or had second thoughts on his worldly mission in life?" asked Madden.

"Through our trusted sources from a couple of tribes in Yemen, Snow is understood to have been captured by the Houthis, the Shiite insurgency group that are by no means friends of al-Qaeda," Meyers replied. "Your alibi will be that you were able to escape from your Houthi captors during a drone attack, found a motorcycle and made your way back to the Shabwah province to rejoin the al-Qaeda jihad—"

"You're crazy and delusional," Madden yelled, "and frankly don't have a clue what you're talking about or know what you're asking me to do."

Attendees figuratively put on seatbelts in preparation for the coming exchange.

"Listen," Madden said, trying to calm his voice, "I have spent months in Yemen tracking down terrorists, including those in the dangerous and deadly Shabwah province. At that time, we did not have so many different terrorist organizations fighting each other, and most important of all, there was an established central government that had a good handle on controlling the terrorists and the petroleum infrastructure.

"Even the President of the United States said Yemen was a so-called model nation for countering al-Qaeda and the other insurgency groups—a true democracy, my ass. Now, there is no government, just very powerful terrorist groups sponsored by the likes of Iran. So if you think my chances are anything but good, why don't you come along with me?" Madden challenged Meyers.

"Okay, Mr. Madden." Klug suddenly rose to address Madden's frustrations. "What do you need or want to make this mission work for you? What support?"

"First, from the time I transition from oil field worker to this al-Qaeda Mr. Snow, I will need two fully armed drones directly overhead supporting me and my mission. This is not negotiable, as my life will very well depend on them," Madden said.

"Col. Graham, can you make that happen?" Klug directed the question to the colonel.

Graham put on his reading glasses and, with his executive officer sitting next to him, began reviewing thick classified documents in front of them and began making calculations regarding drone availability and committed target schedules for the near term when Madden was expected to begin his operations.

"I can guarantee one on Madden's station at all times, but not two—we have priority national commitments all over the region for drone support, and frankly, we'll be lucky to support the one," Graham earnestly reasoned. "I truly understand Madden's request. It makes perfect sense, but we just do not have the drone assets—we are stretched thin as it is."

"What do you think, Rob, can you live with one?" Klug asked Madden.

"Yes, but if shit really hits the fan and that one drone cannot cover the attack or my withdrawal back to Marib, I request a Broken Arrow scenario where all available air assets will be directed to support me getting out of the al-Qaeda camp in the Shabwah province." He knew he needed to negotiate all the air support he could get. One drone would work if Graham kept to his end of the agreement, but Madden had his doubts.

"I will need at least a twenty-four-hour notice prior to you going tactical on your own heading for Shabwah and the al-Qaeda camp," Graham said.

Madden stared at Graham for a moment and nodded his head. He thought to himself, *Game on.*

"Mr. Madden, when you leave this room, you will be officially employed by the Midland Oil Company working under a special contract with Yemen General Corporation for oil, gas, and minerals—in other words, your cover is going to be that of an oil field specialist in petroleum exploration. You're somewhat familiar with this career field are you not, sir?" Meyers knew the answer to the question, but asked it for clarification with the other members in the room.

"My gosh, my experiences in the oil field were in a different lifetime, so much has changed from the days I worked them—I was literally a kid then," replied Madden.

"Thanks, Mr. Madden, but you know the basic operations for oil exploration and know how to talk oil field jargon like a seasoned roughneck," Meyers said. "For clarification here, a roughneck is a slang word used throughout the corners of the world for an oil field worker working the most hazardous jobs on an oil-drilling platform—am I correct?" asked Meyers with a big grin on his face.

"Yes, you might as well call me oil field trash if you like, if you understand what that means."

Laughter arose from the observers, intrigued by Madden's past experiences in the oil field. Col. Graham sat in disgust looking away from Madden, still not understanding why they were bringing Madden back to this operation.

"As an employee of the Midland Oil Company, you are to proceed directly to their field office in Tulsa, Oklahoma, where you will receive a very short orientation regarding your new job duties and all the clothing and equipment needed for your stay with Midland Oil in Yemen," Meyers said.

"Also, your training in Tulsa will include specialized training in the Arabic dialect in Yemen and a review of your communications equipment and procedures for contact with the drone base at Djibouti—all conducted by the Agency."

"Where in Yemen?" Madden asked.

Silence filled the room, as all were straining to hear.

"Rob, your initial destination in Yemen is the town of Marib in central Yemen—are you familiar with this area?" Meyers said.

"Shit!" exploded Madden. "Please forgive my spontaneous answer to your question. Yes, I am familiar with the area."

"For the benefit of the members present, would you provide us with a short description of Marib?" Meyers asked.

"Marib is a most interesting place with an assortment of different oil field companies scattered around the area with a major oil refinery located just outside of town." Madden stopped for a moment to take a drink of water.

"It almost resembles what we would think of as the Wild West, with very tough oil field workers living within an old, established Yemeni religious community. Also, there is the constant threat of al-Qaeda terrorists shooting at the workers and blowing up pipelines."

All eyes were on Madden. "Yemen did have a strong government military presence in Marib, and I remember them putting in a good effort to stop and terminate the terrorists, but as we all know, they required and asked for help from the United

States. And, yes, I would take a trip back to Marib in a minute to take care of Azzam."

"Good," said Klug, "because that is where you are going in Yemen to meet up with your fellow roughnecks with the Midland Oil Company."

Madden nodded.

"We understand what we are asking from you is risky and dangerous at best," Klug announced, standing at his seat, "however, we do believe we have a force multiplier that will ultimately enhance the success of your mission."

Madden and the audience were surprised to hear of a force multiplier and how it applied to Madden's mission. Frankly, Madden was relieved to get some assistance with this crazy task.

"Our British cousins have a Special Air Service detachment working in the area you are destined for," explained Klug. "For those in attendance who are not familiar with the SAS, they are the United Kingdom's version of our Special Forces, Green Berets. They are a low-key group who have been actively conducting covert reconnaissance and counter-terrorism operations in the area Madden is destined for."

"How will I contact them while in Yemen?" Madden asked.

"I was assured by their people that they will find you, Madden, when the time is right," Klug replied while Madden shook his head in approval, admiring the SAS cockiness and swagger—very relieved and more confident now with their participation. "How do I get there?" Madden asked, resigned to the fact he was going back, but with world-class professional support.

"For those staff members requiring information on Mr. Madden's travel arrangements, please stay and we'll begin the briefing in 10 minutes," Klug announced. "For the rest of you, this concludes the operation briefing for Paradise Bound, Special Operations order PB-0009742 and remember, this is a Top-Secret briefing, No Foreign Dissemination—nothing said out of this room about the briefing, understood?" Klug emphasized.

The main lights of the briefing room were turned on, and the members and staff blinked at the sudden barrage of lights while they gathered their documents and folders before hurrying out to the elevators.

Left in the room were a few military and civilian support staff that had been working the details for Paradise Bound for many weeks, looking forward to its execution and the opportunity to meet the famous Senior Master Sgt. Rob Madden

"Rob, you brought up a very good question—how do you get there?" Klug said, almost laughing at the simple question that required a detailed and critical answer. Klug chuckled and patted Madden on the back while making his way to the coffee bar in the rear of the conference room.

Madden returned to his seat, reviewing again the operation plan centered around him getting close enough to make the call for the drone strike. Unbeknownst to Klug, Graham, and the other Pentagon planners for Paradise Bound, Madden had his own agenda for the operations in Yemen. The U.S. military, CIA and now the British SAS were all going to help him—whether they knew it or not.

"Rob, could I meet with you for a moment over here in conference B?" Klug asked Madden, leading him to a vacant, secure room.

Both taking a seat at a small conference room table, Klug asked about how Madden personally felt about the mission and if there was anything else they could do to assist. However, this was not the intent of this short, unexpected meeting between them—Madden did not think so, either.

"Rob, what I am going to relay to you is highly classified, and only a few people are authorized to know what I am going to tell you." Klug's statement immediately got Madden's attention.

"Recently, the FBI raided an al-Qaeda cell safe house in Detroit and discovered credible information that al-Qaeda had stolen a tactical nuclear weapon in Pakistan and somehow transported it to the United States through the border with Mexico."

"Oh my God—it has finally happened," Madden said and continued, "we have always thought a scenario like this could happen—any further details?"

"Plenty," Klug said, "however, it would take too long to explain the details as we know them, but we are quite sure Azzam was the ringleader who knows where the bomb is located and what cell has responsibility.

"When you do get in contact with Azzam, it is imperative you snatch any information you can from him—it just might lead us to where the bomb is and which al-Qaeda cell has it," Klug bluntly stated.

Madden sat back, attempting to comprehend all that Klug had told him. Now he was being asked to go above and beyond his original mission.

"Before I kill Azzam, I'll do my best in taking whatever documents and computers I find," Madden insincerely replied, knowing full well he would kill Azzam first and look for documents later.

Klug just nodded his head as both men left the conference room.

"Rob, if you miss and cannot terminate him or obtain any of his computers or documents," Klug said with deadly seriousness, "we will send in a combined air strike and completely obliterate his camp—regardless of who gets killed."

Madden just nodded his head.

CHAPTER
15

"Ms. Gloria Hawkins, would you please brief Mr. Madden on his itinerary to Yemen?" CIA Special Agent Meyers gestured to a stately woman in her mid-forties wearing a corporate-style blue dress, high heels and gold necklaces plus stylish gold earrings. Hawkins smiled and stood, nodding her perfectly made-up face to Meyers. A strong scent of an expensive perfume trailed her to the podium.

As she adjusted her dress, Hawkins was not shy about showing off her well-toned legs to the obvious stares from the men in the room. Having worked her way up from intern travel specialist at the Pentagon during her college years at the University of Virginia, she was now a top DoD civilian overseeing many sensitive and clandestine travel arrangements for situations such as Madden's trip to Yemen.

It was common knowledge among Pentagon personnel and the rumor mill that Hawkins truly loved her job of arranging travel for intriguing and dangerous men like Madden. One of her many fetishes included sleeping with the men for whom she was making the highly classified travel arrangements. Many looked at it as one of her hobbies—and a bonus for those men traveling into harm's way under her supervision.

But she was also known throughout Pentagon circles as a first-rate, hardworking professional who took her responsibilities seriously knowing her decisions were critical to the safety of her customers—she literally took a personal interest in all of her customers.

To everyone in the room, it was plain to see Madden's eyes light up. He definitely was paying attention when she approached the briefing podium.

"Good morning, all. I am Gloria Hawkins, and I have the pleasure to brief the conference on Mr. Madden's travel itinerary through Aden, Yemen, into Marib." A smiling Hawkins looked directly at Madden and now had everyone's attention.

"Mr. Madden, upon completing your training with the Midland Oil Company in Tulsa, Oklahoma, a chauffeur will escort you to the Dallas/Fort Worth International Airport," she said, briefly glancing at note cards.

"You will board Turkish Airlines flight 401 from Dallas to Chicago O'Hare, with your next connection from O'Hare to Istanbul, Turkey, and from Turkey your connecting flight to Aden, Yemen."

Hawkins kept her attention on Madden.

"One point of information you may be interested in is why Turkish Airlines. At this time, Turkish Airlines is the *only* carrier with stops in Aden, Yemen. The only carrier. The other major U.S. and foreign airlines terminated service to Yemen due to the numerous terroristic threats. Any questions?"

"Thank you, Ms. Hawkins, I do have one—though I am familiar with the Aden airport, how will I make my way to Marib to join the others on the team?" Madden asked.

"Thank you, Mr. Madden, and please excuse me for not briefing you further," Hawkins continued in a very alluring and soothing voice to the point of flirting with Madden. All knew what awaited Madden that night.

"Midland Oil Company operates their own small fleet of airplanes in Yemen, and I suspect you will travel by way of a small, twin-engine de Havilland Otter aircraft, which are known workhorses in oil fields across the world," she explained.

Madden was familiar with the Otter and very much loved and respected the aircraft. In his days of working with the Special

Operations and CIA, Madden spent countless hours riding in an Otter's cargo hold, and in some cases, the reliable Otter kept him and his team out of trouble.

"Rob, for your benefit, we have sent many of our people into Yemen under the same guise of working for various oil companies in the area and are pleased with the operation to date," Meyers added. "Also, the Yemeni government has been easy to work with regarding passport and visas for our temporary oil field workers. They truly appreciate the vast amount of money the oil companies are investing in Yemen and are not about to cause any issues to disrupt the flow," he clarified.

"However, the family clan of Azzam are well informed by corrupt government officials about who arrives in Yemen to work in the oil and gas fields," Meyers continued, "and we have not had any problems with our operatives working with Midland Oil."

"Yes, I recall on several occasions while we were tracking the al-Qaeda terrorist Abu Qasm al-Rimi in eastern Yemen, the many oil production crews were doing their testing and measurements—certainly did not appear to be a fun job," Madden commented.

"Gloria, do you have anything further for Madden in regard to his travel arrangements?" Meyers asked Hawkins.

"Yes I do," Hawkins said. "I would like to go over some last-minute details with Mr. Madden on his travel itinerary prior to him leaving the building today."

There was not one member of the audience who did not know what Hawkins meant by "last-minute details" except Robert Madden. However, the others in the conference room felt it was a rite of passage for Madden to find out on his own what the details were.

"Thank you, Ms. Hawkins, I'll swing by to see you prior to leaving for the night," Madden politely responded.

Hawkins smiled at Madden while gathering her documents and smoothed her blue business dress ensuring her finer assets were properly displayed. She picked up her briefcase and headed for Madden, who was now standing to have a side conference with one of the military intelligence specialists.

"Excuse me, Mr. Madden, I am sorry to interrupt," Hawkins said, positioning herself next to Madden as she handed him a small envelope while lightly touching his arm.

"Thank you, Ms. Hawkins," Madden said, acknowledging her while the intelligence specialist politely excused himself. "I am grateful for all of your work in making the arrangements for my upcoming travel. I understand you have been doing this for years and are a seasoned expert."

"Thank you for your kind words," Hawkins said, intentionally keeping her hand on Madden's arm. "May I call you Rob?"

"Of course, and may I call you Gloria?"

Madden felt somewhat awkward with her sudden closeness and occasionally eyed her hand on his arm with curiosity. He caught a whiff and decided she was a cigarette smoker, liked a strong perfume as a cover-up, and obviously liked to show off her physical assets. In addition, he detected, she was in good physical shape—she definitely worked out.

"Now, Rob, we have you staying tonight at the Ritz-Carlton, Pentagon City." She lifted a large envelope from her briefcase and handed it to Madden. "Are you familiar with the Ritz-Carlton?"

"Yes, probably the finest hotel in the area—I know where it is," Madden replied as he had stayed there in the past when directed to provide briefings to the Joint Chiefs of Staff when on active duty for the Air Force.

"Here is your room reservation, and for obvious reasons, the name on the reservation is a Mr. Jeffrey Stinson," she said, handing Madden the envelope. "We believe it best that we don't advertise your visit with us."

Madden smiled, nodding his head that he understood.

"Now, I'll meet you at the Ritz at seven this evening, so we can further discuss your travel arrangements, and it will give me enough time to have the tickets prepared—okay with you?" she asked, starting to reel in her prey.

"Sure, should I meet you in the bar or dining room?"

"No, no Rob, it would be best if we went over the itinerary and schedule in your room," Hawkins insisted, "too many familiar faces frequent the Ritz—we certainly don't need any unwanted attention for your visit now, do we?"

"Fine, Gloria, I'll be in the room at seven. See you then," he affirmed, finally sensing that Hawkins wanted more than just a review of his travel plans. *Whatever she wanted, she was going to get,* Madden reasoned. *Living a celibate life in an armpit called Tres Rios, New Mexico, for a year doing nothing but teaching neglected children, fighting some doped-up drug lord, and having a terrorist come out of nowhere to try to kill me, you're darn right I'm going to appreciate the assistance of Gloria Hawkins. Well, at least there are some benefits to returning to Yemen,* he reminded himself. But thoughts of Bonnie McCord took over.

Madden grabbed the envelope that Hawkins had provided him regarding the information on their meeting that night in his hotel room.

Sorry, Hawkins, no Madden for you tonight, Madden thought.

Hawkins picked up her briefcase and headed out of the conference room with most of the men in attendance tracking her departure with wonderment and desire.

"Well, another notch on Gloria Hawkins's bedpost," whispered Gen. Klug's aide to another officer.

"At least he'll have some pleasure prior to going to that hell hole in Yemen," the officer replied with a smirk on his face.

16

"Special Agent Bonnie McCord?" the executive officer for the DEA Training Academy politely asked McCord as she was waiting in the conference room adjacent to the academy supervisor's office.

"Yes, I'm Bonnie McCord," she replied as Special Agent Ken Arland took a seat across from her at the exceptionally large conference table. The conference room appeared to be bare of any pictures or posters, which is common for government facilities. McCord's sixth sense told her this was going to be strictly business—no diversions.

Arland opened his briefcase and began organizing many of the documents on the table. McCord patiently watched as he finally completed his inventory. He stared at McCord with an expressionless face. She stared right back in the uncomfortable silence.

Is this some sort of personality screening? she wondered. *Whatever.*

"Agent McCord, you know you are volunteering for one of the most dangerous assignments in the Agency, and I am not sure if you realize and understand the gravity of the situation," Arland emphasized. "Do you have any idea what you are getting yourself into?"

"I trust that if the Agency trains me well, I will be able to handle any situation," McCord said, parroting the standard Agency "book answer" in interviews like this.

Rolling his eyes as though he had heard this reply a thousand times from overzealous, arrogant, and fairly new agents, Arland knew it was his job to purposely attempt to talk agents out of assignments—especially life-and-death duties like this one—when the Agency had grave doubts about their success and safety. He knew McCord's record and reputation and genuinely liked what he had learned, but he was desperately trying to give her a way out—there was no turning back.

"As you well know, the Agency has a lack of information with no eyes on the ground and zero in regard to an informant network in the area of operation where you volunteered," Arland said. "Also, your superiors thought very highly of you, which resulted in your being offered this assignment—you speak perfect Spanish, you survived in the jungles and streets of Colombia, and handle yourself very well when the chips are down."

McCord sat motionless, continuing to stare at Arland.

"Is there anything further you would like to discuss, Agent Arland?" McCord asked, eager to get on with her specialized undercover training.

Taking off his reading glasses and rubbing his forehead, Arland was in deep thought for a minute.

"If you get compromised or your cover is blown, you will have no friends, no help, and no one from the embassy to bail you out—you'll be on your own," warned Arland.

From her past experiences with the Agency, McCord knew there were all types of "under the table" and alternate, unofficial ways to free an agent from a hostile environment, and she also knew Arland was only doing his job by elevating all of the dangerous and potential risks she would be taking in Bolivia. McCord knew her star was rising within the Agency, and this chance to blow the cover of the kingpins in the infamous Sola Mesa drug cartel was a golden opportunity for another rapid career advancement regardless of the risks involved.

"Yes, sir, Agent Arland, I am well aware of the situation and would like to move forward with the assignment," McCord confidently replied.

"Let's proceed with your briefing on your assignment in Bolivia then," Arland said, sounding resigned and knowing nothing was going to stop her.

"Agent McCord," he said, now formally addressing her as a peer, "your undercover training will begin here at the academy with advanced agent training with a mix of classroom and practical drills including small arms training, hand-to-hand conflicts, and probably, most important of all, surveillance techniques."

He looked at her for any sign she might waver. "Also, advanced instruction in Bolivia's drug laws, diplomatic protocol with language training to identify words, phrases, and meanings common in Bolivia," Arland explained.

"Agent Arland, I feel confident with my language skills in South America," McCord replied.

"Yes, McCord, your skills may be acceptable for Colombia, but possibly not Bolivia," Arland said. "For instance, what was an acceptable phrase in Spanish in Colombia might be a slur in Bolivia."

"Yes, of course, that makes perfect sense." A somewhat humbled McCord nodded her head in agreement.

"Your formal undercover training here will be 'practicals' with scenarios matching your mission to be planned and executed by one of our seasoned case agents—I believe that will be—" Arland stopped and put on his reading glasses to review the mission training folder.

"Oh, yes, Special Agent George Vaca is the assigned case agent," Arland said, still scanning the folder, "and I see he was one of our last agents out of Bolivia in 2008 when we were ordered to leave the country. I am sure he is the best we have to train you for your mission.

"After your training with Agent Vaca, you will be assigned for further advanced undercover training at undisclosed locations at the FBI and CIA facilities, specifically for intelligence gathering and surveillance techniques," said Arland.

"In addition, you can rest assured the FBI and CIA will put you through your paces regarding the details of your new identity, authorized activities, and covert handlers and contacts." Arland paused for a moment to reread a note.

"Lastly, McCord, CIA and DEA Agent Vaca will school you in everything you need to know about the Sola Mesa organization," Arland concluded.

"I understand, Agent Arland. However, I am curious to know what my cover will be in Bolivia," McCord asked, knowing full well the training path leading to her assignment.

"We're getting to that," Arland replied. "With your assignment in Bolivia, you understand that the Bolivian government kicked the DEA out in November of 2008 and claims they formed their own special forces to combat drug trafficking—we are unsure of the progress or enthusiasm the government has made in stopping the production of cocaine labs in Bolivia."

McCord was now paying close attention to Arland's words.

"It is widely known the Mexican drug-trafficking organizations are financing and controlling the cocaine labs in Bolivia. However, they don't actually operate on Bolivian land, but rather use their influence via established criminal organizations in Bolivia with the possible assistance of the Fuerzas Armadas Revolucionarias de Colombia, commonly known as the FARC." Arland smiled and asked McCord, knowing she knew the answer: "Are you familiar with the FARC, Special Agent McCord?"

"Yes, and I have the scar to prove it," McCord replied as she pointed to a slight scar on her left check below the ear.

"Well, McCord, you just might have the opportunity to meet up with them again in Bolivia." Arland's mention of the FARC held McCord's full attention. No way did she want another run-in with them.

"Our records indicate you were personally responsible for taking down a few FARC soldiers yourself while defending a helicopter landing zone in Colombia," Arland added.

"I don't recall," answered a grinning McCord knowing full well her actions were still considered highly classified and left it there as a mystery to Arland.

"Legend has it that during the fight, your rifle was knocked out of commission when two FARC soldiers nearly captured you," Arland commented, smiling. "We understand that you yelled at the approaching soldiers while pulling out your bayonet in preparation for being captured, 'You're gonna have to pay the price if you want to fuck Bonnie McCord.'"

She just smiled.

"To our understanding, the two soldiers were taken down just prior to reaching you by Colombian Special Forces soldiers," Arland said, showing his respect and admiration for this special agent.

"Sir, I have no knowledge whatsoever of the operation you described or my participation."

Arland sat back, obviously enjoying his interview with McCord. He continued the briefing.

"The local criminal elements in Bolivia and the FARC oversee the coca leaves grown in Bolivia that are, in turn, processed into paste and packaged into processed cocaine at a drug lab in Colombia. From there the cocaine is loaded on a private aircraft registered in Venezuela and lands in Honduras, where it is shipped through Guatemala and Mexico destined for the United States." Arland was reading from notes and occasionally looked up at McCord.

"Bottom line, McCord—Bolivia is one of the world's largest coca producers, which makes it a priority for the Mexican drug-trafficking organizations," Arland stressed, "and with the government of Bolivia kicking us out of the country, we have no eyes or ears on the ground to help us identify which cartels are involved, who is controlling them, nor how much the government of Bolivia is involved with the drug traffickers."

Arland removed his reading glasses and rubbed his wrinkled temples.

"McCord, your assignment is to gradually immerse into the local commercial workforce at the Georgia Fried Chicken restaurant at the Ventura Mall de Santa Cruz in Santa Cruz, Bolivia's largest city, and seek a way to become known in the franchise circles as just another gringo franchise manager trying to make it big in Bolivia." The glasses were back on Arland as he read the assignment from a secure folder.

"You will be the new manager at the Georgia Fried Chicken franchise," Arland clarified.

"I'm a manager for a fried chicken franchise?" a surprised McCord asked.

"The undercover people at the Agency have gone over this a thousand times trying to work the best possible scenario for you to fit in, and with your attributes and skills, it was determined that the franchise manager would be the best cover," Arland explained.

"Listen," he said, "I don't mean to sound like a sexist, but you are an attractive woman with skills to match your looks to include your proficiency in Spanish, lawyer by training, you have proven yourself in defending yourself and getting yourself out of dangerous situations—to include being very lucky."

"I must say, it beats being a blackjack dealer in Tres Rios, New Mexico," sighed McCord.

"Let's talk about your cover—here is the plan." Arland was now resigned to the fact that McCord was committed.

"Upon your undercover training with the FBI and CIA, you will attend the Georgia Fried Chicken Training Center in Savannah, Georgia. Of course, you will arrive at their school as an out-of-work financial advisor who needs a steady paycheck to pay many of your bills—it's work. In other words, you got into some trouble at your previous job and are desperate for a new job even if it's as a manager of a franchise in Bolivia," explained Arland.

"We'll ensure you know enough about the franchise business to make it look credible when you show up," he said.

"Is this for real?" McCord mocked. "You want me to change my identity and go undercover as a fried chicken manager?"

Arland let her vent her frustrations about the assignment.

"What did you expect, McCord? Did you think we were sending you down to Santa Cruz as a bank president? Get real," Arland snapped.

"Wonderful, and thank you for this grand opportunity," murmured McCord, "but how in the devil am I to gain access to the workings of the cartels and government as a short-order cook?"

"We'll get to that in a minute," answered Arland. "Now please listen very carefully."

"By luck or coincidence," he said, "the Georgia Fried Chicken restaurant is located with the Steel Rock Café in the mall—are you familiar with the Steel Rock Café?"

"Yes," she said quietly.

"It's widely known in Santa Cruz that the high-roller cartel kingpins and government officials enjoy the pleasures and atmosphere of the Steel Rock, just like here in the States— movie stars, celebrities and drug dealers—there is a wealth of information just waiting to be picked at this location," Arland predicted.

"With the GFC being located with the Steel Rock Café, this will give you the perfect opportunity to associate with the workers at the Steel Rock and possibly make friends and associations. Maybe even enlist some informants for our payroll—you'll be trained accordingly in your classes regarding the recruitment of informants," Arland said.

"Again, you'll be the only DEA agent in Bolivia, and it is critical we get accurate information on the Sola Mesa cartel— it is that crucial to us," he said. "Now, before leaving this room for your first phase of specialized training here at the academy, it is imperative that nothing we discussed in this room is leaked—for the sake of your safety and your cover—do you understand?"

"Yes, sir," McCord formally replied. She pushed her chair back and got up to shake Arland's hand.

"Good luck and if you see issues that affect your training schedule, come to me directly—no one else, do you understand?" commanded Arland.

McCord thought for a moment wondering if this might be a good time to share with Arland about a certain FBI agent, also in training at the academy, who had made several unwelcome advances toward her.

"No," McCord thought to herself, she would handle the situation herself.

CHAPTER
17

"Attention please," came the broadcast over the public announcement system at the Aden International Airport in Yemen later that Friday afternoon in September. The temperature inside the airport terminal was a mild 74 degrees, while outside was a hot 115 degrees.

"Turkish Airlines flight 2010 from Istanbul, Turkey, has just landed and will arrive at gate 15," the broadcast announced again in English, Arabic, and French. The airport was noticeably staffed with several armed security guards and dogs in response to recent terrorist attacks and threats targeting the airport. Airline passengers from various countries surrounding Yemen were all represented wearing clothes appropriate to their region. From Hong Kong-made business suits to the traditional Arab robe, Aden definitely took the appearance of an international crossroads.

Among the numerous international parties waiting for flight 2010 to deplane at the gate was what appeared to be a typical Western oil company supervisor picking up one of the many thousands of oil industry workers descending on Yemen for the past several years. With oil and gas being the only viable and profitable export from Yemen, the government was considered friendly and accommodating to the flood of oil and gas technicians entering the country.

The supervisor was a well-tanned, grizzled muscular man who appeared to be in his mid-forties. He wore a khaki shirt, along with a black ball cap that proudly displayed the Midland Oil Company name and logo. Stitched on the shirt was his name— Andy Rikli. Rikli was considered a career oil man at Midland and had served the company for over five years in Yemen during the current boom.

Starting at the lowest and least desirable job possible as a roughneck on an oil drilling platform after his hitch in the U.S. Army, Rikli was a tough supervisor who was known for getting results and working well with the government and the other oil and gas companies in the area. Also, Rikli and Midland Oil were clandestinely supporting U.S. government efforts to track known terrorists in the Shabwah and Nisab regions, also known as the triangle of evil.

Opening his grease-stained notebook, Rikli looked at schedules to find the name of the new employee he was to pick up. Fumbling through the well-worn pages, he came across the name of his new employee: Ron Hanson.

As a large crowd of different nationalities gathered around the gate area waiting for passengers to deplane and make their way through customs, Rikli quietly moved to the back of the area next to the small newspaper stand. He was content to wait there and read the paper as the flow of passengers slowly came through the security area and greeted their waiting parties.

There he is, Rikli thought to himself. *Oh great, they sent me another CIA undercover spook and not an experienced oil field guy.*

Madden had on a pair of worn Wrangler jeans, along with a Decker long-sleeve work shirt that had the Midland Oil name all over it, so to most people, he looked like any of the other company oil and gas workers who were always coming or going in Yemen.

But after a lifetime in the oil business and with his informal links with the Feds, Rikli was quite able to pick out the true roughnecks from the CIA imposters, and Madden was definitely an imposter.

Grinning now and shaking his head, Rikli remembered what Shakespeare said about clothes making the man. Not in Rikli's eyes.

Madden was just leaving customs when he spotted a man, also with a Midland Oil shirt on, approaching him.

"Mr. Hanson, I'm Andy Rikli. Welcome to Yemen," he said, shaking hands with Madden as both got out of the way of other passengers.

"Thank you, Andy, for meeting me," a grateful Madden replied.

"Did you have a good trip?" inquired Rikli as he patiently escorted Madden.

Rikli led Madden through another maze of checkpoints and waiting areas, and without fanfare guided Madden out in short order.

Both men made their way to the arrival parking curb with Madden's gear and luggage. Two Yemeni soldiers were guarding a rather new-looking British Range Rover with the Midland Oil Company seal on the side and back. It was obvious the Rover was parked in a no-parking zone, but no one was going to question the violation with two armed soldiers guarding it.

"Shukran, sabah al-khayr. Thank you and good morning," Rikli greeted the two soldiers and shook hands with each, transferring what appeared to be a wad of U.S. dollars.

"Many thanks, sayyid," replied the soldiers as they quickly placed the dollars in their pockets, picked up their rifles, and headed back into the airport terminal awaiting more "guard duty."

"I can see it pays well being a soldier here in Yemen," a grinning Madden observed.

"Sure does—now let's get your equipment loaded in the Rover and get you something to eat and some rest. I suspect you're probably tired and hungry."

Rikli started the Rover and made his way out of the busy, dirty, and crowded roads leading out of the airport and into the city of Aden. Vendors were all over the Rover pushing their goods and barking at the two men attempting to sell their goods to the rich oil company foreigners. Again, Madden noticed the police and military were aware of the Rover and paid extra attention ensuring there were no traffic problems along their path down the dusty roads heading to the Midland Oil Company headquarters just north of the city before making his way to Marib.

Both men knew everything said in the Range Rover could be recorded by a listening device planted by a soldier, street vendor or literally anyone seeking sensitive information on Midland's operations—both its oil production business and any other support they may be providing to the governments of Yemen and the United States.

"Hanson, you will find Aden a land of contrasts—very modern and prosperous in some quarters, and impoverished in others," explained Rikli. "Have you experience in working any other fields in the Middle East?" asked Rikli.

"Yes, some," an evasive Madden replied.

Picking up his cell and dialing a number while driving the Rover, Rikli contacted the dispatcher at the Midland Oil complex and provided him a status on newcomer Hanson.

"Yes, Red, no problems," he relayed over the phone, "should be at the complex in about ten minutes."

Rikli continued to glance at Hanson occasionally as he finished getting Madden safely to the Midland complex. Approaching the heavy steel security gate of a mammoth concrete entrance, Madden marveled at the huge walls and barbed wire surrounding the perimeter. Inside, Madden noticed yards filled with various types of oil field equipment—all neatly arranged along the roads for easy access. Also, he noticed the support facilities that were common for most oil producers in the area—office buildings, machine shops, vehicle garages, cafeteria, and living quarters.

After the Yemeni guard inspected the Rover at the entry checkpoint and another asked to see the identification of both driver and passenger, the large steel, electric gate was opened and Rikli drove in, heading through the maze of pipes and pumps to the administration building.

Signing into the Midland Oil Company headquarters to drop off his gear, Madden asked, "Andy, do you mind if I keep my gear with me?"

Looking somewhat puzzled by the request, Rikli nodded his head.

"Sure, Hanson, we can load it in the storage locker and pick it up after we get a bite to eat at the cafeteria—okay with you?"

"Thank you and lead the way to the cafeteria—the food on Turkish Airlines was not agreeable with my stomach," commented Madden.

The spacious, modern cafeteria was a typical oil field catering operation. Twenty-four hours a day, meals were served for those working inside the equipment yard and those in the oil and gas pipeline operations. Madden marveled at the fresh selection of food and an international cadre of food service workers serving up a variety of meals. Recalling his days as an apprentice driller on an offshore drilling platform brought back memories of the importance and significance of looking forward to a good meal after one's shift on the platform.

Both men filled their plates with roast beef and cold shrimp. Rikli pointed to a lone table in the corner with few employees in the vicinity. The rumbling of an overhead fan provided a little more comfort in this steaming oasis.

The cafeteria was the hub of activity in the Midland complex with the usual banter, loud chatter, and excessive laughter that provides welcome relief for those working long hours in the excessive heat of Yemen's oil and gas fields.

"Listen to me, Hanson, or whatever your real name is," getting right to the point in his face, Rikli turned from the friendly supervisor to a stern no-nonsense business guy.

"I'm here to run the operations of Midland Oil here in Yemen and ensure the personnel and equipment are producing oil and gas—not distracted from that by wet nursing some employee who may have a different agenda," stated Rikli. "Do you understand me?"

"Yes, I am a proud member of the Midland Oil team," Madden said, attempting to defuse any confrontation with Rikli, "and you, sir, are the boss."

"We've had others like you that somehow found themselves outside of Marib, in Midland vehicles apparently with their own agendas. And somehow, by coincidence I am sure, drones from nowhere were flying overhead and dropping bombs and missiles at cars and huts in the area—can you imagine that! Everything happened when Midland Oil crews were in the area—I wonder how that is, Hanson?" a frustrated Rikli now venting to a pitch that others around the other dining room tables were taking notice.

Madden was just looking nonchalantly at Rikli and shrugged his shoulders. "Beats me, boss. I was told I was sent here to be part of an exploration team looking for possible oil and gas deposits in the area you mentioned—Marib."

Staring at Madden for a half a minute, Rikli was satisfied that he had said his piece but knew any further talks with Madden were fruitless.

While they ate, Rikli provided Madden some updates and what to expect in regard to working conditions in Marib when a woman with large Ray-Ban aviator sunglasses appeared at the table with Madden and Rikli.

"Did you want to see me, boss?" asked the young woman as she politely tapped Rikli on the shoulder. Madden looked up to see a cute woman of about five-feet, five-inches with a nice figure—almost muscular in many ways—under a blue denim work shirt and cargo pants that bore their share of solvent stains.

When she removed the Ray-Bans, Madden saw penetrating blue eyes and a light complexion that had obviously seen too much sun in the dry desert heat. Madden judged her to be in her mid-thirties, and he was curious to find out how she found herself working as a roughneck in Yemen. He also noticed that the various other Midland employees were taking notice of this woman. But then again, Madden mused to himself, "Any woman looks good here in Yemen."

"Yes, Kelly, please take a seat," invited Rikli. "This is Ron Hanson, a new employee."

"Pleasure to meet you, Ron, I'm Kelly Carson—welcome aboard."

Taking off her wide-brimmed Midland Oil hat, she sat down next to Rikli and put her iPad and notebook on the table.

"I sure hope you're our helium welder—we've been waiting for one from Tulsa for over a month now," Carson said.

"No, I'm afraid not," Madden said.

"Hanson here is going to be joining our exploration team up in the Marib area," Rikli said.

"So you're a specialist in oil and gas exploration, huh?" Carson snidely asked, now looking directly at Madden.

"Yes, ma'am, I am, and looking forward to getting to work up in Marib," Madden said. He was having fun playing the inexperienced and naïve oil man with Carson.

"Do you know anything about Marib?" she asked, glaring at both Rikli and Madden.

"I hear there are numerous pipeline problems in Marib—is that so?" Madden put on an act.

"Listen, smart guy, Marib is a dangerous place to work," she said, "and we are finding that more and more every day, especially with terrorists sabotaging the oil infrastructures there and wreaking havoc with the oil and gas pipelines. Do you understand any of this?"

Getting a sense of her pent-up frustration, Rikli grinned at Carson and nodded his head knowing the heat, isolation, and tough production schedule was exacting a toll on his ambitious field supervisor and corporate pilot.

"You're one of them, aren't you, asshole?" Carson blurted out.

Rikli grabbed her hand and motioned for her to keep quiet, "Shhhhhhhh."

Madden remained quiet, knowing anything he said would just cause further problems while a frustrated Carson nervously tossed back her short brown hair and looked away from both men, visibly annoyed.

"Hanson, a while back, Carson had a couple Midland workers lose their lives to terrorist attacks in the Marib area. They were tasked by our contract to work on the pipeline and were ambushed by al-Qaeda operatives just east of the pumping station outside Marib," Rikli explained in a quiet voice.

"We have a large cadre of Midland workers, one hundred and five to be exact, working out of our facility in Marib. It's a comfortable facility for the area where we work and is guarded 24/7 by a Yemeni security service—mostly off-duty soldiers and police officers," Rikli said.

"Please listen to me, Hanson." He lowered his voice and pulled out his dirty notepad and a pen and began writing something on the tablet.

"Here," Rikli pushed a folded note to Hanson. "This is your room number over in the dormitory—your equipment was brought in by the company courier a few days ago. It should be in your room."

"Thanks," Madden replied as he studied the note while finishing off the last of his shrimp.

"What is your business here?" Kelly Carson quietly asked Madden, certain she knew the answer.

"Why, Miss Carson, I was tasked to assist in looking for new oil and gas deposits outside of Marib," Hanson answered.

At that, Carson stared at Madden for a moment, got up from the cafeteria table, grabbed her notebook and iPad and hat, and abruptly left the table.

"Fuck you, Hanson," was heard as Carson slammed the cafeteria door behind her.

Madden and Rikli ignored the commotion of the other employees finishing their meals and now bantered back and forth about what they just witnessed. Just another show.

"Listen, don't let anything that Carson said offend you," Rikli whispered to Madden. "She lost her fiancé last year up near Marib, and he was also looking for new oil and gas fields, like you."

"What happened?" Madden needed to know.

"He was teamed up with a new employee who had other things on his mind besides looking for oil," Rikli said, knowing this would hit home to Madden. "He was accidentally shot by a tribal clan thinking he was working for the CIA while working on a pump station on the pipeline out of Marib to the ship tanker loading terminal at Bir Ali."

Knowing he'd get a rise out of Madden, Rikli said, "Carson will be flying you up to Marib tomorrow morning in the Otter, so you'd better get to your room and check your gear and get some sleep—you have had a long day."

"But is she really qualified to fly a Twin Otter?" Madden said, now a little anxious and showing it about the prospects of flying with Carson as the lone pilot.

"Well, I guess we'll find out tomorrow, huh?" Rikli knew Carson had thousands of hours flying Midland personnel and equipment all over the southern Arabian Peninsula—especially Yemen.

"What do you want—some 10,000-hour American Airlines pilot?" Rikli said, feeling the frustration with what he considered to be a wet-nursing job for some government undercover agent.

"Nah, thanks, Andy, I am sure Carson is a very fine pilot and greatly appreciate the lift to Marib," Madden said.

To the rest of the Midland employees enjoying their late-evening meals, Madden appeared to be just another vagabond roughneck looking for a quick buck while working in a dangerous environment—Madden played his part well.

Near the drop-off station for dirty dishes and trays, a young Yemeni contract worker for Midland stopped his work and took a special interest in Madden as he and Rikli left their dishes. He took a small cell phone out of his back pocket, and the kitchen worker turned the phone toward Madden and immediately acted as if he were making a short call. As quickly as the phone appeared, the worker hurriedly placed it back in his pocket and continued his work.

Later in the evening, the kitchen worker found a secluded area near the trash containers and made a brief call, speaking in Arabic.

"He's here," he said, and sent the stealth photo.

CHAPTER
18

"Good morning, Aden International. This is Midland Air 101, ready for takeoff," Carson announced over the radio to the control tower as she taxied the de Havilland twin-engine Otter to the hold line prior to entering the runway. Carson was routinely running her pre-takeoff checklists while the powerful turbo propeller engines were sending clouds of dust and sand behind the Otter.

Madden, sitting in the co-pilot's seat as a passenger, was impressed by the professionalism and experience Carson was showing in handling her pilot duties.

"Is there anything I can do to assist? I'm pretty handy around aircraft," Madden asked Carson over the plane's interphone while she was still working the radio traffic and completing her checklist items.

"Yah, Hanson, you can strap in and keep your mouth shut," Carson replied while an embarrassed Madden reached down to lock his seat belt.

"Midland Air 101, this is Aden tower, you are cleared for takeoff on runway 260, climb and maintain 12,000, direct course to Marib, maintain radio frequency 119.6 after departure. How copy, Midland Air 101?" relayed the Yemeni air traffic controller.

"Aden tower, Midland Air 101 copies all and have a good day," Carson replied.

As she pushed the throttles forward and adjusted the propellers' pitch for takeoff, the Twin Otter vibrated excessively as Carson maneuvered it straight down the runway pushing more power into the engines for takeoff. Gaining speed, the Otter was now racing down the runway and finding the correct takeoff speed. Carson lifted the Otter into the air, leaving behind Aden International with nothing but blue skies in front of them.

Madden was sitting back, admiring Carson's piloting skills. He had flown with hundreds of different pilots throughout his military career but was truly impressed with her operations in the cockpit—especially with no designated co-pilot to assist her.

"Aden Control, Midland Air 101 is level at 12,000, transponder squawking 4401, proceeding direct to Marib, over," announced Carson while she adjusted the throttles for level flight and set the autopilot.

Adjusting the secondary radio frequency to that of the Midland Oil operations center, she advised the center that 101 was airborne en route to Marib—no problems. Then she had another radio transmission where she was in good humor and laughing with another party, only all was said in Arabic—she continued laughing and looking at Madden.

After Carson completed her personal transmissions on the radio, she sat back and began working her flight plan and fuel management.

"You know what?" Madden said over the interphone.

Carson stopped for a moment and looked at Madden. "What?" an annoyed Carson replied.

"I don't think I'm as dumb and stupid as you described me over the radio to your friend," Madden informed Carson with a large grin on his face.

Carson glanced at Madden trying to ignore his comment while she went back to adjusting the Otter's fuel figures.

The son of a bitch knows Arabic, Carson thought to herself. *Wonder what else he knows?*

Settling back and enjoying the ride, Madden looked down at the sun-parched terrain of southern Yemen with its high terrain features not uncommon in the American Southwest. But he had left New Mexico far behind. He remembered his previous life in

Yemen tracking terrorists for the CIA and Special Operations—probably the most dangerous and challenging assignments in his Air Force career, but by far the most rewarding in regard to making a difference in the world and to his personal satisfaction.

Wearing his aviator sunglasses and sitting back in the co-pilot seat, listening to the rumbling of the two turboprop engines and the constant radio chatter with a female pilot who did not care at all about him—Madden tried to make the best of the situation.

Bonnie McCord. He wondered how she was doing in her new undercover assignment with the DEA—hoping she would stay safe and out of trouble. Like him, he reasoned, trying desperately to stay out of harm's way.

He peered down on the small, desolate town of Nisab in the badlands of the Shabwah province. He was now alertly awake, surveying the town and its many roads and paths around the town—trying to make a quick mental note of the area. Madden knew there would be much trouble in this area—soon. He would make sure of it.

"You're going down there—aren't you, Hanson?" Carson surprised Madden with this sudden question.

He replied with a smile, "Only if Midland Oil needs me there."

"Hanson, or whatever your real name is, you are so full of shit," she said.

"You are correct, I am not an oil field specialist, but a church missionary and I'm going down there," pointing to the province below, "to save all of those heathen souls from damnation."

Carson did not know what to say at this wisecrack. Frustrated, she sat back and made a routine radio call to the Aden air traffic controller. "Yes, roger, out!"

Madden expected some sort of emotional response from Carson.

"Listen, Hanson, whatever you do here during your short stay in Marib, please don't cause any more problems for us who live here. This is my career, and I don't want you messing it up chasing after local bad guys." Carson attempted to temper her frustrations.

Madden nodded his understanding completely. Both sat quietly in the cockpit of the Otter with their thoughts.

"Are you married?" Carson asked Madden as she routinely leaned the engines for best fuel management.

"No, I am widowed," a somber Madden replied. "Why do you ask?"

"Just curious. I see no wedding ring on your finger and just figured if you didn't wear it for your special work or you just take it off when you travel."

Staring at Carson for a minute and realizing she meant no harm by her question, Madden thought about a suitable, balanced reply about his actual work and family, but decided to level with her about his intentions.

Who knows? Madden rationalized and thought to himself, *An oil company pilot with access to an aircraft could be highly helpful to me with my current special tasking while in Yemen.*

"How far out are we from Marib?" Madden asked with an alternate purpose.

"I'm sorry if I went too far with my questions—I was just curious," she said. "To answer your question, we're about two hours out from Marib."

"No, I was not trying to avoid your question, just wanted to ensure we had enough time here in the flight to explain some things to you," Madden said sincerely.

Removing the bulky radio headset from her short brown hair and placing the radio switch to the cockpit speaker so she could listen to the radio traffic, Carson seemed intrigued about what her passenger wanted to talk about.

"Let me be straight with you," Madden began. Carson just stared at him, breathing a little shallower, not knowing what his motives were.

"Some people who live in that little town of Nisab are responsible for the deaths of my family—my wife and two daughters—there is no doubt about it." Madden paused, allowing Carson to take in what he just said.

"What are you talking about? You're a crazy man," a confused Carson screamed, trying to find some task to take her away from what Madden had just said.

"Settle down Carson, and watch the horizon—you're the pilot-in-command." Madden held her by the arm.

"How can you be so damn sure that this terrorist in the town of Nisab is responsible for the deaths of your wife and children?" a calmer Carson asked. "Hold on, I need to make a position call to air traffic control," she instructed.

"Aden Departure Control, Midland Air 101 at 12,000 direct Marib—estimated time of arrival of 1430 local, how copy?" Carson routinely announced.

"Midland Air 101, this is Aden Departure Control, read you loud and clear," the controller replied. "You are cleared to contact the Marib radio on 118.4, have a nice day."

"Copy all," acknowledged Carson as she set the new radio frequency for their approach into the Marib airport.

"We'll talk further on the ground about your mission," she said, the professional pilot side of her kicking in.

Madden just nodded his head feeling somewhat awkward about telling Carson about his true mission in Yemen, but she probably knew all along he was not there strictly for oil. Madden reasoned Carson could be trusted, and besides, her access to a Twin Otter aircraft, where he was going, could be critical to his mission and just might save his life if there was trouble.

Silence filled the cockpit as Carson and Madden scanned the horizon as a sure sign neither wanted to talk further, until possibly later on the ground.

"Marib traffic, this is Midland Air 101 inbound for a straight-in approach to runway 17, over." The silence in the cockpit was broken by Carson's radio call.

"Marib does not have a control tower," Carson informed Madden, "so all operations are visual flight rules meaning coming into Marib, we are on our own and make radio calls in the blind to inform other aircraft where we are."

"Thank you for the information," Madden replied, knowing full well of the air traffic control procedures as his experiences as an Air Combat Controller for the Air Force.

"Midland Air 101, good afternoon, Carson, this is Hunt Oil company dispatcher," said a voice on the radio that had the unique sound of a West Texas drawl. "Carson, looks like we are using runway 17, wind calm, barometer setting appears to be 29.65."

"Thanks, Big Mike, we'll be on the ground in about thirty minutes," Carson acknowledged.

"We are all very close friends in the Marib area, and we work closely with the other oil and gas companies in the region," Carson explained.

As Carson prepared the Twin Otter for landing, Madden took note of the sweet smell of sulfur that entered the cockpit from the burning refinery oil flares and black smoke rising from the various pipeline construction projects centered in Marib.

"Ah yes, there they are," Madden said to himself as he eyed the Yemen Oil Refinery to the left of the airport and the famous Marib–Red Sea oil pipeline—the pipeline made famous by the many local terrorists' attacks on it—also, the main source of revenue for the Yemeni government.

"Hanson! Got your seatbelt on?" Carson instructed as she completed her landing checklist.

"Yes, ma'am, I do," he said pointing to the silver buckled lock while smiling at Carson.

Eyeing Madden with a quick grin, she was anxious to get the Otter on the ground and hear the details of Madden's motivation for being in Yemen—particularly Marib.

"Let's get this ol' girl landed so we can talk," Carson added.

Bringing the Twin Otter in for the landing at the primitive, dirt-paved runway at the Marib airport really took no great piloting skills—the aircraft was designed for such rough landings.

Carson had accomplished this approach a few hundred times, and she gently maneuvered the Otter to a smooth landing, reversing the turbo props on touchdown to save wear on the brakes.

As the Otter was slowing with dust and debris obscuring the view from the cockpit, Madden noticed various signs and logos from the oil and gas companies with taxiways leading straight into their facilities. Carson turned off the runway, applied power to the engines and headed to a taxiway that pointed to a large sign, "Midland Oil and Gas."

She stopped in front of a rather large aircraft hangar with a large office complex inside.

As Carson was busy working her shutdown checklist, Madden noticed one of the many overused, dirty Range Rovers coming out of the hangar heading for the Otter. Turning off the last of the Otter's various switches, Carson unclasped her seatbelt, grabbed her pilot's traveling case from the back, took off her Ray-Ban aviators and neatly stowed them in a holder on the visor.

"Thanks for the ride, young lady, nice flight," Madden said as he also took off his seat belt and opened the Otter's cabin door to find the desert heat as hot as he remembered.

Stretching his body after the long flight under the wing while Carson accomplished her post-flight inspection of her aircraft, Madden saw the Range Rover throw a slight dust trail behind it as it made its way to the Otter.

CHAPTER
19

"Hey, buddy, are you Hanson?" came a call from the driver's side of the Rover as it came to a stop near the wingtip of the Otter.

Madden immediately recognized him from the old days, and grinned.

The driver climbed out of the cab of the Rover wearing his oil-stained Midland cotton blue denim shirt and cargo jeans—also just as soiled as the shirt. An old pair of what appeared to be worn military boots and a straw hat adorned the driver, who also wore a pair of military-style aviator sunglasses.

Madden moved to greet the driver while Carson was still working her post-flight checks and paperwork under the shade of the other wing of the aircraft.

"Hey, Hanson," Carson yelled, "after you give your old friend a big fucking kiss, would you mind getting over here and helping me unload these pump jack bearings, tools, and your shit?"

She added, "It's kind of a tradition around here where the passengers help with the unloading." She shook her sweating ball cap with some disgust.

"Well, Hanson," the driver emphasizing the name and winking at Madden, "welcome to Marib and Midland Oil and Gas—looking forward to getting you orientated and on the job very quickly."

"So, Blake Rhodes, what a surprise. Hadn't seen you since our high school days at the American School in Kuwait—still in the oil business I see," Madden said, delighted to see his old friend in the most surprising of places.

"Later," Rhodes said, obviously not wanting to attract anyone's attention at their meeting, especially wanting to hide any association from Carson who was just coming around from the rear of the Otter looking annoyed at this apparent old friend reunion.

"Hey, Blake, if you and Hanson are through screwing each other, would you mind giving me a lift to the office?"

"Sure, sorry," Rhodes said as he helped Madden and Carson load the equipment and tools from the Otter into the cargo hold of the Range Rover.

Madden instinctively held the passenger side door for Carson to enter the Rover, and she immediately took this as an insult and pressed her middle finger against Madden's face.

"Sorry, Carson, force of habit," Madden apologized. "I have always been taught to open doors for ladies."

"You assholes can kiss my ass and while you are at it, would you mind driving us to the office?"

"Sure, Carson, good idea and glad you thought of that," replied Rhodes, holding back laughter as he shifted the Rover into gear and headed for the hangar.

"Well, I see you two jokers know each other. Let me guess, you worked off a drilling platform in the Gulf." Carson smirked, knowing full well the mission of both men.

"No, we went to school together in Kuwait while we were young—Hanson here was a pretty good soccer player," Rhodes proudly replied. "Watch out for him. He's a real lady killer."

Madden just sat back with his arms folded, shaking his head not knowing how to reply.

Carson never showed it, but she obviously liked working with these men and she could dish it out as good as she got.

"Carson, angel, would you mind if I drop you off at the office?" asked Rhodes. "I need to get Hanson settled down and show him around the facilities."

"Yah, right, you're just going to show him where the beer and booze are hidden," she snapped as the Rover stopped in front of the Midland Oil office complex.

"Not a bad idea," commented Madden.

She pulled herself out of the Rover and picked up her gear from the back of the truck.

"What about unloading the equipment? Some of it is urgent for the onsite welders," the serious side of Carson asked.

"We'll handle it, don't worry," Rhodes replied while Carson slammed the door and headed for the front office entrance. Madden slid out of the backseat and found his way to the passenger seat.

"Is my equipment here?" asked Madden.

"Yes, came by company courier last week and I have it secured in a locked garage—it's titled seismographic instruments," Rhodes answered. "Would you like to check on it now and do a quick inventory—appears to be three large crates?"

"Yes I would, certainly would sleep better knowing it was everything we need—and it works."

"Okay, we'll swing by the garage and check it out of storage," Rhodes said, "then we'll get to your quarters and you can make your inspections."

"You know those instruments can be very sensitive!" Madden turned to look at Rhodes as he navigated his way to the storage locker.

Unlocking the heavy master lock at the locker, Rhodes entered with Madden following.

"There you go," said Rhodes, "the large wooden crates over in the corner."

"Midland Oil and Gas Company, Tulsa OK, Invoice 111784653, Seismographic Instruments, Marib, Yemen, Field Operations Branch," was stenciled on the top of the wooden crates, which were about the size of dishwashers.

"Hey, you fellas need any help?" came an unexpected cry from a mechanic from the machine shop.

"Thanks, Bill," assured Rhodes. "Maybe you can give us a hand getting them in the back of the Rover."

"Glad to help," the mechanic offered as he assisted Rhodes and Madden in getting the bulky wooden crates into the Rover.

"Bill Younger, this is Ron Hanson, our new man from Tulsa." Rhodes made introductions. "Ron here is going to be doing some exploration work for us around the Shabwah province—we got a new contract with Yemen Oil to do some exploratory work in that area."

"Better you than me, Hanson. That place is crawling with al-Qaeda fanatics and their families," Younger said. "Should be okay just as long as Yemeni government troops are escorts."

"Yes, government troops would be very appropriate," added Rhodes, knowing full well Madden liked and would be required to work alone—knowing from past experiences, government troops were often corrupt and not that reliable.

"Hey, nice meeting you, Ron, and if I can help in any way while you're here, let me know." Younger wiped the oil and grease off his hands before shaking Madden's hand.

"Likewise, Bill, and thanks for the advice."

Both men got into the Rover. Rhodes put it in gear and headed for the short drive outside of the large company hangar to an adjacent smaller hangar.

He stopped in front of the smaller hangar, which had nothing but small living trailers parked inside.

"Well Madden, this will be your home for the next few days while you're here," Rhodes said, pointing to the rows of trailers.

"Let's see," Rhodes commented as he was searching his well-worn schedule book for Madden's trailer number. "Ah yes, the presidential suite for you Madden, number 14."

As other Midland Oil employees were coming or going from their own trailers, no one paid attention to the new member of their community. They just figured he was a new guy brought in as a replacement for the many employee losses in the past year.

"Let's get your gear in your trailer and get a bite to eat, then I'll give you a quick orientation."

"Fine with me. Will my equipment be safe in the trailer?" Madden asked.

"Not a problem," Rhodes replied, "Trust me, all the workers

here have more on their minds than breaking down doors and stealing crap."

Rhodes helped Madden move his personal gear and company crates into the trailer.

"What do you think? Pretty nice, huh?"

Madden, a little tired and dirty, just laughed and replied, "You know, Blake, before coming here, I was a school teacher in New Mexico and my residence was a trailer almost like this one."

"Guess you're destined to live in trailers the rest of your life," teased Rhodes.

"Yeah, maybe I'll get a double wide, double tandem one of these days," Madden retorted.

Both men squared away the crates in the trailer's storage closet, locked the door and headed toward the Rover.

A glowing red sun was now falling below the flat desert horizon with the constant, endless sounds of a twenty-four-hour operation at the oil refinery just a few miles from the airport. The gas flares of the refinery and the heavy sulfur smells of oil and gas being refined were now just part of the desert landscape.

CHAPTER
20

"Hanson, why don't you and I take a drive to the refinery—just a quick trip," Rhodes said, almost yelling to ensure those curious minds around heard his intentions. Madden soon gathered quickly, as he had so many times in his prior life working with Special Operations, there were many "curious minds" lurking in the shadows.

"Fine by me, boss," he said, grabbing a bottled water from the crew ice chest in the back of the Rover. Madden slid into the front seat.

"Hanson, grab me a water, too." Madden passed him the water bottle he had snagged and reached back for another.

Taking the time to empty the water bottle in one swig and smiling, Rhodes said, "Sometimes water beats a cold beer—don't you think?"

Each knew perfectly well that there were probably listening devices in the cab of the Rover planted by the Yemeni government, terrorists, foreign embassies, or any group interested in the operations of Midland Oil and their "special" associations with foreign governments. Conversation was often just for the theater of it.

"Well, tell me, Hanson, who's going to win the Super Bowl this year? I've been away for so long that I certainly miss watching the games back in the States," Rhodes added just for effect.

Talk of the football games and the Super Bowl continued between the two men on their drive to the oil refinery now headed east on the main highway.

Madden noticed vehicles of every type coming and going on the road. From municipal to oil company work buses to heavy truck carriers for the oil field equipment, they were all impatient with the slow-moving traffic and bottlenecks caused by the numerous stops at the checkpoints. He also noticed heavily armed Yemeni federal troops and local police officers guarding the many checkpoints at different intervals along the road. Bribes and corruption were a way of doing business in the oil business in Yemen, and checkpoints were no exception—especially for the various foreign oil companies producing oil and natural gas near Marib.

As the Rover slowly approached a government checkpoint, two Army sergeants sitting under a canvas tent next to their American Humvee were slow to get up from an evening nap. They gathered their AK-47s and approached the Rover from both sides.

Seeing the Midland Oil logo and signs on the Rover, the sergeants turned their weapons away and smiled while approaching Rhodes.

"Good evening, Mr. Rhodes," the first sergeant said pleasantly, in broken English. "More work at the refinery this evening?"

"Sgt. Ali Ahan, you know I almost live at the refinery—just to make you rich."

The two sergeants laughed and put down their weapons as Rhodes handed them each a wad of U.S. dollars. As expected, they shoved the bills in their military khaki pants and thanked Rhodes for his generosity.

"Very good, Mr. Rhodes, you are free to proceed to the refinery—we'll radio the other checkpoints and let them know you have taken care of the necessary paperwork here," Sgt. Ahan assured Rhodes while smiling and nodding.

"Many thanks, Ali, and could you do me a favor?" Rhodes asked as he handed him a few more bucks. Ahan was more than happy to listen to the request.

"Ali, this is Ron Hanson," pointing to Madden on his right side, "he is a new member of the Midland Oil team and will be making several trips from the airport to the refinery. Could you ensure, as a new person and guest, that he makes it through the checkpoints with no problems?"

Ahan put his arm and hand through the driver's open window and shook Madden's hand.

"Nice to meet you, Mr. Hanson," Ahan greeted him with a firm handshake.

"Sgt. Ali Ahan, pleasure to meet you, sir," Madden reciprocated.

"I am sure we will be seeing you again, and we are always at the service of Midland Oil," said Ahan, who then surprisingly gave an informal military salute to Rhodes and Madden. Rhodes returned his salute, put the Rover in gear and proceeded slowly away from the checkpoint toward the Marib facility.

"We are very glad to have capable and dependable Yemeni government troops ensuring the safety of our road leading to the refinery," Rhodes stated as he rolled his eyes in disgust at the bullshit he just said.

Madden just grinned and nodded his head, knowing the game well.

Making slow progress to the refinery, Rhodes turned onto a gravel and dirt side road to what appeared to be an old oil drilling platform that had been abandoned for several years. Any roaming eyes would conclude that the two men were inspecting the platform as part of their normal duties with Midland Oil. Also following was a surplus Humvee used by the Yemeni government to provide protection to certain oil company supervisors.

"Why don't we get out? I want to show you how some of the chemical treatment corrosion has affected some of our drilling operations in the Marib area," Rhodes announced as he got out of the Rover and pointed Madden to a couple of industrial steps leading up to the platform.

Rhodes radioed his military escort and informed them that they would not be needed at the platform and requested they wait for them on the refinery highway until the meeting was over. Both soldiers acknowledged and waited outside their vehicle, smoking their much-valued Camels and appreciating the smoke break.

What appeared to be an all-too-common sight of a routine meeting between two foreign oil workers discussing technical, work-related issues could not have been further from the real motives for the meeting.

"Okay Madden, Hanson, whatever. What is the deal, what is the mission, and how are we involved?" Rhodes displayed a now businesslike attitude far from the prying ears of hidden listening devices or curious bystanders.

"Blake, in a few words, I am on contract with the government to direct a drone strike against Azzam or if necessary kill him myself if the drone strike fails," Madden calmly and coolly replied.

Almost falling off his feet with the shock of hearing this announcement from his longtime friend, Rhodes was speechless. He could only come out with, "Why you of all people? I thought the Navy SEALS or Army Special Forces did jobs like this."

Madden smiled at his boyhood friend.

"Madden, Khalid Azzam is a legend here in Yemen and well-guarded, a real bad guy but a legend indeed, and you've come to take care of him—by yourself! You have to be insane and again I ask, why you?"

The sun was now slowing dipping below the horizon, and the slight westerly wind whistled through the old metal support derrick as both men engaged in conversation.

"Blake, you're familiar with the recent failed rescue mission some time back where Special Forces, I believe Navy or Army, attempted to rescue an American journalist and a South African missionary in the Shabwah province." Madden attempted to fully explain his situation to Rhodes. "It truly was a dicey operation from the get-go in my opinion, but it had to be tried."

Madden continued. "Either you take your chances with a rescue, which might, with a little luck, succeed, or you watch two innocent people have their heads cut off on international television with no chance," Madden reasoned. "Rescue was the only way out, and the Navy SEALs and Delta Force had the guts to try."

"So why you, Rob—why not send some undercover CIA folks to finish the job on Azzam or just have the Air Force drop the bombs on where you think he is?"

"The U.S. is catching hell from all over the Arab world regarding the killing of innocent civilians," Madden explained. "What I consider the terrorists' families mostly. And the powers-that-be want this mission to be right on target without deviations and no ties to any U.S. military on the ground."

"So DoD feels that you, as a civilian contractor, will have better success penetrating Azzam's camp?"

"Yes, as you know I had an Air Force assignment working a few months with a CIA team in the Shabwan and Abyan regions tracking targets for the drone attacks. I truly am the best qualified for this mission—especially with my skills with the Arabic language and cultures. I'll get by." Madden fell silent as he scanned the desert horizon, which was reminiscent of his actions several years earlier when targeting and killing the terrorist Anwar Aldawasari and the royal prince from the United Arab Republic.

"I have a very, very personal reason for volunteering to return here and target and take out Azzam," Madden revealed. "'Vengeance is mine,' saith the Lord."

"Excuse me, Rob, what did you say?" Rhodes thought his friend was losing his mind.

"Khalid Azzam is responsible for the murder of my wife and two daughters—any more questions?" Madden had rehearsed and prepared for this moment for days and would attempt to ease the sudden impact of his mission as much as possible, but Rhodes had to know.

Rhodes walked around the old platform for a minute trying to gather his thoughts.

"Listen, Blake, I am very much responsible for the deaths of two of his very good friends and top leaders in al-Qaeda—Anwar Aldawasari and his brother Humza."

"What the hell are you saying—how in the devil could you possibly be involved in the deaths of these two infamous terrorists?" an excited Rhodes tensely asked.

Rhodes's hands were shaking as he pulled a cigarette from the front pocket of his oil-stained work shirt while Madden helped light his friend's cigarette. Taking a puff and exhaling, Rhodes just stared at Madden with the bluest eyes in Yemen.

"You know, Blake, smoking is bad for your health." Madden tried to ease the tension.

"Yes, and being associated with you and working oil in Yemen is ten times more dangerous," Rhodes retorted, exhaling a large cloud of smoke and taking another puff.

"You mean to tell me you are not on some intelligence reconnaissance mission for the government, for God knows what?" Rhodes asked. "We see drones passing overhead all the time flying for targets around the Shabwah area, and frankly, we try to ignore them and just stick to our oil and gas production work.

"Whenever the drones make a strike, we lose production when terrorists make retaliatory strikes against the pipelines running to our offshore fueling ports of Bir Ali and Balhaf in the Gulf of Aden," Rhodes added. "Our people are injured and occasionally we have losses."

Madden nodded.

"This job is dangerous enough working the oil and gas—we certainly don't need the added risk of a bunch of al-Qaeda terrorists getting all pissed off and looking for payback," Rhodes vented, still in motion taking nervous drags from his cigarette, still pacing the old, creaky metal ramp while Madden said nothing to his old friend.

Both men turned and faced the bright orange ball of the sun dropping below the horizon while the Yemeni soldiers radioed Rhodes warning it was time to get off the road.

"Thanks, Sergeant, be right there," Rhodes replied to the radio call. Night was not a time to be out and about.

As they walked toward the Rover, Rhodes turned to Madden and asked, "Okay, what do you need from Midland Oil?"

"Blake," Madden replied, "I would like to go over more of the details tomorrow morning, but for starters, I would like to be assigned some sort of utility shed or small office near the Marib oil refinery and work out of there for the next couple of days."

"Sure, we have just the place for you next to our unused machine shop at the perimeter of the refinery—it has easy access to the entrance, and no one should bother you there," offered Rhodes. "We'll set you up there tomorrow with your equipment and provide you with a Midland truck."

They trudged in silence until Rhodes asked, "I am still confused with all that you told me. How in the world do you plan on getting close enough to Azzam's camp without being assaulted by what is left of the Yemen government, the Houthis, al-Qaeda and even your own drone attacks—who is to say they won't take you out accidentally?"

Madden suddenly realized his friend had a valid point. His old nemesis, Col. Graham, came to mind. Madden's mind began racing with the possibilities of ugly scenarios that were indeed possible. Graham could drop a drone's Hellfire missile on him while he was attempting to evade Azzam's destroyed camp.

Damn! Madden thought to himself. By accident or design, such an attack could cover any U.S. government involvement. And the radio beacons concealed in his regional clothing could track him and zero him in as a target himself. Shit.

CHAPTER
21

Rhodes dropped Madden off at the small company café located just inside the large utility hangar lined with rows of temporary living trailers all with their pulsating air conditioner compressors filling the huge space with their irritating, out-of-sync rhythm.

"Ron, why don't you go over to the café and get yourself something to eat?" Rhodes suggested as Madden was getting out of the Rover. "I'll be back tomorrow morning at six to pick you up and take you and your equipment to your new work site."

"Thanks, Blake. See you tomorrow morning," Madden said as he shut the cab door and headed for the small café with a large sign at its entrance—Last Chance Cafe. *Last Chance*, Madden sighed and thought to himself, *what a very appropriate name for this fine establishment*, as he ordered the special of the day, lamb stew and rice.

Finding a small table near the window and overhead fan, Madden was one of few Midland employees seeking an evening meal at the Last Chance with a case of beer shared by one of the newly arriving roughnecks from the oil refinery.

Enjoying his lamb stew with a couple of German beers, Madden was relaxed for the time being. He reflected on the possible events to come and the many details that still needed to be planned—what-ifs were constantly taxing his tired brain. What if the al-Qaeda zealots don't buy his story of being an American volunteer for the jihad? What if Col. Graham refused to cover him with his assured drone? What if he survived the attack and is able to get back to Marib, but Midland has left with the other oil companies—and their small fleet of airplanes? What if there is a covert agenda to take him out with a drone strike?

"May I join you?"

Madden turned to find an attractive woman wearing a clean, buttoned-down, cotton utility shirt, tight Wrangler jeans and cowboy boots. With her freshly washed hair and an appealing face with a touch of makeup and lipstick, Madden at first did not recognize Kelly Carson until she took a seat directly across from him.

"Carson!" a somewhat bewildered Madden said. "Why yes, of course, please have a seat."

"Thank you, Ron. Glad you found our little café," she said.

One of the other tired and dirty workers also having dinner at the café offered Carson a beer and she graciously accepted, with some kidding from the others at the café that she would not be flying that night after drinking—all laughed including Carson and Madden.

"Do you want something to eat?" Madden politely asked, still pleasantly surprised in the change in her demeanor from this morning.

"I have a feeling we got off to the wrong start this morning," she confided, "but I think you owe me a little more of an explanation regarding what you told me on our flight up here regarding your family and the reason you're here in Yemen."

The café contract worker asked Madden if he was through and removed his empty plate of lamb stew and provided Carson and Madden with bottles of water.

Both sat back, enjoying the cool desert breeze making its pleasant effect in the large hangar complex. A few birds were sweeping through the hangar making their echoing chirping noise. The dry breeze and cackling of the birds reminded Madden of his challenging days in New Mexico.

Carson's voice brought him back to reality.

"Ron?" she softly inquired while momentarily holding his arm and gently letting go.

To the other oil workers and customers in the café, Madden was just another new guy making his way to the Marib refinery or pipeline leading to the seaport at Balhaf on the Gulf of Aden—like so many other oil men drawn to Yemen for the top wages and, most importantly, the adventure.

"Kelly, why don't you and I take a little walk outside so we can talk privately."

"Sure. Why don't we walk on over to the small utility room we have set aside for the Otter's maintenance?"

"Sounds good," Madden followed Carson toward a small hangar adjacent to the main Midland facility.

Scattered in front of the building was an array of roughly constructed outdoor wooden furniture created from some of the thousands of packing crates that passed through the Midland facility.

"Have a seat." She motioned to Madden. "I'll go inside and grab us a couple of beers."

"Nice little hangout you have here," Madden loudly said to Carson, who was inside searching the small refrigerator for beer.

"Yes, we have come a long way here in Marib, both business-wise and quality of life stuff, which we consider a true luxury," she said. "But with the current government barely able to hold power and protect the oil and gas infrastructure, I am sure our days here are close to being gone."

Handing Madden a beer, she found herself a small wooden chair and moved it as close as possible to him so their conversation could be as private as possible.

He took a swig of the cold beer.

"Now, Ron, I have some explaining to do. I know that you are tired and probably have a long day ahead of you tomorrow, but I lost my fiancé a couple of years ago to a terrorist attack on the pipeline in the Shabwah region just southeast of here."

"Yes, I am familiar with what goes on in the Shabwah region—a dangerous and unstable part of Yemen," Madden noted, knowing full well that was his intended destination working his way out of Marib.

She continued, "My understanding is that he was assisting with some sort of CIA undercover team attempting to gather intelligence in Shabwah—he got in the middle during an al-Qaeda strike on the construction crew working one of the many auxiliary pump stations."

"I have also lost many friends in that region," Madden said.

"Okay, now I'm totally confused," she said. "You told me on the plane today something about coming here solely to kill an al-Qaeda leader who was responsible for the deaths of your wife and daughters—I don't understand any of this. Why cause us problems here? We have enough distractions and tragedies—we don't need any more." Carson's lips quivered, and tears were now streaming down her face.

Madden instinctively moved near her and gave her a hug. "It's okay, soon this will all end, and you'll find a much better life wherever Midland sends you," he said and wrapped his arm around her shoulders.

"Now tell me your story," she sniffled, "how did you come to be selected to take out Azzam?"

"First of all, my name is not Ron Hanson. It's Rob Madden, and I am retired Air Force, Special Forces specialist, with skills that include tracking terrorists for our drone operations worldwide, and also I'm pretty good with my Arabic," Madden began. "But please, always refer to me as Ron Hanson while we are in Marib."

"I understand," she acknowledged while wiping away her remaining tears.

"Listen closely and let me explain a little bit about my past and why I am here in Yemen," Madden slowly began.

"Do you remember a few years ago here when Anwar Aldawasari, the top al-Qaeda leader in Yemen, was killed with a member of the United Arab Republic royal family in the Shabwah province by a U.S. drone attack?" Madden asked.

"Why yes, I do," she said. "It certainly caused a lot of confusion in our business and resulted in an increase in terror attacks on our pipeline—nothing we could not deal with or for that matter the government of Yemen."

"The long and short of it is this. I was very much responsible for the deaths of Aldawasari and the UAR prince and, rightfully so, took the hit, the blame, for the killings without permission from the State Department and military—I was literally the government's scapegoat for the incident."

"So you were part of that raid," Carson noted.

"Yes, and after I retired from the Air Force, I became a public school teacher—it was our family dream," he smiled.

Madden continued, "Anwar Aldawasari had a brother, Humza, who was released from the U.S. terrorist prison at Guantanamo and found his way to a terrorist sleeper cell in Detroit."

"Did he attempt to settle the score, get even with you?" Carson asked.

"Yes, he did," Madden said. "I understand when he found out that I was teaching school in New Mexico, he made a nonstop effort to find and kill me to avenge his brother's death. Through official government sources and documents, Humza found I was solely responsible for his brother's death."

Suddenly, a Midland Oil Ford pickup appeared, slowly approaching with a trace of dust as it made its way to where Madden and Carson were sitting outside the utility hangar.

"Hey, Hanson, shouldn't you be getting some rest? You have a long day tomorrow at the refinery," a voiced yelled out of the pickup cab.

"And you, Carson, better get some sleep, you'll need it for tomorrow's flight operations."

"We have no flight operations planned for tomorrow," Carson said to Madden. "I wonder what's going on."

The headlights of the pickup truck shone brilliantly toward the wind sock at the edge of the airport runway as Madden and Carson got up and walked to the passenger side.

"Andy Rikli, is that you?" Madden asked. Rikli, the Midland supervisor, stopped the truck and got out.

"Ron and Kelly, glad I found you. We have problems, major problems," Rikli said as he motioned for Madden and Carson to join him on the open tailgate of the truck. The diesel engine was left running, emitting black fumes into the dry air.

"All hell has broken loose, and the government has lost control," he told them. "Appears the Shiite insurgency group called the Houthis are taking control of Yemen's capital in Sanaa. With al-Qaeda still causing us major problems with no government protection, Midland Oil and the rest of the companies are moving operations and management offshore, mostly to Dubai."

He asked, "Are you familiar with Djibouti? We've made last-minute special arrangements for a temporary location at Djibouti."

"I'm somewhat familiar," Madden replied, "As you probably know, we have a huge Special Operations base at their main airport—in fact, most of the drone missions targeting Yemen are out of Djibouti."

"Where in Djibouti are we going?" Carson asked. "Do we have access to an airstrip?"

"Yes, we are establishing a temporary headquarters near an old, abandoned airstrip near the town of Dikhil, just west of the main city of Djibouti. Why don't you grab one of your sectional charts and let's see what kind of route we're looking at?"

Carson nodded her head and immediately found her way into the lighted hangar where she grabbed a pilot sectional chart, opened it and made a quick review of the distance and terrain. She reasoned she was going to be extremely busy the next few days ferrying Midland crews and priority personnel from Marib, across the Gulf of Aden, to their temporary quarters in Djibouti.

"How soon can you get the Otter ready for shuttles to Djibouti?" Rikli asked.

He took the map from Carson and laid it out on the bed of the pickup truck, pulling a flashlight out of the cab while Carson began preparing a scratch flight plan.

"Boss, I can have the Otter ready to go in one hour and the estimated flight time will be just under three hours," she said. "Will we have access to fuel at this place called Dikhil, and for

God's sake, do they have landing lights if we start tonight?"

"Regardless, we'll have vehicles there with their lights on marking the runway—just get there with what you have in the way of instruments," Rikli ordered.

Sitting back and listening to Rikli and Carson frantically creating an ad hoc contingency for the evacuation of the Midland Oil Company to Djibouti, Madden was thinking how this sudden change of events would impact his mission of supporting the drone strike on Azzam.

"Okay, Carson, get the Otter and prepare for your first shuttle in one hour," directed Rikli. "I'll have your passengers and load ready for boarding in front of the main hangar."

The seasoned oil company pilot that Carson was, she was used to late-night missions and operations that lasted for days. For her, this was nothing new, and it was obvious to all she rather enjoyed the excitement and adventure of the ever-changing flying environment in Yemen—she relished the fact that she was right in the middle of making the evacuation work.

"Okay, boss," she acknowledged.

"If I may add, and you have probably thought of this," Madden commented, "if you have trouble finding or getting into Dikhil, you might want to contact Djibouti Approach Control on 121.5, emergency frequency—the Air Force operations there will be monitoring."

Turning around, she smiled at Madden and quickly headed for the parked twin-engine Otter tied down a few yards away.

"Rob, Ron, whatever your name is, we'll talk later," she added. "Hope you get back during the evacuation—it may be your only way out, and you'll certainly owe me."

Smiling and waving goodbye, Carson was gone getting ready to refuel and configure the cargo compartment on the Otter.

Rikli was still studying the map Carson provided and was on his secure radio, barking orders to the field managers commanding them to start getting Midland employees back to the main hangar. Midland employees also relayed to Rikli that the other companies were doing the same in arranging airlifts out of Yemen due to the increased danger of a Yemeni civil war.

Barking out his last set of orders to his field supervisors over the radio and with limited cell phone availability, Rikli folded up the map, closed the pickup's tailgate and approached Madden.

"You understand quite well what is going on here, so what are you going to do? Do you want to fly out with us or take your chances with your other work?"

Momentarily looking at the sudden activity at the other foreign oil companies around the airport facilities late in the evening, Madden knew his only lifeline for a chance of getting out of Yemen depended on the fleet of airplanes flying out of Marib—if he even made it to Marib after his mission.

"Thanks for your offer, Andy, and I don't mean to bother you now with this sudden crisis, but when do you estimate the last Midland plane will depart from Marib?"

Looking down at his overstuffed clipboard and messages, he pulled out a pen from his shirt pocket and wrote down some calculations.

"I just received word from the Midland district headquarters in Dubai that there is the possibility the Egyptian Air Force may lease out a couple of their C-130 cargo aircraft and crews for the airlift out of here, but there are no guarantees," Rikli said. "Bottom line, we'll be out of here by Wednesday evening, so that gives you three days to work your mission."

"Thanks, I'll proceed with the mission," Madden answered, knowing his coming back was questionable. Rikli assumed the same.

As he climbed back into the pickup, Rikli pulled a card from his wallet and handed it to Madden. "This card has all of the connect information including radio frequencies, phone numbers, and internet addresses you will need to get a hold of Midland if you do make it back here, and I assume you have a variety of communications equipment in your crate.

"I'll ensure our company dispatcher is continually monitoring all communications to include any signals from you," Rikli advised. "We'll provide you with periodic updates on the evacuation as time permits and, most important of all, a good estimated time when our last plane is departing Marib."

Finally he said, "I'll have Blake ensure that your seismographic equipment is moved to the facility we offered you out by the oil refinery."

"Thanks, Andy," Madden said. "Do you mind if I borrow one of your older trucks, with some extra fuel, and I'll head out to the refinery this evening? Mind if I take some of your food stock with me?"

"Take whatever you need, but please sanitize anything that says Midland Oil on it. We don't need to be implicated with your work."

"Will do," Madden acknowledged as Rikli sped across the airport's dirt tarmac and headed for the hub of activity at the Midland hangar.

Madden walked back to the small utility hangar Carson used for the Otter and began inventorying equipment he may need for his work, unsure if Carson would be back here and if she would ever again have need for many of the supplies and equipment. He stuffed articles in a duffel bag that included mobile radios, emergency beacons and tactical aviation charts of the local area. All could be helpful if the situation unexpectedly went to shit.

"Many thanks, Carson, truly hope to see you again," Madden said to himself as he turned off the light, closed the door to the hangar, and swung the duffel bag over his back as he headed for the Midland Oil Company motor pool to pick out the most suitable truck for his mission.

The normal security guard, a Yemeni national, was nowhere to be seen, and it appeared by looking at his guard shack that he had left quickly. His evening meal sat on the table, only half eaten.

Making his way up and down the rows of vehicles, Madden found what he considered the perfect vehicle—an almost new, white Toyota Tundra pickup with easy-to-remove Midland Oil logos on the side doors.

"Perfect!" Madden was relieved to find the truck, knowing that the pickup of choice for al-Qaeda and the jihadists was a Toyota pickup covered with black spray-painted jihad symbols and signs, and some sort of machine gun or cannon mounted in the truck bed. He would take care of the machine gun and the painted markings later, but for now he needed to find black spray paint.

"Yes, this is just right," Madden reasoned as he headed for the empty guard shack and picked up the keys to his new ride to paradise. While returning to his truck of choice, Madden went through the other idle vehicles, looking for any items that would assist him in his mission: several five-gallon gas cans and cases of bottled water—essentials for the trip ahead.

He started the Toyota pickup, headed to the motor pool fuel depot and immediately filled the gas tank and the gas cans.

"Whoa, this is like a new truck," he thought. "The zealots are going to love this one when it is rammed up their ass."

Dark settled around the airport with the bright lights of the Marib oil refinery on the distant horizon. Madden turned on the headlights and the company radio, attempting to follow the progress of the Midland Oil evacuation from Marib. He heard an enormous amount of radio communication—mostly questions with some signs of panic.

Making one last stop at the main hangar, he saw Carson overseeing the loading of personnel and cargo into her Otter.

"Carson!" he yelled to her while stepping out of the truck. "Good luck to you and hope to see you again."

Carson looked up, saw Madden silhouetted against the backdrop of the huge, outside hangar lights and immediately headed toward him, still carrying her cargo manifests and flight plans on a large clipboard.

"Rob, please take care of yourself," she said, attempting to control her emotions as she gave Madden a large hug and held him for a few seconds. "I've got to get going with my shuttles to Djibouti. It appears I'll be the only transport out of Marib for the next couple of days," she explained.

Madden was still feeling the warmth of her unexpected hug.

"Listen," she stopped her frantic pace for a moment, "you have all of our communications data, so when you get back here after your mission, I'll do the best I can to pick you up."

"Thanks, Kelly, I understand I have at the most three days to get back here for a possible lift out—does that figure with you?"

"Who knows," she said and hurried back to her aircraft. Hesitating, she turned and yelled, "You still owe me more of an explanation on why you are pursuing this mission of yours."

Madden just waved and nodded as Carson completed her checklist inspection of the aircraft. He watched as she jumped in the pilot's seat and started the two jet turboprop engines that the entire Midland Oil Company would depend on for the next few days.

From the cab of his new pickup, he watched as Carson taxied the Otter into takeoff position on the lone runway, with the lights powered by a portable electrical generator. The whine of the Otter's engines increased as Carson coaxed as much power as she could and released the brakes, steadily increasing her speed down the runway. As heavy as the Otter was with Midland crew and equipment, it appeared to take forever to get airborne in the desert heat.

The red and green navigation lights and the red strobe light on the tail were a beautiful sight as the Otter gained altitude to navigate over the few four-thousand-foot peaks that covered the route to Djibouti.

"Good luck, Carson," Madden mumbled to himself as he shifted the pickup and began looking for Rhodes or Rikli prior to heading for the makeshift workstation provided him at the refinery.

He found Rhodes, clipboard in hand, designating the priority items for the next shuttle.

"Hey, Blake, I'm heading out to the refinery," Madden yelled from the pickup. "Thanks for everything, old friend."

Stopping what he was doing, Rhodes approached Madden and shook his hand.

"Rob, I had your equipment transferred to your shop at the refinery this evening by a couple of our dependable Yemeni employees—you'll find your stuff there."

"Thanks, man," Madden said.

"Listen Rob," said the out-of-breath Rhodes, "some of my people informed me that a group of strangers, maybe eight or nine, were seen roaming around the machine shop area at the refinery—all wearing typical oil company work clothes from British Petroleum. Now, it may be nothing, but my people have never seen them before."

"That's definitely need-to-know information," Madden said and drove off.

From the lights of the hangar, dozens of people were packing up equipment and what appeared to be binders of reference documents used by the technicians. As the volume and intensity of the work increased, so did the barking of orders and direction by the supervisors while crates were being prepared for the next shuttle out of Marib.

The Midland operations mirrored the other oil companies' movements to evacuate as soon as possible.

In no time, the small, crude Marib airport became one of the most active on the Arabian Peninsula, with cargo planes of every type and size flying into an uncontrolled airport environment and working to avoid a mid-air collision. Besides the ever-increasing intensity and loud sounds of small cargo aircraft attempting to land and take off, the sound of automatic weapons and an assortment of explosions and their flashes could be seen on the distant eastern horizon—right where Madden was destined to go.

CHAPTER
22

"Hey lady, what's that address again?" bellowed the overly heavy cab driver as he turned his tanned head to his backseat passenger.

Fumbling in her large, overstuffed purse, the passenger pulled out a colorful business card and read off the information to the impatient cab driver.

"Driver, the address is 1801 Henry Street in Savannah," she said to the driver as he put the Yellow Cab in gear and slammed the meter handle down to begin a new fare while making a call on his radio.

"At Savannah International Airport heading to the chicken school, OUT!" the driver advised his dispatch controller while smiling.

His passenger was a nondescript woman in her mid-thirties, wearing little to no makeup, with her ponytail pulled through the back of a Texas Rangers baseball cap. Though she may not have been the prettiest woman ever to grace his cab, she had other nice features under a men's blue cotton workshirt and worn blue jeans—all fitting quite nicely for the driver's viewing pleasure.

"Hey lady, are you going to become an expert in frying chicken?" the driver asked while intently staring at his passenger in the rear-view mirror.

Somewhat annoyed by the unexpected and unwanted attention, the passenger just nonchalantly nodded her head while reading the latest edition of *USA Today* she picked up on the flight.

Georgia Fried Chicken, or GFC University, is known worldwide as the corporate training center for all the owners and managers to learn their career skills in frying chicken.

"Lady, we're here—that's twenty-four dollars and eighty-two cents," the driver said.

He hurried around the cab and unlocked the trunk, from which he lifted out two large suitcases like he had done a thousand times in the past, making a show of it for a potentially nice tip for his above-and-beyond efforts.

As the driver opened the door for his passenger, she stepped out onto the sidewalk and opened her purse searching for her wallet while the cab driver patiently waited, always with a big smile.

"Here you go and thank you," the passenger said as she handed him a twenty and a ten.

"Thank you, ma'am, and good luck with your new career frying chicken," said the driver as he slid into the front seat, adjusted the meter and made his usual radio call that he was free.

More students arrived at the university in cabs with suitcases in hand and headed for the initial check-in desk, which was next to a small auditorium.

The woman passenger immediately checked to see that she had all her belongings and headed into the main entrance of the large and colorfully bright GFC University.

As she surveyed the well-decorated reception area, a man approached her dressed in a bright red blazer and a red tie with "GFC" all over it.

"Good morning, young lady—are you here for the GFC Management Training Program?"

"Yes, I am," the passenger said. "Am I in the right building?"

"Indeed you are. I'm Tommy Westgate and am proud to say I'll be working with the new GFC manager class starting today. We had better get you registered—the morning orientation will begin in a few minutes. And I'm sorry, I didn't catch your name," Westgate inquired.

"Oh, I'm sorry. My name is Patricia Turner from Des Moines, Iowa, but everyone just calls me Pat."

"Well okay, Pat, let's get you registered and trained as a manager."

Bonnie McCord made her way to the incoming student reception desk and waited in line a few minutes to be onboarded. She noticed the processing was well organized, with kind receptionists, along with professionally produced name tags and welcome brochures all displaying the bright red GFC logo.

"Can I have your name please," a young and attractive corporate management trainee asked McCord with a distinct Southern drawl.

"Good morning, my name is Patricia Turner—here for the manager's course."

Looking through a folder of files, the trainee looked diligently for Turner's orientation package and checked again, having no luck finding it. Somewhat embarrassed at not being able to locate it, she made a quick call to a supervisor. After a few minutes and with the growing line of new students also waiting, the trainee got off the phone and, ever smiling, turned her attention to McCord.

"Ms. Turner, I am very sorry, your package is in our overseas folder—please just give me a second to locate."

"No problem, take your time," McCord said, knowing she was not in a big hurry anyway—especially just to learn how to fry chicken.

"Oh, Ms. Turner, here you go," a relieved trainee handed her the overseas in-processing package. "Be sure to wear your name tag so we can all get to know you better during the course." McCord's luggage was stowed behind the reception desk with the luggage from the other trainees.

"Welcome, all of our new GFC members, to the manager trainee program," came a sudden loud announcement over the public-address system. "We need all those attending the program to make their way to the GFC University auditorium located immediately to the right of the reception area."

McCord, like the rest of the thirty excited new manager trainees, made her way to the auditorium. She observed that most were a mixed bag of diversity.

A creature of habit, McCord picked a seat in the back row.

Oh, Bonnie McCord, Patricia Turner, or whatever you are called this month, she mused to herself, *you are so lucky that the Agency has picked you to attend the GFC fried chicken school. Maybe this will carry over to a new career when you are retired or fired from the Agency. After all, you've had a wonderful career in the Air Force as a staff judge advocate lawyer and gave that all up to become a special agent for the DEA, where you were wounded in a firefight with the FARC terrorists—but you did learn how to accomplish helicopter assaults in jungles.*

She smiled, hoping no one noticed, and now almost talking to herself, *I got to spend a year as an undercover agent dealing blackjack at a Native American casino in New Mexico monitoring the actions of a local drug producer—where I almost got blown up in a mine explosion. And then there was Madden. Oh, Madden.*

Almost out loud, she said, *Where are you now? Safe, I hope. So now, in thanks for all my superior undercover work, I was selected to be the assistant branch manager at the new GFC branch in Santa Cruz, Bolivia. In a country that hates the DEA. Oh, boy.*

Breathing hard and looking straight ahead, she continued her intense reflections when another student down the row from her, leaned toward her and asked, "Are you okay?"

"Oh, yes, thank you," McCord said. "I'm just a little tired from the trip to get here."

The room immediately quieted as a strikingly regal older woman entered the auditorium. By the attention the other GFC staff were showing her, it was obvious that she must be a higher-up in the corporate organization.

Her air of confidence, despite being barely taller than five feet, was emphasized by her expensive black pantsuit and stylish heels. Her long, highlighted brunette hair touched her shoulders.

McCord had spent her career reading people, and she sensed this woman was capable and powerful.

"Good morning, and welcome to the Georgia Fried Chicken University. "We are so very happy to have you as part of our team," began a young staffer, speaking without notes.

"I am Matt Blomstedt, vice president and director of training here at the university. We'll begin our first day of orientation soon, but first we are privileged to have with us this morning the president of GFC, Dr. Elizabeth Alexander." Blomstedt began clapping and was immediately joined by everyone in the auditorium. The GFC staff showed great enthusiasm for their president, as they were sure their careers depended on it.

Moving up to the podium, as she had done a thousand times before with hundreds of classes like this one, Dr. Alexander acknowledged the warm reception.

"Hello, everyone. Welcome. We are looking forward to working with you and getting you started on your new careers at GFC."

Just for entertainment, McCord studied the woman and could tell Alexander was a tough taskmaster—not one to get into a fight with. Of course, McCord reasoned, she herself was not a woman with whom one would want to tangle.

Alexander saw McCord sitting in the back row of the auditorium and attempted to size her up.

"GFC serves over 11 million customers a day in over a hundred countries and territories around the world," Alexander gave the standard company line, "and GFC operates more than four thousand restaurants in the United States and more than twelve thousand restaurants internationally."

She went on about the history of GFC for another 10 minutes, emphasizing the stake the new managers had in GFC's continued success and growth.

"Thank you and good luck to each and every one of you." As Alexander ended her speech, the audience stood and clapped their approval.

She waved to the staff, shook Blomstedt's hand as she left the stage, turned for a quick second and gave a departing glance at McCord while McCord did the same.

Holy shit, McCord thought. *Can we move on with this theatrical bullshit, so I can learn how to fry chicken and get down to Bolivia and be something I always wanted to be—a party girl at a Steel Rock Café managing a GFC.*

"Thank you, Dr. Alexander, for that wonderful introduction." Blomstedt resumed the day's training as McCord sat back and watched the others go through the motions that seemed so predictable—and downright ridiculous.

"Patricia Turner, Patricia Turner!" McCord suddenly came alive from a short nap while attempting to show interest in Blomstedt's briefing.

"Yes," said the startled McCord while writing in her notebook just for effect.

"Ms. Turner, you are to report to room 205B upstairs, for further in-processing and room assignment," directed Blomstedt, still eyeing McCord with suspicion.

"On my way," McCord said, standing up and collecting her backpack. She maneuvered down the back row to leave, avoiding the openly provocative stares of many men in the room.

Noting the stares, she mused, *Well, I suspect that after two months here of cooking and eating chicken, there won't be many heads turning to see my fat butt, that's for sure.*

To the other students, McCord appeared to be just another middle-aged woman who—either due to a bad marriage or a sudden, unexpected career change—found herself starting again as managing the art of frying of chicken. Except for those who noticed something else.

CHAPTER
23

"Okay, let's get this party started." Madden, trying to make light of the dangers facing him, placed the truck's transmission in drive and headed for the airport's now unsecured entrance. Feeling under the seat of the truck, Madden checked to see that his 9mm Beretta pistol was in place and the AK-47 assault rifle given to him by his old friend Blake Rhodes was loaded and locked. In his military days, Madden was considered an expert with both weapons.

Heading out of the town of Marib, he found an enormous amount of truck traffic heading west from the refinery to the Marib airport. The hundreds of trucks created a small sandstorm along the entire route, and with the endless line of headlights attempting to light the way, the parade appeared to be something out of an apocalyptic science fiction movie.

He opened one of the bottled waters and savored the cool water down his throat—he needed to remind himself to drink plenty of water whenever possible. He searched in a small paper bag that Rhodes had stashed in the truck and to his grateful surprise found a couple of chicken sandwiches and a few bags of potato chips.

"Marching toward hell with a chicken sandwich and a bag of potato chips just does not get any better," he said out loud to the forlorn desert ahead of him, trying to find some pleasure in this increasingly dangerous and unstable world he was headed for.

He noticed he was approaching the Army checkpoint that he and Rhodes had passed earlier, where Army guards were continuing to check papers and collect protection fees from all travelers.

"Stay where you are in the truck!" came the command in broken English and Arabic as floodlights suddenly beamed into the cab of the truck. Two men in uniform approached, and Madden stuck his head out the truck window.

"Good evening, I am Ron Hanson with Midland Oil," he said with a friendly smile. "Sergeant, I remember you from yesterday—I'm the new guy, and I came along here with Blake Rhodes."

With that, the two guards smiled and lit up a couple of Camels while turning off the bright lights. They approached the vehicle knowing that Midland workers were "very generous and appreciative."

"Ah yes, Mr. Hanson, I do remember you," the sergeant answered in broken English while taking the time to exhale cigarette smoke.

"Would you and your friend like some water?" Madden asked in English and Arabic, attempting to continue to build a good rapport with what might be valuable friends in the near future.

Grabbing a couple cold bottles of water from the cooler on the passenger seat, he also retrieved a couple of hundred dollars in twenty-dollar bills, wrapped the bills around the bottles and handed them to each man.

With large smiles on their faces, the two guards hurriedly separated the wad of bills from the bottles and stuffed them in the front pockets of their dusty military uniform pants. After securing the small treasure they had just received, both men enjoyed the cool bottled water as traffic backed up for miles because of their preoccupation with Madden. Horns started blaring and other drivers were cursing the guards while impatiently waiting their turn to pass.

"Thank you, Mister Ron, and thank you for your generosity," said the sergeant while wiping the water from his lips. "You can go—are you heading to the refinery?"

"Yes, my friend Rhodes has ordered me to help him ensure all the Midland people get back to Marib if the bad guys take over the refinery," Madden replied. "Also, I am to travel down as far as I can go along the Marib–Red gas pipeline and check for Midland stragglers on their way back to Marib." Madden discreetly handed the sergeant a half ounce of gold bullion.

The guard's expression at seeing a life fortune in the palm of his hand had served Madden's intentions of creating a short, valuable relationship with local military guards who would never again see a paycheck from their own government and would most likely find other avenues to gain income. Gold was considered the premium trading standard.

"Yes, Mister Ron." The enlightened guard was now more anxious than ever to assist, with the prospects of more tokens of gratitude. "Sir, why don't you park your truck over there on the side of the road," the guard politely asked his new benefactor.

Nodding and smiling, Madden pulled his pickup into a small parking area next to the government checkpoint while watching in his rear-view mirror as the guard continually admired his new wealth in the palm of his hand with the expectation that more could be earned from "Mister Ron."

As various types of oil company vehicles streamed past the checkpoint from the refinery all heading for Marib, all paid their tribute to the guards. Madden waited next to his truck and pulled out a detailed map of the roads and towns situated near the oil and natural gas pipeline leading to the export terminal at Balhaf on the Gulf of Aden.

Madden could hear the guard giving instructions to his fellow soldiers at the checkpoint and noticed that he entered a small, mobile office trailer, most likely donated by an oil company for the guards' "comfort and pleasure."

Madden awaited the guard's return, unsure why he entered the office, but was relieved to see him approach with what appeared to be a large letter folder hidden in his military shirt.

"We'll, let's see what kind of goodwill a half ounce of gold bullion buys in Yemen," Madden thought, knowing from his

Special Forces days years ago in Yemen what a little gold, and sometimes U.S. dollars, could buy.

"Mister Ron, why don't we discuss your travel plans in the back of your truck," the guard recommended, attempting to draw as little suspicion as possible regarding what he was providing Madden.

"Sounds good, sergeant. Let's bring down the tailgate and roll out the map. I appreciate any advice," Madden said, ready to pull out a couple more gold coins if required.

"What exactly are you looking for? What information do you require?" asked the sergeant.

"It is my very risky job," Madden said, "to travel down the road next to the pipeline and check for any Midland Oil employees who may still be working on the line or its many auxiliary pump stations along the way." Madden pointed to his route with a pencil on the open map.

"Yes, I am in agreement with you," the stunned sergeant said while reviewing the map.

"I need to know where the trouble areas are so I can avoid them. If you know areas that are infested with terrorists along my route, I certainly would appreciate knowing about them," Madden told the guard, who studied the map more intently and brought out a file folder in Arabic marked, "Activity Reports—Marib."

Madden was patient enough to let the sergeant take his time studying the map and at the same time review reports from his folder. Occasionally, the sergeant would make small marks on Madden's map and put a few short notes next to them.

"I have marked on your map some areas where we have had terrorist activities in or near the pipeline area—both Houthi, al-Qaeda, and some anti-government protesters," the sergeant confidently said. "However, a warning to you, Mister Ron—I would stay very clear of the area near this small town of Nisab in the Abyan province. It is rumored that al-Qaeda has a major base camp just north of the town in an old school building."

He pointed to the area on the map. "We have had many attacks on the pipeline and some drilling platforms planned from this al-Qaeda base."

"If it is well known, as you say it is, that it is a terrorist base camp, how come the U.S. has not taken it out? Seems like they have no problem taking everything out," Madden questioned, acting the part of a naïve, new oil field worker.

"Mister Ron, I need to get back to my duties and wishing you a safe trip and also be aware that this checkpoint will be most likely disbanded by the time you finish your work," he said and started walking toward the trailer.

"Wait, sergeant," Madden called as he quickly folded up the map and secured it in its carrying pouch.

The sergeant stopped and turned to look. Madden had something in his right hand.

"Thank you again, friend. I cannot tell you how valuable your information is to Midland Oil and my own safety, again, thank you," he said and handed the sergeant during a second handshake another half-ounce of gold bullion.

"Again, I do appreciate the critical safety information you provided, but I am curious, if everyone knows these buildings north of Nisab are a terrorist base camp, why haven't the U.S. drones taken it out?"

"Mister Ron, that is an easy answer you as a Westerner, infidel, will very much understand. Besides being a base camp for al-Qaeda, it also functions as a full-time school and camp for the local children in the villages and towns."

Madden had heard and seen in his prior Special Forces work in Yemen that al-Qaeda used hospitals, churches and even mosques as safe havens, but never a school with children camped around it to shield the al-Qaeda leadership from destruction.

Climbing into the cab of his pickup, Madden watched his new friend disappear into his duty station and thought and prayed, "I certainly hope to see you again."

For a few moments, before maneuvering the truck on the crude asphalt leading to the refinery, Madden made notes regarding what the sergeant of the guard had told him. The sergeant's information seemed to match the intelligence he had received at the Pentagon weeks earlier when assigned to this mission, but the school cover for al-Qaeda north of Nisab was possibly the missing link regarding the whereabouts of Azzam's camp.

Grabbing a bottle of water and placing the truck in gear, Madden headed east toward the refinery—one of the few vehicles traveling in an easterly direction.

At the main entrance, a lone security guard and a few Yemeni Army soldiers were sitting on wooden benches with their weapons scattered in disarray.

The amount of traffic leaving the oil refinery was beginning to slow as Madden drove up to the open gate and was slowly motioned forward by the lone guard. The soldiers turned, looked Madden over and went back to playing cards on a rotting wooden picnic table.

"What business do you have here?" the guard asked Madden in broken English, looking inside the truck cab for weapons or explosives. Realizing Madden was probably one of hundreds of Western oil field workers, the guard felt more at ease in approaching Madden's open driver-side window.

Eyeing and trying to measure up the guard's possible ability to assist him, Madden spoke to him in Arabic and handed him a few twenty-dollar bills, attempting to hide the transaction from the lethargic soldiers.

"Good afternoon, sir, I'm Ron Hanson with Midland Oil," Madden said.

"Yes, Mr. Hanson, how can I help you?" The guard instinctively moved the wad of twenties to his back pocket. Keen in observing his actions, Madden was satisfied that he was a man he could deal with—he needed all the friends he could buy now.

"Officer," Madden using the title to build up the guard's ego and respect, "I understand Midland Oil has a building here they want me to work out of until events get straightened out around here."

Using a flashlight and grabbing a disorganized clipboard and reviewing the top sheets, the guard found an authorization for Hanson to proceed to the vacant Midland machine shop on the refinery premises.

"Mr. Hanson, you are cleared to proceed to building number 45," the guard announced. "It is an old Midland facility, but I understand some Midland people were up here earlier today to get it ready for you. Do you wish to have an escort to your building?"

"No thank you, officer, I'll be coming and going for the next few days," Madden mentioned, which raised the guard's curiosity.

"Sir, what exactly are you going to be doing?"

"Friend, I have been tasked to proceed as far as I can along the pipeline road and notify all Midland Oil people to make their way to the refinery or Marib until things calm down here."

"Very well. Please let me know if I can assist you in any way," the guard said.

"Thank you, officer, and I would appreciate it if, during my travels down the pipeline, you would keep Midland Oil at the airport advised if you do not hear from me for a few days," requested Madden as he handed a few more twenty-dollar bills to the guard.

"As you wish, and you are cleared to proceed, and may God be with you."

With a mock salute, Madden drove forward on the freshly paved asphalt road leading through the lighted refinery to Midland's building number 45. He stopped the truck in a small, seldom used parking lot, reached under the seat of the cab for his pistol and ensured it was loaded.

Slowly and silently, he held out his pistol and flashlight as he walked on the narrow gravel walkway leading to the metal industrial door, which was illuminated with a bright industrial light hanging from a steel pole. Above the door read, "Midland Oil Company Machine and Tool Die, Building #45."

A strong sense of uncertainty fell on Madden as he cautiously made his way to a few of the covered windows that prevented him from looking in the building with his flashlight. Turning around and heading back to the entrance, he thought he heard a noise coming from inside the building that sounded like a human cough. The height of his anxiety had been reached as he chambered a round, unaware that his every step was being watched by men posted around the outside of the building.

Madden's heartbeat was racing, and every ounce of energy was now focused on self-preservation. Madden knew someone was close—or as he called it in the Air Force, "Danger Close."

"DROP YOUR WEAPON AND HANDS UP NOW!" came the sudden order in broken English as Madden froze, feeling the barrel of a gun pushed against his back.

Madden followed the assailant's orders and dropped his gun, raised his hands and said nothing as his arms were pushed down and tied to his back with plastic flex cuffs used by most police departments when arresting suspects. A black cloth bag was jerked over Madden's head.

"KEEP VERY STILL," came the order as Madden was body-searched and several of his personal documents were taken from his pockets.

"MOVE FORWARD SLOWLY," again came the broken English. "YOU WILL BE GUIDED WHERE TO GO."

Madden could sense whoever was abducting him was very much a professional and took great pains not to injure him. *But why*, he wondered. Usually, from his past experiences with hostages and terrorists, when they took someone down, it truly was a hard take-down with no pleasantries or considerations involved. Humiliation and hurt was one of the key goals.

Madden suspected his cover was compromised. He was probably in for a huge interrogation. He heard others approach him through his black head bag. The door to the facility squealed open while he was guided in. Again, the soft nature of the abduction made Madden wonder, "Who are these people?"

Guided by two men, Madden was placed in a chair and told to remain seated. Through the heavy black cloth, he could see the motion of men pacing around him and that the lights inside the facility were on.

"Now, Mr. Madden, be a good bloke and don't cause us any problems when we take your hood off, do you understand, sir?" asked someone with a thick English accent.

"Yes," Madden answered.

The hood was removed, and Madden was dumbfounded. He saw several muscular men with long beards and hair of a typical Yemeni male and wearing the traditional male garb of a white sarong matched with a shirt, turban, tribal scarf, and armed with menacing daggers. The men in the room were taking delight in seeing Madden's reaction to their presence.

On the wooden table in front of him were laid out all of his personal belongings seized in his quick abduction. Also on the table was a platter of fruits, bread, and meat that was being enjoyed by the various people in the room.

Out of the corner of his eye, Madden noticed a man who did not appear to have the same characteristics as the other Yemeni men. He was of lighter complexion, with a scruffy brown beard and with distinct, long brown straggly hair reaching well beyond his shoulders. This stranger, perhaps the one with the English accent, appeared to Madden to resemble the famous English soldier Lawrence of Arabia. This stranger was staring at Madden and eventually moved forward and took a seat next to him on one of the many simple wooden chairs surrounding the table as the others helped themselves to the food and continued their informal conversations.

"Well, mate, what have we got here?" the strange-looking leader of the bunch with an English accent asked Madden—the same voice that apprehended him outside the building.

"Sir, you have me confused with someone else," Madden tried convincingly to hold on to his cover. "I'm Ron Hanson, a seismographic specialist with Midland Oil Company here in Marib, tasked to run the pipeline to ensure all Midland people get back to Marib."

"Oh, is that right, mate," the Englishman pondered laughing while the others in the room also joined in the charade.

"While traveling along the pipeline road to assist your fellow oil field workers, did you have any other tasks in mind, Mr., uh, Hanson?" asked the Englishman, carrying the entertainment a bit further.

"No, just doing my job," Madden answered, knowing full well the less he said, the better.

Madden had no clue who these strange and professional officers were. Friend or foe was the question Madden was hoping to find out soon.

"And we are doing ours, Sgt. Madden," the leader quickly replied while reviewing an official-looking folder as the others anxiously awaited Madden's reply.

"With all due respect, gentlemen, you must have me confused with someone else." While still playing his cover, Madden noticed a distinctive tattoo on one of the men in the room. He noticed it appeared to be similar to the U.S. Army Special Forces insignia with the words, "Who Dares Wins."

He finally recollected that tattoo's insignia was of the British Special Air Services, SAS, the United Kingdom's equivalent in operations and mission to the Army's Green Berets and Navy SEALs.

"Mr. Madden, would you please stand and take off your shirt," instructed the leader. He clipped the flex cuffs off.

All eyes in the room were now staring at Madden as he slowly stood and began unbuttoning his stained, sweaty, soiled Midland Oil cotton shirt.

With all the buttons undone, he took his shirt off, revealing a dirty, strained muscular chest with an assortment of tattoos running from his chest to the top of his left arm. Madden had a hunch that was the reason for the removal of the shirt—to show his new friends his tattoos. All the men in the room gave approving looks. Men of equal bravery and distinction were now commenting to each other about the significance of the tattoo markings.

Unbeknownst to Madden, the leader and every man in the room was familiar with who Madden was and what his mission actually was—to ensure the death of the al-Qaeda leader Azzam using American drones from their base at Djibouti in eastern Africa.

From his airline arriving at Aden, Yemen, to his orientation at Marib by his Midland Oil boss, Blake Rhodes, the SAS knew—through their paid informants—the exact whereabouts of Madden, and they sometimes shadowed him with a protective eye.

"Mr. Madden, Sgt. Madden, Rob, whatever you like to be called, I'm Capt. Lee Terry with the British Special Air Services," the leader introduced himself to Madden while also introducing the remaining team members in the room.

Looking surprised and relieved, Madden grinned and shook each of the men's hands attempting to remember each of their names while all the men gathered around the food-filled table for a late, informal dinner.

"Mr. Madden, for your benefit," Terry announced while grabbing a thick folder and large, geographical map of the area and returning to the table, "we have been tasked to support your mission to take out Azzam.

"Simply put, Mr. Madden, Azzam is as much a menace and threat to the United Kingdom as he is to the United States," he said. "Anyway, we have been tracking the bad guys for a few months here in Yemen and don't mind helping you."

He added, "Besides, we have been ordered to."

Tired and attempting to understand this unexpected and surprising development of British military support in his mission to kill Azzam, Madden simply smiled and answered, "Sure. Why not?"

CHAPTER
24

"Turner! Where is Turner?" a loud voice suddenly interrupted the class regarding the proper temperature for storing freshly fried chicken wings.

The intruder in the class appeared to be slim and middle-aged, with a crew cut and well-fitting pinstriped suit with a matching monogrammed, starched white shirt. One would suspect by his bearing and clothes he was high up on the GFC food chain and was not shy about showing others his importance.

"Who in the hell is that?" one student said. "Seems in a big hurry to find her."

"Turner, Turner. Where in the devil are you?" the man shouted as he hurriedly made his way through the maze of students working their assignments on the training fryers with little regard for his awkward interruption.

"Mr. Barrett, good morning, sir." The class instructor literally ran to the unexpected visitor as the class was completing temperature calculations for storing chicken. All eyes now turned to McCord and why this anxious, rude man wanted to speak to her in such a hurry.

After cleaning the hot chicken storage compartment she was training on, McCord was taking off her red GFC apron and safety goggles when she heard her name being called by this strange man.

She crouched low behind a stainless-steel broiler and immediately began reaching to her waist for her 9mm service pistol—an ingrained reflex from another world she had come from—but there was no pistol, and she was not in danger.

Regaining her composure as if nothing had happened, McCord rose and brushed the burned oil and flour mixture from her already red-stained apron. Her face was also smeared with the grease and chicken spattering that accompanied work with a deep fryer.

"Ms. Turner, would you find your way up to my desk, please?" the instructor announced over the class public address system as Barrett was still combing the classroom searching like an animal seeking its prey.

"I'm Turner—what do you want?" She stood up, continuing to brush chicken particles from her clothes and wipe the grime from her face. The entire classroom of over thirty students stopped their training tasks and were quite taken by the entertainment of all the excitement over management trainee Turner.

"Are you Turner?" Barrett said, pointing his finger at her while approaching, pushing students and equipment aside to meet up with her.

McCord nervously pondered the best way to take him down if it came to that. She figured she would just kick him in the groin and explain she learned this at a YWCA self-defense class. Anything else would draw attention. Decking Barrett in the middle of the classroom would evoke problems—major problems.

Standing her ground and attempting to act like a frightened student, McCord played her role well.

"Are you Turner?" asked Barrett, raising his voice and pointing his finger at her as if he were a prison warden.

She nodded.

"Well, come with me," he ordered as he grabbed her by the arm and attempted to lead her out of the classroom. The class was now stunned, but mostly entertained by this spectacle.

"Mr. Barrett, could I assist in having Ms. Turner escorted out of the classroom?" the classroom instructor meekly offered his services while not wanting to get on the wrong side with Barrett, but at the same time feeling responsible for the confusing conduct delivered to his student.

"No, just get out of the way—we have an urgent meeting with Dr. Alexander. Now beat it," Barrett shouted as he held McCord by the arm and attempted to force her out of the room.

McCord leaned closer to Barrett and whispered in his ear, "If you do not let go of my arm, I will kick you in the nuts—do you understand?"

A startled Barrett released her arm slowly and then turned to view the spectacle he unintentionally created in the classroom. He hoped there were no security cameras.

"Okay, Turner, follow me," he said, attempting to regain his composure while leading the way with McCord following. The only sounds were the ringing of the timers on the fryers.

"This guy Barrett sounds like a hatchet man to me," one student said to another. "I bet Turner is in a world of trouble. What do you think?"

"Yeah, by the looks of things, she isn't coming back," the student replied.

"I bet she's in trouble over drugs, man," said an older, long-haired student who looked like a hippie from days past. "I could just look at her, and she had the look."

Following Barrett down the long, colorful hallway of framed GFC history and memorabilia, McCord had no clue where she was going. All she knew was that no matter what happened, she needed to keep her cover. She was drilled in her extensive training for undercover—keep and live your cover. And most important, keep your mouth shut, regardless of the circumstances.

Barrett continued straight ahead toward the university's front doors where McCord had entered the school just seven weeks earlier. She followed him in silence—both not saying a word until he opened the main entrance doors for McCord. She never looked at him or acknowledged this courtesy but just stood outside almost enjoying the warm sunshine and the birds chirping in the nearby oak trees. There McCord stood in her stained, red GFC apron, wondering if she were being expelled from the school.

She watched Barrett as he spoke in hushed tones on his cell phone. When he finished the call, he politely approached her.

"Ms. Turner, wait here. We'll be leaving shortly for the corporate headquarters for a meeting with Dr. Alexander, president of the GFC Corporation," he said as if speaking to his best friend. "Any questions?"

McCord just gave Barrett a quick glance and shook her head no. In Tres Rios, New Mexico, she had enjoyed listening to the birds chirping and the company of her longtime friend, now lover, Rob Madden. She often thought of Madden. The active and pleasantly noisy birds provided her with a tranquil distraction from the weeks of training and now a run-in with some overzealous executive regarding who knows what.

McCord's dream-like musing was interrupted when a large, flashy black limousine pulled into the well-groomed driveway leading up to the reserved executive valet parking area. With so much happening that she did not understand, she eyed the black limo wondering who was so important to arrive in such a nice ride. The limo stopped only a few feet away from where she and Barrett were standing. The driver, with black cap and suit, got out of the limo and moved to the rear passenger side and opened the door with a large smile.

"Ms. Turner, Mr. Barrett, please," announced the driver. A very tall African American man, six-foot-four at least, he appeared to be more of a basketball player than a chauffeur.

Looking at Barrett out of the corner of her eye, McCord did not move as Barrett headed for the limo's rear door and proceeded to make himself comfortable in the back as the chauffeur continued to hold the open door for McCord.

"Ms. Turner, if it is not too much trouble, would you mind getting in the limo?" said Barrett. "Dr. Alexander is a very busy person who does not have all day waiting to entertain a management trainee."

She balked.

"Turner!" Barrett firmly reminded her, "You work for us— remember that!"

The glare and expression Barrett conveyed to her from the back of the limo said it all. She was now concerned about her mission and her safety.

Keep the cover alive, do not talk, she repeated over and over again in her mind as she slowly made her way to the door of the limo. The chauffeur, smiling away with some of the whitest teeth she had ever seen on a human being, helped McCord in, immediately shut the door behind her and worked his way back to the driver's seat, where he tuned the radio to a classical music station.

Sitting in the back of a limo configured to carry more than eight people comfortably, with a well-stocked bar, McCord felt awkward sliding around on luxurious leather seats next to a man who a moment ago had been restraining her with his hands. She was quiet as the limousine headed east on Interstate 16 for downtown Savannah.

Barrett opened his briefcase and portfolio and began reading many papers and writing notes on documents while at the same time always glancing at his iPhone for messages.

McCord, ever vigilant, just stared straight ahead with no trace of emotion or caring.

"Ms. Turner," the silence was surprisingly broken by the chauffeur with a strong Southern drawl. "Ms. Turner, do you like college basketball?"

For a moment, McCord was surprised at the sudden question from the chauffeur and was attempting to determine if this was some kind of trick or staged maneuvering by Barrett or some other interested party.

Did I like college basketball? the question raced through her mind—*why that particular question?* she pondered. *Did they know that I did play varsity women's basketball for Louisiana Tech University? Be very careful how you answer the question and live the cover, live the cover,* she repeated to herself.

"Yes, I followed women's basketball when I attended Kansas State," she replied politely. "Why do you ask?"

"Well, ma'am, over there is the Savannah State University, and I am proud to say I play basketball for the Savannah State Tigers," he said, obviously showing his pride in playing and attempting to break the awkward silence to the point of feeling sorry for the woman who, with her dirty work apron and messed up hair, was heading for God knows what at the headquarters.

"You play basketball for Savannah State and at the same time have time to drive a limousine—and study to boot," McCord said, feeling a little bit more at ease with the driver.

"Yes, ma'am," the driver replied. "You see, during the off-season, I am blessed to be hired as a chauffeur for GFC. I feel like the luckiest guy in the world. GFC is a big booster of the university's basketball program and during the off-season, the team is given jobs, you know, to give us some spending money."

The chauffeur glanced in his rear-view mirror.

"What are you studying and what career field do you want to go into?" McCord curiously asked, somewhat starting to like the athlete/chauffeur.

"Ma'am, thank you for asking," he said. "I am studying to become a lawyer."

McCord just nodded her head and smiled, venting to herself with sarcasm, *Smart move, become a lawyer and possibly later be selected to attend the GFC University and learn a real trade, like frying chicken.*

No, it gets better, she continued thinking, *after learning the art of frying chicken, you get to move to Bolivia, South America, and manage a GFC branch—yes, yes by all means get that law degree.*

McCord sensed their destination was close when the chauffeur placed his hat back on his head and Barrett, ignoring their conversation, stuffed all of his documents and papers back into his briefcase.

The limousine went past the main entrance to the headquarters and slowly made its way to a ramp leading to an underground parking garage. The security guard at the checkpoint waved them through while Barrett looked at his watch and began dialing numbers on his phone. Showing relief that his errand run to pick up some student at the university was about over, he barked some orders to the chauffeur, who drove the limousine to a secluded corner of the underground garage.

McCord noticed the limo was slowly approaching a small utility elevator door with a couple of security pass locks.

Live the cover, keep quiet. Live the cover, keep quiet, she reminded herself while attempting to stay as cool and unfazed as possible.

The chauffeur stopped the limo and immediately followed his normal routine of making his way to the passenger doors allowing Barrett to depart first, followed by McCord.

"It has been my pleasure escorting you to headquarters," the smiling chauffeur announced as if he had made this same statement a thousand times in past assignments.

Barrett pointed McCord to the elevator entrance while he placed the appropriate codes in the code box. A humming sound marked the elevator car's approach to the garage level.

"Thank you, driver, and good luck with your law career," she said as she shook his enormous hand. "I'll watch a Savannah game just to see you in action." The chauffeur nodded his head with a large grin and returned to the limousine, where he immediately turned the big Lincoln around and headed out of the garage.

"If you don't mind, Turner," Barrett scolded McCord while he held the elevator door for her to enter while he followed and pressed a button on the menu of floor numbers. The elevator car immediately responded and began lifting them up.

McCord thought, *Here I am, looking like I just got off the night shift at a local GFC branch while being escorted by an arrogant clown executive wearing Armani.*

At the final ding on the eighth floor, the doors opened. Barrett motioned for McCord to depart and take a seat in a small, ornate private reception area. Gone were the flashy and colorful GFC logos and banners, replaced by fine framed and lighted portraits of the past and current presidents of the corporation. Two large windows opened to panoramic views of downtown Savannah and the Savannah River rolling to the sea coast.

Barrett quietly conversed with the two receptionists and suddenly disappeared down a hallway that had more lighted portraits of corporate officials.

They sure like themselves around here, she thought to herself as she moved to the windows to enjoy the scenery afforded by the views from the top floor. She noticed a nice park next to the river with green grass, tall trees, and a jogging path along the river— if only she could be down there now.

The morning newspaper sat on the coffee table in the reception area. One headline caught her eye: Oil Companies Exit Yemen during Civil Strife. She tried to be calm as she casually picked up the paper and read the story. What would these developments mean for Rob in the Feds' plan to eliminate Azzam and his organization? With what she read in the story regarding the instability in Yemen, she was now more worried than ever about his safety.

The two receptionists paid little attention to the odd woman with the stained GFC apron in their world of high corporate opulence.

McCord was still staring out the window when one of the young women announced, "Ms. Turner, Dr. Alexander will see you now."

CHAPTER
25

"Please keep in mind, when the tactical decisions are required for the authorization for any drone strikes, they will come through me and me only. Is that acceptable?" said Madden to Terry, captain of the British SAS detachment.

Terry nodded his head in approval. After asking one of his sergeants to move the remaining food off the large worktable, Terry spread out his detailed map of the pipeline area leading to a small town called Nisab located in what is considered an al-Qaeda stronghold with little road access.

Madden observed on the map a large circle around a cluster of buildings north of Nisab with pinpoint descriptions and updates linked to the circle. He was impressed with the attention to detail of the intelligence.

"I take it that the buildings you have highlighted here are schools and also serve as a camp and headquarters for Azzam," Madden said to Terry.

"Yes, they are. How in the devil did you know that, Madden?" Terry asked.

"I greased a few Yemeni security guards' palms on my way up here with some gold and greenbacks. They were very helpful telling me where the bad guys were and areas to avoid," replied Madden.

"Just confirms our intelligence also," Terry said as the other operators in the room took notice of Madden's information on Azzam's whereabouts. "I got to ask you this question because we are dying to know, but how did you intend to accomplish this mission by yourself, mate?" Terry took a seat at the table and grabbed a can of fruit to eat.

Madden took advantage of the opportunity and picked up some bread and cheese. He took a few bites and washed them down with a fresh bottle of water before responding.

"One of the roving CIA drone target teams last year picked up an American al-Qaeda volunteer—a Johnny Snow—who was lost and attempting to make contact with Azzam's people, but the CIA apprehended him and got him to sing like a bird regarding the al-Qaeda organization and his recruitment," Madden said.

He added, "I am assuming the identity of this guy Snow with all the right papers and even his laptop with all sorts of good information—especially his contacts."

Noting this was all news to Terry, Madden continued, "I feel good about being able to penetrate the al-Qaeda headquarters at the school and ensure we target Azzam and his lieutenants, but I am concerned about the collateral damage that two Hellfire missiles will have on the students and families surrounding the school."

Terry nodded in agreement.

"Captain, do you or any of your team have any ideas?"

"I suspect you Yanks are trying to avoid what has happened in some of your past Special Operations rescue missions—operators detected and killed by terrorists and civilians killed by drones," Terry surmised.

"Exactly," Madden said. "If we can eliminate him surgically, as a last resort, it may be a drone Hellfire missile that takes him out. According to Snow's interrogation, he also confirmed the presence of a school front for Azzam just north of the town of Nisab that confirms your intelligence and the paid information from the security guards."

Other SAS members in the room slowly made their way to the table to listen more intently to Madden's plan.

"In back of my pickup, in crates with signs that say seismographic equipment, are my weapons, communications equipment, and different sets of various clothes to match the region and circumstances I may encounter."

"First class!" one of the SAS members spouted out, impressed with Madden's risky plan to track Azzam.

"So, let me get this straight," Terry said, trying to understand Madden's almost suicidal mission, "you were literally going to drive yourself down to Nisab, changing clothes as the situation dictated, hunker down somewhere in view of the school, and call in and confirm the drone strike?"

"Yes, but under the guise of this American-turned-al-Qaeda cover and a very good working knowledge of Arabic, I feel confident I could get close enough for the kill if the drone mission failed or was aborted."

The eyes in the room were wide open, and the stunned faces told the tale.

Terry stared at Madden for a moment, thinking he was a crazy man, and the members in the room were thunderstruck at this lone man's mission.

"Very good, Mr. Madden," Terry acknowledged. "You are a better man than I am, Gunga Din. Do you want to work this mission solo or do you want our support?"

Terry knew full well what the answer would be but added, "We have been ordered to work with you, but it's your call."

"Let us make this a joint effort, and I must say I am relieved to be working with SAS on this mission," Madden surprised them, "but I do have one request to make of the team: I'll be the one to pull the trigger on Azzam. Any issues with this request?"

"Mate, I don't see a problem with you making that call, just as long as we kill the ruddy bastard," answered Terry.

"Why is it so important for you to be responsible for the call to the drone and the possible shot?" asked an SAS member.

"Azzam is responsible for murdering my wife and two daughters," Madden quietly replied.

Quiet filled the room as the SAS members sat in silence after hearing Madden's reason.

"Sgt. Smadi, would you please assist Mr. Madden in moving his equipment in here for his checks?" Terry directed.

The refinery machine shop turned into a Special Forces forward strike base, with all the members hurriedly unloading packages and crates of gear for their mission. From food stores to hand grenades, all was accounted for and organized for the long, perilous mission ahead. Like the procession of an orchestra, members of the British SAS team professionally readied themselves and knew they could count on each other as they had so many times in the past during their deployment to Yemen.

As for Madden, they considered him a crazy bloke they would come to trust and admire.

CHAPTER

26

"Ms. Turner, Dr. Alexander is ready for you." The request was repeated while McCord slowly turned to look at the receptionist and acknowledged the request with a nod.

After she was escorted into the office of the president of GFC, the receptionist closed the doors behind her.

My gosh, this is a working president—not some token woman figurehead, McCord told herself as she surveyed the president's office: plain and ordinary, with stacks of reports and files filling the room's tables and desk. A small conference table next to the desk had more piles of paper cluttering its working surface. Also, with McCord's years of experience with the Agency, she assumed the room was wired and that everything she said would be recorded.

Be careful what you say, she reminded herself, *and live the cover.*

Bewildered there was no one in the room, she again took a few moments to view the sights from the large windows—sunshine was making a pleasant, strong presence with small shadows behind the many tall stacks of papers.

After hearing what sounded like a toilet flushing, she turned and was confronted by the president who had welcomed her the first day of class—Dr. Elizabeth Alexander.

"Well Ms. Turner, it is so good to see you again. Why don't we make ourselves comfortable over there at the conference table?" Alexander led the way and moved a few stacks around to give both of them a place to sit.

"Thank you, Dr. Alexander," McCord acknowledged while following her to the conference table.

"Would you like some coffee or something to drink?" Alexander offered. "Oh, and please call me Beth."

"Very well, Beth," McCord replied, "now would someone please explain to me why I was literally dragged out of my class by one of your executive goons and then hustled over here in a limousine?"

"Ms. Turner, please...may I call you Patricia or Pat?" Alexander calmly asked while McCord remained standing red-faced and shaking mad. Calming down and regaining her composure, all for show and the cover, McCord sat down, staring at Alexander.

"Yes, you may call me Pat, and yes, I would like a Diet Coke," McCord replied.

Alexander smiled, hit a switch on her telephone monitor and ordered a Diet Coke and a hot cup of tea.

"I suspect you are wondering why you were brought here," offered Alexander. "We did it for your own good and career here at GFC. You see, Pat, we found you were hiding drugs in your apartment room and thought it best if we took care of it in-house, where the authorities are not involved or bothered."

Her mind racing, McCord was attempting to decipher the meaning and reasoning behind this absurd allegation—why was Alexander to be the messenger?

Not saying a word to Alexander's remarks and accusations, with an indifferent facial expression, McCord just stared at Alexander while sipping her Diet Coke.

"Actually, Pat, I believe we just did a huge favor for you—you may not realize it now, but possibly later," Alexander said.

McCord shrugged while showing no emotion, figuring that GFC would hold this little incident as blackmail on her at a later time if required—but why?

"Dr. Alexander, oh I'm sorry, Beth. May I now return to my training unless you have something else for me besides your people planting drugs in my room?"

Alexander smiled and moved herself away from the conference table with her tea, gently and intentionally touching McCord on her neck as she glided herself to the windows overlooking the south downtown area of Savannah.

McCord suspected the touch was not unintentional and suspected Elizabeth Alexander had something else in mind. She just glanced at the strange woman drinking her tea with an eerie grin on her face.

"Let's see, Patricia, you are scheduled to depart for Santa Cruz, Bolivia, after graduation next week," she said, remaining at the window and not facing McCord as she spoke.

"Yes, that is correct, I am assigned the new GFC branch in the Steel Rock Café at the Ventura Mall in Santa Cruz," McCord replied, not having a clue where she was going with this conversation, but it concerned her.

"Oh, Patricia, why did you ever volunteer for such an assignment so far away from home in what appears to be a dangerous area with corrupt officials, terrorists and drug trafficking?" Alexander slowly turned to McCord with a sinister grin.

McCord was well prepared to answer her informal interrogation as she had practiced so many times in the past few months—real world and training exercises by the best the Feds could offer.

"I was recruited to join the GFC team as an assistant manager in Bolivia because I have a good, solid accounting background and I speak fluent Spanish," McCord said. "Also, I was assured I would receive extra incentive bonuses for accepting the assignment."

McCord was well aware that Alexander knew her application and résumé very well and probably had her corporate security check out the background thoroughly for any holes or questions.

Alexander, for a moment staring at McCord, made her way back to the conference table while going by the coffee table for more tea.

"Would you like another soda, Pat?"

"No, thank you," replied McCord, now cautious that Alexander might place a drug in her drink.

Taking a quick sip of her tea, Alexander seated herself close to McCord and again sipped her tea with no comments, keeping an eye focused on McCord.

The buzzer suddenly rang out of nowhere while Alexander grabbed a cell phone, annoyed at the interruption.

"Yes, I understand the audit committee is waiting for me," she snapped over the phone. "Tell Senior VP Emerson to take it for me."

Alexander tossed the phone onto the conference table and moved ever closer while a bewildered McCord became more suspicious of her every move.

It finally dawned on McCord that her cover may be too tough, too practiced to the point of being too perfect, and that would certainly draw suspicion.

Shit, McCord thought to herself, *you need to start acting more like a scared and intimidated management trainee versus some tough and cold undercover agent.*

In her new, intimidated persona, McCord said, "What is it you want from me?" and added a little trembling.

"It's okay dear, it's okay," Alexander repeated as she slowly began placing her arms around McCord's shoulders and closely embracing her. McCord wished to take physical action against the unwanted advances but decided she would play this part for all it was worth.

"Pat, for your benefit, I would like to explain a few facts of life to you that are very important to us here at the corporation," Alexander said, pulling back from the embrace, but not far enough for McCord's liking.

"As it has been preached to you over and over again in your classes, GFC has over twelve thousand restaurants internationally, and you are probably wondering why I am so excited and interested in the Santa Cruz, Steel Rock Café venture."

Alexander leaned in and practically whispered, "We did not place that particular restaurant there in Santa Cruz as a money-making venture or investment—we placed it there as a personal favor to one of our most trusted and dependable bankers in South America."

"I don't understand. Why would you spend thousands of dollars on a restaurant you foresee as having no future for cash flow?" McCord questioned with a curious look on her face. "You sent me to seven weeks of training to assist in managing a restaurant that you know is going nowhere. I just don't understand."

McCord thought she was going to suddenly get the mother lode in some important intelligence regarding possible relationships between banks and narco drug traffickers in Bolivia.

"I'm not sure I was cut out for this position in Bolivia," McCord said, now putting on a convincing act for Alexander's benefit. "Can I change my assignment to someplace where GFC wants to make money, where there is a career? Someplace not as dangerous as Bolivia?" McCord asked, knowing they needed an immediate fill for the Santa Cruz restaurant. She played her poker hand well, realizing it would take months to recruit and train another candidate equal to her qualifications.

"No, no Pat," Alexander said, now holding McCord's hand and slightly brushing her hands through McCord's flour-filled hair. "GFC has many, many friends and business associates in the region, and they all very much like our chicken. In fact, many of our friends in Bolivia are graciously helping us to expand to other areas in South America with generous assistance in loans and property purchases—it is in some ways like a trade-off—goodwill." Alexander remained uncomfortably close.

"And you, Patricia, are responsible for making our special customers happy—any questions?"

"What about the bogus drug raid in my apartment—why?" McCord sternly asked.

"Pat, if you venture out and attempt to work for someone else or talk about things you see in Santa Cruz, that could be rather embarrassing to GFC, and we would be forced to bring your drug problems to your next employer," she said, continuing to stroke her hands in McCord's hair.

"I'm so sorry, dear, but we do need to take precautions in the event you attempt to leave our family," said the spider to the fly. Alexander turned her attention from caressing McCord's hair to placing her hand on McCord's grease-stained pant leg.

"Do you understand, dear?" Alexander whispered.

"Yes, I do understand, and there will not be any problems," McCord professionally replied, wondering what card to play next in this game of poker.

"Fine, Pat, now what do you think about having dinner with me tonight—let's say about seven?" Alexander said, breathing heavily now as she moved her hands over McCord's breasts, becoming more excited.

Sitting as still as a department store mannequin, watching the president of GFC fondling her—no less in her office—McCord thought of a few often-used scenarios to get out of this awkward situation.

"Dr. Alexander, I mean Beth, I would truly love to have dinner and spend some more time with you tonight, but I must tell you up front that I am currently taking antibiotics for a sexually transmitted disease—I just thought I should tell you this before we got too far along in our friendship," McCord said.

The hands that seconds before were caressing and petting McCord's finer qualities immediately were withdrawn. Alexander pushed herself back from the conference room chair and got up to take another chair while showing signs of embarrassment and frustration. McCord expected this sudden action.

"Beth, do you still want to meet tonight? Sounds like we could still have a good time," McCord asked.

McCord stared at the flustered Alexander attempting to regain her composure, looking for an excuse to leave this embarrassing situation. Alexander nervously picked up her iPad and announced she was late for another meeting.

"Ms. Turner, thank you for your time and please remember what I just told you—do you understand?" While placing her business suit jacket on, she added, "Please wait in the reception area where you came in, and Mr. Barrett will escort you back to your class."

Standing and looking hurt and dejected, still wearing her dirty red GFC apron, McCord made her way to the door.

Adding a little salt to the wound, she turned to Alexander, who was attempting to hide her disappointment by diving back into her corporate work.

"Do you still want to meet tonight?" McCord asked, egging on an already embarrassed Alexander.

"Out of the office now, Ms. Turner." The corporate bitch was back.

Quivering with hurt feelings, McCord made her way to the reception room where Barrett was waiting for her.

"Let's go, Ms. Turner—hope you learned your lesson," he commented while escorting her back to the GFC University.

Once in the limousine, Barrett put down his portfolio for a minute and looked with interest and curiosity toward the dirty though attractive trainee and wondered how the ass chewing from Alexander went. As far as Barrett knew, it all had to do with the drugs in her room and nothing to do with her upcoming assignment.

"Listen, Turner," Barrett unexpectedly broke the silence—almost caring, "you've only got one more week until graduation and off you go to Bolivia—God only knows why you volunteered there."

The limousine pulled up to the main entrance to the university and parked as the new chauffeur was just about to open the passenger doors.

"Henry, that's okay, we'll get out on our own," Barrett directed. Henry knew very well that meant Barrett wanted a few private words with the passenger.

"If you get in a situation that you feel is dangerous and a threat to your life while on your assignment, go to this address," Barrett quietly whispered as he handed her a plain white card with an address in Santa Cruz.

"Also, Turner, you help me out and I will try to help you," Barrett said. "Now go."

Without a word, McCord got out of the limo and stared at the card and then back at the departing limousine.

What a bizarre morning, McCord thought to herself as she returned to class with the stigma of hiding drugs in her living quarters.

Proud of her theatrics in her meeting with Alexander, McCord was attempting to analyze and review all that was said—she had already received a fair amount of information from Alexander herself, and she was getting a feel for what was happening in Bolivia.

"So good to have you back, Ms. Turner," the instructor announced for all to hear.

McCord nodded, put on a clean apron and began cleaning the deep-fat fryers.

CHAPTER
27

After all the equipment checks had been accomplished, the SAS team began moving and packing their equipment into three Toyota pickup trucks.

"Capt. Terry, if I may make a request, sir," Madden asked Terry, who was following his team's contingency checklist prior to departing.

"Yes, Rob, go ahead." Terry stopped and gave his full attention to Madden.

"Sir, we all know as a team that our communications with the Special Operations base at Djibouti is critical—for the mission and possibly our survival," explained Madden while the other team members slowed their preparations, now taking an interest in where Madden was going with his statement.

"Yes, I believe we all know that's a given—where are you going with this?" Terry asked.

"Lee, if something happens to me, and it possibly could, I would feel a lot better knowing we had a backup person who is familiar with our communications systems, frequencies, passwords, you know," Madden reasoned while Terry rubbed his face and thought for a moment.

"Yes, right on you go," Terry replied. He looked to his men and called, "Sgt. Ryan."

"Yes, sir," replied a fit team member who had the cherubic face of a Brit. His long red hair and beard certainly did not match the typical features of an al-Qaeda member, but he would pass as just another crazy Western youth looking to join al-Qaeda, and there were plenty of them in Yemen.

"You were trained and skilled in communications, were you not?" asked Terry.

"Yes, sir, I have skills in communications," Ryan assured Terry while looking at Madden.

"Captain Terry, with your permission, I would like to review our communications checks with Sgt. Ryan." Madden nodded at Ryan.

"Righto, lad, please get together with Madden and ensure we have a backup in you," Terry said, nodding his head in approval.

With Ryan feverishly taking notes, Madden began setting up and explaining features of the various communications gear for satellite communications, cell phone and internet communications, and Very High Frequency (VHF) radios for contact with aircraft. Ensuring all was in order and enabled, Madden made sure Ryan was listening as he made contact with the Joint Special Operations Command, known as JSOC, and the Special Operations duty controller at the drone base at Djibouti, Africa, whose radio call sign was Angel Fire.

"Angel Fire, this is Black Jack, how do you copy? Over." Madden, holding the headset to his ear, attempted to double-check the assigned radio frequencies.

"Angel Fire, this is Black Jack on primary and secondary frequencies. How copy? Over."

After a few seconds, the satellite speaker came to life: "Black Jack, this is Angel Fire. How copy?" the duty communications officer replied from his command post at the Special Operations drone base at Djibouti.

"Angel Fire, this is Black Jack, request further contact with the duty controller. Over," Madden requested.

"Stand by, Black Jack, duty controller will be with you momentarily. Over."

While waiting for the duty controller, the SAS team members finished their jobs of loading and organizing the specialized equipment in the three trucks, grabbed a chair and some bottled water, and gathered around Madden and his satellite communications setup to monitor this critical contact that would affect all of them and their survival.

After a couple minutes, the satellite speaker came to life: "Black Jack, this is Angel Fire duty controller, prepared to pass your message to Sky King. Over."

"Angel Fire, request you authenticate Foxtrot Charlie. Over." Using the day's scheduled authentic codes matrix to ensure the positive contact, the duty controller was obligated to reply with the correct alphabetic reply—if not, there would be no further contact.

"Black Jack, this is Angel Fire, authentic Zulu. Over."

"Roger, Angel Fire, please pass the following message to Sky King," Madden continued. "Have joined up with friends at the Marib oil refinery and am now heading with team to Yemen grid coordinates Y2401Bravo and Y6708Tango, repeat coordinates Y2401Bravo and Y6708Tango, how copy? Over."

While waiting for the confirmation from the duty controller, Madden asked Capt. Terry and Sgt. Ryan to double-check his grid coordinates to ensure they were exactly as relayed for the al-Qaeda headquarters at the schoolhouse north of Nisab—the final destination and last known whereabouts of Azzam.

Carefully studying the coordinates with personal navigation devices, Terry and Ryan nodded their heads in agreement. "Looks good, sir," Ryan confirmed.

"Black Jack, this is Angel Fire, passed your information to Sky King." The duty controller then asked, "Do you request your drone support to begin immediately as directed in operation plan Paradise Bound? Over."

"That is affirmative, Angel Fire," Madden confirmed, "request drone surveillance and loitering in corridor between Marib and relayed coordinates. My electronic beacons are now activated for positive identification by the drone pilots—we may look like a bunch of al-Qaeda thugs from the drone's sensors, but we are the good guys."

The SAS members were more relieved and a bit more confident knowing an American drone would be monitoring their every move.

"Black Jack, be advised, your dedicated drone will be launching soon, but I have been instructed to inform you one drone will be available for your mission. How copy?"

"That damn Col. Graham." Madden shrugged while the others in the room did not understand Madden's frustrations. It was not worth arguing with Graham at this advanced stage of the operation, and he certainly did not want to raise any concerns with his new SAS teammates. He would keep his frustration to himself.

"Roger, Angel Fire, copy and understand our one drone mission is operational and executed," Madden said. "We are depending on you, Angel Fire."

"Roger, Black Jack, drone will be airborne in one hour," the duty controller confirmed, "use preset satellite communications channels 45 as primary and 46 as a backup to contact pilots. Over."

"Thank you, Angel Fire, we are moving now heading for destination and will monitor this frequency for further contact with you. Out."

"Good luck, Black Jack, Angel Fire is out," the duty controller signed off.

"Let's get a go on Madden, we have to depart now!" Terry strongly urged Madden to collect his communications gear, package it up and get it in the trucks.

"Terry, hold up for a couple more minutes," Madden replied. "I need to check with our friends at Midland Oil who just might be our last chance to get out of here after our mission—when we get back here."

With prospects of an extraction after the strike on Azzam, Terry and his SAS members were not as eager for a quick departure.

"Okay, but please hurry it up," Terry replied with his team nodding their heads in agreement. All were now watching Madden, wondering what else this strange American had in his bag of tricks.

Madden methodically pulled out the communications information from a small travel-all suitcase provided him by Blake Rhodes and Kelly Carson before departing from the Marib airport. Both contacts with Rhodes and Carson were good on primary and secondary radios, plus the cell phones were operable but sporadic, understandably so with all the turmoil in the region.

He reached them on the radio. Both advised Madden that the other oil companies were increasing their tempo of having their people airlifted out of Yemen with the assistance of Egyptian Air Force cargo planes.

I'm sure the Egyptians also love all of that oil money paying for their Air Force, Madden thought to himself.

"Rob, one last piece of critical information you need to know," Carson relayed to Madden. "We are all expected to be out of here by Wednesday night, and by that time who knows who will be controlling the airport."

"Kelly, we'll do all we can to get our work done prior to Wednesday evening—can you stand by just for a minute?"

"Hurry, Rob, I'm on descent now into Djibouti," replied Carson, who was making one of her countless airlifts from Marib.

"Capt. Terry, sir, it is urgent, I need to speak with you for a moment," Madden requested while holding the radio's headset in his hands.

"Bottom line, how were you planning to withdraw from the region after the strike?" Madden asked Terry. The other SAS members slowly stopped their preparations to listen to Terry's response. They, too, were concerned about their withdraw plan after the strike on Azzam.

"Men, may I have your attention, please? Mr. Madden here has just broached the subject we had not planned well on—how to get out of here when all hell breaks loose."

Addressing Madden and his team members, Terry advised all that the British Petroleum officials at the airport complex had arranged for their airlift out, just as long as the airport was in the hands of some friendly authority. Now, Terry was more concerned about the airport being in friendly hands after the strike. His concern was evident.

"Carson, this is Rob," Madden said, motioning Terry to get closer so he could listen to his conversation from the headset.

"I have a few friends here with me at the refinery who are also going to assist me in tracking down the Midland workers on the pipeline." Madden attempted to keep his communications as benign and normal as possible. "Worst case, Carson, how many additional passengers can you airlift out?"

"Maximum of ten with no equipment," she replied, "on glide path for approach, got to run. OUT!"

Turning off all of the communications equipment and putting down the radio headset, Madden turned to Terry.

"It appears, just in the event British Petroleum cannot get out in time," Madden emphasized, "Midland Oil has a Twin Otter cargo plane that may be available—if we can get back to Marib by Wednesday evening or even sooner."

"Yes, we have all seen it flying around the pipeline and refinery since we have been here," Terry observed. "Nice that you have a friend with an airplane, but what happens if we can't get back to Marib?"

"I have an idea," Madden said, with every member of the SAS team intensely listening as he again pulled out from his shirt pocket one of the many tactical maps they had been poring over.

Unfolding the map and laying it on the top of a pickup, Madden pulled out a pencil and pointed to what appeared to be a flat, primitive dirt road a couple miles from the hideout area, just above the horizon of the school.

"Capt. Terry," said Madden, "a possible alternate way out would be for us to work with the Twin Otter pilot in landing on the road and extracting us—we are talking worst-case scenario."

"How in God's name are you going to convince an oil company pilot to land their only air asset in the middle of our fight," Terry vented loudly, probably due to his anxiety about the mission and possibly lack of sleep, "and then airlift us out?"

"I feel your concerns," Madden acknowledged. "However, the pilot has agreed to wait for us in Marib until Wednesday night, now we are just asking her to pick us up about a hundred miles away.

"Tell you what, when given the opportunity on our way down to Nisab, I'll contact the pilot and see what is possible," Madden said. "No harm in asking her."

"Her?"

"Yes, you heard right. Her," an annoyed Madden replied. "Do you have any problems with that, captain?"

"All I mean is—" the captain was cut off by Madden.

"Yes, I know full well what you were meaning and let me assure you, if you continue to have problems with a woman pilot in the next few days, you can kiss my ass," Madden sternly lectured.

"Madden," Terry retorted, "I'll be the first to kiss her ass if she gets us out of here. Is that clear?"

Madden smiled.

"Okay, you dirty slobs, secure your gear and equipment and make your way out to the trucks," Terry ordered. "We have a long way to go tonight."

CHAPTER
28

While Turner was completing her assignment disassembling the fryer, GFC company president Elizabeth Alexander returned to her cluttered office and made a beeline to her formal desk still showing telltale signs of frustrations after her interview with Turner—not to mention the sexual rebuff. Frustration turned to anger after her embarrassing interlude with Turner. Alexander was concerned that maybe she spoke a little too much about the Santa Cruz GFC situation and the unorthodox reasons for providing the "government officials" with such a restaurant.

"Get Roy Baker, Corporate Security, in my office immediately," barked Alexander to her private executive secretary.

"Yes, ma'am. I understand he is briefing our board of directors on some recent security issues," the secretary said.

"As soon as possible, have Roy meet me in my office."

Two hours later, Roy Baker was indeed heading up to the president's office.

"Please go in, Mr. Baker. Dr. Alexander is waiting."

Roy Baker was a seasoned security expert in military and corporate environments, and had been head of GFC corporate security for ten years. He was used to Alexander's sudden requests—and quick temper. Also, he was aware of her many strange idiosyncrasies including sexual liaisons in her office during the day and occasionally at night. Some had become public and embarrassing for the corporation, but she had mostly been successful at covering up her affairs.

Usually when Baker was summoned immediately to the president's office, it involved covering up a perceived scandal or working a private or confidential issue involving an employee's background.

"Dr. Alexander, good afternoon," Baker politely greeted her as he made his way to his customary seat inside the small corporate conference room adjacent to Alexander's private office.

"Good afternoon, Roy, thanks for coming on such short notice," she insincerely replied, knowing he'd better get his tail up there quickly if he wanted to remain her security chief.

The usual salutations and small talk were dispensed with as she immediately opened up a single personnel folder lying on her desk. Baker, knowing Alexander's personality and bizarre whims, quickly prepared his notebook and personal laptop for the president's tasking.

"Roy, I want you to find out some background, personal information for me on a certain employee we are sending to Santa Cruz, Bolivia, next month."

"Yes, of course, Dr. Alexander," Baker replied as he booted up his laptop, which contained highly sensitive personal background information on all GFC employees—especially the candidates scheduled to work in foreign countries.

Baker's experience had taught him that many GFC candidates volunteer to work in foreign countries thinking they can do drugs, sell drugs on the side, or get involved in credit card scams on their customers. It was a constant problem for security and the human resource office. The candidates scheduled for foreign duty were known for having the most rigorous background checks. Finding qualified candidates in the States was tough enough, but finding those for overseas was brutal.

"I want you to dig deeper in your background investigation for one of our management trainee candidates named Patricia Ann Turner," she directed as she sat back in her custom-fitted leather chair. "Something about her appears maybe a little bit too perfect."

He scanned her info in the laptop. She appeared qualified for her scheduled position in Bolivia—especially her Spanish language skills.

"I'll have our background investigation contractor do another review and see if we find any irregularities that are out of line with our normal trends for such a position," Baker assured Alexander as he had so many times in the past.

"NO, ROY!" she screamed and threw the closest stack of papers within her reach at him.

Used to such outbursts, Baker sheepishly found his way to the floor and began picking up the scattered mess of paper strewn on the floor. He put the collected papers on the conference room table, resumed his seat, straightened his tie and opened his notepad.

"Roy, listen to me." Alexander raised herself from the table and began pacing the room fixated on the background and possible real identity of Patricia Turner.

Turning and pointing her finger at him, she ordered, "You'll get us another background investigator to validate what we already know about Turner—do you understand me?"

"Yes, I understand," he replied. Though visibly shaken, he was used to her drastic mood changes. "I'll contact one of our freelance investigators, Brisco & Sons, to accomplish this task. They have accomplished sensitive background investigations in the past."

"Also, I want this investigation accomplished in less than a week," she commanded, emphasizing, "no more than a week."

"Dr. Alexander, it will take at least twice that time to get just a preliminary background investigation." He realized he may have been too quick with his reply and added, "Possibly a week can be arranged, but we'll certainly pay for the short notice."

"Listen, I don't care what it costs, just get me that investigation—now!"

"What is so important about a second background check on an assistant manager going to Bolivia? I just don't understand," a frustrated Baker replied while collecting his laptop computer and portfolio, preparing to leave.

"Get out of this office now and get back to your job," she said, pointing her finger in his face, "and get me that investigation as soon as possible—if you're still working here then."

He turned and headed for the office door.

"Oh, Roy," she calmly called as she made her way back to her desk, "ensure no one sees that investigation. Only you and me, do you understand?"

CHAPTER
29

The sun was just coming up when a ragtag caravan of small pickup trucks departed from the Midland Oil machine shop facility at the Marib oil refinery heading southeast along the pipeline road heading straight to Nisab.

By all accounts, the caravan looked like a normal operation of oil and pipeline workers heading down the dusty road inspecting the pipeline for possible terrorist damage—typical operations. To add to the authenticity of the trucks, SAS members in Yemeni Army uniforms traveled with the caravan in a "borrowed" Army Jeep. Everything looked like it was part of day-to-day operations to support Yemen's only source of income—the oil and gas pipeline.

The caravan, like a chameleon changing color to the current environment, made changes to its appearance along the route to Nisab—from looking like typical pipeline workers to passing for Shiite insurgency groups or al-Qaeda jihad terrorists—the team was well versed at adapting to the environment.

The caravan passed through one checkpoint after another with the usual bribe of gold and dollars. But as it approached Nisab and al-Qaeda strongholds, the gold and dollars were replaced by religious fanaticism aimed at avenging the Great Satan.

Of great surprise and relief to Madden, a couple of the SAS members were Yemeni nationals who were very convincing when negotiating through the various roadblocks.

Later in the afternoon and getting ever closer to Nisab, the caravan took a short stop behind an abandoned auxiliary gas pipeline pumping station. Black spray paint was brought out from one of the equipment crates in the truck, and Madden watched with interest as the two Yemenis began painting fanatic al-Qaeda slogans on the sides of the trucks.

"I am sure Midland Oil is not going to appreciate this type of addition to their trucks," Madden said jokingly.

"Come on, Madden, let's get out and help set up the guns," Terry said.

"Guns are good," Madden commented as he assisted the SAS team in configuring a heavy machine gun in the cargo bed of each truck.

"Watch out, Azzam, the Great Satan is coming your way," Madden mumbled to Terry in the cab of the lead pickup truck. Terry just shook his head and grinned, "You are either the craziest, stupidest, or bravest Yank I have ever had to work with."

With the machine gun configured, Terry gathered his team and Madden together around the back of the pumping station and pulled out his map of the area, laying it on the ground for all members to see. The map was worn, with numerous marks and annotations.

"Lads," Terry directed with all eyes on the map, "as we briefed at the refinery, from here we'll make our way just a few more miles ahead to an old abandoned equipment depot filled with nothing but rusting old oil and gas equipment once used by the Yemen National Oil Company." He pointed to their current location on the map.

"We have pretty good intelligence no one cares about the depot, and it's deserted except for a few goats and snakes," Terry continued. "We'll hunker down there this afternoon and move out at dark on this dirt side road leading off of N-17 that will take us in sight of the school by tomorrow morning."

He surveyed his troops. "For now, let's move forward to the depot, set up and check our communications and get some rest for tonight. Any questions?"

"Yes, Captain, I have a question," said a young, burly, bearded SAS sergeant. "When we get Mr. Madden here close enough to that bloody al-Qaeda school north of Nisab, how will he take care of Azzam? What is the plan? What is the plan after the hit— how do we extract ourselves when hell breaks loose?"

The SAS sergeant was unknowingly speaking for every person on the team. Madden sat back, thinking to himself, *Darn good question, Sarge.*

"Well, Mr. Madden, do you have a good answer for the sergeant?" Terry asked, smiling at Madden while making room for him around the terrain map.

"Thank you, Capt. Terry," Madden politely replied to Terry as he knelt down near the map and pointed to the intersection of National Highway 17, which they were currently traveling, to a narrow dirt road leading a few miles north of Nisab and the school.

"If Capt. Terry and your team can get me here by early tomorrow evening," said Madden, pointing to what appeared to be the end of the dirt road just a few miles from the school, "I'll take it from there."

All eyes were now focused on Madden as he was intensely studying the terrain features.

"Terry, all I ask in return is if you would set up a makeshift command/communications post near this point here," Madden pointed to a deep, hidden ravine that would also serve as a secure hiding place for the team and vehicles while he was moving forward alone to the al-Qaeda stronghold.

"Once you are hunkered down in the ravine, with a good view of the school and have communications connectivity with our friends at the Special Operations base at Djibouti," said Madden, "I'll begin my journey as the American al-Qaeda recruit Johnny Snow to the school and take out Azzam—either by knife or drone."

Terry's tanned, dirty sweaty head nodded in agreement.

"Anything else, Rob?" Terry asked, knowing the team— especially Madden—was getting more anxious the closer they got to the school.

"All right, if shit does hit the fan and we do need to escape and evade immediately, the trucks will definitely be our first option," Madden rationalized for the team. "We could plan on limited cover by the drones." Only one drone had been earmarked for his operation, but more could be available if Madden or Terry initiated a Broken Arrow call.

"However, if we get engaged with al-Qaeda fighters, our only way out may be the help of a small cargo plane picking us up at the primitive road we were discussing earlier," Madden said, again raising the hope of an air rescue.

"When we get to our forward hideout here," Madden said, now pointing to a spot on the map, "I would recommend that a couple members of your team make a quick reconnaissance of the possible aircraft landing site here—just in case."

"Sgt. Evans and Corp. Williams!" Terry ordered, "Please join Mr. Madden and me here."

Both Evans and Williams joined Terry and Madden in studying the map and the location of the possible landing strip.

"When we get to our hideout here, we need you two to make a reconnaissance run to this primitive road located here." Terry traced his finger on the map from the hideout area to the landing strip.

"No problem, mate, but what are we looking for when we get to this possible aircraft landing site?" Evans asked. "I frankly don't know shit about what to look for or make a judgment whether it is suitable for aircraft operations."

"No problem, mate," said Madden, now mocking Evans's British accent and patting him on the back.

"I'll make up a little checklist for you to use when you get there that pretty much explains what we need to know about the road and especially the terrain near it," Madden offered.

"I hope for our sake that little road is suitable for your friend's aircraft to land," Evans said nervously.

"Well, Mr. Madden, you are just a jack of all trades, are you not?" Williams said.

"Okay, Evans and Williams, with Capt. Terry's permission, let's talk about what you will be looking for at the road airstrip site."

Madden drafted a checklist for Evans and Williams to follow on their reconnaissance mission.

"Thank you—we'll see what we can bloody do," a perplexed and concerned Terry replied, not knowing what else to say to a man who was just going to walk into an al-Qaeda stronghold dressed like an American-recruited al-Qaeda member, kill its leader with a drone or knife, then walk away.

"Yes, we will see what we can bloody do," Terry repeated, still trying to grasp what Madden was proposing and still thinking this Yank was probably the looniest CIA operative he had ever met.

CHAPTER
30

"Dr. Alexander, a Mr. George Pablo Quezada is on line four wishing to speak with you," the GFC president's admin announced on the intercom.

"Thank you, Mary," Alexander nervously replied as she thought for a few seconds before picking up the receiver.

"Good afternoon, George. How is the weather in Santa Cruz?"

"Ah, valued friend, so good to hear from you and I am well, thank you," Quezada commented in a thick Castilian accent. "Are we any closer to getting our GFC restaurant running down here? I hear from sources we are having management issues."

"George, thank you for caring, and I do apologize for not getting back to you sooner, but we are confident we have the perfect candidate coming your way next week," Alexander said. "In fact, our candidate graduates soon and will be on her way immediately following her graduation—okay with you?"

"Elizabeth, we have heard this before from you a couple of times, and we still do not see our assistant manager," his tone conveying his frustration. "The current Bolivian manager is swamped, and as you know he has not been afforded the opportunity to attend the training."

In other words, Alexander angrily thought to herself, *the restaurant is not open due to the fact you don't have an American management flunky to run the operation while the Bolivian manager just sits around picking his nose.*

"You do remember our initial agreement that the manager will be from Bolivia and the assistant manager will come from the GFC Corporation— for obvious reasons."

"Of course, George, I do remember, and we have placed a priority on getting the assistant manager to you next week." She worked to sound sad and sincere. "We will not let you down this time—you have my word."

"There will be no more delays, or we might have to reevaluate our relationship with you, Dr. Alexander," Quezada warned. "We'll wait for her arrival. What is her name again?"

"Patricia Turner."

"Okay, Dr. Alexander. I truly hope for your sake that this Patricia Turner will be what you Americans call a 'team player' in our primary business," warned Quezada.

Alexander shuddered, knowing full well what he meant by primary business.

"Hasta luego, Dr. Alexander."

Alexander attempted to be calm, knowing the assistant manager's job was solely to show legitimacy to the GFC Bolivian operation while the manager dealt with relations with the Sola Mesa drug cartel, which was funding much more than a GFC.

CHAPTER
31

"Alright, mates, this is it," Terry announced from the lead truck as they arrived at the dirt road and ravine leading off from Yemen Highway N-17. "Men, let's get established here prior to the sun coming up—you know what to do," Terry ordered as his team methodically hunkered down and established the command post hideout.

All were now clothed in standard tan al-Qaeda battle dress, with all carrying AK-47 assault rifles—the weapon of choice for al-Qaeda fanatics.

As the team was preparing the hideout to be operational, Terry found Madden checking radios and personal gear in preparation for his mission the next day.

"Hey, Rob," Terry called out, breaking Madden's concentration, "how about you and I do a quick survey of where you're heading?"

Madden looked up, nodded at Terry and grabbed sets of binoculars for both of them.

Moving up the side of a sandy, dusty, lifeless ravine, they came to the edge where they peered down and saw, a mile away, the lighted school building with al-Qaeda members milling around the premises. They were surprised to notice a well-concealed storage and garage facility next to the school.

"If not for the school and the children in it, this place would have been destroyed months ago by drones, but the children are human shields for these mutts," a frustrated Madden said.

"They are aware and confident that a ground operation against them would be virtually impossible with the network of informants and spies in the region—they own it," Terry reasoned.

The spies and informants had reported to Azzam the movements of a normal al-Qaeda patrol roaming the backroads near the highway heading for Nisab. Cell phone pictures of the caravan were taken and forwarded to one of Azzam's lieutenants, who passed it off as a routine patrol of brothers searching for ways to cause more havoc to the oil pipeline. He assumed they would make their way to the school and report in.

"We'll await their arrival," the lieutenant mumbled and scratched his thick, black beard while reviewing the pictures.

As the local school-children began playing soccer on the run-down soccer field, the al-Qaeda members and their recruits were meeting in a small training center a few yards from the schoolhouse.

A class of recruits newly arrived from all over the United States, Europe, and Africa were being lectured by one of the many bearded al-Qaeda religious instructors on topics including basic weapons training and demolition techniques.

Madden and Terry were both studying every aspect of what they were observing, taking quick notes on potential threats. It was clear to both men that there were significantly more soldiers, recruits, weapons, and trucks—maybe fifty or more bad guys—but most disconcerting was the number of heavily armed surplus military Humvees—originally provided to the Yemeni military and police, but now in the hands of al-Qaeda.

"All those vehicles, especially the Humvees, could be a real challenge in us getting out with our trucks," sighed a surprised, disheartened Terry.

"Yes, and well camouflaged and hidden next to the school," Madden replied. "It's obvious our drone reconnaissance of the school prior to getting here didn't show the Humvees and the various recruit groups al-Qaeda was training here."

"Yes, and drones can carry but a few missiles to handle anyone chasing after us," Madden replied.

"Recommend we get your friend with the airplane on the line as soon as possible—it may just be our only saving grace," Terry suggested. "I would like you to see what the chances are of her landing on the road near us."

Madden just kept his eyes trained on the facility through the binoculars.

"Madden!" Terry wanted Madden's full attention while both men continued to survey the school area and its unexpected surprises. "If we can't get a good, solid commitment from your pilot friend, I recommend we abort the mission and head back to Marib as soon as possible."

Both men looked at each other knowing the gravity of the situation with the sudden change in intelligence.

"All right, Terry," Madden nodded his grimy, unshaven face. "I'll contact the pilot and see what the odds are that she can get to us here by Wednesday morning." Madden paused for a minute. "It would be suicide under the present conditions."

CHAPTER
32

"Sir, what do you think?" Sgt. Evans asked Capt. Terry as he and Madden arrived at the now operational hideout hidden under camouflage netting to protect against the sun and extreme desert temperatures. Everyone on Terry's team waited for the answer to the sergeant's question. They all knew the dangerous situation they were in, being so close to the largest al-Qaeda safe haven in Yemen.

"Lads, if I could have your attention and please gather around," Terry said as the men took their places around their commander. Madden sat away preparing for the communications he would be having with Kelly Carson about a possible lifesaving extraction by her and her aircraft.

Terry briefed his men on the observations at the school and explained that it appeared much more active and operational than what they had expected, with numerous armed, fast-moving Humvees parked and camouflaged next to the school. Also, he told them about a large contingent of foreign recruits being trained there.

"Unfortunately, our intelligence did not find or report this to us prior to our jump off," Terry continued. "However, if Mr. Madden's pilot friend can land near us and extract us before all hell breaks loose, we may have a chance of completing the mission. If we cannot get a solid commitment from the pilot and Midland Oil, we will abort the mission and return to Marib as soon as possible—are there any questions?"

"Sir, when will we know if we will be airlifted out? What about Mr. Madden's mission?" asked a corporal.

Capt. Terry and his team were now staring at Madden, looking for answers.

"I should let you know within a half hour if an airlift is possible," Madden said. "If not possible, I recommend you head back to Marib immediately. I don't believe our drone support would increase our chances against the force we are seeing at the school."

He scanned the faces. Some showed disappointment. "Regardless of the situation, I'll be continuing on with my mission, and your departure would be a good diversion for me to get close enough to Azzam," Madden said.

Kelly Carson was at the Midland Oil facility at the Marib airport, loading equipment and fuel in her twin-engine Otter for one of her last trips to Djibouti. The unstable political situation and repeated attacks by various local and international militias, including al-Qaeda, made Midland operations at Marib highly dangerous.

Carson was just topping off her fuel tanks at the Midland facility when the call appeared on her cell phone.

"Kelly, this is Rob Madden. We need your help."

Carson secured the tank caps, then went inside the cockpit and grabbed her clipboard from the passenger's seat, all while keeping the cell phone to her ear.

"My goodness, Rob, how and where are you?"

"Kelly, I am with a team of pipeline maintenance specialists north of Nisab, and we urgently need your assistance in getting out of here." Madden asked, "Is your offer of an airlift still good?"

"Sure, if you can make it back here to Marib by tomorrow evening—if we have that long." Carson added, "You just might be my last shuttle out of Marib for Djibouti."

"Kelly, would it be possible for you to pick us up at a small strip above the town of Nisab?"

Carson could hear the anxiety in Madden's request, and she thought there must be more to this than he was relaying. She didn't like it.

"You want me to do what?" Carson exploded over the radio. "Let me grab another sectional map to see what's possible."

Finding the appropriate aeronautical map for the area from her case full of local maps, she located Nisab and could not find anything in the way of an airstrip or airport. Also, she knew from many company reports that heavy al-Qaeda activities were in that area, so flying near it was considered risky and prohibited by Midland.

"Rob, I can't find any airstrip near Nisab. Am I not finding it on the map?" a somewhat weary Carson replied. "Are you sure you have the name right and town right?"

"Listen to me very carefully," Madden began, "we need for you to land and pick us up on a primitive, flat dirt road near our present location. The coordinates are as follows."

Seconds passed as Carson removed her gloves and sunglasses and began making an intensive study of the location that Madden had described to her. Stunned at this request, she sat back for a minute in thought. She figured the group was potentially in danger if they did not get an airlift.

"Kelly, are you there? Over." Madden transmitted.

Madden knew he had thrown an impossible request to Carson and understood her need for time to sort it out.

"Shit, this lady has balls if she volunteers for this mission," one of Terry's sergeants mumbled aloud. All nodded their heads in agreement.

"I'll have to get permission from Rhodes. I suspect he won't have a problem, just as long as we have completed transferring all of our Midland personnel and critical equipment to Djibouti by this evening," Carson said.

"Thanks, Kelly. So I take it we can count on you being at our designated landing area tomorrow morning?" Madden asked.

"Yes, if we have no major maintenance problems, I'll start working on a flight plan to your area," Carson said. "I'm going to need an exact time when you need a pickup. Also need to speak with you or anyone about the conditions of this road I am to be landing on."

Madden handed the phone to Evans and said, "By the way, this is Evans. He has a British accent. Part of the British Petroleum team I am working with."

"Miss Carson, good morning to you. This is Bob Evans, do you hear me, love?"

"Cut out this nice love shit and tell me what I need to know to safely land there," Carson demanded.

For a few minutes, Evans briefed Carson on the conditions of the proposed landing site and their efforts at making it as accessible as possible for her arrival the next day.

"First, I need to know if when I land, will there be enough level ground on either side of the road for me to turn the aircraft around, taxi down the road, turn around and line up on the road for takeoff." Carson ticked off her list of must-haves.

"Second, I will need to see either smoke or flares at the beginning of the landing area on the road."

"Third, I will need to be in radio contact with you prior to landing—no buts about it. If I don't hear from you by my arrival overhead, I'm returning to Marib."

Evans looked at Madden and Terry for their reaction, both nodding their heads with approval.

"Fair enough," Madden replied, speaking for the team.

"Miss Carson, all of your conditions will be met, and we'll notify you of any changes here," Evans reported back.

"See you tomorrow," Carson sarcastically replied, "and please relay to Madden he is a stupid, dumb-shit motherfucker for thinking this one up. OUT."

"Rob, you did not mention to her the true reason why she is picking us up here?" a concerned Terry inquired.

"She's got enough on her plate right now and just getting to us is going to be a major feat—no use adding more than what she needs to know, for now," Madden said.

Sensing that Terry was not pleased with his holding back information from what appeared to be a brave pilot coming to rescue them, Madden understood completely.

"It had to be done this way," Madden said. "We'll see what tomorrow morning brings when we make the hit on Azzam."

CHAPTER
33

Late in the evening, as the sun was setting below the range of mountains and ridge to the west, Capt. Terry's team and Madden were actively preparing for the morning raid on the al-Qaeda schoolhouse, with all members in al-Qaeda tan military dress and carrying AK-47 assault rifles and black flags.

Madden had nothing but respect for the well-seasoned SAS team he was working with. It was evident to him they certainly had been in Yemen for a while to mirror the dress and day-to-day routines of the terrorists.

Terry's team was just finishing dinner of U.S.-donated Meals Ready to Eat (MREs) and some modest foodstuffs normally carried by Special Forces members. Terry opened his military-issued notepad/map case.

"All right, gentlemen, hope you enjoyed your early dinner—let's get going with this." He was visibly anxious to get the operation started. "Oh, before we begin, want to thank the ol' boy for arranging transportation out of here tomorrow morning." The team nodded at Madden.

"Gentlemen, I am handing the execution phase of this operation over to Rob here."

Pulling out of one of the trucks a large, clean piece of plywood that he situated within the group for all to see, Madden uncapped a black marker, ready to brief the mission.

"Thank you, Capt. Terry, and allow me a few minutes to lay out our critical sites and make a talky pointy for all of our benefit."

The team watched with extreme interest as Madden began noting all the various critical sites on his plywood briefing aid, including marked locations, landmarks, and notes on radio frequencies and channel settings.

As Madden continued marking and writing on the plywood, team members pulled out their personal notepads and began writing down everything Madden was marking—now focused on Madden's markings and quietly asking each other questions as Madden's concept briefing was being brought to life.

With the team's present location being marked with a large X in the middle of the board, other points included the al-Qaeda school with its tents and vehicle lot next to it, the dirt road a few hundred yards away leading into the school, and the improvised airstrip to be used by Kelly Carson and her aircraft for the team's extraction from the area.

Other features such as ravines, hills, accessible roads and wadi—dry river basins—were identified because of their relationship to the three main points of interest. The team's hideout, the al-Qaeda school and the makeshift landing strip.

Madden intentionally wrote 0900 in large, black numbers above the mark showing the airstrip. Madden allowed the team to make notes and write down all that he had transcribed on the plywood board. Many team members moved near the board for a better look as Madden was making his own notes.

Satisfied the team members had sufficient time to make their notes and with Terry gesturing his approval for Madden to continue, Madden stood next to his plywood briefing board, marker in hand. Looking at his dirty, dusty audience of professional British soldiers, Madden was gaining more confidence this mission might succeed—especially his ambitious role.

"Okay, men, allow me to proceed with this briefing and please take notes accordingly and questions after the brief," Madden announced.

All eyes were now on Madden and his planning board as he started the briefing.

He began with their current location hunkered down at their well-hidden staging area.

After thirty minutes, the briefing ended with the sun just going down.

"Gentlemen, that concludes the plan," Madden added. "I know y'all are tired of me mentioning it, but we have to be at the designated airstrip at nine in the morning for the ride home—regardless if the mission is a success or not."

All were stunned at the audacity of Madden's plan, with Terry rising to take a better look at the plywood board that now resembled a complex military operation.

"Let me summarize what you just relayed to us, Rob," Terry said. "You are going to just walk on down to the al-Qaeda school house dressed in local garb and pass yourself off as this American recruit, Snow?

"Then you are going to rig grenades or explosives in the surrounding vehicles and with the explosions and certain confusion, you are going to make your way into Azzam's tent and drug him—or kill him," Terry stated.

"Yes, Capt. Terry, sir," Madden calmly replied.

"And you are confident the mustard gas grenades will take down Azzam's bodyguards and any others rushing to his assistance?"

Madden nodded.

"Then you plan on loading Azzam in one of their pickup trucks—if you don't kill him—and just drive away, making your way to the airstrip. Am I listening correctly?" Terry asked in disbelief, shaking his head.

"If things go wrong for me down at the school and I can't get out, I recommend you and your team get the hell out of here—either high-ball it out of here with your trucks or wait for the airlift," Madden advised.

"Since this is a joint effort," Terry sarcastically said, "what exactly again do you want my team to do—just watch?"

"When I do make it out of the school compound in one of their trucks and if anyone cares to follow, please position your guns focused on any vehicles pursuing me," Madden emphasized.

"I also highly recommend that Sgt. Ryan remain with the communications and radios during the entire operation—especially maintaining contact with the pilot and the drone handlers at Djibouti Special Operations center." Madden could not emphasize enough the importance of Ryan's role.

"Lastly, it's imperative that Sgts. Evans and Williams ready the makeshift airstrip with the necessary smoke and flares marking the landing site for the pilot," Madden concluded.

"Okay, gentlemen, you heard Mr. Madden's request," Terry said. "Let's make a go of it. Everyone get some sack time, with three in the morning coming early."

"Capt. Terry, sir!" said Nasser Saeed, a young Yemeni national on contract with the British SAS team because of his knowledge of the area and family vengeance toward the al-Qaeda on the Arabian Peninsula. "Sir, I have a request."

Saeed had been a military intelligence officer in the Yemeni National Army, and he was considered one of the most knowledgeable officers regarding al-Qaeda operations in Yemen. With the outbreak of civil war and the overthrow of the Yemeni military, his station and mission were eliminated. Also, his father and brother were murdered by al-Qaeda for their support of the former president of Yemen during a political rally.

Saeed was known by British intelligence agency MI6 as being very familiar with the many different tribes in Yemen and, most importantly, for proving his loyalty and bravery. British intelligence actively recruited Saeed to work with various clandestine British Special Forces operations in Yemen. His knowledge of the local languages, customs, and culture made him invaluable to any team he was on.

"Yes, Nasser?" Terry answered.

"Sir, I would like to volunteer to join Mr. Madden on his tasking down to the school," Saeed said.

Any team member would have bet their month's pay that Madden was not coming back from his mission and were now in awe that Saeed wanted to volunteer to go with him.

Silence fell over the team hideout. Terry and Madden, both taken by surprise at this request, stared for a moment at Saeed to comprehend this unexpected development.

"Mr. Madden, could you use a volunteer?" Terry offered.

"I would be honored to have Saeed join me," Madden said, "I certainly could use the help."

"All right then, Nasser, please get together with Mr. Madden, and I am sure he will detail where you can assist."

"Very good, sir." Saeed stood and saluted Terry.

No one had provided Terry with a military salute in several months due to the nature of their mission—it was just not required or appropriate with Special Operations in the field.

Somewhat surprised by the salute, Terry rose and returned the salute while the remainder of the team smiled and chuckled at Saeed for being a kiss ass.

CHAPTER
34

"Halt and identify yourselves," came the command from a young al-Qaeda guard, pointing his AK-47 assault rifle at Madden and Saeed from behind a stone wall a couple hundred yards from the school. Suddenly, the bright high-beam lights of a pickup truck were shining directly at them. Both men froze and greeted the guards with the customary al-Qaeda gesture of respect and allegiance.

"Brother, I found our lost recruit from America," Saeed very convincingly relayed to the guard. "Thank Allah we have found you—we have come a long way."

"Stop where you are and keep your arms raised!" commanded the guard while Madden and Saeed followed the orders and Saeed continued to praise Allah for reaching this final destination. Madden followed Saeed's lead playing the role of a very tired and confused al-Qaeda recruit from America.

Two men casually dressed in dirty battle dress exited the pickup and approached Saeed and Madden with rifles pointed directly at them.

"What is your business here?" one of the men from the truck asked in an Arabic dialect not commonly spoken in the region.

"My brother, praise Allah for our safe journey, we have had a very challenging journey to reach you," Saeed said, "and now we must continue and do work of Allah."

The guards approached closer and lowered their rifles. Madden started to begin measuring their next moves in dealing with them.

"I am Hamid al-Sowmeli from the Islamic Emirate in Azzan," Saeed identified himself, "with important messages and directives to be directly given to our leader Azzam."

"Let me see the messages," demanded the guard.

Saeed took off his brown canvas backpack and laid it on the ground. He opened the top flap and pulled out a computer CD, showed it to the guard and placed it back in the backpack.

"Only the great one is authorized to view the information, and I must get it to him immediately," Saeed insisted, attempting to motivate the guards into taking them to Azzam's location.

"And you," the guard pointed the barrel of his rifle at Madden, "so you are one of our new recruits ready to wage war on the infidels for our Islamic state—from America, yes?"

Madden knew how to play his part well after personally interrogating the real recruit Johnny Snow and gaining all the information he needed to pass himself off as an idealist Western recruit for al-Qaeda.

Madden acted as if he did not understand what the guard was asking, so Saeed took the cue and translated the guard's statement in English for Madden.

"Yes brother, I am here to do my duty for the Islamic nation," Madden replied, handing all of Snow's al-Qaeda identity papers and passes to the head guard, who appeared with a flashlight to inspect the documents.

"Why did you arrive here so early in the morning and why are you walking?" the head guard asked suspiciously, still holding Saeed and Madden by gunpoint.

"Allahu A'lam," Saeed began, "we had difficulties getting by military checkpoints but convinced the soldiers we were working with the oil pipeline company and of course we had to use bribes to get by."

He told them, "We were able to confiscate a truck from the oil company up near the pipeline and made it as far as we could with the gas available—we ran out of gas and had no other option but to walk in.

"We wanted to use the cell phones to make contact and ask for assistance from you, however, we all know the phones are intercepted and unreliable," Saeed continued. "Most important, the documents and messages I have for Azzam must not fall into the wrong hands, so I played it safe."

The guards lowered their weapons and began speaking softly among themselves. Saeed and Madden still stood motionless in front of the high headlight beams of a Toyota pickup.

Pulling handheld radios out of their jacket pockets, the guards began conversing with one of their leaders at the school regarding what to do with the two unexpected al-Qaeda members who suddenly showed up. Discussions went on for several minutes, with a few pauses and some confusion among the parties on the radio transmissions.

"Your stories check out," announced the head guard as he placed the radio back into his military-style jacket. "I am to take you, Hamid al-Sowmeli, to Azzam's deputy, Qaed Salim, where he will safeguard the documents for Azzam."

"And you, Snow," laughing and pointing his dirty, scarred finger at Madden, "I am to take you to the new recruit camp near the schoolhouse."

"I am ready to serve Allah in any way," Madden played it safe by just providing an enthusiastic reply and acting as if he didn't understand what the guard just relayed to him.

"All right then, get in the truck and I will take you where you need to go," one of the guards ordered. The other guards hunkered down behind the stone wall, getting a few more hours of sleep before the sun came up and it was time for morning prayers.

As Madden and Saeed were being driven down to the al-Qaeda school and complex of tents, Terry and his team were monitoring every move—prepared for any possible contingency. The radio transmissions from Madden's well-hidden personal transmitter were clear to the point of being able to hear the comments of the truck driver as he explained the setup and organization of the al-Qaeda base to Madden and Saeed. Terry was relieved and amused to hear the talkative driver brag to his two passengers about his fighting abilities against the Great Satan.

"We are here," announced the driver as he brought the pickup to a stop in front of a small complex of tents south of the school where an awakened al-Qaeda officer exited a large tent—carefully cradling his AK-47.

"What are you doing here?" the officer demanded. "What important messages do—?"

His sentence was cut off as Madden fired two rounds from his silencer-equipped 9mm Beretta SF pistol into the officer's face, cutting off half of his head.

Seeing Madden pull his pistol, Saeed immediately pulled his service commando knife and pressed it against the throat of the driver.

"You can live or you can die right now," Saeed firmly stated. "Do you understand?"

A slight nod came from the surprised and scared driver as Saeed kept the knife so very close to the driver's neck.

Madden manhandled the bloody corpse and dragged it to the side of the first tent, but not before relieving the dead officer of his radio and gun. Covering the body with a canvas tarp found in the truck, Madden made his way to the driver's side window.

"Okay, brother," now speaking to the driver in perfect Arabic, "you do exactly as we say and will have the choice to live. If not, I will shoot you like your brother."

Gasping for air, the driver nodded his terrified face and asked, "What do you wish from me?"

Madden, having previous experiences in dealing with al-Qaeda prisoners from his Air Force Special Operations and CIA missions in Yemen, knew the driver was probably an al-Qaeda fanatic who would turn on Saeed and him if given the opportunity. There would be no deal-making with the driver—just use him for as long as possible, until he became a threat.

"Where is Azzam's tent?" Madden pointed his pistol at the driver.

"I will not tell you," the driver boldly answered, testing Madden's resolve.

"Kill him and let's put him in the back of the truck and send him to paradise with his brother," Madden ordered, knowing Saeed probably knew his game with the driver while the pressure from the knife was literally drawing blood.

"Kill him and kill him now," Madden firmly ordered Saeed.

"No, no, I will tell you where he is," the now crying and bleeding driver spoke. "Azzam and his family are living in the large, lighted tent—there." He pointed to a nicer and larger tent than the others in the complex. Also unique about Azzam's tent was the proximity to a portable power unit and latrine.

First-class operation, Madden thought to himself, seeing the makeshift latrine.

Swiftly, Saeed wrapped duct tape around the driver's head to ensure his mouth was covered and pushed him out of the truck while Madden tied his hands and feet together. Throwing him into the back of the truck, Madden advised him that he just might live if he stayed put—any moving around or sudden noises would ensure a quick bullet to the back of the head.

"Saeed, where is your backpack?" Madden whispered.

"Let's kill Azzam now and get out of here while we can," an anxious Saeed said.

"Wait, Saeed!" making a halting sign with his hand, Madden thought for a moment, looking frantically for the backpack.

"Head on over to the truck parking area, find us another truck to get us out of here with and set some of the timer grenades out of your backpack in as many vehicles as you can," Madden directed.

"Set them to go off in half an hour. Do you understand, Saeed? Get back here as soon as you find another truck and set the explosives," Madden said. "If something happens to me, you get the hell out of here and head back to the team's hideout."

"Yes, sir, I understand," Saeed said.

"Capt. Terry," said Madden, whispering low on his hidden radio transmitter, "Do you copy what I instructed Saeed to do?"

"Affirmative," Terry confirmed, "your radios are working well."

"Do you have time for a short update on your extraction plan?" Terry asked.

"Standby, Captain, I'm ensuring Saeed is receiving your transmissions."

Holding off starting the truck, Saeed gave Madden a thumbs-up that he was receiving the radio transmissions and waiting for Terry to relay the details of the plan.

"Your friend with the aircraft relayed to us that she would be able to make the landing at the road," Terry continued. "She was madder than hell for such a short-notice request but confirmed she would be here at 0800 hours versus our planned 0900 hours. Will that affect your plans?"

A surprised Madden looked at Saeed for his reaction and got another thumbs-up and a nod from his scarved head wrap.

"Does she have a clue what we are facing?" Madden asked, almost afraid of the answer.

"No!" Terry confirmed. "She believes it is just a routine pickup of oil pipeline workers needing a lift out of an inaccessible area."

"You might relay to her there may be some hostile forces near the landing site and that we will be very much in a hurry to load and take off immediately—is that clear?"

"Anything else, mate?" asked Terry.

"In about five minutes, I'm going to be entering Azzam's tent and finishing the mission," he told Terry, knowing full well everything rested on the next few minutes.

Now, more than three years after his wife and two daughters were blown to bits by Azzam's assassins in Florida, Madden had his own plan for the demise of this terrorist leader. Unbeknownst to Saeed and the SAS team, Madden planned to conduct a brief, painful interrogation of Azzam in an attempt to find who in al-Qaeda was responsible for the heist of the Pakistan theater nuclear bomb—then he would be executed.

"Terry, this is Madden. Over."

"Go ahead, Madden, copy you loud and clear."

"I'm going to use the nice camp radio that we took off one of the al-Qaeda guards and start a little diversion prior to entering Azzam's tent," Madden explained. "Saeed, you copy?"

Now at the truck parking lot, getting ready to set the timers for the explosives, Saeed replied. "Copy. Setting the charges now."

"Terry, in a few minutes, have your team shoot some flares on the other side of the school near the new recruit camp," Madden instructed, "and at the same time the flares are landing at the camp, I'm going to get on this captured radio and announce in Arabic that Israeli commandos have been detected raiding the camp from the wadi south of the school. That should give us a quick diversion to snatch Azzam and give Saeed time to get a truck around here to pick me up and make a dash for you and the landing site."

"You crazy Yank," Terry mumbled over the radio. "Firing red flares off in five minutes. Over."

"Thanks." Madden thought for a moment. "Saeed, did you copy?"

"Yes, I have a commandeered Humvee ready and will have the explosive charges situated in the truck parking lot ready to go off when you give me the word. Over."

CHAPTER
35

"Attention, brothers, we have spotted Israeli commandos on the north side of the school near the recruit training center." Madden made the excited announcement in Arabic as Terry's team continued to fire flares.

Complete confusion followed as men and women staggered out of their tents while seeing the menacing and sinister glow of red flares near their camp and hearing the incredible announcements on the radio that Israeli commandos were infiltrating the compound.

"Hurry, brothers, hurry in the name of Allah, God is great! We have discovered the Jews' assassin group and are fighting them now." Madden sounded convincing as he made more radio calls calling for action by the compound while keeping a keen eye on Azzam's tent. The tent's lights immediately went off, but no one emerged from the tent.

The crescendo of AK-47 rifle fire was increasing throughout the compound, with tracer bullets filling the clear, brilliant night sky. Madden listened to the excited voices over the radio as al-Qaeda officers and leaders tried to determine the extent of the Israeli raid and plans to counter it. Numerous orders were being given by various leaders, with no clue of the circumstances surrounding them.

"BOOM!" A deafening, bright explosion suddenly lit the night sky with an apocalyptic black mushroom cloud rising above the truck parking area.

Madden immediately hit the ground, as more and more al-Qaeda were racing toward the flares, half dressed, with their weapons.

"Nice work, Saeed," voiced Madden over the radio, praising the sudden explosion. "Have you still got us a ride out of here?"

No contact with Saeed could be heard. Madden desperately attempted contact several times.

Capt. Terry was also monitoring every radio transmission between Madden and Saeed and was concerned about not hearing from Saeed. Terry's team knew that without Saeed's ability to pick up an escape vehicle, Madden had no hope of survival, and the team members would need to extract themselves without Madden.

"Saeed? Over." Madden continued to attempt contact while monitoring the confused guards stationed around Azzam's tent. Picking himself off the ground and still wearing his al-Qaeda battle dress clothing, he ran toward the guards with a captured radio in hand, yelling at the guards to join the fight against the Israeli commandos.

The scared, excited guards pointed their weapons at Madden, not sure if he was friend or foe, while inside the tent a voice was heard that Madden knew most distinctly.

"Brothers, God is great," came the man's voice from inside. "I order you to proceed to the attack and repel the invaders. I will follow you soon to the attack."

As the guards hurried to join in on the diversion attack, Madden made one last attempt to make radio contact with Saeed prior to entering Azzam's tent.

"Saeed this is Madden, over." Nothing.

"If you can hear me, I am a minute away from entering Azzam's tent and completing the mission," Madden coolly stated. "Again, if you hear me, please get over here with an escape vehicle now. Over."

Order was slowly being restored to the al-Qaeda compound, with the red flares burning out and no sign of Israeli commandos. Sporadic gunfire lingered as leaders gathered their members back to their tents, and a small team of al-Qaeda guards searched for the party setting off the flares and causing the commotion over the radios.

Many reasoned it was an ineffective harassment operation by Houthi rebels.

Pulling out his 9mm Beretta pistol and silencer, preparing to enter Azzam's tent to complete the mission, Madden noticed an Army surplus, olive-drab Humvee heading his direction with full head beams bouncing up and down on the impoverished road heading straight for him. Hitting the dirt and preparing for the worst, he saw the front headlights begin flashing on and off. Staying low on the ground in the dirt, he readied his AK-47—he was prepared to kill the driver and steal the truck for his getaway.

"Shit, it's Saeed," a relieved Madden murmured as Saeed used a flashlight beam to code out the friendly signal. Lifting himself up from the dirt path, Madden ran to the driver's side of the Humvee, still steadying his pistol in the event it was not Saeed.

"Damn, Saeed, it's good to see you," Madden gasped.

"Let's get out of here while we still can," a nervous and excited Saeed pleaded. "Is Azzam dead?"

"Madden, this is Terry over, get the hell out of there," was heard over Madden's radio.

"On our way," Madden calmly said. "Saeed, move the Humvee over to near that sewage ditch near the junction in the road." Madden pointed to where he wanted Saeed to wait for him.

"Saeed, Terry, give me five minutes to get back here. If I'm not here, get the hell out," Madden instructed.

Bullets now ripped up the dirt and ricocheted off nearby structures. Madden looked up at the ridge where the flares were shot and saw most of the terrorists and their recruits still attempting to determine where the Israeli commandos were. They were sure putting up a good fight against a bunch of burning red flares.

"Saeed, hold up for a moment." Madden grabbed his arm inside the Humvee and said, "Listen to what I am instructing Terry to do now—it will be quick."

"Terry, this is Madden, do you read me over?"

"Damn it, Madden, get the fuck out of there now," an excited Terry transmitted.

"Do we still have drone cover overhead now?"

"Yes, the drone is prepared to cover our withdrawal if required," Terry answered, annoyed that Madden was taking too long to depart.

"Terry, contact the drone operations center and have them drop their two Hellfire missiles on the red flares immediately," Madden added, as the intensity of chaotic gunfire was increasing from all directions. "Advise them the target area is well out of range of collateral damage to the school."

"Calling it in now and get out of there now—that is an order, Madden!"

"Saeed, get to the meeting-up point," Madden yelled over the barrage of explosions.

Saeed nodded and accelerated up the road to the designated rendezvous point while Madden headed again toward Azzam's tent. Reloading his pistol and placing it back into its holster, he ensured his stolen AK-47 was loaded and his al-Qaeda tan battle dress fatigues could pass as any recruit in training.

Cautiously, Madden made his way to the entrance of Azzam's tent and pushed away a flap, attempting to find Azzam while giving particular care to positioning the rifle if required.

"One good shot and I am out of here," Madden thought to himself, searching desperately for Azzam inside the tent lit only by a single kerosene lantern. Still hearing the explosions and rifle fire surrounding the schoolhouse and the camp, he was just about to turn around and head out toward the waiting Humvee and Saeed when—CRACK!

Madden fell to the ground from a hit to the side of the head by the butt of an AK-47. A dazed Madden lay on the ground with a severe cut to his ear and neck. His hands were roughly tied behind his back and he was dragged to a small, well-worn, wooden chair where he was clumsily manhandled in place.

In a semiconscious state, trying desperately to regain some sense, he heard two men speaking in Arabic as they ripped his clothes off looking for anything to identify the intruder. One older, bearded guard continued holding a Russian-built pistol to Madden's head.

"So is this one of our new recruits from America? A Johnny Snow?" a cynical and very calm al-Qaeda officer asked, looking at the nearly naked body of Madden sitting on the chair.

"Well, Mr. Johnny Snow, we find it interesting that you have various American military tattoos," said the senior al-Qaeda officer. He swung back his fist and punched Madden hard, knocking him to the tent's floor rug again.

Two officers threw him back into the chair.

As Madden slowly regained some awareness, he heard sounds of rifle fire and explosions, even as the guards repeatedly knocked him out of the chair by blows to the body and face.

"I seek protection in Allah from the American Satan," a barely audible Madden said in Arabic as the bodyguard and officer stopped their beatings, now confused how this recruit spoke passable Arabic.

"I believe you *are* the American Satan," came a voice in very proper English from one of the al-Qaeda officers.

Out of a dark corner of the tent, Madden made out a person sitting on a rug watching the entire encounter while slowly smoking a cigarette. He sat motionless observing Madden while stroking his long, gray beard. Madden could only surmise this was Azzam, who he knew spoke perfect English with all the al-Qaeda propaganda programs he had reviewed prior to the mission.

Slowly the man got to his feet and entered the lighted area of the tent, glaring down on Madden with a slight grin on his face and a glare from the John Lennon-style eyeglasses he was wearing.

Madden's bruised, bleeding face turned to look up at the man. No doubt in his mind, he was facing Azzam—the architect of thousands of murders of innocent people.

"In the name of Allah, let's kill him now and be done with him," yelled one of the heavily armed, gray-bearded lieutenants pressing the barrel of his rifle against Madden's neck.

"Not so fast, al-Awlaki," Azzam directed, cleaning his glasses with a white cloth—still smiling at Madden. "There is much to tell Robert Madden before he departs for his Great Satan."

Azzam knew the al-Qaeda recruit, Johnny Snow, was indeed Robert Madden. The mastermind of directing a U.S. drone strike against Anwar Aldawasari, their beloved al-Qaeda spiritual leader in Yemen, and the killer of his brother, Humza, in some place called New Mexico in the United States.

"Robert Madden," one guard said, using his rifle to turn Madden's face toward Azzam.

"Yes, Madden, as you probably already know, I arranged for your wife and two daughters to enter hell," Azzam grinned. "You'll be seeing them soon, very soon."

Boiling with uncontrollable anger hearing Azzam's testimony, Madden jumped up from the wooden chair and launched at Azzam, only to be restrained and severely beaten by the guards.

Azzam nonchalantly cleaned his glasses again, smoked a cigarette, and looked down at the beaten Madden on the floor.

"Interesting, Madden. I must credit you for getting this far to kill me, but that little charade of Israeli commandos was too much. We had a good idea this new recruit of ours, Johnny Snow, was compromised a while back, but we did want to see who would take his place." He sneered.

"Did we put on a good show for you here, Mr. Madden?" Azzam laughed while he translated what he said in Arabic.

"Take him down to the recruit firing range and tie him up to one of the posts holding the targets," Azzam ordered his top lieutenant. "Tomorrow we will film Madden's execution at the hands of our recruits and spread the pictures around the Arab world to our brothers in jihad."

"Our recruits' first kill, first blood," added one of the guards, roughly pulling Madden's shirt back on him.

Azzam was pleased about the publicity and notoriety his al-Qaeda family would gain by the online, real-time execution of the Great Satan Robert Madden by fanatical recruits. What a recruiting opportunity for al-Qaeda and headline news for Al Jazeera.

"Give my best to your wife and daughters in hell," Azzam gleefully commented as Madden was brought to his feet by two guards.

Both grabbed an arm, pulled him out of the tent and dragged him across the gravel road to the empty firing range. They tied Madden's body to one of the range's wooden target posts that was nearly shattered with all of the bullet markings due to months of firearms training.

"What a great opportunity for our recruits—the opportunity to have a shot at Rob Madden," one guard laughed.

"Praises belong to Allah," the other guard said excitedly, raising his hands to the heavens.

THUMP. THUMP. The two guards fell to the ground, and Madden was left clumsily hanging on a range target, conscious enough to see the two guards fall to the ground.

Now struggling to free himself, Madden viewed what appeared to be a lone al-Qaeda recruit moving fast toward the two downed guards and placing one more round in each guard's head. He reloaded his pistol and reattached the silencer to the barrel.

The recruit turned his attention to Madden, who was still strung up on the range target, resigned to the fact that he could be in his last moments of life.

"Madden!" the recruit yelled, attempting to get his attention while holding on to him and shaking him. "Madden, look at me, can you move?"

"Yes, I can walk. Saeed, is that you?" a confused Madden asked.

"Keep quiet and continue to play the role of a prisoner."

Madden nodded his head while Saeed loosened the ropes tying him, the pistol still pointing at him for show.

"Thought you left to get out of here with the SAS boys—that was the plan," Madden muttered quietly. "Did they get out all right?"

"Your wireless hidden in your clothes was not found by the guards, so we have been listening to everything including your little reception with Azzam," Saeed whispered while untying Madden from the target.

"Capt. Terry ordered a hold on the extraction time and authorized me to turn around in an attempt to find you among all the damn confusion around this hell hole."

As Saeed helped Madden get to the hidden commandeered Humvee, the confusion and sporadic gunfire and explosions were slowly subsiding. Al-Qaeda leaders were on their radios ordering all to return to the recruit camp and stop firing their weapons. As Madden and Saeed monitored an al-Qaeda radio taken from one of the dead guards, it was obvious the diversion actions taken by Capt. Terry's team were effective, but finished.

"Capt. Terry, this is Saeed. How do you read me, over?"

"Loud and clear," Terry immediately replied. "Do you have Madden? Over."

"Yes, sir, he is rather beaten up, but okay," Saeed replied, carefully observing Madden, who gave him a thumbs-up.

"Saeed, are you able to depart the school area in your Humvee without getting into a firefight on your way back here? Over."

"Negative, from what we are observing, it appears the little diversion we created is over and the al-Qaeda leaders will soon discover the results of some of our handiwork, including a few dead guards scattered around the road and camp areas," Saeed said as Madden dressed his wounds.

"Okay, Saeed, here's the plan. Sit tight where you are for now," Terry instructed. "We have two backup drones in position over us now, and in two minutes one will release two of its Hellfire missiles in the recruit camp—be prepared to move quickly out of there once they hit, do you copy? Over!"

"Yes, sir," Saeed replied.

"What about Kelly Carson and her airplane?" Madden said to Saeed. "Will she still be able to help us?"

Terry transmitted, "I heard your conversation and yes, she said she would be there."

"Good ol' Kelly," Madden muttered to himself, trying to force a smile on his bruised and battered face.

Sitting in the cab of their al-Qaeda Humvee waiting for the two missiles to strike their targets, Saeed and Madden briefly discussed their best course of action.

"Saeed, there is no way we are just going to escape here without taking care of Azzam—either we take him with us or throw a couple grenades in his tent."

"Are you out of your mind? You're lucky to be alive and even luckier I came back to look for you. I could have been killed, you asshole," a distraught Saeed vented. "When the two missiles explode, I am heading straight for the hideout and hopefully your friend with the airplane will fly us out of here—you got that, Madden? No stupid detours to pick up or kill Azzam."

Madden didn't say anything—just nodded his head allowing Saeed to speak his mind and let out his frustrations, knowing full well he would probably change his mind.

"Okay, Saeed," Madden replied, uncharacteristically calmly.

"Oh, fuck you, Madden," Saeed said. "So what's your plan for Azzam?"

Madden and Saeed had just finished discussing the plan for Azzam when massive explosions ripped apart the al-Qaeda recruit training center and the vehicle assembly area next to it. Both men held their hands to their ears due to the deafening blast so near them and watched orange fireballs erupt into the night sky followed by thick, swirling black smoke that caused confusion and havoc among the survivors of the attack.

Loud screams and yells for help could be heard coming from all directions within the al-Qaeda camps, but to the amazement of both men, the school and its nearby village of families were not targeted or touched.

"Step on it, Saeed, let's go while the getting is good," Madden yelled.

"What does that mean? 'Step on it' and 'Getting is good?'" Saeed asked, not knowing the American slang.

"It means let's get the hell out of here!" Madden said.

With that, Saeed slammed the Humvee into drive and raced across the firing range heading for the al-Qaeda camp, encountering many dazed al-Qaeda members searching for friends and medical assistance. While heading straight for the camp and Azzam's tent, they passed various vehicles heading toward the missile strike site with their headlights bouncing up and down as they navigated across the barren, rocky camp interior. Survivors of the attack were yelling, "There is no power nor strength except with Allah."

Shouting fake, useless orders in Arabic out the windows of their fast-moving Humvee and on their stolen al-Qaeda radios, Madden and Saeed returned to within a few yards of Azzam's tent. Madden held a loaded AK-47 ready to mercilessly spray Azzam's tent with lead, hoping to kill everyone inside.

As Madden lifted the rifle, Saeed held Madden back as he pointed to a group of what appeared to be senior al-Qaeda leaders heading for the school. Madden also noticed the group and immediately tossed the AK-47 on the floorboard while asking Saeed for his 9mm pistol.

"Looks like they are running for the safe haven of the school building, knowing it will never be targeted—smart move on their part," Madden said.

Mass confusion and terror were evident throughout the compound as al-Qaeda members saw the school and found no collateral damage to it.

None of the al-Qaeda members paid any attention to the Humvee as it dashed for Azzam and his senior leaders, who were running for the sanctuary of the school building.

"Slow it up and get as close to Azzam as you can," Madden ordered as he positioned himself in the left rear window of the Humvee with his pistol in hand and AK-47 on the seat next to him. "Saeed, don't get into this fight, you just prepare to get us out of here once I hit Azzam."

Now nearly on Azzam and his group, Saeed began yelling out his window in perfect Arabic, "Azzam, get in! Let us seek the safety of the school immediately, in Allah's protection."

Azzam's group stopped in front of the headlights of the Humvee and were very much relieved and thankful for the offer of a ride to the school.

"Barakallahu feek, May the blessings of Allah be upon you," was shouted as the al-Qaeda leaders made their way to the Humvee.

With the leaders within pistol range and the headlights providing decent illumination on the targets, Madden jumped out of the Humvee, moved to a shooter's stance and fired his pistol at each al-Qaeda leader—careful not to hit the distinct body profile of Azzam. Madden's Special Forces training came back as he reloaded the pistol and again searched for targets until there was only one left standing—Azzam.

Azzam was confused and dazed, being in the center of a group of his leaders suddenly slaughtered by an unknown assassin. He immediately turned and scurried for the school while Madden and Saeed were in hot pursuit with the Humvee.

"Why didn't you kill him?" Saeed screamed at Madden. "What are you doing?"

"Get as close as you can to him, and I'll take it from there," a seething Madden directed.

"Oh, screw you, Madden," Saeed replied while driving the Humvee directly to the side of the running Azzam.

"Stop now!" Madden yelled as he jumped out of the rear door. With all the energy and pent-up rage he could summon, he ran after Azzam.

Within a few feet of the international terrorist, Madden jumped on Azzam and threw him to the ground, landing blow after blow to Azzam's face and body, like a rabid dog attacking its prey.

Saeed released the safety on his AK-47 and was a moment away from firing a few rounds into Azzam when Madden sprang up and pushed the barrel away as the rifle fired a short burst.

"We're taking him with us," Madden shouted. Azzam's body lay motionless in the lights of the Humvee.

Madden searched the Humvee for rope and belts to tie up Azzam.

"Madden, have you gone crazy?" Saeed attempted to reason with Madden in the middle of the al-Qaeda assault, surrounded by explosions, gunfire and the screams of those seeking safety from the apocalyptic scene in the camp.

"Get over here, Saeed, and help me tie this bastard up and put a gag in his mouth."

Suddenly, from the scattered fires caused by the Hellfire missile impacts and the early morning rays of the sun reaching over the lifeless ridge, Madden made out several small bands of disorganized al-Qaeda members, leaders and recruits approaching from the north side of the school. Green-colored tracer bullets from several AK-47s were whizzing past, with a couple dinging the Humvee.

Both men hit the ground hard to avoid any gunfire and awkwardly dragged Azzam to the cargo compartment and threw him in the Humvee, not sure he was even still alive after Madden's beating.

Madden retrieved a small leather purse concealed under Azzam's clothing. At this, Azzam stirred, semiconscious, and knew only too well the significance of what had just been just taken from him.

Saeed sped off, with Madden covering their escape with gunfire using rifles taken from the dead al-Qaeda leaders. Saeed hit the accelerator and headed for the gravel road they had previously entered from earlier, leaving behind the mayhem, destruction, and death they were totally responsible for.

"Capt. Terry, this is Saeed. How copy? Over." Saeed tried to raise the team. "Capt. Terry, do you read me?"

Terry and his SAS team had seen the whole operation from their hideout several hundred yards away, feeling somewhat guilty that they were not joining in the fight with Madden and Saeed, but they were all professional soldiers and knew their responsibilities. The SAS team had readied their vehicles for their risky departure and were prepared to provide Madden and Azzam with any covering fire support as they departed the camp.

"Sgt. Ryan!" Terry barked as he continued to monitor the action at the camp while trying to make out with his binoculars the escape vehicle supposedly coming their way.

"Sir!" Ryan immediately responded.

"Make sure you are in constant contact with the Special Ops command at Djibouti and stress our immediate need for another armed drone to cover our escape," Terry ordered and added, "and make sure you keep us advised of your contact with this pilot friend of Madden's."

"Sir, recently advised by Djibouti that an additional drone is airborne and on its way to our position," Ryan said.

"Good!" Terry muttered while still eyeing the slowly decreasing action at the camp with his long-range binoculars, still searching in vain for the escaping Humvee.

"What about the aircraft?" Terry asked. "Any further word from her?"

"Sir, last transmission from her came through our VHF radio an hour ago stating she planned to be at the landing strip at 0730," Ryan reported, "and it's currently 0700 now."

"Okay Ryan, continue to broadcast in the blind across all radio frequencies and let her know we will be ready for her now, do you understand?"

At the makeshift airstrip on the dirt road, Sgts. Evans and Williams posted various small colored flags along the length of the airstrip and finally placed two of the team's pickup trucks on each side of the estimated touchdown area, facing away from the airstrip. The lights from the trucks would help the pilot make the early-morning approach.

"Evans and Williams, over!" Terry transmitted over the team radio network, "is everything set up as Madden instructed? Any problems?"

"All set, Captain," Evans replied.

"Expect aircraft arrival at 0730," Terry announced over the radio, "all team members check in and acknowledge. Over." That's when he heard Saeed radioing in.

"Saeed, relieved to hear from you, what's your status? Is Madden okay?"

"Sir, Madden is beat up a little but fine, and we are rapidly moving toward the airstrip now," answered Saeed as Madden was positioning himself in the Humvee's roof opening with an AK-47. "Request assistance from your team in marking the way to the airstrip with flares—it is the only way we will find the airstrip from here."

"Roger, Saeed. Copy all," Terry affirmed. "From our position, we'll provide you with enough covering fire as possible until you are right up on the hideout, then we will all race to the airstrip."

The SAS team readied what weapons and ammunition they had at the hideout, then took up various positions around the empty desert landscape, prepared to challenge al-Qaeda members pursuing Madden and Saeed.

"Saeed, we have visitors coming our way," Madden yelled down to Saeed as the sound of bullets began whistling around the Humvee, with numerous green tracer flashes racing by into the dusty terrain.

"Faster, Saeed. Faster!" screamed Madden as he began firing at pursuing vehicles rapidly approaching their rear.

As the hurtling Humvee came closer to the hideout, Terry's team began firing their weapons at the pursuing vehicles on Madden's tail, with many taking direct hits and suddenly stopping as smoke and flames erupted.

The race continued, with the Humvee taking various hits and Saeed attempting to navigate the dirt-and-gravel road as the dark of night faded away, with the sun rising on the ridges to the east.

"Madden, Madden, I got the flares in sight," Saeed shouted.

Reloading his AK-47, Madden turned his attention to the road ahead and could make out the team firing from the hideout and the lifesaving flares marking the way to the airstrip.

"Terry, this is Madden. If you hear me, we are following the flares to the airstrip. Many thanks for setting them up—you'd better be hauling your asses, too."

"See you at the airstrip," Terry acknowledged as the remainder of his team members picked up their weapons and rejoined at the hideout, preparing for the quick dash to the airstrip and possible covering fire for the arrival of Madden and Saeed.

"Sgt. Ryan, any words from the aircraft?" Terry asked, hoping for some kind of reassuring words as their vehicles bounced their way to the airstrip. They could still hear the sound of small-arms fire being targeted at Madden's Humvee.

"Sir, the last transmission from the pilot was that she would be here at exactly 0730," Ryan answered nervously. "I'll continue to attempt contact, sir."

"When we arrive at the airstrip, we'll set up a defensive perimeter twenty meters from the approach end of the runway," Terry barked into the radio. "Evans and Williams, is everything ready for the aircraft arrival?"

"Sir, we have the aircraft in sight," Evans announced over the radio, "and we are popping smoke now on the airstrip—green and red. Over."

"Midland Team, Midland Team, this is YN78765 on final approach, do you copy? Over."

Suddenly the VHF radio came to life with the voice of Kelly Carson and her twin-engine Otter broadcasting her arrival to the makeshift airstrip.

"YN78765 we are certainly glad to see you. Wind is coming from the southwest at six knots, red and green smoke are in line with the runway," Ryan relayed. He couldn't hold back his relief in seeing the aircraft. "Ma'am, we certainly are glad to see you."

"Knock off the ass-kissing and tell me what the hell is going on down south of the airstrip—looks like a bunch of vehicles racing this way," Carson noted anxiously and screamed, "and it looks like they are firing on another vehicle in front of them!"

Still in awe of the drama she was witnessing from 500 feet above the ground, Carson was just completing her final approach checklist of setting flaps, engine settings, and monitoring airspeeds for a short, rough landing when she noticed a couple of tracer bullets whizzing below her aircraft. Carson was configured in a deep descent to the airstrip and adjusted the throttles and airspeed for a very slow, soft landing on a rough gravel road.

"Thank God she made it, she made it," roared Terry as he and his team observed the plane make a steep drop to land a few hundred yards in front of them. Relief could be seen on all the faces of Terry's team as they hit the accelerator to reach the landing site as quickly as possible.

"Saeed, this is Terry. What is your status? Over."

"Madden and I are just over the rise heading for the landing site, and we're still heavily engaged in running firefights with al-Qaeda in pursuit."

Terry could hear the fire from Madden's AK-47 in the background as he continued to spray the approaching vehicles with deadly accuracy.

"Sir," a very nervous and stressed Saeed called to Terry, "recommend you use every available weapon to cover our arrival. They are coming in force."

"Very good, Saeed, we'll cover your ass when we see you approaching. Out," Terry said. His team was just arriving at the airstrip and taking up defensive positions. There was only one way out—the girl and her twin-engine Otter.

"Shit, what have I gotten myself into?" Carson vented as she expertly dropped the twin-engine cargo plane onto the improvised airstrip. Dust and rocks were swept behind the aircraft as the powerful turboprop engines were idled back.

As the aircraft slowed and began making a U-turn, vehicles and men made a quick dash toward her.

"Screw you, Madden, screw you, you son of a bitch," a scared and frustrated Carson screamed as she focused on turning the aircraft around for immediate takeoff.

Once in place, she began following her short and rough field takeoff checklist, praying that the group of armed men wearing tan battle field clothes approaching the aircraft were friends of Madden.

As the propellers were adjusted to idle, blowing back hot wind and sand, two men made their way to the nose of the aircraft. To protect their faces from the gale-force winds of the plane's jet wash, they covered their eyes with goggles and the traditional scarves that were part of their disguises. Carson slid back the cockpit window and motioned for the men to make their way to the cargo hatch on the rear, left side of the aircraft. Both nodded while making their way around the spinning propellers.

They found the latches that opened the cargo door and the access ladder. The men boarded quickly and made their way, passing the empty cargo area, to the cockpit where they found Carson at the controls of the aircraft.

"Who in the fuck are you, and where the hell is Madden?" Carson screamed at Terry while chewing a wad of bubble gum and clutching the sweat-drenched collar of his shirt as if she were going to punch him in the mouth.

After their brief encounter, Terry knew who was in charge— she was.

"Carson, we do not have time now," Terry stressed. "Recommend you prepare to get us out of here at once—I'm loading my team's wounded and equipment now."

"Team!" Carson yelled, bewildered and wary of the passengers who she could see taking up firing positions around the parked trucks near her aircraft.

"Where the hell is Madden? I was told by that son of a bitch that he needed a ride for himself and a few of his co-workers out on the pipeline doing some routine maintenance."

Helping some of his team load equipment onto the aircraft through the cargo hatch, Terry heard Carson yelling at him through the sound of the aircraft's idling propellers. Shaking his head in frustration, he directed his men to get the equipment and wounded men secured as he made his way again to the cockpit and sat in the co-pilot seat, which was strewn with aviation charts and aircraft performance manuals.

"Where's the co-pilot?" Terry asked.

"You're it, asshole!" Carson replied. "Don't need no stinkin' co-pilot. The company saves a ton of money by not hiring one. Anyway, they ask too many questions and get in the way. Anything else, smart ass?

"Who are you, and where is Madden?" Carson asked again, wondering what a team of oil and gas line maintenance workers did to have half of the al-Qaeda soldiers in Yemen coming after them with trucks and guns.

Terry looked back into the cargo compartment and was satisfied his team was taking the necessary precaution of loading required survival equipment, as others held defensive positions around the trucks surrounding the aircraft. His men were now actively engaged in providing covering fire for Madden's Humvee, aiming at the parade of al-Qaeda vehicles—from small pickup trucks to confiscated military personnel carriers.

"Ma'am, Mr. Madden is in that lead Humvee you see just coming over the rise in the road," Terry said as both looked out the right cockpit window at the approaching firefight. "We're British Army soldiers. My team's covering him until he arrives. Then you can fly us the fuck out of here."

As the rifle fire and explosions drew closer, Terry's team members increased their rate of fire to cover Madden's Humvee. Madden and Saeed were now a hundred yards from the aircraft.

Getting her mind back to the task at hand, Carson nervously and quickly reviewed the Twin Otter's takeoff performance requirements for a primitive runway and short field takeoff. Though she was very experienced at takeoffs and landings near the hostile oil and gas fields around Yemen, never had she faced the daunting task currently before her. She could make out tracer bullets hitting and ricocheting off the trucks defending her aircraft as Madden's vehicle drew closer.

"Carson, I'm going out there till Madden gets here," Terry hollered up to the cockpit. She nodded her head while running some figures on her weight and balance sheet.

Terry grabbed some extra ammunition and a couple of rocket-propelled grenades as he and two other team members headed back out to provide cover fire for the quickly approaching Madden and Saeed.

"Sgt. Ryan!" Terry found that his communications specialist was remaining in contact with Special Operations at Djibouti while at the same time firing his AK-47 to provide cover fire.

"Ryan," said Terry, who was yelling in Ryan's ear due to the intense noise of gunfire and explosions, "immediately relay to our drone people that we need those Hellfire missiles executed now on the targets behind Madden. They should see them on their sensors."

"Tango 5674, we are Danger Close and declaring a Broken Arrow, requesting priority close air support from all available drones and allied aircraft—how copy Tango 5674?" Ryan yelled over the satellite communications radio for a second time.

The drone pilot acknowledged the Broken Arrow distress call and relayed to Ryan that they had positive optics on the chase and had directed two more drones toward the fight.

"Ryan, this is Tango 5674," the drone pilot acknowledged over the satellite phone. "I have good acquisition on the targets, positive contact on your beacons, more drones on the way—when do you want it?"

"Now, now, now!" Ryan roared over the radio, with Terry preparing his team for the upcoming drone support and close explosions.

BOOM. BOOM.

Two huge explosions threw orange fireballs into the dawn, filling the skies with black smoke and debris falling to the desert floor. The sounds of gunfire subsided. The pursuers were either dead or injured due to damage from the missiles.

"Sgt. Ryan, please pass on to Special Ops and the drone pilot that they just saved our lives, and we will be departing here pronto," Terry said, adding, "great job in keeping contact with the outside for us, Ryan. We depend on you."

"Yes, sir, it was close," Ryan said, his voice shaky.

"Too close. Let's get out of here while we can," Terry commanded while helping Ryan gather up his communications gear and sprint to the waiting aircraft.

"Oh my God," Carson mumbled as she witnessed the deadly devastation of men and vehicles just a few hundred yards from where she and her aircraft were sitting. "Madden, where are you?" she said to herself, searching the massive cloud of dust and debris for his vehicle.

After what seemed like an eternity, Madden and Saeed's bullet-ridden Humvee broke through the cloud and limped into the cluster of vehicles near the plane. All eyes now watched Madden and Saeed as they opened the Humvee's rear cargo compartment.

Pulling out what appeared to be a bruised and injured al-Qaeda officer, tied up but very much alive, Madden and Saeed worked to get the man out of the cargo hold as other team members ran to assist.

Terry hardly recognized Madden and Saeed, who in their filthy, blood-soaked tan uniforms could have easily been mistaken for al-Qaeda soldiers. Madden, who looked as though he had been in a barroom brawl, was limping and had many cuts and bruises to the head. Saeed looked about the same, except for the head injuries.

"Good to see you, old boy," Terry said to Madden as they watched the tied-up bad guy being carried to the loading area by Terry's team. "Who you takin' prisoner now, Madden?"

Madden turned around with a slight smile from a face that looked as if he had been in the ring with a professional boxer.

"Good to see you, Terry, never thought we would make it," Madden added, having a difficult time talking with his busted lips. "Thanks for waiting for us."

Terry's team remained poised at their assigned defensive positions covering the plane, waiting for orders to board the aircraft.

"Okay, men, let's get a move on and get loaded on the aircraft," Terry ordered as his team members made their way to the cargo hatch while the blast from the hot exhaust sprayed dust and debris on them.

While Madden and Terry were discussing their escape flight out and the team was finishing up loading the prisoner and themselves, Carson pulled back the cockpit window and raised her middle finger at Madden. He just smiled and waved at her.

"Let's get the hell out of here, Terry—we've had enough for one day."

Madden made a beeline to the co-pilot's entry hatch as Terry entered the plane from the side cargo hatch. As Madden buckled himself into the co-pilot seat, Carson reached over and gave him a hug, then shoved some paper towels into his hands to clean his wounds.

"Thanks, Carson. We owe you our lives," Madden whispered to her as her large sunglasses masked the tears coming down her face.

"Hurry, you assholes, hurry up and get tied down," Carson yelled back to the cargo compartment.

Terry was sitting in the austere jump seat between the pilot and co-pilot's seats, which was typically used by an instructor or student pilots to monitor the pilot's performance. He had a full view of the landscape—primarily the dirt-and-gravel runway ahead of them.

"My God!" Terry yelled loud enough for the men in the back to hear, "we have two light pickup trucks with heavy machine guns coming at us from the road to the east."

"Everyone on the floor," Terry ordered as Carson quickly accomplished critical takeoff checklist items.

Without a word, Carson set the aircraft's trim and pushed the throttles forward for full power while adjusting the variable pitch propellers for maximum thrust on a short field takeoff. Carson was facing what in aviation terms is called "cockpit saturation," where a lone pilot must fly an aircraft under catastrophic, dangerous conditions without help from a co-pilot who would normally be responsible for backing up the pilot-in-command.

But Madden, who was sitting in the co-pilot's seat, had flown hundreds of hours in a Twin Otter and would assist Carson as needed by calling off airspeeds and monitoring engine gauges, leaving the burden of flying the aircraft to Carson.

The two powerful Pratt & Whitney engines roared to full power, with the propellers spraying dust and sand a hundred yards behind the aircraft. The Otter slowly began its bumpy takeoff roll down the dirt road. Carson meticulously managed the control wheel, holding the aircraft steady while accelerating to takeoff speed with no relief from the potholes in the dirt road.

"Madden, call the airspeed off to me and hold the throttles full forward," Carson ordered.

"Thirty knots," Madden announced, staring at the airspeed indicator while holding the throttles to their maximum power settings.

All eyes in the cargo compartment were focused on Carson as she skillfully began raising the nose of the aircraft while the main wheels continued their rough roll down the road.

"Forty knots, forty-five," an excited Madden yelled as he and Terry watched the two al-Qaeda trucks fire on the quickly accelerating aircraft. Tracer bullets darted across the early morning sky. One slammed into the cargo compartment and exited out the other side. The men in the compartment were now making every effort to lie as low as possible while surrounding themselves with equipment and cargo to protect themselves from the spray of bullets.

"Fifty knots, oh shit," Madden screamed in pain as a bullet creased his right shoulder and slammed into the Otter's instrument panel, knocking out all flight instruments. Besides the various debris floating in the cockpit from the instrument panel's implosion, there now was a large hole in the nose of the aircraft. Strong streams of air were blowing in, but the aircraft was still flying.

"Help me with the throttles," Carson ordered as she continued working the controls—seemingly oblivious to the catastrophic event in the cockpit. Terry, now realizing the gravity of the situation, leaped forward from his jump seat and held the throttles while attempting to assess Madden's injury.

BOOM, BOOM, BOOM! Suddenly, the right engine was hit by machine gun fire, causing fire and black smoke to spew from the engine cowling. The immediate effect of losing any engine on takeoff is a critical lack of airspeed and control. Carson took quick action to configure the aircraft flight controls to fly on one engine—a dangerous situation even under normal circumstances. If the correct rudder control inputs are not applied instantly, an aircraft will certainly crash on takeoff.

Carson heard the explosion in the right engine and saw the flames and smoke trailing behind the aircraft. Still working to control the difficult short field takeoff, she immediately took all necessary actions to save and control the Otter.

"Madden, Madden," screaming in his ear, "push all you can on the left rudder—NOW!"

With the right engine out, the Otter was drifting sideways off the road. The left rudder inputs by Madden stopped the uncontrolled drift and began straightening the Otter's takeoff path while Carson fought the controls to compensate for the lost engine.

Fighting frantically to maintain control, she began turning off, from the overhead control panel, the right engine switches to stop the flow of gas, preventing a catastrophic fire. Due to the bullet penetrating the instrument panel, there was no way of monitoring the left engine, which appeared to be running normally. Carson was now flying, as the old saying goes, "by the seat of her pants."

Now moving straight down the road at a slower pace, in an instant Carson determined that at the current rate of acceleration, they would never make the minimum 70 knots required for takeoff.

"Madden, back me up on the wheel and hold it steady," directed Carson as she turned her attention to the above control panel engine switches that were still functional. For Carson, there was only one way to get her Otter off the ground with the major hits it had taken: she was going to over boost the remaining left engine to get the required power for takeoff.

Over boosting an aircraft engine is highly discouraged and potentially very dangerous, as it requires the engine to perform well above its safe operating limits. The resulting extreme stress and heat can cause the engine to explode.

With the two al-Qaeda trucks catching up with the now slower Otter, Carson over boosted the engine and readjusted the propeller pitch. Her passengers all felt an incredible new burst of thrust.

"Madden, I got the controls, but continue to give as much pressure as possible on the left rudder until I can get the manual rudder trim working."

Now bouncing down the road at a good rate of speed, with no functional instruments to tell her the airspeed, Carson would have to use her judgment and instincts when she felt it was time to rotate the Otter to take off. With Terry still holding the one throttle to full power and Madden, regardless of his wounds, continuing to hold the left rudder pedal, waiting and praying for Carson to pull the controls back for takeoff—no one was questioning her judgment. She definitely was the aircraft commander.

The clanging of broken metal and the strong inflow of wind increased as the men inside prayed to their God for deliverance at the salvation of this girl piloting the Otter.

"Rotate!" Carson declared as she very slightly pulled the control wheel back, confident she had the right airspeed. From the overstressed one engine to the many critical damages incurred, the Otter was flying by the grace of God and a highly competent pilot. Yells of praise and applause for the pilot could be heard from the men in the cargo compartment, who slowly began rising from the cargo deck floor and taking stock of their own injuries and equipment they were able to load prior to the quick takeoff.

"Looks good on our rate of climb," a shaken Carson informed Madden and Terry as she monitored the emergency backup altimeter while slowly bringing up the flaps and adjusting the trim for a slow climb to 5,000 feet—just enough to get over the ridge looming off in the distant south.

"Mr. Terry, you can let go of the throttles now," a relieved Carson told Terry while bringing the engine back from the stress of the over boost to its normal operating limits and easing the Otter into a slow cruise speed. "Madden, please continue to hold the left rudder until we can ensure the manual trim for the rudder works."

"Madden, are you okay?" Carson was shocked at his appearance and did not realize the extent of the many wounds he had received from the al-Qaeda and the bullet grazing him in the cockpit. She just wanted to reach out and hold him.

Terry unlocked Madden's seat belt and helped him to the cargo compartment, where the team medic could care for him. Terry moved into the co-pilot seat and would have nearly nodded off asleep had it not been for the tremendous noise of a much-damaged aircraft filling the cockpit. Like Terry, the rest of his SAS team was getting some much-needed rest.

"Okay, Mr. Terry, you have a barely flyable de Havilland twin-engine Otter," a more subdued Carson said as the pulsating hum of the lone engine became reassuring. "Either your queen or my Uncle Sam is going to be buying the Midland Oil Company a new one."

"Love, please charge it to Uncle Sam," Terry smiled and winked.

"Terry, forgive me for being a smart ass, but where are we going? I suspect the airport at Aden."

"Just a moment, ma'am," Terry replied. "I'd like to get our communications man up here to possibly set up some sort of contact with Djibouti and the Special Operations command post."

"What the fuck for? Let's just land at Aden International Airport, get Madden and your team some medical attention, and grab some commercial airline tickets out of here while the airport is still operating," Carson stressed and added, "if we can even make it that far in the condition we are in."

"Carson, there are a few reasons why that is not such a good idea," Terry went on. "For starters, I don't think Yemeni Customs would be too kind to a bunch of British Special Forces members landing at the airport in a commandeered aircraft—we might all be arrested."

She sighed.

"Also, not sure if you are aware of it, but we have a captured al-Qaeda leader tucked away and very much tied up in the back," Terry told Carson. "I don't believe the current Yemeni government, whoever they may be today, would appreciate us abducting an al-Qaeda terrorist and taking him to the United States for a little, uh, questioning."

"Who have you got back there of any value?" a curious Carson asked while taking the opportunity to grab a bottled water from the personal storage bin.

"We have Azzam. Are you familiar with him?" Terry jokingly asked, knowing the entire Middle East and the Western world knew of the most famous and notorious al-Qaeda terrorist leader living in Yemen.

Carson nearly choked on the water. She looked straight ahead at the Al Bayda ridge in the distance. After flying over the ridge, the Gulf of Aden immediately appears in just a few miles. She was still trying to weigh in her mind the impact of flying the world's most wanted terrorist out of Yemen. Then it dawned on her that last time she heard, there was a multi-million-dollar reward for the death or capture of Azzam—she was now getting excited about the prospect of earning a large chunk of that reward for her services in his capture.

Again trimming the Otter for possible updrafts from the ridge below, Carson slightly tweaked the throttle and propeller pitch for less strain on the engine and adjusted the feed from the fuel tanks to ensure a good weight and balance for the next part of the journey—to where she did not yet know, but would be ready.

"Say, Terry," Carson said while cleaning her sunglasses with a piece of torn cloth from the debris in the cockpit, "does the reward still apply for anyone bringing in Azzam?"

"As far as I know, love, and am confident Madden and I for sure will vouch that you were instrumental in bringing in him," Terry replied. "In fact, you might even get a medal from our countries."

"I'd rather have the money," a now smiling Carson replied, knowing she might get a piece of a few million dollars.

"So where in the fuck are we going? We are just about to make contact with the Gulf."

"Head west to Aden, and I will have more information soon—all right with you?"

"I'm going to take her down to a thousand feet in the event we have other problems with the good engine—at least we'll be able to survive an emergency landing on the beach."

Terry just nodded his head.

"Sgt. Ryan," Terry yelled over the deafening noise in the aircraft, looking back in the cargo compartment for his communications specialist.

Having a good idea of what Terry wanted, Ryan grabbed what functional communications gear he was able to bring aboard the aircraft before takeoff.

"Sir."

"Do you have any means to contact Djibouti Special Ops?" Terry asked while Ryan stared at the destroyed instrument panel with its twisted mess of broken wires and tubes strewn everywhere.

"I'll get right on it."

Ryan inventoried his communications gear and made contact with the Special Ops Command Post at Djibouti using a satellite phone.

An excited Ryan handed the phone to Terry. "I have the Djibouti Command Post on the line."

Terry relayed to Djibouti their location and flight plan, along with the need for a helicopter pickup at a small airport near the coastal town of Dhubab. From past experiences in Yemen, the Dhubab airport was a favorite and logical airport for extracting Special Operations teams from the country. It was controlled by a friendly government, not to mention the special and lucrative agreement with the local authorities, which made it the perfect site for a helicopter pickup and ride to Djibouti.

Most important, Terry added, "Madden says 'mission accomplished' with Paradise Bound and the main target is in custody and aboard the aircraft."

"You actually got him?" the Special Operations Command Post senior officer asked.

"Affirmative," Terry acknowledged, having a difficult time receiving and broadcasting information due to the strong winds and rattling in the cockpit.

"Djibouti Command Post, request immediate extraction from country with the on-alert HH-53 helicopter at rendezvous point Yankee Quebec, how copy? Over,"

Terry transmitted, fully aware of the grid coordinates for the landing site, and added, "Also, Djibouti, be aware, this satellite communications channel we are currently using is our only means of communication. Out."

"Roger, sir, currently working helicopter support," the officer acknowledged.

"Thank you, Djibouti, and also be aware our aircraft has sustained numerous battle damages, and we are currently flying on one engine with a few wounded on board, including Madden—request medic be aboard arriving helicopter. Over."

"Excuse me, Capt. Terry," Carson broke in after Terry made his last radio transmission passing along estimated time of arrival, souls on board and other pertinent information for their reception.

"Yes."

"Now let me get this straight about Azzam—the reward is good dead or alive, is that correct?" The worries and dangers of flying a damaged Otter on one engine to an unknown isolated airstrip were being replaced with the thought of the millions in reward money she would be eligible for.

"Carson, if I were you, I would be more worried about getting us to the helicopter versus your reward money," Terry answered with a grin. "Besides, as you Yanks would say, 'meat ain't meat until it's in the pan.'"

Carson just nodded her head while adjusting the one engine and the pitch of the propeller for their final leg to the helicopter rendezvous airport at Dhubab.

"If it is not too much trouble," Carson asked, "since I am going to be landing our damaged aircraft at a primitive airstrip I've never used before, would you be so fuckin' kind as to tell me about it, like runway length and headings, plus anything else you can help me with?"

"Of course, good idea and glad you thought of that," Terry replied and began providing Carson an update on what she could expect at the airfield.

Both searched the terrain below, looking for distinguishable landmarks from their out-of-date pilot maps. The damaged Otter followed the Yemeni coastline west to their final landing area, unaware their satellite communications transmissions had been intercepted by an Iranian radio intercept and decoding station.

When word worked its way back to the al-Qaeda headquarters at the Islamic Emirate in Azzan, Yemen, that Azzam was possibly still alive and in the hands of the Great Satan, the United States, directives went out to all al-Qaeda members to kill Azzam—he was soon to be compromised under interrogation by the CIA.

The nuclear bomb heist Azzam had been planning for a year was in jeopardy of being compromised by its main architect. Besides being a treasure trove of information about al-Qaeda leadership on the Arabian Peninsula, Azzam most importantly knew the names and addresses of sleeper cells and agents tasked to steal the bomb from the Pakistani nuclear depot and transport it to the United States.

Azzam had to be killed for jihad—Allah willing!

CHAPTER

36

The Special Operations Command Post at Djibouti was abuzz with excitement as word circulated that one of the world's most wanted and sought-after terrorists had been captured by a Special Ops team and was being picked up by one of the base's alert helicopters.

The commanding officer of the joint military base at Djibouti, Col. Mike Dulaney, immediately entered the command post and ordered that no mention of the capture of Azzam would leave the facility. He reminded his staff that it would be considered a major breach of security if any information were broadcast to the outside world, and he would hold those staff members accountable. Only secure, top secret communications with the U.S. Special Operations Command at MacDill Air Force Base, Florida, would be authorized.

The commander convened his battle staff, which was executing plans to dispatch two giant cargo HH-53 helicopters to pick up the escaping Special Operations team and the huge prize—Azzam. One helicopter would add an Air Force flight surgeon and medical assistants, plus boxes full of sandwiches and fruit for the Otter pilot and Special Operations team. The other helicopter, dedicated only for the transport of Azzam, included a military physician and a contingent of federal agents whose specialty was the onboarding of foreign terrorists in preparation for interrogation.

"Col. Dulaney, sir," the command post duty intelligence officer stood and addressed the colonel. "Sir, the deputy commander of the National Command Center would like to speak with you on secure voice in the SCIF."

"Okay, captain, I'll make my way down there and see what the Pentagon wants," replied the colonel.

Wondering why the National Command Center wanted to talk with him, he suspected it had everything to do with the approaching arrival of Azzam. Everyone who knew about that was feeling a little giddy—and relieved.

Upon entering the secure facility, the colonel picked up the secure phone and was immediately in contact with the senior general officer at the center, who was quick to get to the point.

"Colonel, we understand Azzam has been captured and is on his way to your base with a group of British Special Forces in a commandeered cargo aircraft—we understand the details of its damaged status."

"Yes, sir, we are doing everything possible to get the crew and Azzam back here as soon as possible with special accommodations for Azzam," the colonel said.

"All right, here's the deal," the general continued, "our intelligence agencies are confirming large amounts of recent al-Qaeda message traffic confirming the abduction of Azzam by Israeli agents. It has been confirmed by the Department of Defense that there has been a very secret and sensitive mission titled Paradise Bound led by one of our operatives named Madden."

"Yes, general, that is correct, our drone operations here at Djibouti provided robust support to Madden and Paradise Bound with the most recent support as of early this morning—it was a real firefight in Yemen's Shabwah province, but Madden and the British team were more than lucky to escape.

"Frankly, general," the colonel proudly stressed, "they would not have made it out without our drone support."

Col. Dulaney could sense that the general did not call to discuss Madden's team's escape or the incredible capture of Azzam.

"Very good, colonel." The general shifted the conversation to a more urgent matter. "Colonel, is there anyone else in the SCIF with you?" the general asked. "If so, please ask them to leave—I need to speak only with you."

"Sir, I am alone in the SCIF," assured Dulaney.

"Colonel, for your information, an al-Qaeda sleeper cell in the United States, in all probability, has possession of a theater nuclear bomb."

The colonel took a deep breath, shocked.

"We have confirmed just recently that a group of al-Qaeda sympathizers, working undercover at a Pakistani nuclear storage depot, heisted a nuclear weapon and transported it to the United States through our border with Mexico," the general said. "Also, this heist had been planned and financed for years by al-Qaeda leader Khalid Azzam in Yemen. This intelligence was confirmed by a recent FBI raid on an al-Qaeda safe house in Detroit."

The general paused for effect: "There is no doubt Azzam is responsible and is probably one of few leaders who know the exact location of the bomb and the cells responsible."

The colonel almost dropped the secure phone in shock, knowing their worst nightmare had come true—a terrorist group had obtained a nuclear bomb.

"Colonel, are you still there?" the general asked, knowing he had thrown the colonel an unimaginable apocalyptic scenario.

"Yes, sir, what are my orders?" the colonel replied.

The general went on to brief Col. Dulaney that for some time, U.S. intelligence agencies had determined, via decoded al-Qaeda message traffic, that al-Qaeda leader Azzam was now on the most urgent priority hit list for assassination by the al-Qaeda supreme leaders due to his complete knowledge about the Pakistan bomb heist, and, most importantly, he was probably still alive in the hands of the United States or Israel.

"Colonel, I want you to place the highest security restrictions on your base—restricting all nonmilitary members from having access. Do you understand, colonel? This is imperative," the general ordered.

"We have very reliable sources telling us that al-Qaeda will go to great lengths to assassinate Azzam prior to him falling into the hands of the United States. I am sure you are presently taking measures to establish a very safe and secure facility at your base where we can detain Azzam and interrogate him immediately upon his arrival," the general emphasized. "There is a special interrogation team in the air now heading your way—we've got to find out what Azzam knows about the heist and where the nuclear bomb is."

"We'll have all that you ordered ready," assured the colonel as he signed off with the general.

The colonel returned to his key staff members and began giving direction and orders for the closing of the base and the arrival of Azzam, interrogation team, and the surviving members of Paradise Bound.

CHAPTER
37

"Carson, do you see it?" Terry yelled across the strong winds and rattles of the aircraft's junked cockpit. "Off to your two o'clock."

"Yes, I see it," Carson replied as she began a gradual turn to align her aircraft with the landing site. With all the instruments destroyed during the takeoff and only one functioning engine, there would be one opportunity to land the aircraft—no second chances.

"Terry, get everyone buckled in or tied down for landing—it may be pretty rough on this wonderful airfield of yours," she ordered. "Especially that Azzam, I have a vested interest in keeping him alive."

"So does the free world," Terry commented as he left the co-pilot seat to ensure his team, Madden, and Azzam were all prepared for a rough landing—or crash.

The aircraft descended slowly as Carson feverishly worked the controls and engine throttle, bringing the plane to a soft landing on the gravel airstrip.

Yells of jubilation and great relief were heard from Terry's team in the cargo compartment as Carson taxied the aircraft down the remaining airstrip runway to what appeared to be a small parking ramp. She immediately shut down the engine and locked the brakes. Her hands shaking, she grabbed a bottle of water and had a difficult time opening the cap.

"Well done, love, well done!" could be heard while the team hurriedly grabbed what weapons and equipment they had been able to bring with them and immediately formed a defensive perimeter around the aircraft until the Special Operations helicopters from Djibouti arrived.

Carson made her way back to the cargo compartment and saw her banged-up and bruised friend Madden sitting on one of the passenger web seats just staring at the dazed and confused Azzam still tied up and lying on the floor.

Madden produced a small commando-type knife he had strapped in a side pocket of his torn and dirty pant leg. Now, Azzam's excited eyes followed Madden's hands as he positioned the knife to cut Azzam's throat.

"Damn you, Madden, don't you dare kill him," she screamed as she grabbed his hand with the knife and tried pulling it away. With his wounds and injuries, Madden didn't have the strength to resist, and Carson worked the knife out of his hands and threw it on the floor—barely missing Azzam's head.

"You kill him, and I could be out twenty-five million bucks for the reward," she scolded Madden with some theatrics. Carson knew the value of keeping Azzam alive—until his interrogation was completed. She also knew Azzam was responsible for the death of Madden's wife and two daughters—his vengeance would have to wait. Money talks.

"Damn you, Carson!" Madden said, barely able to talk, "We need to get a good blood sample from Azzam to prove we have him—do you understand?"

Reasoning for a moment, she reached down on the cluttered cargo floor and retrieved the knife that Madden was to use to get a blood sample and made the cut herself and placed the blood in a small vial provided by the SAS medic.

After taking blood from Azzam, Carson found a web seat next to Madden and wrapped her arms around him, sitting in silence until the thunderous loud thumping noise of two huge HH-53 military helicopters could be heard approaching their location.

Cheers and excited hand waving by Terry's team lasted for several minutes as the helicopters circled the airstrip with their booming rotor blades slapping the air and eventually landing on a gravel road adjacent to the parked Otter. Several hardy-looking men in military battle dress and carrying weapons raced out of the helicopters and were immediately greeted with hugs and handshakes from Terry's team.

The Americans were not expecting to pick up a Special Operations team with thick British accents. A couple of tanned, lean-looking men in blue jeans and denim shirts wearing baseball caps exited the helicopter and made a beeline for the aircraft.

Terry ensured all his men were accounted for and directed them to proceed to the number one helicopter and follow whatever instructions were given to them by the crew chief—he would catch up with them later. Walking back to the aircraft, he was joined by the two men dressed in civilian jeans.

"Sir, I'm Bryce Wilson and this is Shane Rhian," Wilson introduced himself and his partner to Terry while pulling his Department of Defense identification package and orders out of his jeans pocket. The roar and thump of the helicopter blades threw dust and rocks against them as they spoke.

"Glad to make your acquaintance. I'm Capt. Terry in charge of this team with the British Special Air Service," almost yelling now to each other due to the noise of the helicopters' jet engines.

"I assume you are here to collect Azzam?" Terry jokingly stated as he led the two men to the open aircraft cargo door where they found Azzam still bound, lying among the debris.

They observed Carson caring for Madden on the side web passenger seats examining and cleaning his wounds using the plane's medical kit. Madden looked up and smiled at the two men, knowing who they were and what they were there for—they would begin preparing, or in Agency terms, onboarding Azzam for immediate interrogation upon their return to Djibouti.

"Are you Madden? The guy responsible for operation Paradise Bound?" Wilson asked while making his way into the cargo compartment, preparing to move Azzam to the waiting helicopter.

"Yeah, I'm Rob Madden and I don't know anything about Paradise Bound," Madden replied, giving a quick wink to Wilson. "And Kelly Carson here is the pilot of this aircraft who saved our lives and is responsible for bringing in Azzam. She's the only one on the team eligible for the reward."

Carson, still caring for Madden's wounds, looked up and smiled, still feeling the emotional effects of what they had just been through.

"Let's all move quickly over to the first helicopter—we do have an Air Force flight surgeon ready to care for Madden's wounds. Shane and I will escort Azzam here over to the second helicopter reserved just for him," Wilson directed.

With Madden helped aboard the first helicopter by Carson and Terry, both were enthusiastically hailed by a jubilant bunch of grateful members of Capt. Terry's SAS team. The flight surgeon immediately assessed Madden's gunshot wound while Carson was being endlessly saluted as their hero—"Hurrah for Kelly Carson, for She's a Jolly Good Lady." Carson was not used to such adoration and was frankly embarrassed by all the attention.

"Knock it off already," she told them.

"Welcome aboard," the helicopter crew chief announced, "on behalf of the twentieth Special Operations Squadron, we are proud to have you on board. At this time please be seated and fasten your seat belts."

Both helicopters were revving up their powerful engines for takeoff, with dust, rocks, and debris thrown in every direction. Thumbs-up was given by all crew members as the number two helicopter, carrying Azzam, lifted off and headed south across the Bab-el-Mandeb strait directly to the military base at Djibouti, where all was ready for Azzam's reception.

The second helicopter waited a few minutes, lifted off and began circling the airfield while a crew member set up a standard 20-millimeter machine gun in an open side hatch.

"What's with the gun?" a curious Carson asked the crew chief.

"We have orders to destroy the aircraft—make it look like it crash-landed with no survivors," the crew chief answered, not realizing the plane was Carson's life and livelihood for her years in Yemen.

Carson watched out the observation window as the powerful machine gun tore into the disabled Otter, leaving it a hulk of shredded metal. Tears fell from Carson's face. Others got up and observed the destruction, knowing full well the plane had to be destroyed and look like a horrible crash landing to curious al-Qaeda members and their affiliates.

Carson continued to stare at her dying Otter as the helicopter headed south toward Djibouti over the majestic blue waters of the Gulf of Aden.

CHAPTER
38

"Ramrod Control, this is Flankerback 20, heading inbound, my feet are wet, how copy on secure VHF 122.1?" the pilot of the helicopter carrying Azzam was checking in with the military air traffic controller at Djibouti using secure communications. The mission was classified top secret with no air traffic reporting provided to any of the surrounding countries. The transponder usually providing air traffic ground controllers with the location of all aircraft in the vicinity was turned off.

"Flankerback 20 and Flankerback 21, this is Ramrod, you are both cleared straight in, will keep you advised of aircraft traffic for your route of flight. How copy? Over," the military air traffic controller at Djibouti directed.

"Ramrod control, this is Flankerback 20, I have flight—" the co-pilot's transmission abruptly ended.

An enormous shock wave and huge explosion with a ball of fire shook the immediate vicinity as the pilot of helicopter one, call sign Flankerback 21, took evasive action to control the helicopter and steer away from the flying debris of the catastrophe just ahead of them.

"Everyone strap in and ensure you have your life vest on," ordered the shocked helicopter pilot to the crew chief as he quickly maneuvered his craft around the explosion site of the disintegrating Flankerback 20.

"Chief, make sure everyone is prepared for a possible ditching or crash landing," he ordered as the gravity of the situation was making itself clear—their helicopter could also have an explosive bomb on board or a terrorist could be sighting them up as the next target for a surface-to-air missile.

The pilot, not taking any chances, immediately dropped the nose of his copter and leveled off as close to the water as possible and turned off any unnecessary electronic equipment that could spark an explosion or attract a missile launch.

"Mayday, Mayday, Mayday. Ramrod Control, this is Flankerback 21 on secure frequency declaring an emergency. Over!" the co-pilot transmitted while the pilot was focused on flying the huge helicopter just above the waves.

"Flankerback 21, are you in contact with 20 over? We are not able to contact them. Over!"

"Ramrod, Flankerback 20 is down due to an explosion approximately four miles north of the town of Moulhoule over the strait of Bab-el-Mandeb," relayed the co-pilot. "We are currently taking evasive action and request an emergency landing at Djibouti."

"Flankerback 21 you have pilot's discretion and cleared to deviate. How copy? Over," the controller announced and added, "We are launching the alert rescue helicopter to the last known location of 20. Over!"

"Ramrod Control, this is the pilot of 21," still working vigorously to fly as low as possible over the strait, "highly recommend the alert rescue helicopter be sanitized and checked for hidden explosives prior to takeoff. Over."

The radios were silent for the next few minutes as the crew of Flankerback 21 was vigorously preparing for a possible water ditching or crash landing. Capt. Terry found a seat in the aft passenger section next to where Rob Madden was being treated for his shoulder wound by the flight surgeon. Terry observed Madden getting his senses back, and the surgeon gave Terry a thumbs-up on Madden's condition.

"Hey, mate. Got any ideas what we can be doing to assist the crew in getting us all back—alive?"

"Terry, survey your team to see if they saw any type of missile approaching the helicopter prior to the explosion or anything that looked peculiar from their views out the windows and hatches—I am sure someone on your team may have seen something," Madden said. Terry nodded his head in agreement.

"Good idea, but what do you really think caused the explosion?" Terry earnestly asked, knowing it was likely not some sort of surface-to-air missile.

"My personal views from experience here in Yemen, as you also well know, I believe it was a cell phone-activated, improvised explosive device, or IED, that was planted on the helicopter, possibly some foreign contract worker—God only knows how or when," Madden speculated while rubbing his greasy hair and chugging down a bottle of water.

"I have to believe that there is probably also one on this helicopter that malfunctioned and did not go off at the same time as the one that destroyed the other copter," Madden reasoned. "I am truly shocked by what happened to the crew, with the only redeeming sense of all this is that Azzam is dead and gone."

Madden did not share his real theory why the IEDs were planted on the rescue helicopters. He suspected that the explosives were purposely planted by al-Qaeda operatives to ensure Azzam did not talk during interrogation concerning the Pakistani bomb. Others in the raid had no clue of the consequences of Azzam's death and unimaginable consequences in regard to the security of the United States.

Madden winced in pain as the medic started bandaging his shoulder. "Again, the terrorist who worked this is still probably dialing the cell phone for the IED on this copter, hoping to get it to work," Madden said. "The lower we are, the better the chances the IED will not explode due to cell phone coverage and reception—just a guess."

A tired and strained Terry nodded his head and patted Madden on the back as he headed up to the cockpit to discuss Madden's recommendation with the pilots. The pilot brought the copter ever closer to the lapping waves below them.

CHAPTER
39

"Flankerback 21, this is Ramrod Control," the military air traffic controller announced. "What is your status? Over."

"Ramrod, this is Flankerback 21, we are thirty miles out and are at low level, on the deck, with a possible bomb on board," the co-pilot calmly relayed. "Request landing in a parking ramp as far away from the base as possible for obvious reasons. Over."

The senior military controller was closely monitoring the approach of the copter over the shoulder of the duty controller and realized immediately the gravity of the situation—the pilot suspected a bomb on board.

"Flankerback 21, this is the senior military controller, you are to land at the dirt area just northwest of the helicopter parking ramp—we'll mark the area with red flares, and a controller will be on the ground to guide you in. How copy? Over."

"Roger, sir, we'll be skimming over the base at low level and am familiar with the directed landing site," the pilot acknowledged.

"Recommend you and your passengers egress the copter as soon as possible after landing—we'll have the necessary rescue crews on the scene," added the senior controller.

"No shit, Sherlock," the pilot mumbled to anyone who could hear.

"Hey, Terry," the pilot yelled toward the back as Terry made his way up to the cockpit.

"We'll be landing soon in a deserted landing area near the base, so get your people strapped in tight. When we land, get all of your people in the back out of the copter immediately—I'll ensure the back-cargo ramp is deployed for your exit and will sound the crash horn when it's time to depart the helicopter. Do you understand?"

Terry returned to the passenger compartment and briefed Madden, Carson and his team members on the upcoming landing situation with the emphasis, "WHEN THE HORN SOUNDS, GET OUT IMMEDIATELY THROUGH THE CARGO RAMP!"

Flankerback 21 flew so low over the base at Djibouti that the hurricane force winds of the helicopter's rotors blew dirt and debris everywhere in the air while angry Djibouti citizens raised their fists and gave universal hand gestures as the copter passed over. The Djiboutis also threw rocks at the helicopter's belly. When the rocks hit, the resulting banging sound only heightened the tension.

The pilot sighted the red smoke rising from the designated landing area and gradually slowed the copter with a gentle descent to the ground—the horn blasted, and the cargo ramp fell while the huge blades of the helicopter continued to create a small dust storm as they gradually slowed.

Terry's team helped Madden, Carson, and the flight surgeon down the cargo ramp and into the swirling dirt and sand as they were guided by Air Force rescue specialists to emergency vehicles a short, safe distance away. The helicopter crew quickly sanitized the copter of any classified material and exited quickly to the safety of the waiting vehicles. Suddenly, emergency fire and crash emergency vehicles entered the area followed by a team from the ordnance disposal team to check the copter for any type of hidden bomb.

After helping Madden and Carson to an awaiting military ambulance, Terry and his team relaxed in what they thought was paradise—a clean, roomy, air-conditioned bus with a cooler filled with ice and Foster's Lager. Terry's team was totally exhausted and filthy, so they shed their undercover Yemeni male garments for their just as dirty and sweat-soaked oil field clothes of blue denim and cotton workshirts. Their baked, black grimy faces spoke volumes about their weeks in Yemen's harshest and most dangerous regions.

Madden's appearance mirrored those of Terry's team, with blood stains punctuating his already grimy clothing, as a reminder of the ordeal he had survived.

Carson did not quite mirror the men's appearance, but showed noticeable cuts and bruises to her face and arms due to the shattering of the plane's instrument panel. And like the men, she was coming to grips with what they had been through in the past few hours, knowing it was a miracle they had made it out with Azzam—and feeling lucky they were on the helicopter that did not explode in mid-air.

Madden relaxed in the ambulance, owing his tranquility to some drugs the surgeon provided. Carson sat next to him, gently washing his filthy face and arms with alcohol towels and dressing.

Upon arriving at the base hospital, he was immediately offered a wheelchair and orderly, but flat-out rejected the courtesy, and walked himself into the emergency room with Carson's support. A cordoned-off section of the emergency room was secured for Madden as a team of doctors and nurses began their work on this ragged stranger. Many assumed he was just another Special Operations operator coming out of a mission in Yemen—they had seen many in the past few months.

The hospital staff tactfully attempted to restrict Carson's access to Madden, but she insisted on sitting in the emergency room during his entire stay—in some cases providing her own expertise to the doctors regarding his care. She also demanded a hospital room next to Madden's—the staff relented, not wanting to tangle with this tough woman. She was still the pilot-in-command.

CHAPTER
40

"Atten-Hut!" yelled the base executive officer as the Djibouti commanding officer entered the base officer's club. The British SAS team found themselves there after commandeering the bus taking them to the visiting officers' quarters.

Col. Dulaney judged by the mountain of beer cans on the floor that his guests were now just trying to dull the pain of losing the brave men and women in the helicopter explosion, with each realizing it could very well have been them.

Regardless of their reason for dulling the pain, each was trying to recount what had taken place in the past week, knowing they were the lucky ones.

Upon hearing the order of attention, the men stopped their drinking and helped each other up—trying to show some semblance of respect for military order.

"As you were, gentleman," Dulaney ordered, trying not to burst out laughing at the bizarre scene in his officers' club.

"Gentleman, could I have your attention please," he said.

"Sir, would you like a pint?" SAS member Sgt. Evans offered Dulaney his just-opened can of Foster's.

"Sergeant, greatly appreciate the offer, however I'm still on duty, and you will be soon," Dulaney informed the SAS members.

"Gentlemen, please listen up. Your SAS regimental commander is flying in this evening from Great Britain to meet with each of you and observe the mission's debriefing."

The announcement that their commanding general was arriving soon sobered up the men, who awkwardly attempted to clean up their beer cans and trash. Dulaney, more than anyone, knew these men deserved a break, but an immediate debriefing was required.

"Please see fit to make your way to the club entrance, where your bus will be waiting to take you to the visiting officers' quarters where you will be provided all the clothing and bathing articles you may need. Do you gentlemen understand?"

"Sir, yes, sir!" replied the SAS members as they slowly headed for the bus, making it a point to finish off their last cans of beer. Capt. Terry winked at Dulaney as he led his men to the bus.

Later that evening, all the survivors of the raid for Azzam were escorted to the secure conference room where specialized teams of military intelligence, CIA, FBI, and an intelligence officer from Britain's MI6 awaited. All nine members of Capt. Lee Terry's SAS detachment were present, as were Kelly Carson and Rob Madden, who were escorted from the hospital by military police. Madden was still recovering from his shoulder surgery and several other less-severe wounds, but he emphatically demanded that he attend the debriefing.

Capt. Terry began the debriefing with his team's operations in Yemen the six months prior to recently being ordered to support Madden's tasking, Paradise Bound. He went on to relate the first meeting with Madden at the Marib oil refinery. Terry and his team's briefings lasted approximately an hour, with several questions from the various intelligence services. Terry said he would draft the appropriate award packages for each of his team members, including the Victoria Cross for the actions of Nasser Saeed and his induction into the regular British Army.

Next, Rob Madden, now showered and dressed in jeans and a denim workshirt, still groggy from surgery and wearing a shoulder bandage and sling, methodically provided a summary of his tasking from his Pentagon briefing to his actions with Azzam—when the terrorist was alive.

All eyes were now on Kelly Carson, who appeared at the debriefing in a surprisingly clean summer dress that an Air Force intelligence officer had given her, plus makeup that was used to try and conceal many of the cuts and bruises—especially on her face and arms. All were in awe of her. They also were intrigued by her actions and aware their lives were saved when she volunteered to help Madden, not to mention her exceptional skills as a pilot. They could not thank her enough, except for the $25 million reward she was expected to earn for her part in bringing to justice the world's most wanted, deadliest terrorist.

Terry's team members and Madden were not eligible for the reward due to their government employment status, but Carson was, and she agreed to give members of Terry's team and Madden a million dollars each when the reward was approved for distribution. Carson made a lot of people happy during the debriefing.

With many questions being asked by the various intelligence agencies, the debriefing ended late in the evening. All were reminded of the following day's schedule of more debriefings and a warning that all the information and discussion was considered top secret. All were filing out of the conference, being escorted by military personnel back to their secure quarters, when the CIA and FBI agents in attendance requested a few minutes in private with Madden.

Carson was assigned, due to her demands, to a room next to Madden's at the base hospital—it was of particular interest to all that she would take the lead in his healing. It was obvious Madden was very tired and feeling the effects of the pain-blocking drugs, but he realized time was critical now with the upcoming news to the world that Azzam was dead. He was disappointed and saddened that they had come so very far in taking Azzam alive and getting him on a military helicopter heading for a critical interrogation. He was depressed, knowing that the opportunity to find the Pakistani nuclear bomb through Azzam had come to a tragic end.

"You just may be interested in these—not sure if they will do you any good." Madden, working hard to stay coherent while the painkillers were wearing off, handed the agents two small pouches of computer disks. Their excitement showed as the two agents carefully handled the drives and immediately placed them in a classified and secure briefcase.

"Rob, how in the devil were you able to obtain these?" an agent asked, stunned by their possible good fortune.

"When the drones began the attack on the camp near the schoolhouse, the SAS Sgt. Saeed and I saw Azzam and his personal lieutenants running away from their tent for the safety of the school. We immediately raced after him in our Humvee and killed many of his bodyguards," Madden recollected.

"When I got to him, I quickly subdued him with many body blows to the head, that fucker, and noticed even with all the blows he was taking, he guarded a pouch he was wearing around his neck under his clothes."

Madden thought for a moment, still struggling to stay awake. "I ripped the small pouch from his neck and placed it in my back pocket, not really knowing or caring what it was, but it sure seemed important to him.

"I hope they do us some good, fellas," Madden struggled to say as he slumped down in his chair exhausted and in pain.

"I suspect when the drone's bombs started dropping near Azzam's tent, he figured he had better take his backup computer files in the event his computer and files were destroyed," offered a CIA official and again praised Madden for grabbing the pouch.

Security guards and hospital attendants immediately carried Madden out of the command post briefing room to an awaiting military ambulance—Carson was waiting inside to ensure he was comfortable.

Holding Madden's hand while making the short trip to the hospital, Carson's incredible performance, lack of sleep, and mourning the death of so many outstanding airmen in the helicopter explosion—she broke down and cried while gently rubbing Madden's hand.

CHAPTER
41

"Are you Rob Madden?" An official-looking stranger approached Madden while he was reading a book and recuperating at a small patio area just outside the Army's Landstuhl Regional Medical Center in Germany. Madden had arrived at the center a few weeks earlier and was expecting to be transferred back to the United States within a week.

The death of Azzam was continually being reported in the newspapers, with the official version being that he was killed by his own people—al-Qaeda. After reading the reports from the papers, Madden just smiled, looking forward to getting back to the United States and maybe finally getting back on the road to his degree in education—plus a million bucks to blow from Carson's reward money.

"Yes, I'm Rob Madden, what can I do for you?"

Madden sized up the man in his mid-fifties, six feet tall, and in good physical shape as most likely some sort of federal agent or intelligence officer. Madden surmised he had spoken with dozens since his arrival at the hospital and told the same account of his actions in Yemen.

"May I have a seat, Mr. Madden?" the man said, pulling a wooden patio chair closer.

"I'm Dr. Dan Schuster," he said, shaking Madden's left hand. The right was still in a sling. "I'm a special assistant to our ambassador here in Germany."

Schuster knew Madden's reputation and history enough to know that Madden knew he worked for the CIA.

"Good for you, Dr. Schuster, now what can I do for you?" Madden asked patiently.

"First, on a personal note, and I know you have heard it from hundreds of others, but we all salute you for your incredible bravery in the face of such overwhelming odds."

"Thank you, but I attribute the success of our actions to those brave and unsung heroes of the British Special Air Services and that gutsy and brave pilot—Kelly Carson. They are the heroes, not me. Would you like to meet Kelly Carson?" Madden politely asked. "She has taken it upon herself to ensure I recover—I think she figures she is a multimillionaire because of me, and she owes me.

"Of course Kelly and I have somewhat of a special relationship now. She saved our lives with her heroic piloting skills getting us out of the al-Qaeda camp, which resulted in her being awarded the $25-million-dollar bounty for the capture or death of Azzam."

"No doubt, you are in good hands," Schuster agreed, nodding his head.

Madden replied, "Now what can I assist you with?"

Schuster looked around to ensure they were indeed alone and pulled his chair even closer. "Do you recall the two computer pouches you took off of Azzam and were able to provide us at your debriefing when you returned from Yemen?"

"Yes, I do recall. I was wondering if you found anything of value on them."

"To put it lightly, it was a treasure trove of information connecting many of the al-Qaeda sleeper cells, including their planned operations and financing. We have already stopped and apprehended a couple of cells in Spain that were planning on bombing a military base in Zaragoza," Schuster said.

"However, the big win with your disks was the discovery of the al-Qaeda cells that were able to heist the nuclear bomb from the Tarbala Underground Nuclear Depot. They eventually found their way to Mexico and across the border to the United States.

"For your information, Madden, we have been monitoring tons of highly classified message traffic between various Pakistani intelligence agencies and military authorities—all centered on the location of a theater nuclear bomb. Either the Pakistanis lost track of the bomb, or al-Qaeda undercover operatives were able to heist it out of its storage area."

Madden was smiling, elated to hear that besides killing Azzam, by a miracle, they were able to uncover the terrorists responsible for stealing the bomb.

"What about the nuclear weapon—the bomb. Did we find it?" Madden now sat on the edge of his chair.

"We got it back," Schuster confirmed. "After our recent sweep and arrests of the local identified al-Qaeda cells in the States, there will not be any further threats against your life—remember, you're still technically a doctoral student at Stanford University."

Schuster got up out of his chair, smiled, and winked at Madden while shaking his left good hand.

"Oh, Madden." Schuster stopped and turned while walking away. "The president is planning on giving you some sort of medal when you return, and military sources tell me you are being promoted to Chief Master Sergeant—does that mean anything to you?"

"Hey listen, Schuster—if that truly is your real name—do me a favor and go back and tell your people all I want is to get my Honda from Albuquerque, New Mexico, and head out to Stanford University."

"Will do—just don't get into any fights with drug lords along the way," Schuster joked.

Madden just shook his head and smiled as Schuster left him.

Tres Rios, Tres Rios, Madden repeated to himself, reflecting back to those terrible, but very satisfying days of mentoring and teaching the impoverished and lost students that everyone had forgotten about. But not Rob Madden. *I wonder who learned more in Tres Rios—the young students or me?*

While recovering in the hospital with Carson, he had time to reflect about his relationship with Bonnie McCord and where it would go. Somehow he knew, deep in his heart, they were destined for each other. Possibly to settle down with her after her return from DEA undercover work.

"Rob, may I join you?" came a soft voice as Madden was napping in the late afternoon sun on the hospital patio.

"Ah my dear Kelly, please, please have a seat with me," said Madden, who was coming out of his fitful nap very pleased and excited to see Carson. "Come here and sit next to me."

Wearing stylish black slacks and a brown leather bomber jacket with a white scarf, Carson looked like a dashing aviatrix model out of Cosmopolitan magazine—with a total makeover in hairstyle and makeup. Madden definitely took notice.

"Well, who is this beautiful lady?" Madden said, now wide awake and enjoying the sight of Carson's new fashions.

"Ah yes, you are a multimillionaire now, and the clothes have to reflect your jet-setting lifestyle," Madden said while eyeing Carson.

"Oh, Rob, would you knock it off," she quipped, smiling and holding Madden's hand.

"Rob, I'm leaving for Tulsa tomorrow morning," Carson said. "Midland Oil has a new job for me as a pilot on one of their corporate jets."

Tears could be seen coming from Madden's eyes at the prospect of Carson's departure.

"Kelly, I believe it is safe to assume we have strong special feelings for each other, but we both know it's time to move on," Madden said as tears also began streaming down Carson's face.

Both stood and wrapped their arms around each other in a passionate embrace.

"Who knows, Kelly?" Madden said, regaining his composure, "it will be nice knowing a girl piloting a Gulfstream G650 corporate jet in addition to a twin-engine Otter."

Carson just smiled and gave Madden a quick jab to his unhurt shoulder, suspecting one day he might show up in Tulsa, Oklahoma.

She gave Madden a kiss on the check, turned and walked away to the patio exit as Madden eyed her departure.

Damn, she looks good. Sure didn't look like that in Yemen, Madden mumbled to himself.

After weeks of debriefings, a nondescript government aircraft landed at Kirkland Air Force Base outside Albuquerque, New Mexico, and deplaned one passenger.

As he gathered his luggage, Madden recognized a man coming directly toward him with a large grin on his face.

"Rob Madden, good to see you," DEA Special Agent Steve Webb greeted him. Another agent grabbed his bags and took them to a waiting vehicle with a New Mexico Publishing Company logo on its doors.

"God, Webb, I was hoping I would never see you again—bad things happen when I'm around you," Madden laughed, shaking Webb's hand and patting him on his back.

"Yes, that may be true, but I have always been your guardian angel—well, at least in New Mexico," Webb replied, escorting Madden to the company car that would take him to the Publishing Company building in downtown Albuquerque.

While the younger agent drove the vehicle off the base and onto the busy thoroughfare of Broadway Avenue, Webb briefed Madden that he was taking him to pick up his Honda Element and trailer for his trip to Stanford University. According to Webb, special arrangements had been made with the university to ensure Madden began his studies immediately upon arrival. Webb added that the officials at Stanford were very aware of the circumstances resulting in his delay and were grateful for his service to the United States and his dedication to the education profession—all would be taken care of at Stanford.

Arriving at the basement of the New Mexico Publishing Company, the DEA agents loaded Madden's bags and luggage in his Honda and bid him farewell. He headed north to Interstate 40 West. Just outside Albuquerque, Madden was tempted to return to the Flying Buffalo Casino, La Mesa Uranium Mine, and Tres Rios Rural School, but decided against it—it was time to move on.

CHAPTER
42

"Welcome to Santa Cruz, Ms. Turner, we are so happy to have you here!" A handsome and stylishly dressed stranger in an elegant Italian suit approached McCord as she was gathering her luggage at the arriving flight carousel at the Viru Viru International Airport, a few miles north of Santa Cruz, Bolivia.

"Many thanks," she replied, suspicious yet tired as she continued to watch the carousel for her belongings.

"I am so, so sorry," the stranger conveyed with pearl white teeth and a well-tanned face, plus a hint of alcohol on his breath. "Let me introduce myself to you. I am Antonio Juarez, the Georgia Fried Chicken restaurant manager at the Ventura Mall in Santa Cruz."

She eyed him, quickly surmising he was the token manager who probably never served a customer or fried any chicken in his life. His job was marketing and public relations, she reasoned— in other words, schmoozing.

"Thank you, Mr. Juarez, for meeting me here," she acknowledged. "I see my luggage coming this way, so please excuse me for a moment."

"Here, here, let me help you." He followed her to her luggage and ordered a porter to take the bags out to a waiting white late-model Mercedes in the temporary arrival parking area.

"We are so looking forward to getting you on board as soon as possible," he added while they walked together out to the car. "With no assistant manager, I have had a very challenging time running the restaurant and my own job alone."

"I see," McCord replied, knowing he probably had accomplished nothing except filling the role as the national figurehead. "I suspect as your assistant manager, I'll have my work cut out for me. You can call me Pat, and if you feel more comfortable, I do speak Spanish very well."

"Thank you, Pat, and you may call me Tony," he said, opening the door for her as he guided her to the Mercedes—the porter was just putting the luggage in the trunk. Juarez immediately slipped a twenty-dollar bill in the porter's open hand.

"Muchas gracias, señor," the pleasantly surprised porter acknowledged quickly and put the bill in his dirty, torn shirt pocket.

Suddenly, an airport police officer confronted Juarez about his parking too long in front of the arrival terminal. In a matter of seconds, he shook the officer's hand, which held a couple of twenty-dollar bills. The officer smiled at McCord and informally saluted Juarez as he turned and wished both a good day.

Aware of the recent "legal" transaction between Juarez and the police officer, McCord was reminded of her times in Colombia and Mexico where a few twenty-dollar bills could move mountains.

Juarez headed the car toward the airport's exit, not noticing that McCord had clandestinely placed a small radio beacon and listening device behind the glove compartment rear panel. She had great expectations for the amount of human intelligence she would gain from these hidden devices.

"Well, Pat, again I'll say how happy we are that you arrived to us safe and sound," he said, lighting up a Camel. She found the cigarette smoke nauseating but was used to such environments.

"Let me explain our game plan for getting you on the job as quickly as possible," he said. He was racing the Mercedes in and out of traffic and taking long puffs on his cigarette.

Oh, brother, McCord thought. *Thank goodness he'll be out of the restaurant doing his PR or marketing thing.*

"I'm going to drive you by the Ventura Mall where the GFC is located and then swing around and show you where you will be living during your stay with us."

"Thank you, Tony. Greatly appreciate the tour."

"You will be staying at a luxury condominium we have arranged called the Condominium Montana—it is just a couple blocks from the mall."

Juarez continued his fast driving while providing more details regarding her work and responsibilities. She pulled open her purse, grabbed her day planner and began taking notes, asking questions as they traveled down the highway. It was obvious to her, after the few brief conversations with Juarez, that she would literally be running the restaurant on her own while Juarez was out and about, but he would occasionally check up on her to see, as he put it, "how things were going."

Well, with him out of the way most of the time, she reasoned to herself, *I'll be able to concentrate on other issues.* She faintly smiled about how some good fortune might come of this.

She noticed that he was taking more of an interest in her to the point of watching the road and eyeing her, and she knew what was coming next.

"Tell me, Pat, are you married, have any steady relationships?" he calmly inquired while taking the last drag from his cigarette.

"No, I am not married, but divorced. I am engaged to a special lady back in the States and plan on tying the knot when I return," she said, almost laughing out loud at herself with such a dramatic, but convincing lie.

"Well ah, okay, Pat, ah, well whatever you do is your business, but don't let your romantic, social life interfere with the restaurant's business—it could be embarrassing and cause problems for us." His eyes were now directly on the road while he fired up another Camel. "Understood?"

"¡Claro, jefe!" McCord replied in Spanish, still amused at his questions and the answers she had given and especially tickled about her bogus response.

An uncomfortable silence filled the Mercedes as Juarez was trying to comprehend any problems with her statement about being gay—he did not know if this would affect his business and her relationship with the other employees. She could sense this troubled him significantly.

"Tell you what. I will not let the word out about my sexual preference and will act the part of some hot, horny broad—would that satisfy your concerns?"

"Yes, I believe that would be appropriate," he said. "You understand, here in Bolivia, that could be very bad for business." He was now looking at her and trying to move on to work-related duties which he knew very little or nothing about.

"Now, in the morning when you sign in you should…" the briefings went on with McCord making notes in her notebook.

The job expectations suddenly stopped when the car exited Highway 4 and headed south on the busy main highway loop in Santa Cruz, Cuarto Anillo. Heading for a very modern and attractive shopping mall, Juarez found an owner's parking slot near the mall's main entrance.

"Would you like to take a look at your new office?" he asked, knowing full well she would probably be living there for the first year while he observed and evaluated her performance in producing a cash flow for his salary.

"Sure, I look forward to seeing the restaurant," she replied. "This is exactly what I have been training for."

She mused, *Between lying and acting, the DEA has trained me well—should have been a lawyer.*

CHAPTER
43

The DEA operations center in Arlington, Virginia, was clandestinely linked to Turner's email messages and also received the confirmation that she was established in Santa Cruz with current contact information. The security technician monitoring the terminal reviewed an incoming message from Turner and immediately picked up the secure telephone and relayed the information to her supervisor.

"Ma'am, this is Lisa Carter in the Tactical Information Center, we have just received a confirmation email from Special Agent McCord," the young technician announced, following her directed checklist items when reporting the arrival of a DEA undercover agent in a foreign country.

"Thank you, Ms. Carter. I'll be down there directly to review it," said Jean Hurst, the DEA watch supervisor.

Hurst, a seasoned and well-respected African American agent recently promoted to a director position, also followed her executive checklists. She stopped working on one of her many reports and made her way to the office door and ensured it was locked. She opened a large, wooden cabinet door and gradually pulled it open revealing a large vault. Placing her hand on the security pad and inserting the six-digit code into the master panel, the vault door opened.

Hurst grabbed the folder containing the identities of DEA agents working undercover at the various locations around the globe. Searching the highly sensitive and top-secret list of agents, she found the name Bonnie McCord.

"Okay, McCord, let's get an update on where this is going," Hurst murmured to herself as she made her way to her conference room table and reviewed McCord's assignment and any other significant items on the standard field report.

After her second cup of coffee, and the third re-read of the documents, Hurst sat back rubbing her forehead—something bothered her about this undercover assignment. Frustrated, she did not like the idea of sending such a "green" but very ambitious agent out on an uncover assignment such as this one. She could not put her finger on it, but she did not like it.

Well, McCord, good luck to you and hope you enjoy frying chicken, Hurst commented to herself as she placed the sensitive documents back into the vault and again set the alarm.

"Mr. Whitehouse," she said over the intercom to her executive assistant.

"Yes, ma'am."

"Bill, I'll be down in the Tactical Information Center reviewing some messages."

"Anything wrong?" he asked, knowing the boss only went down to the center when there were potential problems.

"I hope not, but I have a sixth sense about this Bolivia operation with McCord," Hurst shared with Whitehouse.

"Well, she always has the safe house to fall back on. We certainly ensured it was located in a neighborhood near her condominium," Whitehouse added.

"Yes, but who else may know about the safe house outside of the Agency?" Hurst questioned.

CHAPTER

44

"I need to see Dr. Alexander immediately!" Roy Baker yelled in the phone to Alexander's executive assistant.

"Mr. Baker, Dr. Alexander is in a financial forecast meeting with the directors—could I leave a message for her?" the assistant grudgingly offered, not appreciating Baker's tone.

"Listen, you break into that meeting and inform her that I need to see her PRONTO," Baker ordered. "This is an emergency. Dr. Alexander needs to know now!"

The assistant interrupted the meeting and gave the message to Alexander. She exploded in front of all of her directors and threatened to fire Baker, their head of security at GFC, on the spot and immediately opened up her cell phone to see what the emergency was all about. All the directors were intrigued by this emergency phone call from security and wondered if it affected them.

"Damn you, Baker, this better be important—talk fast, you fucking idiot!"

"Ma'am, I believe it a good idea if we talk down in the patio area off by the river," Baker emphatically suggested, "and recommend you come by yourself—no one else."

Upon hearing the request from Baker, she threw her cell phone against one of the many paintings in the board room—leaving cuts and gash marks on the rare masterpiece.

Alexander instructed her directors to continue working the forecast, and she would be back in just a few minutes after "straightening out my idiot security director."

Rushing to the elevator, she hurriedly punched the button for the atrium that led out to the well-groomed patio area. Just pushing the glass door open to leave the building, she saw Roy Baker sitting alone at one of the secluded picnic tables.

Wearing her usual blue corporate suit, literally almost running, she went as fast as she could in her high heels, with every step agitating her further until she came close to Baker.

"Baker, you stupid fool." The whack was heard all the way up to the atrium level as Alexander slapped Baker across the face and continued until her frenzy wore her out to the point of panting.

"Listen to me, Elizabeth," Baker now ordered, "we need to talk right now, right here, it is that important—do you understand?"

Regaining her composure and vanity, she straightened out her business suit and sat opposite him on the wooden picnic table.

"Why such urgency in seeing me and why away from the office?" Alexander calmly asked.

"First, what I have to say, you will agree, needs to be said away from the office—it is that sensitive," Baker said, "and you'll understand why in a moment."

Alexander was now thinking of various scenarios within GFC that could be considered an emergency, which was usually handled by the director heads of the staff—*but why the secrecy and urgency now,* she pondered.

"A few weeks ago, our human resource office received an anonymous letter informing us that we were unknowingly training an undercover federal agent," explained Baker. "There were no details who this person was or where in the organization he or she was going to work."

"Oh my God, oh my God," Alexander continued to repeat as she began to figure out who this employee may be that in reality was a federal agent—any scenario was catastrophic to her.

"Elizabeth, we get hundreds of crackpot letters every day from all over the world regarding our people. Many from jilted lovers, ex-spouses, jealous friends—you know where I am going," Baker said. "In regard to this letter on the federal agent, it was not taken seriously by our personnel but filed accordingly."

Alexander put her head in her hands.

"Elizabeth, you'll find this troubling. The detective service of Brisco & Sons called this morning, and their informal, but reliable, sources stated that our Pat Turner, the new store manager in Bolivia, is a bogus person and name." Baker now prepared Alexander for what he knew would be a life-or-death situation for both Alexander and Pat Turner.

"Tell me, Roy!" Alexander ordered, with her face turning beet red and her lips quivering.

"Pat Turner's real name is Bonnie McCord, and she is a special agent with the Drug Enforcement Agency—DEA," Baker replied, knowing his days were numbered as the security director head at GFC.

"Are you absolutely sure?"

"Yes. I was able to find through our friendly government and elected office holders that there is indeed a DEA Special Agent Bonnie McCord whose record is flagged as unavailable—usually meaning she is on a special, sensitive assignment."

Alexander just sat back and thought for a moment of the horrific future awaiting her and GFC if this Bonnie McCord was able to make a connection between her friends at the Sola Mesa drug cartel and GFC. If she was not murdered by the cartel, she definitely would spend the rest of her life behind bars. There was no doubt in her mind that McCord, Turner, or whatever her name was had to be taken care of quickly.

"Roy, this is completely confidential between us—no mention of this will be shared with anyone. No one but me. Do you understand?"

"Yes, ma'am," Baker nodded.

Alexander hurriedly returned to her office and had her executive secretary cancel all meetings for that day. While in the office, she opened her private, secure safe. She grabbed an unmarked, heavily wrapped envelope and a cell phone.

Stuffing both in her purse, she hurriedly left her office, instructing her executive assistant that she would be gone for the rest of the day and could not be reached until the next day.

Impatiently waiting for the elevators to reach the underground garage, she raced to her Mercedes sports car, frantically found the keys, left the garage and headed for a large cemetery near GFC headquarters. There, she found a small marble bench under a cottonwood tree where she would open the envelope and the cell phone—reflecting for a minute how it all came to this.

Alexander configured the new, secure cell phone and opened the sealed envelope containing other secure cell phone numbers. After going through a secretary and assistant, Alexander finally reached George Pablo Quezada.

"Sir," she said, "Our newly assigned GFC manager in Bolivia. Her name is Patricia Turner. But she's really a DEA Special Agent working undercover. Her real name is Bonnie McCord."

CHAPTER
45

"Please contact Director Hurst immediately and ask her to report to the DEA Tactical Information Center as soon as possible," the center's duty controller directed the communications officer.

With the phone call from the center awakening Hurst at three in the morning, her family was used to the various calls at all times during the night and day—all part of the job for Hurst.

Arriving at the center at four o'clock in the morning, Hurst was immediately escorted into a secure conference room where Ryan Floor, duty controller, reviewed new message traffic they had just received from South America—Bolivia, to be exact. Floor explained the center had monitored some cell phone conversations involving various Sola Mesa cartel members, which were mostly routine and of no consequence. However, that morning, Floor found a few conversations, in the open, regarding a federal undercover agent they had just discovered and compromised in Santa Cruz posing as a manager of a GFC.

"Ma'am, please clarify for me, do we or do we not have agents in Bolivia?"

CHAPTER
46

"The theories we once held true for developmental and physiological science are now being challenged by—" The professor abruptly stopped his lecture as a gentleman entered the classroom.

"Please forgive me for the interruption, Dr. Epler," the gentleman quickly apologized while scanning the classroom. In a second he found who he was looking for.

"Mr. Madden, could I see you for a minute?" asked Dr. John Schwartz, dean of the Graduate School of Education at Stanford University, Madden viewed Schwartz with a suspicious look.

Madden got up from his seat and followed Schwartz out into the graduate school hallway heading for the dean's office. Schwartz made simple small talk with Madden during the walk.

"Please, Mr. Madden, come on in my office," directed Schwartz as he opened the large oak door leading to an impressive office with many plaques, awards, certificates, and pictures of well-known personalities befitting a university dean of education. Madden nearly burst out laughing observing the office, for it mirrored the appearance of a military high-ranking officer who thought a lot of himself with a universal "I Love Me Wall." However, at a rather large, cherry wood conference table two men and a woman sat. Madden immediately sized them up as being federal agents—he would know.

"Mr. Madden, I would like to introduce Mr. Bill Roberts, Mr. Joe Martin, and Ms. Judy Case." Schwartz made the introductions as all stood and shook Madden's hand.

"Rob, these people have a special interest in your academic progress and would like to talk with you further about your future goals," explained Schwartz.

Bullshit! Madden thought to himself—standard procedure is to appear to be normal legitimate college recruiters so as not to involve the dean in the event there were unauthorized listening devices in the room. Protects everyone, especially the dean.

Let me guess, Madden thought, *they're going to offer to go outside with me and walk around the campus and find some nice bench to sit at and talk about my future.*

"Mr. Madden, would you feel more comfortable if we went outside and maybe found a nice comfortable place to talk?" Roberts asked.

Madden stared at Schwartz, who in turn nodded his head having a gut feeling Madden would not be coming back—at least for a while.

Leaving the dean's office, all four made small talk about the weather, college football, and various family issues. Madden just listened while being purposely led to a secluded area with a park bench and chairs. All took their seats as the small talk subsided.

"It is pretty obvious you know where we're from," Roberts spoke first with a few seconds of silence following.

"Mr. Madden, we are very well aware of what you have been through these past two years, and we cannot thank you enough," Judy Case stated, with both men thoroughly in agreement. "Frankly, you are a legend at the Agency."

"Well that is really nice for you to pull me out of my studies to tell me this," Madden vented. "Now what the hell are you doing here and why contact me with this cloak-and-dagger bullshit?"

No one spoke except for Joe Martin, who reached into his briefcase and pulled out an official-looking government report.

"Rob, I'm being up front with you," Martin said, preparing Madden for the worst.

"We know you and Bonnie McCord are very close and—"

"Where is she? Where is Bonnie?" Madden demanded to know. "I'll go get her, I can go get her, I know how."

"Yes, we know you can, but first let me update you on what we know now about Special Agent McCord," Case spoke softly and gently. She was brought along just for this moment—to calm Madden.

"Rob, as far as we know now, Bonnie is alive," Roberts said.

"What are you trying to tell me," Madden demanded, "tell it to me straight right now!"

"Bonnie's cover as a Georgia Fried Chicken assistant manager in Bolivia was blown—we are not sure how, but an investigation is under way now," Roberts continued. "Her whereabouts are unknown right now."

Madden stood, clenching his fists.

"There is a rescue team being formed in Texas with a forward operating base in Colombia," Roberts said. "Are you interested in joining this team?"

ACKNOWLEDGMENTS

I would like to thank the staff and associates at the City of La Vista Public Library in Nebraska for their most generous support with resources, technical guidance, and outstanding research facilities.

Professional editing support provided by Dr. Nancy Thomlinson, Margaret Nordland, Mimi Dreiling and Sandy Wendel. With their seasoned and professional editing skills, this book came to life. Also, invaluable artistic support provided by Cynthia Cronn.

Special thanks to Lisa Pelto, Ellie Godwin, and Olivia Nixon of Concierge Marketing Publishing Services for their magnificent job in finalizing *Saving Vengeance*.

I also thank my fellow members and staff of the Air Commando Association for their exceptional reporting and documenting missions the Air Force Special Operations members face daily— they are truly the "tip of the spear."

And finally, I greatly appreciate the advice and expertise of professional educators at the Nebraska Department of Education, National School Board Association, Nebraska Association of School Boards, and the Nebraska Council of School Administrators.

ABOUT THE AUTHOR

Growing up in the petroleum business in various states across the United States, John Witzel learned firsthand the challenges our young people face in attending several different schools prior to graduation—he attended four different high schools due to the demands of his father's career.

John was fortunate to attend college on an Air Force scholarship and graduated from Louisiana Tech University in 1974 and earned a master's degree from Ball State University in 1979. Later, after retiring from the Air Force, he earned degrees at Bellevue University in accounting and computer information systems.

Commissioned in the Air Force in 1974, he served twenty-two years and retired as a Lieutenant Colonel, and served as a navigator, public affairs officer, academic instructor, combat operations planner, and director of quality improvement. He has served at various locations and assignments around the world including being a volunteer with the Iranian Rescue Attempt in 1980, and appointed and served as Director of the Strategic Air Command Airborne Command Post (Locking Glass) in 1990. He has deployed several times overseas.

Following his military service, John began his second career as an accountant at a national bank headquartered in Omaha, Nebraska, and subsequently was asked to return to the military as a defense contractor where he supported command and control systems at U.S. Strategic Command.

Currently, he is serving as President on the State Board of Education and represents District 4, which includes North and South Omaha, Midtown Omaha, and large sections of the suburban cities of Papillion and Bellevue. Prior to serving on the State Board, John served as a local school board member at the Educational Service Unit 3 for fourteen years supporting eighteen local school districts, 58,000 students, with education programs and technology services.

His first book in the Rob Madden action thriller series, *Saving Tres Rios*, was a finalist in a national book award program. This book, *Saving Vengeance,* continues the saga of Madden, an Air Force Sergeant turned public school teacher and the many challenges he faces in and out of the classroom.

John lives in Papillion, Nebraska, where for over twenty-eight years he has served the military at the nearby Offutt Air Force Base, and the community in public education where he oversees many of the state policies and programs he initially started, including a new accountability system, career technical education, and early childhood development. His passion is closing the achievement gap and providing world-class college and career-readiness education for all Nebraska students.

ANOTHER BOOK IN THE
ROB MADDEN SERIES!

Buy it today at **Amazon.com.**
Also available on Kindle!

ISBN: 978-0-9911029-1-4
Paperback Price: $15.95
Kindle Price: $3.99

www.ingramcontent.com/pod-product-compliance
Lightning Source LLC
Chambersburg PA
CBHW030648260626
47157CB00007B/2549